CATALYST

HOTEL ST KILDA

CATALYST

For Helen

With very best wishes

Michael Knaggs

MICHAEL KNAGGS

Matador
9 Priory Business Park
Kibworth Beauchamp
Leicestershire LE8 0RX, UK
Tel: (+44) 116 279 2299
Fax: (+44) 116 279 2277
Email: books@troubador.co.uk
Web: www.troubador.co.uk/matador

ISBN 978 1783062 348

British Library Cataloguing in Publication Data.
A catalogue record for this book is available from the British Library.

Typeset in Aldine401 BT Roman by Troubador Publishing Ltd
Printed and bound in the UK by TJ International, Padstow, Cornwall

Matador is an imprint of Troubador Publishing Ltd

For Carol

'The wicked draw the sword and bend their bows
to bring down the poor and needy,
to kill those who walk uprightly;
their sword shall enter their own heart,
and their bows shall be broken.
The righteous shall be kept safe for ever,
but the children of the wicked shall be cut off.
The righteous shall inherit the land,
and live in it for ever.'

Psalms, 37

PROLOGUE

The rocks were exceptionally hot to the touch as the eight men dropped down onto their stomachs and squirmed forward towards the edge of the escarpment which overlooked the focus of their mission. Like stepping into a hot bath, it took several seconds for their bodies to adapt to the new environment before they could relax without being conscious of the discomfort.

Three heads pushed up slowly over the edge and looked down in silence for a full minute, taking in the scene before them. The ridge to the left of where they lay curved round in a tight arc through ninety degrees then straightened again to continue directly away from them for as far as they could see. The ground fell away steeply along the whole length of the ridge to the flat rock-strewn bed of a dried-up prehistoric lake.

Some distance away and about 100 feet below them on the flat ground, they could make out two dozen or so men in military kit milling around beside a couple of tents pitched, like sentinels, at either side of the entrance to a large cave in the basin side. The men were chatting and smoking, and occasionally looking into the distance directly away from the three observers.

Captain Malcolm Randall, commander of the small operational unit, spoke to the man on his right. "This close enough, Major? I don't think we can get any nearer."

The man didn't answer immediately but took his time looking round the site. He was tall and slim, with square shoulders and a narrow waist, but without the highly developed muscular frame of each of the rest of the group. He was also the senior by ten years of the next oldest there. His intense dark eyes set in a sharp-featured, handsome face took in all the factors of terrain, light, target angle, range and position that would contribute towards or detract from their chances of success.

"This should be fine," he said, eventually, turning to the third man.

"Right?"

"Sure. You're the man, sir," said the young soldier, grinning.

"Okay," said the Major. "Range check."

The Captain slid back the few yards to the other five members of the team.

"This is it," he said. "We wait."

On the ridge, the two men dropped down below the sight line and the Major unslung the two rifles he was carrying, a signal for the other man to do the same. They each rested one against the rock beside them and slowly pulled the other up over the parapet, shouldering them into position.

"Guy closest to the first tent," said the Major.

He steadied his weapon and peered through the rifle scope. The two lines of mil dots at right-angles to each other, intersecting in the centre of the reticle, formed the cross-hairs and provided the means of estimating the range. He focused on the man nearest the tent. Assuming his height to be six feet and noting that his image through the scope covered four-and-a-half spaces between the dots, he was able to convert this information quickly into a range of 445 yards.

He turned to his partner.

"Have you got your dress on?"

Corporal Mike Hanson smiled. "I prefer to pronounce it 'drez', sir."

"Tell me again what it stands for."

Mike sighed.

"'Digital range estimation system' and I admit, before you say anything, it's nowhere near as accurate as you."

"Just as long as you realise that. What do you make it?"

Mike focused on the same man through the rifle scope, and then held down a button which changed the image to a small screen showing the estimated range in both metres and yards.

"Four-o-six metres – four-forty yards," said the Corporal. "Drop of five inches, adjusted for altitude."

"What?"

"Takes into account height above sea level; bullet travels faster where the air's thinner."

The Major shook his head in disbelief.

"Jesus! In other words, a rifle with a built-in barometer. What next, for Christ's sake? No wonder the old skills are dying out."

The young soldier looked across at him and grinned.

"So, did I get it right, sir? Based on your ancient skills?"

"You always were a precocious little shit, Hanson, right from the first training session. You were five yards out, if you must know."

'Little' shit was hardly an appropriate description. Mike was well over six feet tall, broad-shouldered and with a ruggedly attractive face that gave him an air of authority and toughness. That is when it wasn't smirking, which it usually was.

They adjusted their scope elevation to account for the drop and the young Corporal slid below the level of the ridge and turned onto his back, closing his eyes against the sun. The Major continued to survey the scene around him.

"Four-forty yards," he said, to himself. "That's good. All in range, and a walk in the park for old faithful." He tapped the barrel of his rifle affectionately; an Accuracy International L96A1, generally accepted as the best sniping rifle in the world. Certainly the Major thought so and, as a consequence, so did Corporal Hanson.

"Absolutely no wind for a change. One thing less to worry about."

Looking across to the right where the ridge continued, rising gradually upwards, he noted a distinctive and familiar protrusion of rock sticking out from it, looking a bit like a private box set slightly forward from the Circle in a theatre or concert hall.

"I've been here before, you know," he called down to Mike.

"When? What for?"

"Twelve years ago: it was over there." He pointed to the rocky outcrop. "Doing the same job as today."

"Successful trip, was it?"

The Major shook his head.

"No?"

"No."

"You probably didn't allow for altitude," said Mike, with his hallmark grin.

The Major smiled, although the memory was not a pleasant one. Right now, however, he fixed his eyes again on the direction their present target would arrive from. There was no sign yet. He glanced down at the young man by his side who now seemed to be sleeping peacefully without a care in the world. He hoped that was true, and that it would remain that way.

The waiting continued. Eventually, Captain Randall appeared anxiously by his side, looking at his watch. The Captain was half a head shorter than the two marksmen, stocky and broad-shouldered, with sandy hair and eyebrows, and a round face which seemed to be set in a permanent frown of concentration.

"We need him to get a move on; he's two hours behind schedule already," he said. "Apart from anything else, we're going to get some snow in the next hour or so and I don't fancy being far from the transport when that comes down. I expected we'd be done here by now. I hope to God he hasn't been tipped off," he added as an afterthought, "in which case I guess we should be looking behind us."

Almost as he finished speaking, the welcome cloud of dust appeared in the middle distance.

"Someone's on his way," said the Major, nudging the somnolent Corporal. "Care to join us?"

The three men lay flat and still, watching the dust cloud get closer. The Captain steadied his binoculars.

"Three vehicles – Defenders. Short wheel-base at the front – just two men – driver and one passenger in the front seat beside him. Guess that's our man. Two long wheel-base pick-ups behind; one driver and looks like about six men in the back of each."

He lowered his bins.

"What do you think?"

"Suggest we get the guys in place right now," said the Major. "Don't want any movements on their sky-line when they get close. We'll try to take him in the car as he arrives – but no promises. Depends on position of the vehicle when he stops. Target won't normally move from his seat until the driver opens the door for him. He usually goes round the back of the vehicle to do that. We could have ten seconds at best. Be ready to start countdown from when he puts the handbrake on. Mike, find your position – now!"

He could feel his excitement rising and surfacing in the way he snapped out the last word to his co-marksman.

The Captain turned and waved the men forward.

"Positions!"

They fanned out along the ridge on either side of the three already there, slipping their assault rifles from their shoulders and settling themselves in readiness. The dust cloud moved closer – now less than half a mile from its destination below them.

The Captain went through the briefing with his men.

"We'll try to take him inside the car as he arrives, so Major will initiate countdown. Count of six. Mike fires on three, Major on two; all fire on zero. Check?"

"Check!" All seven responded as one.

"Only Major to stop count if necessary. If count stops hold positions perfectly still. Check?"

"Check!"

"Okay. Still from now."

It was standard practice when firing through a window or windshield. Two shots, one second apart. The first would take out the glass, removing any risk of deflection for the second.

Captain Randall watched the final stages of the approach through his binoculars as safeties came off and fingers gently touched the sensitive triggers ready for action. The leading vehicle stopped as it drew level with the cave, about twenty yards away from it. The first pick-up eased alongside, between the car and the cave, and the second one pulled slowly round to stop at the other side.

Luck was with the patrol; the leading car was facing directly towards them. The two occupants were clearly not intending to get out until their escort was in position, with the vehicles parked on either side.

"Okay, Mike?" asked the Major.

"Okay."

"Count!"

The Captain called out the seconds.

"Six…five…four…three…"

Mike fired.

"…two…"

The Major fired.

"…one…zero"

Seven rifles opened up on the shocked group below them.

Mike's shot destroyed the windscreen of the Defender half a second before the bullet left the Major's rifle. The victim was thrown backwards in his seat in a double jerk as both shots found their mark. The insurgents, some of whom were still climbing down from the pick-ups, scattered from the point of the attack, running into the cave, dropping behind rocks or rolling underneath the vehicles.

"Hit!" yelled the Captain. "Complete! Near certain! And two more, perhaps three! Keep firing!"

The rest of the rebel group were trying to get into the cave, making darting runs to safety from their temporary cover and firing in the general direction where the shots were coming from. The Captain let the assault continue for another thirty seconds, and then yelled for them to stop.

"Hold fire! Let them get to cover!"

The firing stopped and the remaining rebels scrambled for the relative safety of the cave.

"Okay. Into the entrance – open fire, *now!*" His voice was calmer now that the level of excitement had reduced in the relative quiet of the last few moments.

The seven rifles barked again briefly, peppering the opening.

"Cease fire," said the Captain. "Just to let them know we're still here, if they're thinking of coming out. Okay let's move it!"

As they made their rapid descent back from the edge of the escarpment, the euphoria of the mission's success, in spite of admirable attempts to suppress it, was unmistakable. The grins on the faces of the patrol members were evidence to that and Mike was subjected to a battery of congratulations as they headed home.

"Anyone can hit a windscreen," said the Major.

As they neared the point where they had left their two all-terrain vehicles, the wind and snow came at them together and the light faded. At this altitude and time of the year, the temperature could drop twenty degrees Celsius in a couple of hours. They were within half a mile of their destination, half-walking, half-stumbling along a rough track through a narrow steep-sided gully. The Major was at the head of the group as they approached a blind right turn. Suddenly, he stopped, raising his right arm high to halt the column, and turned to face them.

"Wait!"

They all stopped and instinctively slipped their weapons from their shoulders, the Captain and the five soldiers behind him each throwing over the small lever on the 9mm conversion unit which effectively turned the assault rifles into SMGs.

"What is it?" said the Captain, who was third in line behind the Major and Corporal Hanson.

"Thought I heard something. Stay!"

The Major edged forward slowly to the turn in the path and peered round the corner. A few yards ahead the gully widened out into a circular flat basin, the sides still steep and high, before narrowing again into a similar passageway.

"Wait there."

The Major's instruction was mouthed rather than spoken and reinforced by his hand outstretched towards them, palm vertical and restraining. He was about thirty yards ahead of them as he disappeared from view round the corner. The Captain stepped past the Corporal to the front of the waiting group.

A minute passed, seeming much longer.

Mike at the Captain's shoulder was becoming agitated, and edged forward level with him.

"Sir, shouldn't we…"

"Wait!" The Captain put his arm across the young soldier's chest and held him back.

Then came the first explosion, from not far past the turn in the track. The men behind the leading two pressed themselves instinctively against the side of the gully and hands moved to triggers. They looked anxiously towards the turning, and then to their leader for the order for action. The expression on the Captain's face was of confusion rather than horror.

"Something's wrong," he said, more to himself than to his men.

"Fucking right it is!" yelled Mike. "The Major!" He pushed past the Captain and ran down the track.

"Corporal! Mike! Wait! *Wait!* Stop *now!*"

CHAPTER 1

It was 2.00 am in the morning and Tom Brown was nowhere near completing his preparations for the coming afternoon. He went through to the kitchen.

Taking a mug from the draining board he scooped a heaped spoonful of instant coffee into it. As he replaced the coffee jar, he caught a second mug with his elbow, knocking it onto the stone-flagged floor. It shattered loudly. He looked bleary-eyed in surprise at how far the half-dozen fragments had scattered across the floor. He was too tired to be angry; he reached for the pan and brush from under the sink to start the clean-up operation.

The kitchen door, which had been partly open, swung back further with some drama. The tall, slender figure of his wife, Maggie, stood in the doorway, bare-footed and in a short, hastily-donned dressing gown.

"What the hell is going on?" she said. "Have you any idea what time it is?"

"I've broken a mug and it's just after two o'clock," he said, without expression.

"Yes, I'm aware of that," she said.

"Which?" Tom asked. "The breakage or the time?"

"Some of us are trying to get some sleep."

"Us? I see. Well, whoever it is you've got up there with you, thanks for keeping the noise down. You weren't always so quiet in bed."

"I'm amazed you can remember that long ago," she said, and then saw the shattered fragments in the dustpan in his hand, "Oh,

1

no! That's the mug Katey got me for Mothers' Day; the first present she ever went out and bought for me on her own. I've had it for seven years. Well, thank you very much for that!"

"For God's sake, Mags, I didn't throw it at the wall or hit it with a hammer. It was an accident. I'm very sorry. I'll get you another one exactly the same. Katey will never know."

"What's that got to do with it? *I'll* know!"

"Of course you will," he said. "How silly of me. I won't buy you another one and Katey can be upset as well. A problem shared is another bugger depressed, I always say."

"That's a nice word to use to describe your daughter."

"Oh come on! It wasn't directed at her and you know it!" he said. "Please go back to bed, Mags, I've got to get on with this. I'll tiptoe around and use a plastic cup from now on. And I am sorry about breaking your mug. Really."

"Anyway, what's so absolutely critical that you have to do it in the middle of the night?" she asked.

"I'm meeting Andrew at eight this morning to go through my speech to the House later this afternoon." He glanced at the wall clock. "That gives me about four hours before Paul arrives."

"I can't believe it. You've been going on about this speech for weeks; how come you're working on it now? It's a bit cavalier to leave it this late, isn't it? I mean, I'm assuming it must concern the fate of the nation, otherwise you wouldn't be bothering with it."

"It's what I like to do – as I've explained before God knows how many times. The later I prepare, the more genuine and spontaneous it comes over."

Mags snorted. "Well, there'll be no problem with spontaneous, will there? At this rate you'll be making it up as you go along. I wouldn't care if all this was going to have any lasting value. I just don't know what's going on in your mind these days. I can't believe that you still think it's the right thing to do."

"Look!" said Tom, now finding no difficulty at all in getting angry. "It's already done! I am not prepared to discuss this with you any more. It's what people *want*. How is it that the vast – *vast* – majority of people in the country must be wrong because their opinion differs from yours? Are they all idiots – is that it? I respect your opinion – I'm very familiar with it – you are entitled to it – but

I don't want to hear it over and over again! Can't we just accept that we have different views on this *one* thing and get on with the rest of our lives? This is destroying us. You're letting it destroy us. You won't leave it alone."

"No, I won't, because I can't! It's not possible for me to just accept it when I feel so strongly about it. Don't you understand that? And if you're saying that everything else is okay, and it's just about this 'one thing', then you must have completely lost track of reality. I can't think of *anything* we see eye to eye on now. You've lost me. Completely."

"What do you mean 'lost you'?" snapped Tom. "I don't understand. Lost you how – to someone else? Explain please!"

"Does it matter? Do you *really* care what I mean? You have absolutely no interest now in what is important to me. It's all about your career and this… NJ-bloody-R! And you know very well that there isn't anyone else – yet!"

"Yet! Look neither of us is getting any younger, Mags. If we're heading for a split, then let's get on with it."

"It wouldn't make any difference to you, would it? Having me somewhere else with someone else wouldn't change your life one bit. In fact, that's not true – it would improve it immensely. You have absolutely no interest in me or your family. All we are to you is an unfortunate distraction as you pursue your pitch for fame; your place in history. If we weren't in your life at all it would be so much simpler."

"It's always the same," said Tom. "You invariably reduce the discussion to a bloody vote of confidence. I am now supposed to say, 'that's not true, darling, you know you all mean much more to me than anything else'. It's a cheap emotional trick you pull when you run out of anything constructive to say. Well actually, *darling,* I'm not getting involved in an argument on your level; I'm afraid I can't function at those extreme depths."

"Oh, that's charming!"

"But seeing as you brought it up," went on Tom, "I think you've got a nerve accusing me of not caring about the family when I seem to spend most of my time – when they choose to honour us with their presence – talking to them about what's going on in their lives right now. And it's a good job I do, because you don't seem to give a shit what they get up to and who they're with."

"'Talking to them about what's going on in their lives!'" Mags almost shouted his words back at him. "You don't *talk* to them. You *tell* them what to do. 'Talking' implies a two-way exchange of information. 'Talking' suggests they have a right to express *their* views and opinions. That's what 'talking' means. That's not what you do with your children!"

"Are you suggesting that they don't need any guidance?" said Tom, now raising his voice.

"Guidance, yes," said Mags, "not bullying! They're not kids any more who can be threatened with petty retribution. You can't ground a seventeen-year-old, for God's sake, let alone a nineteen-year-old. They are good kids. Not perfect, but better than most. Better than the vast – *vast* – majority, in fact. But they have to spread their wings. You'd be worried if they stayed in all night reading or watching TV. Well perhaps you wouldn't be, but I would. I just don't know what you expect of them."

"A bit of discipline, that's what!"

"Oh, for God's sake… " Mags looked away.

"*Self*-discipline, then. There must be some middle ground between staying in all night and staying out all night. Where are they now, for Christ's sake? It's nearly two-thirty in the morning. They're both at college in about seven hours' time, and what sort of a state are they likely to be in. And you know why I'm concerned about them – it's the crowd they knock about with. Had you forgotten? Mickey What's'isname and his cronies… "

"And Jason," Mags interrupted. "Don't forget Jason. That nasty piece of work your daughter's in love with."

"I've nothing against Jason and you know it. And Katey is *not* in love with him. She knows nothing about love – she's only seventeen and… "

"That's how old I was when I fell in love with you."

"… my only thing about Jason is that the relationship seems to have gone too far too quickly. Everything considered," said Tom.

"Everything considered?" said Mags. "You mean because he's black, one parent family, no money… ?"

"That is fucking nonsense!" blazed Tom, slamming the flat of his hand down on the kitchen worktop. "You know it's nothing to do with that!"

4

"Yes, okay, I'm sorry," said Mags.

They were both silent for a while.

"No, I'm not comfortable with the relationship," he said, calmly now. "But Jason's okay – and one of the brightest kids I've ever met. He wouldn't have gone to Bishop's if he wasn't – I mean, he must have got a scholarship entry. In fact, he's going to be a brilliant engineer by all accounts. A software, hardware and digital communications genius, so I'm reliably informed. I might be able to use him to hack into a few files," he added, offering a small token of humour, which Mags accepted with a brief but genuine smile.

"I could take the Jason thing, anyway," he went on, "if it wasn't for the fact that he's the one who got Katey and Jack involved with this Mickey. I don't believe anything but pain will come from that association. And I'm not the only one who believes that, am I?"

"That concern isn't by any chance anything to do with the NJR, is it?" Mags asked.

"I don't follow what you mean," he replied. "Is that an attempt to get the argument back on track again?"

"No, I just wondered… but if you really don't follow… then I guess the question's answered."

"What the hell!" Tom's anger was quick to rise again. "We're into riddles now. Just say what you mean; put me out of my misery. On second thoughts, don't bother. Whatever you think of it, I have to get this work done, so would you please go to bed and let me get on with it. Please, Mags."

She sighed, suddenly weary of the conversation, and turned to leave the room. Tom was momentarily overcome by a feeling of regret.

"Mags!" he shouted after her.

She turned in the doorway and stood, hands on hips, feet slightly apart, to face him. Her short robe, with its belt pulled tightly around her, hung loose and wide from her shoulders and gaped open below her waist. Even with her mass of golden-blonde hair tangled by her restless sleep and without a trace of make-up, she was almost impossibly beautiful.

"Do you remember how we used to resolve these differences?" he said, gently. "I used to enjoy the arguments then, knowing how they were going to end."

Mags said nothing.

"It was nice, wasn't it?" he went on. "And not that long ago."

She looked at him sadly, with glistening eyes softened by her own memories. "Yes," she said, in a whisper. "It was nice, then. More than just nice." Then the moment was over; her expression changed again. "But you're wrong about the timescale. It was a *lifetime* ago."

She turned and completed her exit, calling back to him as she left. "Tell Katey when she gets in to come and see me if she wants to."

"Okay," Tom called back, and then much more loudly, "How is it that you've been stomping around for half an hour because I allegedly woke you up with the gentle tinkling of a breaking mug, and now you want me to set up a meeting *later* tonight with your daughter?"

Mags was back again in the doorway, startling Tom with her sudden reappearance.

"Yes, if that's okay," she said. "I thought it would take the pressure off you having to make a speech to her while you're preparing this one. And I just happened to be getting up to go to the bathroom when you assassinated my mug; that's how I came to hear it."

"Well that was lucky, wasn't it?" he replied. "It saved you having to lie on the carpet with your ear to the floor hoping to hear some noise to complain about. Perhaps we should take the carpet up altogether and you might be able to pick up the sound of my breathing."

"Now that's a sound I wouldn't miss," she said, turning majestically away to leave the room again. "Good night," she shouted back, with exaggerated good humour.

Tom called after her. "Do you want me to tell Katey about the broken mug, or shall I just put the pieces in her room so she can find them?"

There was no reply. He watched her go, the sadness returning.

A lifetime ago. Not quite…

CHAPTER 2

Three years ago…

It was eerily dark for an early evening in the first week of May. The advancing storm clouds, like a gigantic blue-black carpet unrolling across a marble floor, had brought on the night a couple of hours earlier than the season intended.

On the ground, violent normality prevailed.

It was the classic trap – bait and wait.

The two howling police cars were confronted by a two-deep line of wheelie bins as they swung into Kingdom Road, which was the only vehicular access to the square. The roaring flames behind the bins showed the obstacles in stark silhouette along with the figures dancing back and forth on top of them, preventing the police from just driving through and pushing them aside.

Kingdom Road was a rather grand name for the 200 yards of tarmac with four closes leading off it – two either side. At the end was the square – a rectangle, in fact – the back of which comprised a row of ten garages, with two lines of parking spaces forming its sides. Three cars were ablaze at one side of the area, with the fire threatening to spread rapidly.

The fire station was just three streets away from Kingdom Road and the mob had banked on the appliances getting there ahead of the police. The bins had been hastily pulled into place as soon as the second fire engine had arrived on the scene, an impressive two-and-a-half minutes after the first emergency call had been received.

Their appearance had been greeted with the usual resounding jeers and abuse which the fire officers both expected and feared. Their unease was heightened considerably by the absence of the police. Nevertheless, they alighted quickly to begin the well-oiled routine they had rehearsed on hundreds of occasions. Only here it was very different.

As they released the hoses from their mountings, they were assailed by a hail of stones, bricks and bottles from the crowd of around sixty youths, mainly in their early to mid-teens but some even younger, and two officers went down under the attack. The crews were forced to retreat immediately back into their vehicles carrying their wounded with them.

A large number of the gang advanced, screaming and shouting and climbing onto the appliances, unravelling the hoses and swinging from the ladders. Some started to smash the cab windows with iron bars, pieces of concrete and the metal nozzles of the hoses. The fire crews covered their heads inside to protect themselves as best they could.

The arrival of the police cars, having negotiated the barriers and now backed up by two armoured anti-riot vans, served only to switch the point of attack. As they sprang from the vehicles to tackle the youths surrounding the appliances, a second wave came screaming at them.

It was a well-orchestrated ambush with the police caught by surprise by another salvo of missiles. They had arrived in numbers, however, with most of them in full protective riot gear, and both groups began to fall back away from the square as the line of officers advanced behind their shields. The fire crews got to work on the burning vehicles attempting to stop the fires spreading to the garages and the other cars. Two ambulances arrived at the scene and the paramedics attended the injured crew members. The crowd was still retreating slowly away from the square before the advancing police line and the worst of the incident seemed to be over.

At the perimeter of this mayhem, three men, older by a few years than the rest of the mob, were watching the events unfold with smug satisfaction. With all attention focused elsewhere, the smallest of the three broke from cover and threw something over the emergency vehicles into the road. He retreated quickly, diving behind a wall and covering his ears, as the stun grenade exploded, blinding everyone facing the explosion for a few seconds and temporarily deafening everyone in the square. The man in a black baseball cap standing behind a white van parked near the corner of one of the closes, ducked back quickly behind the vehicle and covered his ears just in time to avoid the incapacitating effect of the explosion. Several upstairs windows in the houses closest to the scene were shattered and glass fell onto porch roofs and into gardens.

The police and fire crews recovered quickly as another appliance arrived along with two further police cars and a third ambulance. The three men were smoking and chatting casually again as they continued to watch the action in the aftermath of the grenade. The man behind the van had barely taken his eyes off them as the carnage escalated. With so much to deflect his attention, it was surprising that he could stay focused on three stationary forms for so long, but his mind was consumed by his interest in them and all else around him was incidental to the scene, except as justification for his obsession.

His only small distraction was to notice that, despite the blitz happening on their very doorsteps, not one resident around the square was watching. Earlier, every curtain had been pulled back and lights were already on in many of the houses. However, as the crowd had gathered, curtains were quickly closed and lights extinguished. The man thought of the people sitting fearfully in the near-darkness, with only the firelight from outside dancing on the windows to illuminate their lives.

The police held their line well without yielding to the temporary effects of the explosion, and with the arrival of reinforcements, they looked like they were containing the situation. Suddenly, the intense black canopy was split by a blinding white gash and a sound like the crack of a thousand whips as the storm broke. It started raining, heavily and mercifully.

The flames were rapidly quenched by the combination of nature and human resolve and the crowd dispersed, hurling a few token missiles as they left the area. The physical crisis was over. Smoke and steam rose silently in ever decreasing plumes from the metal wreckage; but more clouds of despair had gathered over the Cullen Field Estate.

★

The arrival of the three brothers at the Wild Boar Inn, a few streets away from the disturbance, had an immediate impact. Up to that moment it had been just another Saturday night, with the atmosphere increasing in energy and volume. Conversations which had been light-hearted and animated suddenly stopped altogether or continued in subdued tones. All the good humour seemed to have been sucked out through the door as the men entered.

They looked round the place as they walked across to the bar, leaving a trail of water on the floor, and challenging anyone to make eye contact. A few nodded and a couple offered a muted greeting.

"Three pints, Ned," said the eldest of the men. He was tall and muscular, and wore a dark brown canvas jacket over a tight black tee shirt, blue jeans and sand-coloured desert boots. His head was shaved and his neck heavily tattooed in a continuous design stretching from behind his ears and round beneath his chin, disappearing under his shirt. His face was hard and challenging.

They each pulled themselves up onto a bar stool and leant in a line at the bar.

"Don't know what's happening on Kingdom," said the barman, as he pulled the pints. "Sounds like a fucking air-raid."

"Kids, probably," said one of the other two men and all three laughed. This second man was much the smallest of the three, just under medium height and lightly built, with black hair long enough to hang over the neck of his grey hooded top. He wore matching grey jogging pants and expensive trainers. He had a twitching, fidgeting manner and a permanent scowl, compensating for his lack of stature with an attitude of simmering aggression. He unzipped his top and pulled it open, shaking off the moisture onto the floor.

"You guys okay?" said Ned, gaining in confidence and relaxing a little. He was a smallish man, pale and balding with a hunted look which made him seem totally unsuited for this sort of charged environment.

"Apart from being pissing wet through and dying of thirst. Just get the fucking drinks, for Christ's sake!" said the first man.

The landlord, who had just finished serving another customer, walked up.

"Okay, Ned, I'll take over," he said. He finished pulling the last pint and handed it to the eldest man.

"Ten pound fifty," he said.

"Can't believe you can charge that much with a straight face for this fucking whippet piss," said the man. "Start a tab."

"You can start another tab when you've paid off the last one," said the landlord. "In the meantime, ten pound fifty. And if the lager's that crap, Jimmy, I'd be delighted if you'd go and drink somewhere else."

Max Jordan was a very large man. Most of his weight was now in front of him and his shirt gaped open between every button. But he was a formidable presence all the same, with a bull neck, shaved head and thick, muscular forearms covered in tattoos. Even so, more than anyone he had encountered in thirty years behind a bar, these three pushed his courage to the limit. He knew this could turn bad at any time. But not tonight; not yet.

"Give him the money, Kev," said Jimmy to the small one.

"Fuck off. I didn't even want to come in here tonight," replied Kevin. Even so, he took out a twenty pound note and handed it over.

"Shall I knock the change off your tab?" said the landlord.

"Don't fucking push it!"

"Fine." He handed over the change.

During this exchange, a stranger had entered the pub and taken up a position on a stool next to them. The man was in his early forties, with a dark beard which was not much more than a few days' stubble. His eyes were intense and alert, but not unfriendly. He was tall and slim, and wore a black baseball cap pulled down low over his forehead, a long black leather jacket and a pair of faded jeans.

"Yes?" said the landlord.

"Very large Jameson's, please." The man spoke with a thick Northern Irish accent, returning the landlord's tentative smile.

"Triple?"

"Aye, at least."

The man paid for the drink then drank half of it in a single swallow, exhaling a satisfied 'aaah' as he placed the glass back on the bar. Then he reached along the bar, behind Kevin, the nearest of the three men, towards a bowl of peanuts. In doing so, he caught Kevin's arm, causing him to spill some of his pint down the front of his shirt. Kevin whirled round, dropping from his stool and slamming his glass onto the bar. He grabbed the stranger by the lapels of his coat, leaning backwards slightly as if he was about to head butt him. The man raised his hands

11

instinctively in front of his face to prevent the attack, at the same time crying out, "Sorry, sorry! It was an accident. I'm really sorry!"

The three men had surrounded the stranger who was still on the stool, his back arched over the bar with Kevin's clenched hands holding his collar and his knuckles pressing against his throat. The landlord reached across, pushing Kevin gently but firmly in the chest to ease him back.

"Come on, Kev," he said. "It was just an accident, like the man said. No need for this. He'll get you another drink, won't you?"

"Yes, of course," said the stranger, choking out the words. "Get them all one, please. I'm really sorry."

"You will be fucking sorry!" Kevin snarled, almost spitting out the words, his eyes still blazing. "And what about my fucking shirt?"

"Well, I… "

"It's fucking ruined!"

"Okay, look, I'll give you some money to replace it. But it *was* an accident. Really."

Kevin let him go and the stranger slowly and very deliberately took out his wallet. Jimmy grabbed it off him.

"Good shirt, that, Kev," he said, sniggering. "How much did you say it was?"

"Eighty-five quid," said Kevin. All three laughed.

"Well, there's plenty in here," said the man looking in the wallet. "Let's say a hundred shall we, to cover bus fare there and back to Saville Row. What do you reckon, Karl?" He turned to the third man.

"Uh-uh-uh," his brother made a grunting sound which just about passed for a laugh. Karl was the same height as Jimmy, but much bigger all round. His bulk was mainly excess weight and he had none of the other's muscle definition. In every other way, he was exactly like him. He had the same shaved head and tattoos, and had copied his elder sibling's outfit right down to the colour of his boots. His face was round and full, with none of the hardness of the other two.

"You okay with that, mate?" said Jimmy. "Reckon you've got off lightly so far."

"Now come on," the landlord stepped in again. "Give the man back his wallet and let him buy you all a drink. Those few drops aren't going to spoil a shirt – certainly not such an expensive one," he added.

"Who are you, Max, his fucking nanny?" said Jimmy. "Let him speak for himself. Well, fuck-wit, what do you think? A hundred quid's fair?"

"Yes, of course," he said, "if the shirt was really that much."

"You calling me a liar?" shouted Kevin, renewing his grip on the man. "First you throw a fucking drink over me and then call me a liar. You got a fucking death wish?"

"No, no. A hundred's fine. Then I'll buy you that drink."

This time the stranger pushed Kevin away firmly himself, and then reached over and took back his wallet from Jimmy. He took out five twenties and handed them to him.

"Now three pints, wasn't it?"

"Tell you what," said Jimmy, "Just to make it right – I mean, we were all having such a good time until you came in throwing your weight about – I think you ought to get drinks all round. Then you might even get out of here alive."

"Right, that's enough, Jimmy," said Max. "It was just a little accident and this has gone too far… "

"Let's ask the lads, then," said Jimmy. He turned to the room in general. "Who wants to have a drink with me and my brothers, on our Irish friend here?"

No-one spoke.

Jimmy's eyes swept the room, finally fixing on a table covered in empty bottles close to where he was standing. The three men at the table were all in their mid-thirties, with bulky frames and hard-looking faces. Collectively, they looked as though they would be more than a match for the three brothers, but they became agitated and nervous as Jimmy picked them out.

"You three – would you like a drink with me and my brothers?" he shouted.

"Yeah, that would be great," said one of the men, quietly and without enthusiasm, and the other two nodded.

"Good!"

Jimmy looked up and round the room again; everyone either muttered a 'yes' or nodded or raised a reluctant hand.

"Look," said Max to the stranger, "you don't have to do this, friend. And if you want your hundred quid back… "

"No, that's okay, thanks anyway," he said. "But I've got to be

13

getting along. So, if I just give another hundred to Jimmy, here, then that should easily cover a round for everybody, I guess."

He took five more twenties from his wallet and handed them over. Jimmy took the cash as the three brothers sat down again. He held each of the notes up to the light in mock inspection of the money, while the other two laughed. The stranger, looking relaxed and composed, drained his glass and put it down on the bar. He nodded to the landlord but before he could move, Kevin turned round on his stool to face him.

"Where the fuck do you think you're going? You haven't asked if you can leave yet."

"Let him go," said Jimmy. "At least let's give the poor bastard a start."

They all laughed again.

The stranger stood up very calmly, smoothed the creases from his jacket and pulled down the cap a little further.

"Five seconds," said Jimmy. "You've got five seconds to get to that door and away. Then we're after you. You'd better run like fuck!"

The man smiled, thinly.

"Oh, I will," he said.

Without warning, he lunged forward and shoved Kevin in the chest. The force of the attack knocked Kevin into Jimmy and the three bar stools and their occupants crashed to the floor like falling dominoes.

He moved quickly across the room and through the door into the street. Outside he was confronted by a group of around thirty youngsters, mostly in their early teens, who had been hanging around the pub in the pouring rain. As if by a collective reflex, they all started shouting abuse and insults at him, but did nothing to impede his flight. He set off down the road out of the estate.

In the bar, the brothers scrambled to their feet, taking a few moments to fully realise what had happened to them.

"Stop the bastard!" yelled Kevin, pointlessly.

They raced out into the street. The crowd of youngsters picked up the story as they saw the brothers emerge.

"That way!" they shouted.

"Right!" yelled Jimmy, seeing the running figure already two streets away. "Get him!"

14

The stranger set a challenging pace. The three brothers, at the vanguard of the pursuing pack, initially made no impression on him and Karl soon fell behind. But after several minutes their quarry began to slow down. The road had left the estate behind, passing through an open area before entering an old business park of factories, yards and warehouses, currently deserted.

"This is fucking perfect," panted Kevin. "No witnesses."

The man, who had been running purposefully in one direction, suddenly turned right into a side street.

"Shit, we're going to lose him."

"I don't think so," said Jimmy. "More like he's just committed suicide."

Jimmy slowed down as they approached the corner of the street, and the pack reduced their pace to keep behind him. Most of the gang from outside the pub had stayed the course and fanned out across the entrance of the street as the brothers turned the corner. Karl arrived, gasping for breath, and pushed his way through them to join his brothers.

The street was an old cobbled cul-de-sac, with red brick walls of ancient warehouses rising high on both sides and huge cast-iron factory gates across the end. The stranger was about a hundred yards away, with his back to the crowd, and holding on to the vertical bars of the gates as if supporting himself. He looked totally spent from his exertions.

The three men started towards him; the others followed, still spread across the full width of the cul-de-sac. Jimmy stopped suddenly and turned on the crowd.

"Right, fuck off, you lot!" he shouted.

"Oh, come on, Jimmy," someone called back, and there were mutterings from many of the others.

"Did you hear me? Get the fuck out of here!" Jimmy yelled at them again.

"We won't say anything, Jimmy. Just let us watch," shouted someone else.

This time Jimmy strode across to the Asian boy who had spoken. He grabbed him by his hair, pulled back his head and yelled into his face, "Are you fucking deaf or just stupid?"

Then he slapped him twice very hard across the face – forehand and backhand. Tears welled in the boy's eyes and blood ran freely from his nose. Jimmy pushed him to the ground and kicked him three times as he lay there. He squealed with pain, dragging himself to his feet, half running, half limping away.

"Anyone else want to stay?"

The rest of the crowd quickly started to leave the street and head back the way they had come, following the injured boy.

Kevin and Karl had not taken their eyes off the motionless figure at the factory gates. When the last of the crowd had left the end of the street, Jimmy joined them again and, with him leading, as he always did, they set off walking towards him.

The torrential rain bounced off the cobbles. They were about forty yards away when the man turned to face them. The brothers slowed down, cautiously anticipating the pending action.

The man noted that they looked like three gunslingers on a western street, line abreast, arms hanging loosely but in readiness by their sides, waiting for the first move. He smiled at the image.

"Why, look'ya here," he said, in an authentic cowboy drawl, "It's the good ol' Brady bunch. The Hole-in-the-Head gang. Howdy, boys. Welcome to Dead Man's Canyon."

The brothers stopped.

Jimmy screwed his face into a snarl.

"Who the fuck are you? You're a fucking weirdo, I know that!"

"Why, what a hurtful thing to say, Jim-boy. That sure ain't friendly-like," said the man, still in character. He looked around him at the sombre walls of the buildings.

"Just look at this shit-hole," he said, dropping the fake voice. "What a hell of a place for you to die." He looked up into the sky and felt the rain beating down into his face. "At least the blood will get washed away," he added. His voice was soft and refined and there was now no trace of the Ulster accent.

The brothers had not moved. The initiative had been taken away from them completely by the unnerving composure of the stranger.

"So here we are," the man went on. "The brothers Brady. Jimmy, nearly twenty-one, and Karl and Kevin, eighteen. Twins – nowhere near identical; in fact, amazingly different. One a big, fat slob; the other a pathetic little runt. Only one thing in common – neither possesses a single brain cell."

"You're a fucking wanker!" shouted Jimmy. "And if you think

you can talk your way out of anything, you're fucking stupid as well. And how come you know us? Are we supposed to recognise you or something?"

"No," answered the man, "you don't know me. But we do have a mutual acquaintance. An elderly lady on the estate. Acquaintance might be the wrong word, because I don't know if you ever actually met her, but some very bad things happened to her front door. Someone painted some really bad words on it, then smashed it in a few times with a sledge hammer or something and put dog-shit through the letter box. I guess that was all your doing. She tried to kill herself three times because of you guys."

As he was talking, the man had moved slowly away from the gates towards the brothers until he had halved the distance between them.

"You look a bit worried, Jimmy," the man continued. "I'm surprised really, considering you're just about the hardest guys on the planet, aren't you? Terrorising all those defenceless people; getting children to do the dirty work while you hide in the shadows. And I mean, just look how you dealt with that kid just now. How old was he – twelve, thirteen? You showed him, didn't you? Don't mess with me! Fucking big hard-man me!"

He paused, giving them a chance to respond. No-one spoke.

"Hey, but that's not fair, is it?" he went on. "I could see how it was with those guys in the pub. Nobody wanted to look you in the eye. They were even too scared to turn down a drink with you, even though they would've probably choked on it. How does it feel knowing that every one of the guys in that place wishes you were dead? Come to think of it, I guess that's going to make me a hero after tonight."

The twins kept glancing nervously at Jimmy for some sort of signal. Jimmy stared straight ahead at the stranger.

"Are you carrying any tools, by the way? Knives? Guns? Guns, I reckon. Knives are for small time cowards, aren't they? If you want to be a really big coward you have to carry a gun these days. Tell you what, you show me yours and I'll show you mine."

No-one spoke for half a minute. The stranger broke the silence.

"Look, are you guys going to do anything? I mean you put in a lot of effort to get here. Or are you just scared shitless by one old man?"

The twins reacted instinctively to the challenge. Suddenly they both had knives in their hands, and the sneer had returned to their faces.

"Right, you fucking twat," Kevin snarled. "Piss-taking over! This is it! Get him, Karl!"

Together they rushed forward. In what seemed like a single, blurred movement, the man pulled aside his jacket with his left hand to reveal an automatic pistol in the belt of his jeans; then the gun was in his right hand, arm extended, aimed, fired. The shot signalled the end of Kevin Brady who, with his twin brother, had covered no more than half the short distance between them. He crashed to the ground and lay twisted in death on the street, the rain washing around him, a hole in his forehead.

Karl stopped, frozen in his charge. The man dropped his arm to his side and spoke.

"Well, Karl. You haven't said a single word all evening. Wouldn't you like to say something now? What about, 'Please don't kill me'?"

Karl dropped to his knees on the cobbles. He stared across at Kevin and started shaking with fear. He seemed incapable of speech. The man shouted impatiently, "Well, come on! Are you going to fucking say something or not? I'll count to three – one, two… "

"P-P-Please," stammered Karl, in a barely audible whisper, "don't k-k-kill me. I d-didn't… "

The man furrowed his brow and pursed his lips in an exaggerated expression of concentration. Then his face relaxed.

"No, sorry," he said. His arm came up to the firing position again. His second bullet dispatched Karl with the same precise head shot. Jimmy had not moved since the first shot. His eyes were open wider than seemed possible as he looked from his two dead siblings to the stranger.

"Well, what do you think of *that*, Jimmy?" said the man, nodding towards the two bodies on the cobbles. "That'll be you in a couple of minutes. Tell you what, though," he went on, replacing the gun in his belt. "I know you're packing a shooter, so we'll do this cowboy style. And as you're the baddie, it's a sort of tradition that you get to draw first. I guess you must know, though, that you don't have a fucking snowball in hell's chance. Right?"

They looked at each other in silence for a full minute, Jimmy's lower lip trembling like a child's. Then, suddenly, his expression changed; his eyes flashed and he reached quickly inside his jacket. His gun had hardly cleared the pocket when the stranger fired. The shot shattered Jimmy's right knee-cap, tearing ligaments and sending splinters of bone up into his thigh. The impact of the bullet lifted his leg up behind him and sent him crashing onto his face on the cobbles, his body sending up a spray of water. The gun flew out of his hand and bounced across the street coming to rest against the kerb. He rolled onto his back into the gutter, jerking his head from side to side and screaming in his agony. The blood pouring from the wound was carried away with the rainwater.

The stranger stood motionless for a long time watching his suffering before walking across to him.

"Does that hurt a bit, Jimmy? Don't worry, it won't be for long. I just wanted to make sure that you had a minute or two to think about what's going to happen to you. It doesn't do to rush these things." His tone had hardened and the real obsessive hatred came through in his voice. He put his gun back into his belt then took a pair of surgical gloves from a pocket in his jacket and pulled them on.

"I guess you won't be needing the money for Kev's shirt and the drinks after all. I'll take it back now, if you don't mind; I've got no stomach for robbing a corpse."

He crouched down beside Jimmy, who had raised himself up on one elbow and was clutching his injured leg with his other hand and crying uncontrollably. Reaching inside Jimmy's jacket he pulled out a wad of bank notes from the inside pocket. Silently, he counted out ten twenty-pound notes and pushed the rest back into the same pocket. Then, taking his time, he counted them again, out loud this time as if to show that he had only taken back the amount he was entitled to.

Finally he stood up, taking out the gun again. Leaning forward, he placed the muzzle against Jimmy's forehead.

"Time's up, Jimmy. This is for your neighbours hiding behind their curtains, for the guys you injured tonight and other nights, and for the misery and pain you've inflicted on hundreds of nice people. Oh yes, and for the lady I told you about. I don't think I mentioned it before, but the third time she tried to take her own life, she succeeded.

"Go straight to hell, you evil bastard!"

He pulled the trigger.

CHAPTER 3

At the end of the eighth fruitless day since the killings, Detective Chief Inspector David Gerrard finished reading the final offering, closed the file on his PC and leant back in his chair. His Detective Sergeant, who had supervised the latest information search over the past two days, had been sitting across the desk from him for around two hours as he read through them. DS Joannita Cottrell was thirty-one years old, just under five-and-a-half feet tall and 'three-quarters West Indian', as she described herself – her maternal grandfather was white. Her long black curls with their auburn highlights were pulled back in a ponytail. She was slim without being slender, with an attractive rounded figure and large dark eyes set in a disarmingly pretty face, which for most of the time displayed a friendly smile. However, this was not her preferred way of spending a Sunday evening and the smile had long since been replaced by a mask of boredom.

"That's – what – seventeen in all out of how many checked?" said David, at last.

"Five hundred and thirty-five," she said, grateful for an end to the silence.

"Covering a period of… ?"

"Twenty-six weeks."

"And that's every complaint and call-out we've had on the estate during that time?"

"That's right, sir. Three a day on average. Oh, and none at all since the killings. When we do find this guy, perhaps we should give him a list of our most wanted and let him get on with it."

David snorted a laugh. "Hold that thought, Jo. Well, nothing hits the spot from that lot. There are a couple we could follow up, just so we can tell the press and the boss we have 'new lines of investigation'. But, gut-feel, I don't think so."

"There were others involving the Bradys which we discounted," she said. "Would you like to see them?"

"Why aren't they with these?"

"Because we didn't think – I didn't think – they would lead us anywhere."

"Then I don't need to see them," he said. "I'm sure you're right."

"What now then, sir?"

"Well, we'll get Mutt'n'Geoff to follow these two up," he said, reaching over to the printer where he had run off a dozen or so sheets of information. He shuffled through the papers, separating them into two piles and putting each into a plastic wallet folder. "Give them one each," he said, passing them to the Detective Sergeant. "It doesn't matter who gets which. And make sure they don't spend too much time on them."

"And then?"

"I think tomorrow after the meeting you and I will have another stroll round the estate, just to take the air and join in the carnival."

★

In his office in the Norman Shaw Building at 8.30 am on Monday morning, the Leader of the Opposition was leaning back in the leather tilt-and-swivel behind his vast walnut desk. The office was large and expensively appointed with a rich long-pile carpet and matching walnut cabinets and console tables. The two seats facing his desk across from him were ornate wing chairs, luxuriously upholstered.

Andrew Donald himself was a large man, over six feet tall, and although he was somewhat overweight, he carried the surplus evenly about his body, with no unseemly bulges, front or back. He had a round, rather chubby face and dark hair with a side parting, giving him an old-fashioned schoolboy look. Even so, his appearance was always effortlessly fashionable without surrendering any of the dignity of office. Overall, he looked what he was; an Old Etonian pitching for the job of Prime Minister. Today he was

21

wearing a charcoal grey two-piece suit which the man occupying one of the chairs opposite estimated would have cost him around £2,000.

"Right, let's get straight to it, shall we?" said Andrew, in open irritation. He waved his hand over a collection of Sunday newspapers and national dailies in an untidy pile on the desk. "Would you mind explaining to me why you told the press that you think it's a really good thing that three young men were executed in your constituency?"

Tom Brown was an inch shorter than Andrew and a completely different build: broad-shouldered and muscular with a narrow waist and hips, he had a natural spring to his step and an athletic fluency to his movements. His ruggedly handsome face was accentuated by a pair of pale blue eyes that could burn or twinkle to order, and had the effect of making him – according to popular female opinion – irresistibly attractive. Right now, they were focused and angry.

"That is not what I told the press," he said, "otherwise that's what they would have printed, wouldn't they?"

"Okay, I'm paraphrasing, but… "

"No, you're not," interrupted Tom. "Paraphrasing is when you state the *same* message in a another, usually more succinct, way. Not when you invent something completely different that isn't true."

"For God's sake, Tom! You're not in the bloody House now! You don't have to dissect my sentences to discredit what I'm saying. You know very well what I'm getting at. You have been our most forthright champion of law and order up to now, and we have put you up there as our key spokesman on the issue. That's why we've given you a research team and an office manager and skimmed off so much of our short-money for you. I can't believe you've betrayed that investment and positional trust to get a few brownie points with that rabble."

"That is completely out of order!" Tom shouted, slamming the flat of his hand on the desk and half rising to his feet. "Don't you dare talk to me about betrayal! And they are not rabble, they are people! *My* people!"

Andrew took the outburst unflinchingly and with mild amusement.

"*My* people," he echoed, with a smirk. "It's a shame you don't like them enough to want to live with them, instead of in your walled palace thirty miles away."

Tom could feel his face reddening with anger.

"Now come on, Andrew, I thought we'd drawn a line under that. I spend at least three nights each week at the apartment there, and it couldn't be more central to the constituency. And I'm there most of every Saturday... "

"Yes, but nobody sees you just around and about, do they. They don't regard you as one of their community; just a do-gooder who pops in occasionally."

"What is this about?" Tom shouted. "Why all this again? I suppose you and Isobel can be spotted most weekends queuing at the local butchers! "

Andrew laughed and held up his hands.

"Okay, Tom, I guess I shouldn't take your 'good guy' image lightly. God knows it's been a great weapon for the Party. And 'betrayal' – wrong word. But let's calm down, shall we."

"Would you like to know what really happened?" said Tom, easing himself back onto the chair. Andrew waved an arm inviting him to continue. "I went to the estate on Friday along with Grace and some of the local Party guys, the objective being to reassure the residents – you know – that this sort of thing couldn't be allowed to go on, etcetera, etcetera. And it was like a street party; the only thing that was missing was the bunting. It sort of caught us off-guard... "

"Don't you read the papers? The press have been all over the estate since the killings; the dailies have been full of the festival spirit for a week now. That's another thing; I'm not sure why it took you so long to get round to visiting *your* people."

"Okay, point taken," said Tom, "in retrospect, perhaps an earlier visit would have been appropriate, and yes, I have read the media accounts of the collective mood in the aftermath. But it was the *intensity* of the feeling that took us by surprise, and the openness of their apparent joy at the death of these three brothers. They didn't see the killings as part of the problem; they saw it as part of the *solution*. There was no way I could simply condemn the act without alienating just about the whole estate."

"So what are the lessons you draw from that? Put a sniper on every high-rise in every rough estate? I expect you're still in touch

23

with some of your soldier friends. It's only been, what, six years since you were out there killing people yourself."

"Look, Andrew," said Tom, getting angry again. "We are on the same fucking side and want the same fucking thing. And I'll tell you something – there are a hell of a lot of people out there who'd vote for your sniper scenario. But I prefer to think of that as Plan B. Perhaps when you're feeling more objective and less cynical, we can discuss Plan A."

"Okay, Tom," said Andrew. "*Your* point taken." He checked his watch and stood up to signal that the meeting was over. "I'm just very concerned that whatever you said and whatever the papers printed, the message, as I read it, is that the man who did this was right in taking the law into his own hands and that, in doing so, he did the estate a big favour. Now whether you actually believe that… "

"Oh I do," Tom interrupted, "well the second bit anyway. He *did* do the estate a big favour. He just about set them all free."

Andrew stood motionless for a few moments, looking at his colleague with a quizzical frown and absorbing his words.

"Okay," he said, finally, "let's pick up Plan A tomorrow."

⋆

The Major Incident Team room on the ground floor at Parkside was unremarkable in almost all aspects. One wall was completely covered floor-to-ceiling with white matt-finish panels that served as write-on boards, magnetic display boards and projection screens. The room contained twenty work stations arranged in groups of five for the four teams of detectives working there, and there were four doors leading off it down one side. Two of these opened onto small meeting rooms and a third led to the Detective Inspector's office, currently unoccupied due to its normal resident being on maternity leave. The fourth door represented the single exception from the norm; it gave access to the office of Detective Chief Inspector David Gerrard. Someone of David's rank would usually occupy an office 'upstairs' with the Senior Leadership Team, but at the time of his promotion he had managed to pull a few strings in order to remain with the 'ground forces', as he called them.

At 9.00 am prompt, he pulled on his suit jacket and emerged

from the office, briefly filling the doorway as he passed through it. David Gerrard was huge – a colossus. He stood six feet five inches tall in his bare feet, and weighed in at a shade over eighteen stones – or 1.96 metres and 115 kilograms, as his official record stated. A former Saracens and England Saxons flanker, his career as a full-time professional had been cut short by recurring back and hip problems, but he had since worked hard – and successfully – to retain his physique and fitness. His craggy face was round and full and friendly – some said too friendly for a senior police officer, although his fearsome bulk more than made up for it. Now in his fifty-third year, his slightly receding dark brown hair showed only the faintest traces of grey.

As always, the group became instantly silent as he entered the room. He moved over to the large map of the estate and its immediate surroundings which spanned two A1 size sheets of fibre-board resting side-by-side on a pair of easels in front of the white-panelled wall. To the right of it, an image thrown onto the wall from the ceiling mounted Lite-Pro projector showed a blank background with a number of icons round the edges. To the left of the map were pinned photographs of the three brothers and around a dozen images from the scene of the killings. David turned to face the group, which comprised two of the four detective teams.

"Right," he said, "before we move on, let's recap on what we've done so far. In the absence of any progress at all in finding this guy, it might be therapeutic to remind ourselves that we've been working bloody hard all the same. Catherine, tell us what we know about motive."

He addressed DC Catherine Baxter.

"Almost certainly a revenge killing, sir. Could be personal or contract, related to drugs, protection or social disorder activities – and, just possibly, sectarian."

David nodded, appreciatively. "Thank you, Catherine. Very snappy – you've set the standard. Omar, rationale for drug-related?"

DC Shakhir responded. "None really, sir. Doesn't fit the normal pattern for a gang reprisal. Contract killings are very rare. The Bradys would probably have recognised the guy if he'd been from a rival group and he would most likely have shot them there and then."

"Okay, thanks. Siobhan, what about protection?"

"Also unlikely, sir." DC Wheeler had been seated and stood up to give her reply. "It's hard to believe any of the major chains would risk hiring a contract killer – it sort of goes against their corporate charters and mission statements – and the smaller outlets just couldn't afford it. So we reckon that's a 'no'."

"Good enough. Geoff. Sectarian?"

"Man had a Northern Irish accent," DC Drury answered, "and Brady clan used to live in Donegal. But no history of sectarian involvement and family relocated to London during the Troubles, long before Jimmy and the twins were born. So that's a 'no' as well, sir."

"Which leaves – DS Cottrell?"

"Possible link to street violence and intimidation. On the night of the killings, the man was observed at the scene of the disturbance watching the Bradys. Less than half an hour later the killer entered the Wild Boar and – it seems certain now – deliberately singled them out."

"You said 'killer', Detective Sergeant. Just for once, you're allowed to state the bleeding obvious. Why do we believe the man in the pub is the killer?"

Jo looked surprised at the question.

"Well, sir, he was seen by about thirty kids alone with the Bradys in the cul-de-sac where they were found dead."

"Okay… "

"And," she went on, "the two hundred pounds Jimmy had taken from him in the pub was missing from the body."

"Right. Forensic evidence? Robbie?"

"None, sir," said DC Burns. "No identifiable prints on the stool or glass in the pub, nothing from Jimmy's clothing or the other notes in his pocket. Firearm used was 9mm, quite probably a Glock, but the gun's signature on the bullets can't be matched to any from other shootings."

David nodded and paused for a moment.

"Okay, thanks everybody; so that's what we've got so far – not exactly sweet FA, but not much more. And without anything else, we still can't be sure exactly why this man did what he did. And without knowing *that*, we can't narrow down the search."

He paused to look round the anxious faces.

"Now I know a number of you grabbing bastards put in a lot of overtime this weekend."

The group relaxed for the moment into a collective smile.

"Three hundred and thirty-odd records checked – very impressive – but, I'm afraid, nothing to celebrate. Geoff and Murray have got a couple of leads to follow up, but I won't be asking anyone to hold their breath. So, where do we go from here?"

He turned to the map which was exhibiting signs of wear, with frayed edges and finger marks all over it, reflecting the amount of attention it had received, being the only material focus of the meetings – and the case – so far. The scene of the disturbance, the location of the Wild Boar Inn and the place where the Bradys died – on the very edge of the area covered – were marked with red circular stickers. Scattered over the rest of the map were a number of smaller green ones, fifteen in all.

"I know that the initial team visited every house and apartment on the estate during the door-to-doors. I am also aware that some residents were not at home when they called the first time and that they followed up with further visits to talk to them. In fact, I know by that time some of you were involved in follow-up visits." He pointed to the map. "These green dots represent houses where residents have not yet been spoken to. These are the addresses – DS Cottrell."

Jo clicked on an icon on her laptop and the image next to the map changed to display a list of addresses with the tenants' names. David continued.

"I'd like, say, three or four of you, to split this list and do a final check this morning, and speak to neighbours if we still draw a blank at the addresses themselves. Any questions?"

No-one spoke.

"Detective Sergeant?" he said, inviting Jo to add anything.

"Nothing, sir, except that copies of the list are on my desk."

"Right, we'll get back together again here at four o'clock for an update. Okay, let's go."

★

"What exactly are we looking for, sir?" asked Jo, as they strolled through Cullen Field Estate.

"Anything," said David, "and just as likely, nothing."

"Will we know it when we see it?" she asked, smiling.

"Doubt it," said David.

The Cullen Field Estate was home to around 3,000 people. It had been conceived twenty years ago as a celebration of council accommodation, providing aesthetically pleasing housing with a sense of individuality. Throughout the estate there were wide margins of grass, expansive flowerbeds and small parks dotted around, avoiding any over-concentration of red brick and white rendering. One third of the residences were apartments, but these were accommodated in three-storey blocks designed to look like large houses. The houses themselves, of which there were six different designs, were built to the highest architectural and environmental specifications, and each one had an open plan front garden and enclosed rear one. From the air, the estate as a whole was precisely symmetrical, but at ground level it was pleasingly varied from road to road, close to close, which achieved that feeling of individuality.

On the edge of the estate was a large shopping mall, designed to attract shoppers from a wide surrounding area as well as to provide for the residents themselves. Cullen Hall, like the estate itself, was a high quality show-piece, with domes, arches and manicured gardens giving it the appearance of a huge ancient temple from the outside.

Early signs had been encouraging. Community pride was clear to see in the neatness of the gardens and quality of both internal and external décor. Coach parties flocked to the mall and local businesses thrived. Then the street gangs took over, culminating in the iron grip of the Bradys and their disciples. For the past few years, the estate had been in freefall.

David and Jo turned into the road leading to the square where the disturbance had taken place on the evening of the killings. As they walked together towards the end of the road, Jo stopped and looked round, getting her bearings.

"I have a feeling there's a green dot around here somewhere," she said. Taking a battered notebook from the inside pocket of her jacket, she opened it and removed a folded A4 sheet with the list of addresses. "This is Kingdom Road and the four closes off it are St

Andrew's, St David's, St Patrick's and – bet you can't guess. And here we are," she added, as they arrived at St George's Close. She checked the sheet. "Number 12 is on our hit list. A Mrs Alma Deverall. Shall we take a look?"

They walked down the close. The front gardens were all lawned and fairly well tended. The houses themselves looked neat and clean.

"I spent nearly a full day around here just after the disturbance – and the killings," she said, "and it didn't look anything like this. It fits the pattern of pride returning to the community. All these gardens were overgrown and full of rubbish only a week ago, and there were broken windows and graffiti all round the close. Whoever our killer is, he's touched this place with the hand of God."

The one exception was Number 12, where the grass was over a foot high and the weeds were already wrapping around the 'For Sale' sign which reached up out of the undergrowth. The front door was slightly damaged but someone had daubed a couple of coats of paint on it to try and make it look respectable.

"I'm sure the sign wasn't here before, either," said Jo. "Mind you, they make great kindling, don't they? I couldn't imagine one lasting very long on this estate before the Bradys left us. Do you know that over three hundred of those five-hundred-and-odd cases involved arson, usually along with something else?"

"Those bastards really did run the place, didn't they? Run it *and* ruin it," said David. "Good riddance, I say. Not officially, of course," he added.

They walked up the path to the front door of Number 12. There was no point in knocking; it was clear no-one was living there even though a few items of furniture remained inside.

"Stuff must have been moved out since I was here," said Jo, consulting her notebook. "I would have made a note if any of the houses had been unoccupied."

"So someone might have moved out immediately after the killings," said David. "Killed the boys and ran away… " But he seemed unable to link the fact to anything relevant. "Anyway, worth checking, I suppose. Could you find out who the vendor is and the timing and stuff?"

"Okay, I'll try to get the info for the meeting at four."

"Well, don't kill yourself, I don't suppose it's going to lead anywhere but it's a loose end we could do with tying up. In the absence of any actual leads, loose ends start to look quite attractive, don't you think? Anyway, we haven't finished our constitutional yet. Let's keep going and see if we can scrounge a cup of tea from somewhere. Might as well cash in on the euphoria."

★

George and Irene Holland pulled into the huge car-park at Cullen Hall at just after 10.00 am that same morning. They were on their two-weekly shopping trip from their home in Meadow Village, just a mile and a half away. They regarded this fortnightly event as a sort of raid, the aim being to get in and out as quickly as possible with a minimum of human contact.

George was sixty-five years old, a retired school teacher. Slightly less than medium height, he was a little overweight due to – he was quick to explain – 'the natural slowing down of his metabolism'. He was dressed trendily in blue jeans, checked shirt and casual jacket and his open friendly face sported a small neatly-trimmed goatee beard. His head was naturally bald except for a semicircle of hair round the back at about ear-level which he fashionably removed with un-guarded clippers every other week.

He opened the boot of the Fiesta and Irene lifted out the shopping bags. Irene was the same age as her husband, but looked ten years younger. She was petite and pretty with a trim little figure that most women half her age would die for. Her fair hair, though thinning a little now, retained most of its natural colour with only the slightest hint of grey visible in places.

"Morning, lovely day."

They both looked up in surprise at two smiling women walking past them, and instinctively looked around to make sure they were the target for the greeting.

"Yes, beautiful," said Irene, smiling back when it was clear that they were. The women passed by and George and Irene looked at each other with eyebrows raised in astonishment.

"Well, that's a first," said George. "They must be tourists."

"Perhaps they are," said Irene, pointing to a line of coaches parked in front of the entrance to the shops. "The place looks like it's back in business."

They went into the mall with its impressive marble floors and columns, fountains and sculptures. The place was bustling with people, in contrast to previous visits. They made their way towards the Food Hall at one end of the complex, past large groups of shoppers moving around together visiting the High Street retail stores; clearly day trippers from the coaches outside. The collective mood was relaxed and happy.

As they waited with a full trolley at the Tesco check-out, they chatted amiably to a couple about their own age who were behind them in the queue.

"I'm sure I've seen you here before," said the woman. "Do you live on the estate?"

"No we're from Meadow Village, just down the road," Irene replied, "but we come here to shop."

"Oh, Meadow Village. It's a lovely place isn't it? We've been to the Dog and Duck a couple of times for a meal, haven't we, Seth?"

"Yes, really nice food," said Seth.

"We're very lucky having an excellent restaurant like that in such a small place," said George. "We tend to take it for granted."

"There are some very good eating places in Cullen Field," Seth said, "but people tend to stay in at night. We hadn't had a night out on the estate for months until last week, had we Cathy? You had to be very careful before."

"Before?" asked Irene. "You mean before the shootings?"

"Yes. Things seem quite different now," said Cathy. "Well, they have been so far." She held up her hands with fingers crossed. "Don't want to tempt providence."

"You mean it's all changed in just a week?" asked George. "It was only three kids, wasn't it? How can their not being around make that much difference?" He was thinking back to the last time the gang had descended on the village. There had been fifty or sixty of them then.

"Well, the Bradys weren't kids for a start," said Seth, "and they were behind just about everything, apparently. I don't think anyone realised that, especially the police. Then all the aggro just seemed to stop when they got killed. Everybody's talking to everybody else, the atmosphere's completely changed. It's as if this guy is out there watching over us. It must sound weird to an outsider, but that's the way it feels."

"As I said – *so far*," added Cathy. "I suppose it might be just until the gangs get organised again. Even so, hopefully it won't go back to being as bad as it was."

"We've had problems with them in the village," said Irene, "but not that often. Enough to keep you on your guard all the time, though; like you can't relax completely, you're always listening out just in case."

They'd reached the check-out and the conversation stopped as they loaded the bags and put them back in the trolley. Having paid and stepped out of the way, they waited for Cathy and Seth and walked back with them to the exit to the car park.

"So what are you planning to do now?" asked Cathy.

"Well, normally we just head back home," said George, "but I think we might drop in to Waterstones and have a browse. I guess we could have a coffee there as well." He turned to Irene who nodded.

"Just as long as we get back with the frozen stuff in time," she said.

They pushed through the doors and into the car park to unload the trolley.

"Actually, if you fancy a coffee and a look at some books," said Seth, "at the far end of the precinct – the end opposite the Food Hall – there are a some tea rooms and cafes set out round a little village green along with a couple of craft shops and a little bookseller."

"Right, thank you," said George, "we'll definitely give that a try. I'm George, by the way, this is Irene."

"Seth and Cathy."

"Lovely to meet you," said Irene. "I really hope we'll see you again."

They shook hands and said their goodbyes.

"This is nothing short of a revelation," said George. "Come on, let's do the village green thing and then get back. We'll have to come again soon to have a better look round when we've not got defrosting burgers to worry about. And I think we should mention it at the meeting tonight after the talk."

Jo Cottrell flicked through the pages of her notebook until she found the right place.

"Right," she said, sitting back in her chair. "After I left you, I called on the houses at either side of Number 12 – that's 11 and 14, they're numbered going round the close, but there's no Number 13. Tenants of both of these houses had been spoken to before, but not specifically about Number 12. There was no-one in at Number 11, but the lady on the other side, a Mrs Maxine Johnston, said the house had been empty since she and her husband had moved in – that was five months ago. She said that she understood that the elderly lady who lived there had become ill and left to live with a friend. But the house went up for sale only on Saturday – two days ago. The vendor is Marlburgh Borough Council. They have a policy whereby when a rented property becomes available they put it up for sale for a period of six months before re-letting it if there are no takers. Incidentally, so far they haven't sold any houses on Cullen Field. It'll be interesting to see if that pattern changes now."

David was pacing round his office, an activity which always made it look much smaller than it was. The twelve-foot square room was very sparingly appointed. Apart from David's desk and large swivel chair, the only items of furniture were an old unused filing cabinet in one corner and two dining type chairs pulled up to the desk opposite his own, one of which Jo was currently occupying. On the back wall were a number of framed photographs – mostly team pictures from his rugby days – with half-a-dozen more standing in frames on his desk arranged around his PC.

"And the lady who left?" asked David. "Mrs… ?"

"Deverall, Alma Deverall. I've spoken to the council; they didn't know she'd moved out of the house. Last Tuesday they received a letter, posted the previous day, informing them that she wished to terminate the tenancy with immediate effect, and requesting details of any final settlement in lieu of the contractual notice period. The sender's address at the top of the letter was 12 St George's Close and it was signed by Mrs Deverall. Anyway, they sent her the information on Wednesday."

"What about the rent payments to the council during the months she was away?" asked David.

"Apparently she had an agreement to pay it in cash at the council offices. They stopped accepting cash payments around five years ago but made concessions for several elderly tenants if they were already paying by cash, and Mrs Deverall was one of them. So these cash amounts were paid in by someone claiming to be a carer who turned up each month, just as she had, to pay the rent."

"Did the carer give her name?"

"*His* name," Jo corrected, "and no, he didn't."

"Can we get his name?"

"I assume we can. I'm waiting to hear from Social Services."

"Next of kin?"

"Initially there was a son designated as a prime contact, but his name was removed two-and-a-half years ago. No-one kept a record as to why, but one of the people in the rent office thinks that he was in the armed forces and had been killed in action."

"How do they know when the name was deleted?" asked David.

"When they change any field on the record, they have to insert the date of the amendment before they can save it. The prime contact field now just states 'None' and the date of that change was two-and-a-half years ago. By the way, the name wasn't deleted as such; it's automatically stored in a history file. His name was John Alexander Deverall. Could this be something, do you think, sir? Should we keep digging?"

"It's a bit of a stretch even for the most committed conspiracy theorist, isn't it?" he replied. "But there's just something… " he added, screwing up his brow in thought and leaning against the wall.

"What?" asked Jo, frowning herself as if in sympathy with her boss.

"I'm not sure," he said. "It's just that the timing is a bit of a coincidence. The house is empty for at least five months – all the time Mrs Johnston's been next door – and no action is taken. Then, a few days after the killings, the council receive a letter that the tenant will not be returning. And if we hadn't gone for our walkabout today, we wouldn't have picked up that it was for sale. It's as if someone timed it so we wouldn't see it during the door-to-doors… God, what did I say about conspiracy theorists?"

"You're not thinking, are you," said Jo, "that this lady might be a master of disguise and a brilliant shot with a pistol?" David gave a chuckle. "Much more likely the timing's just a coincidence, sir. Or perhaps she thinks that now there's a real chance of a sale, what with the change of atmosphere on the estate and all."

"It would be a bit soon for anyone to be drawing conclusions like that, and it's not the case, anyway. It's not the resident who's selling the property, it's the council. In fact, the reverse applies; it's more likely now that the tenant would return with everything looking so much rosier, rather than choosing not to come back."

"That's only if her leaving was in any way linked to the problems on the estate," said Jo. "If what Mrs Johnston heard is right, she left because she was ill, and if she moved in with friends or family, they might have simply offered her the chance to stay indefinitely. As I said, the timing is most likely just a coincidence."

"Even so, I think we need to find out a bit more about Mrs Deverall before we can rule her out of the equation. And it's not so much about the timing issue. Think about it; if you were acting on behalf of this woman, would you want to be trekking in to the council office every month, probably to stand in a queue, to pay over some money that you've got, quite likely, by standing in another queue at a cash point? Surely not when you can phone the council and set up a direct debit for everyone's convenience. *Unless* you didn't want to leave a trail. And why would a carer be paying it for her, anyway, and not the people she's staying with?"

He sat down and thought for a few moments.

"Five months," he said. "We know that Mrs Deverall moved out *at least* five months ago, according to Mrs Johnston. Perhaps we've not gone back far enough, Jo, and been spreading our net too wide. Let's follow this up tomorrow. Go back further and look for any incidents involving her specifically. I assume you're going to speak to the person or people at Number 11 and see if they can shed some light."

"Yes, sir," said Jo. "Planned for this evening."

David looked at his watch, suddenly aware of people milling about outside his office. "Right, let's get out there or I'll never be able to yell at them again for being late."

He stepped into the operations room and the customary silence descended. "Okay, everybody, how did it go today? Have we now seen everyone we are ever likely to see?"

DC Baxter spoke for whole team. Catherine was the MIT's sweetheart. Five foot two, eyes of blue, she had platinum-blonde hair which she normally wore in bunches – sometimes plaits, which usually devolved to bunches anyway during the course of a day. She was slim and pretty and fragile-looking, which belied an inner toughness and confidence which always saw her at the forefront of any action, and made her a natural spokesperson for the group.

"Yes, sir, and I think we've got as much as we're going to get. At twelve of the addresses people were on holiday when we did the first and second rounds; we spoke to someone at all of them this time. Two of the others are furnished lets, but the signs have only just gone up, which is probably why we thought they were still occupied. And," she nodded towards Jo, "I know the sarge is picking up the one in St George's Close."

"Thanks, Catherine. Dare I ask, anything helpful forthcoming?"

"Plenty of theories, sir, and reasons why we should stop trying to catch him, but nothing in the way of information, I'm afraid."

"Okay." He turned to Jo. "Detective Sergeant?"

"Well, as Catherine said, I've been looking into Number 12 St George's Close. This is another empty property, but it's as much a case of a missing person as a straightforward vacancy. Until less than a week ago the official tenant was a Mrs Alma Deverall. She terminated the tenancy by letter to the council last week. But, prior to that, she had been away from the house for at least five months, and during that time no-one seems to know where she has been. There was no forwarding address; and her rent was paid monthly in cash at the council rent office by a male carer. Presumably – although we don't know this – he's been picking up her mail from the close during that time. Somebody must have been because I've checked with the post office and they have no forwarding address for the property.

"Two points make this interesting. Firstly, the long gap between her leaving and deciding to end the tenancy – and the timing of the latter, just after the killings; and secondly, the lack of any clue to her whereabouts during that time – almost as if she's been deliberately covering her tracks. There might be a simple explanation, but it's worth checking further. This evening, I'm going to visit... " – she consulted her notebook – "... a Mr and Mrs Ambrose at Number 11. Apparently, they've been there a long time and might be able to shed some light on Mrs Deverall's disappearance."

David took up the story.

"We know that Mrs Deverall left her house *at least* five months ago, so there's a very good chance it could have been more than six months. In which case, if there is some connection between her leaving and trouble on the estate, we wouldn't have picked it up from the record search. So, unless DC Cottrell comes up with something sensational at the Ambroses' tonight, we need to look further back – let's say, initially, twelve months – and narrow the search down to any incident involving Mrs Deverall or anything that happened in St George's Close, even if it didn't directly concern her. Remember, ideally, we're looking for a link to the Bradys, but as they orchestrated just about all the trouble on the estate, any incident would probably lead us back to them anyway. Any questions?"

"Is there no record of a next-of-kin?" asked Omar Shakhir. "I would have thought the council would have some details."

"None held now by the council," said Jo. "Her son was named until a few years ago. Not checked with the DWP yet."

"What about the carer?" This time it was DC Emma Banks. "The NHS must have his details. He must know where she is."

"Not the NHS; they say he definitely wouldn't be one of theirs. So he must be Social Services. I've contacted them and they're going to get me his details. Once we get to speak to him, you're right, Emma, that might well eliminate Mrs D from our enquiries."

"That's true," put in David, "this may well turn out to be nothing to do with the killings. But we've got nothing else, so I want this search to go ahead – full steam. Any more questions?"

No-one spoke.

"Okay," he said. "Let's get all hands to the pumps starting tomorrow as near to dawn as we can – we'll forego the coffee morning for once – and see what we can turn up for... let's say... usual time, 4.00 pm tomorrow. If anyone comes up with something before then, let me know and I'll get us all together right away. As I say, I'm not sure whether there really is something for us here or whether we've reached the straw-clutching stage. Let's find out as soon as possible tomorrow."

CHAPTER 4

Jo Cottrell went round to Number 11 St George's Close that same evening, after the team briefing, and met with Lucille Ambrose and her husband, Barney. She remembered Lucille from the day she had spent at the scene of the disturbance immediately after the killings – how she had come out to talk to Jo, given her a cup of tea and desperately tried, without success, to appear properly horrified and upset. Like almost all of the rest of the estate, Lucille was delighted by the brothers' departure.

She was a lovely, friendly woman, West Indian, as was her husband. She was large and bubbly, bright-eyed and quick to smile, and wore a colourful floral-patterned dress over yellow trousers. They had known Mrs Deverall for over ten years, she said, and although she had generally kept herself to herself, they had had a good relationship with her. It was strange, looking back, said Lucille, that they had not once stepped into each other's houses in all that time, but they had often chatted over the back garden fence, sometimes for hours. And on occasions, when they were both leaving their houses at the same time, they would walk down to the shops together and have a drink in one of the cafés.

"There's no Mr Deverall," said Lucille, "but Alma used to have a son – John, I think his name was – yes, John. I never actually met him come to think of it, but Barney chatted to him a few times when they met out the back. They both served in the army in Northern Ireland, you know, but not at the same time, of course."

"What happened to him?" asked Jo. "You said she *used* to have a son."

"Yes, he got killed in action. Where was it, Barney?"

"Afghanistan," said Barney. Mr Ambrose was a large, well-built man with short-cropped grey hair, dressed smartly in shirt and tie and a dark blue sweater. He was sitting stiffly to attention in an easy chair with his back to them, but clearly listening to their conversation.

"But before that," went on Lucille, "I think they had some sort of falling out. We hadn't seen him visit her for it must have been well over a year, and I asked her one day how her son was doing. She just said 'What son?' and that was that. I didn't press her any more, of course. Then a few months after that, two men in uniform – soldiers – came to her house; they went in and a few minutes later I heard her through the wall crying bucket-fulls. I suppose we knew what must have happened; I used to worry so much about Barney when he was away." She looked wistfully at her husband.

"After that we didn't see her for weeks, then one day she was out in the garden. I asked her if she was okay and she told me about her son."

"Can you remember when she moved out, and why?" asked Jo.

"Well, a couple of years ago – not long after her son was killed, actually – we had a lot of trouble in the close – we have since, but this was really bad. I think it started after Alma reported some lads she'd seen wrecking a car on the square. Anyway, some of the lads must have seen her watching them and recognised her. They must have known or found out where she lived. They gave her a really bad time – put graffiti all over the house – really bad words – and stuffed dog... well, you-know-what, through the letter box... "

"Dog shit," put in Barney.

"Yes, thank you, love," said Lucille, rolling her eyes at Jo. "Oh, yes, and a few times while she was out, they smashed in the front door. It was awful."

"Do you know who it was who did this?"

"No, but those brothers would have been behind it. The kids just do whatever they tell them to do. I should say 'told' not 'tell', shouldn't I?" and she allowed herself a little smile.

"So what did she do; did she tell the police?"

"She was too frightened. It was going to the police in the first place that started all the problems. She got very down, as you can imagine, really depressed, and frightened, of course. Then she took some tablets – you know – to put herself to sleep. Anyway, the window cleaner saw her lying on the floor of the kitchen and banged on the window. When she didn't move he broke in and phoned for an ambulance."

She shook her head thoughtfully.

"It wasn't her time to go, was it? The window cleaner only comes round once a fortnight. How lucky was that?"

"Is that when she left the house?"

"Oh, no. She tried again – you know, with the tablets – a few weeks after that. This time she seemed to change her mind and rang the ambulance herself. They were there in no time and took her away. But she was back the next week. And she still got pestered by those hooligans. You'd think even they would have left her alone after all she'd been through, but they didn't."

"So when did she leave?"

"It would have been, let me see, seven or eight months ago – October, I think. She'd stopped eating and drinking properly, you know – all the stress I suppose – and got this infection – *in her water*." Lucille respectfully whispered the last three words. "Then this chap started coming round to see her. About once a week he came; a male nurse, she said, just to keep a check on her. And after a few weeks of this, one evening a taxi turned up outside. Alma came out with a couple of suitcases and knocked on our door – the first time she'd ever done that, come to think of it – and told us she was going to stay with friends until she got better. And we haven't seen her since."

"This nurse," said Jo, "did you ever get to speak to him; could you describe him?"

"No, he only came in the evening, and only about half-a-dozen times; we were always inside the house when he came. But whoever he was he seemed to cheer her up quite a lot. She was a different person during those last few weeks. We could hear her laughing away, really loud."

"Can you remember if he was young or old, short or tall?" pressed Jo. "Anything might be helpful."

"We didn't see his face at all," said Lucille, "so I've no idea how old he was. But he was quite tall, I think, and he walked kind of straight up, I seem to remember. That's right, because Barney said he looked like he might have been in the army."

She smiled at her husband.

"Barney always reckons he can tell if someone has been in the forces by the way they walk," she added.

"Has anyone been back to the house since she left, as far as you know?" asked Jo.

"The same nurse has been a good few times; I think to pick up Alma's mail. In fact he came last week – Friday, I think it was. We've been trying to catch him to ask how she was, but each time he seems to be in such a hurry; he was in his car and away before we got chance. Then on Saturday two men came with a van and took a lot of the furniture, and the 'For Sale' sign went up the same day."

She shook her head, sadly.

"I suppose we guessed she wouldn't be coming back, but it's a shame we won't see her again. She was a nice lady. I hope she's alright."

"I hope so, too," said Jo.

★

Squadron Leader Arnold Danby (retired) beamed at the ninety-seven members of the local branch of the Third Age Forum who virtually filled the Meadow Village Community Hall. They were staring wide-eyed at the projection screen behind him, as they had been for nearly forty minutes.

"And now for my big finish," he said. "This is a training film taken by a camera in the nose of one of the same type of combat aircraft used during the Falklands conflict."

The static image on the screen changed to one showing a section of an aircraft carrier deck which began to move downwards as the Harrier rose vertically. The ocean horizon came into view and quickly into focus then swung rapidly round and tilted as the jet turned towards land. For five minutes the audience were treated to a breathtaking sequence showing a simulated attack on a munitions storage centre on a remote island. As the carrier deck came into view again, rising as the plane landed, Arnold steeped in front of the screen and bowed theatrically to his audience.

"Thank you," he boomed.

The group broke into spontaneous applause, the majority rising to their feet. As the noise died down, the Branch President rose from his chair and walked to the front to shake the speaker's hand.

"Thank you so much, Arnold, for that amazing talk," said George Holland, as Arnold left the small stage and returned to sit with the rest of the group. "Not sure how anyone could follow that, but we must try because we have another exciting item before we get our prescriptions filled at the Dog and Duck. Any other business. Has anybody got anything?"

There were a few calls of 'no' around the room as people started to rise from their seats. George held up both hands to stop the exodus.

"Just a moment, please. I have just one item. Thank you."

They all sat down again, some with muted grumblings.

"Irene and I would just like to share with you our experience in Cullen Field today." Irene joined him on the stage and they sat down on a couple of chairs facing the group. "We won't take more than a few minutes of your time, but we think this is important." He turned to his wife. "Do you want to start?"

Irene nodded. "Okay. Well, we went to the mall this morning to do our two-week shop and, in a nutshell, we just didn't recognise the place. People were friendly and open; the precinct was just full of shoppers; coach loads of them, all lively and happy. The Food Hall was full as well, and people were taking their time – there was none of that rushing in and out. It was like a different place. We're planning to go back later this week when we can spend more time there – perhaps a full day."

"So the press weren't exaggerating," said someone at the back. "It really is like a street party?"

"Well, we only went to the shopping centre today," said George. "But we had a good look round in there. Usually, like most of us in the room I think, we just get what's on our list from the Food Hall then get out quick. But today we went right through to the other end where they've got cafes and craft shops and a village green, no less."

"And we met some really nice people," put in Irene. "A couple in the Food Hall then some more in the café. In fact, the place was full when we went in, so these four people on this table invited us to pull up a couple of chairs and join them."

"And is this all because they've got rid of these three brothers?" asked someone else.

"It would seem so," said George.

There was silence for a few moments, followed by a number of whispered side conversations.

"We just thought we'd let you know," said George. "It seems like it's not a no-go area any more, just a really nice place to shop and look around. Questions, comments, anyone?"

"Are you saying, George, that the people on the estate are actually *glad* about these murders?" The question came from Clive Taylor, the 3AF Treasurer.

"I think, Clive, they are glad these three lads are no longer around, so if that's the same thing, then I guess the answer's 'yes'."

"But that's barbaric!" said a lady at the back of the room, and then, suddenly doubting herself, "isn't it?"

"I don't think it is, Emily, in the sense that, as I said to Clive, they're just glad the problem – or the biggest part of it – has gone away. Honestly, you just wouldn't believe the atmosphere there. It's a real eye-opener. I think Irene and I genuinely felt that everyone in Cullen Field was tarred with the same brush – were like the crowd that invades us every few months or so. But when you hear them talking, we've got off really lightly. It was the same every night over there – police, ambulances, sirens going all the time – well, we've all heard them, haven't we? And in the last week or so since the deaths – nothing at all, except a few minor incidents which they've dealt with themselves. They say that the only police on the estate since the deaths have been those working on the case."

"But it was only three people," said someone else, "so how come it can make all that much difference? I mean, the last time we had some trouble there must have been at least fifty of them."

"Apparently the Bradys were notorious for planning virtually all the disturbances. They say that last one, on the night of the murders, was carried out like a military operation. Different groups all set up to do different things to create the most damage and chaos. It was all planned with – well, as I say – military precision. So getting rid of the ringleaders seems to have stopped the rot, for now anyway."

There was a momentary silence.

"And another thing," said Irene, "they talk about this man who did it like he's a super-hero, the 'Caped Crusader' or something. They all said they hoped he was still around, and they think that's what might be curbing the other trouble-makers. That, and the fact that people seem to be more prepared to confront any problems. Actually, I think that's all part of the same picture – it's like they now dare go out to tell these kids off, because this person's watching them from round the corner. The kids might very well be thinking that as well."

"Excuse me, Irene, but shouldn't that be '*Capped* Crusader'?" asked the Branch Secretary.

"Thank you for that incisive contribution, Fred," George laughed, along with everyone else.

"Well, good luck to him, I say," said Emily. "I hope they don't catch him. If he's done Cullen Field a favour, then he's done us one as well."

Others nodded in agreement, and Arnold Danby raised his hand to speak.

"Yes, Arnold," said George.

The Squadron Leader got to his feet.

"During nearly a lifetime in the military, I like to think that I have been fighting for what is right and for the upholding of the law – international law in my case. But more important than the law is justice. It seems to me that, in the space of less than an hour, a single person, now being hunted as a triple murderer, and whose freedom – and, effectively, whose *life* – will end when he is caught, has put to rights something that all the agents of the law have abjectly failed to do for God knows how many years. Isn't it ironic that justice, it seems, has finally been done, and the law is such that it will now punish the person who achieved it?"

For the second time that evening, Arnold Danby sat down to enthusiastic applause.

★

Andrew Donald sat motionless, his eyes widening with increasing disbelief and scepticism.

"Jesus, hold it right there!" he said, interrupting Tom whilst he was in full flow. "Have you ever visited the planet earth, by any chance? This is the *real* world, for God's sake. That's just pure fantasy. We have a legal framework to comply with, or had you forgotten? None of what you have said – or very little of it – falls inside that."

"I'm not suggesting we should operate outside a legal framework," said Tom. "Give me some credit, Andrew, how could I possibly be suggesting that? But the legal framework didn't just happen; no-one came down a bloody mountain with it on tablets of stone – well, not in its current format, anyway. *We* put it together. Governments and their advisors. And it's been developed and modified constantly through the centuries in response to natural and manufactured shifts in human needs and standards. What met the requirements of the people a hundred years ago would be mostly unacceptable today. The framework of the law is evolving all the time. We just need to shift it out of second gear – and up into about seventh!"

"But you're not talking evolution, you're talking about… "

"A sea change. A quantum leap. A giant step for mankind. Don't worry, Andrew, I'll write the speeches."

"But, much as I hate to say this, things have moved recently on that front. The government *are* making progress; a quarter less drug crimes; a fifth fewer carrying weapons. Things are improving."

"Have improved," corrected Tom, "not 'are improving'. There's a difference – a big difference." He paused.

"Go on."

"Those figures are twelve months old," said Tom. "We've seen no further change in that time. Exam's over – pens down, no more writing. The papers have been marked. And you won't find anywhere in the world where twenty or even twenty-five percent gets you a pass. Twenty-five percent is an abject failure. Put it another way – they've been seventy-five percent *un*successful, after nearly nine bloody years, for goodness' sake!"

"Good spin, Tom, but there's a wealth of opinion out there that says they've done as good a job as they could. I don't necessarily disagree with that, in fact. You can't compare it with an exam, surely. There aren't a hundred percentage points out there to be had. I'm not sure it's a good idea – in fact, I *am* sure it's a *bad* idea – to try to take apart the government's record on tackling antisocial behaviour. We'll shoot ourselves in the foot with that one."

"Totally agree," said Tom. "What I'm saying though is that, in spite of the efforts, and actual progress, made by the government, there remains three-quarters of what is still regarded by millions of people as the biggest single domestic issue still to be addressed. And don't forget, those are national statistics; they don't tell the story of where things have got worse, in the FSIAs. What they have done, however laudable, has simply not been enough, and is having no further impact on the issue. I repeat, twenty-five percent success equates to seventy-five percent failure. In mathematical terms, at least."

"Okay," said Andrew, holding up his hands in a gesture of surrender. "I agree with your rationale for focusing on this as one of the main priorities of the manifesto, and I really do like the spin on those percentages. But we are *not* going to directly challenge them on their record on this issue. As I see it, the only way we can use that spin is to be very specific about what *we* propose to do to address the remainder of the problem. And, I agree it's got to be radically different from what's in place now. But you'll have to work hard to convince me that what you've just outlined is the way to do it. It certainly isn't the *only* way.

"However, let's not lose those thoughts; I'd like you to put a bit more meat on the bones and look at the *very significant*" – he drew out the words – "hurdles to be jumped before we sprint for the line. Okay?"

"Okay, Andrew," said Tom, like a little boy who has just been told he can go out to play, but not near the main road. "I'll try and find some time to start on it today."

"Hold on, Tom, there's no rush. We won't be talking about it again until I see the final outcome of this Brady affair. I want to see for myself its effect on urban hysteria, given it was that which enticed your revolutionary instincts out of hiding."

★

Jo was already at her desk when David arrived. She handed him a sheet of paper and followed him into his office.

"I've told the guys to hold off on the records search, sir," she said. "They won't find anything. Mrs Deverall did get harassed by the gangs but chose not to report it."

47

David raised his eyebrows with the unspoken question.

"Because it seems that reporting something to the police was the reason she got targeted in the first place."

David's eyebrows dropped and his whole body seemed to sag. "Jesus," he sighed, then looked at the sheet Jo had handed him. "What have we got here?"

"Quite a bit of stuff came in late yesterday afternoon after I'd left to see the Ambroses. That's just a summary."

"Okay, how did the interview go last night?"

"Well, they said Mrs Deverall was harassed by the gangs, although not the Bradys directly, to the extent that she twice tried to take her own life."

"Jesus," said David, again.

"Apparently, she then became ill after her second attempt and that's when the carer made his first appearance. He started making regular visits and soon after that she moved out to stay with friends. That was last October. They couldn't give me much of a description of the man, just that he was tall, very upright. So we won't be able to say for certain whether it was the same man who paid her rent."

David looked down again at the sheet of paper.

"Date of birth, NI number, bank account details, maiden name Coleridge, son's name and date of death, no other children, possibly one surviving sister in Canada – no known address. So we know pretty much everything about our Alma except where the bloody hell she is."

"There's one very interesting bit of information which isn't on there," said Jo. "It came in by email just a few minutes ago. Social Services, like the NHS, have no record of any nurse or carer having been assigned to Mrs Deverall's case."

David's eyebrows shot up again, this time in surprise. He leant back in his chair and tapped the tips of his fingers together, lost in thought for a long time.

"So Alma Deverall is hounded by thugs, gets clinically depressed, tries to take her own life a couple of times, becomes ill and eventually moves out.

"Given the time of year, it could have been a friend – even an old flame – who took her in initially for a few weeks and ended up asking her to stay over Christmas. Anyway, she either doesn't get well or is invited to stay on indefinitely; but whatever happens, she doesn't return. Then, around about the time of the killings she makes a decision not to return at all. This could have been decided weeks before or prompted by the killings themselves – reading about them in the newspaper or seeing it on TV. She just couldn't face coming back and decided to give up the house and stay put. That wouldn't be a surprise, except if that *was* the reason, it took her less than forty-eight hours to make up her mind. But nothing exciting about that; all perfectly logical."

He leant forward now, elbows on the desk, a clear sign of his growing intensity.

"*Now*," he said, "for the exciting and *ill*ogical bit. It appears she lied to her next door neighbour about the identity of her visitor. Mrs D and her new companion either forget – I don't think so! – or take pains not to leave any trace of her new whereabouts. Her doctor, the bank, the council rent office, the DWP all have 12 St George's Close as her current address, which – since last week – is incorrect. Okay let's not get carried away; perhaps she wanted to keep that address because she expected to return up to a few weeks ago. And perhaps she just hasn't got round to writing to them all yet. But that just doesn't stack up, does it? Because now she'll never get her mail because neither she nor anyone else on her behalf has access to the property. How will she receive her bank statements, pension payment slips and all the other stuff she needs?"

"Just a thought, sir," said Jo, "do you think it's possible she died? I mean, that would explain why no-one would care about the mail and why she didn't even visit the house to sort out her things. I know about the letter last week, but a signature can easily be forged well enough to fool somebody who isn't looking for a forgery. I'll check if a death has been recorded in that name recently."

"Okay, Jo, quick as you can."

★

George and Irene returned to Cullen Field earlier than planned, swept there on the wave of curiosity they had generated the previous evening. They drove the short distance to the estate in the vanguard of a convoy of six vehicles carrying nineteen villagers on a tour of inspection of the new world right on their doorstep.

They split up into smaller groups on arrival arranging to meet at the village green in Cullen Hall at 1.30 pm for lunch. Between them they went in almost every outlet in the shopping mall, visited the library, the leisure centre, the college's adult learning section, and a few even risked a quick drink in the Wild Boar Inn, escaping unscathed. As planned, they all met at the allotted time, but four of them had decided to have a game of bowls in the municipal park instead of eating with the others. Immediately after lunch, seven of the group returned to the village; the remainder continued to explore the estate – or played bowls – for the rest of the afternoon.

★

"Who's going first? Come on, make our day, Murray."

"Can't I'm afraid, sir," said DC Murray Davenport. "Spoke to all three shopkeepers; they admitted they had threatened to take care of the Bradys the last time they put in a complaint, but there's no way they're up to that sort of thing. Showed them the identikit – though, as you know, it's all cap and stubble. No reaction at all."

"Department of no surprises. Okay, Geoff?"

He addressed the other half of 'Mutt'n'Geoff'. The two young officers were so alike in appearance that they had been allocated this single identity. Both an inch under six feet, slim, fresh-faced with dark hair, spiked and held with gel, it was easy – and very common outside the team – for one to be mistaken for the other.

"Nothing either, sir," said Geoff. "This was the complainant whose description seemed to match the killer's, but in fact he's about a foot shorter and in his early sixties. So, no joy, I'm afraid."

"Thanks, Geoff. Moving on; as a result of DS Cottrell's meeting with the occupants of 11 St George's Close last night, we now know that Mrs Deverall *was* targeted by the gang on the estate, but she *didn't* report it. I'm sure you'll all want to buy the sergeant a drink for saving you from another record search, but that will have to wait for now."

He turned to Jo. "Detective Sergeant?"

"I bet they're all gutted really, sir. Anyway, we now know just about everything there is to know about this lady from Number 12 except the one thing that no-one seems to know. That is, her current address. And when I say no-one, that includes the bank, the council, her doctor, the DWP. Essential contacts. *And* – as it turns out – Social Services, who also have no record of the carer. So why has she not made any arrangements for people to get in touch with her now she's officially given up her address in Cullen Field?"

"Could she have died, do you think, sarge?" asked DC Shakhir.

"If you'd stop trying to spoil it for me, Omar, I'm coming to that."

Omar shrugged and looked round the room. "I can't help being brilliant."

"I checked this out," Jo continued, "and there is no record at all of the death of a Mrs Alma Deverall anywhere in the country over the last twelve months – that's going back to well before the last time she was seen by her neighbours. However, as we know, great efforts seemed to have been made to keep Mrs D's whereabouts a secret. If she'd died, registering her death would immediately give away her present address – I mean, a doctor would need to attend and the funeral director would have to collect her from somewhere. Unless, of course, her death was registered under a false name, but that's difficult, for all sorts of reasons. So perhaps not a false name, but a real name that she hasn't used for a while."

"Her maiden name?" said DC Omar Shakhir.

"Well thanks again, Omar!" said Jo, with a touch of genuine annoyance. "You've just spoilt my big finish!"

There was some laughter and gentle applause.

"Yes," she went on, "her maiden name. And guess what; a Mrs Alma Elizabeth Coleridge died just over four weeks ago at an address in Hammersmith. Cause of death – a self-administered overdose."

★

All nineteen day-trippers made an appearance in the Dog and Duck that evening. As they drifted in, in twos and threes, they gravitated to the area in front of the large bay window, pulling together a few tables and crowding round them, seated in a tight circle. They were joined by ex-Squadron Leader Danby, who was staying at the pub for a few days. There was only one topic of conversation. All agreed that George and Irene's assessment the previous day had been borne out by their visit.

If anything, the ambience and tangible friendliness of the place had surpassed their expectations and all were enthusiastic about making this a regular trip. They laughed when someone suggested it was as if they were deciding where to go for a weekend break, with someone else developing the idea by offering to check out whether the Wild Boar did bed and breakfast. What lightened the atmosphere so much was the feeling, expressed by Emily the previous evening, that the removal of the threat in Cullen Field would quite clearly be reflected in Meadow Village. The continuous, if almost subconscious, fear that clouded the villagers' lives, particularly in this very situation as they relaxed in the pub but always with one ear to the door, now seemed a thing of the past.

"I think we should have a meeting to discuss this," said George.

"I thought we'd had one," said someone. "Last night we talked about it for nearly two hours, at the hall and in here. I'm not suggesting we shouldn't discuss it some more, but with what in mind?"

"What about a debate?" suggested Clive. "Taking up Arnold's point. Proposal – the man who shot the Bradys is a hero and should be allowed to continue the good work. Please discuss. Something like that."

There were a few chuckles around the tables, but a majority of support as well.

"That's a great idea, actually, Clive," said George. "The usual format; we get someone to propose the idea with a brief speech, someone to speak against it, then throw it open to the floor."

"The problem will be getting someone to speak against it," one of the women said.

"Not really, Joyce," replied George. "We just need a volunteer to oppose the motion. They don't have to mean what they say; it's just to start the ball rolling. I'd be quite happy to do it if someone else will chair the meeting. What about you, Fred?"

"Yes, I don't mind."

"Good," said Clive. "So Fred chairs the meeting, George opposes, and the person proposing the motion can form an orderly queue… "

They all laughed.

"Yes," said George, "we might have to draw straws for that privilege."

"Tell, you what," said Fred. "It might be worth putting up a notice on the estate somewhere. You know, show a bit of solidarity. I can't imagine anybody would be interested, but… "

"I think that's a great idea," said George. "Those in favour?"

Nineteen hands were raised.

★

The expression on Mags's face was similar to the one with which Andrew had received the same information, but about a thousand times more intense.

"I can't believe I'm hearing this," she said. "Have you turned into a fucking monster?"

Tom was realistic enough to have anticipated a negative response, but was taken completely off guard by the ferocity of the attack.

"Look, obviously there are lots of details to be sorted out and I'm sure… "

"It's nothing to do with details. It's *fundamentally* wrong. It goes against every human principle… "

"Every Margaret Tomlinson-Brown principle, you mean. Can't you just for once see the bigger picture? Can't you just for once apply your human rights doctrine to the wider population rather than limit it to the ones that you and your tea-sipping cronies, sitting in your designer clothes on your expensive settees, *choose* to regard as the down-trodden and underprivileged."

Mags's eyes were blazing as she struggled to remain calm.

"I see," she said, softly, after a long silence. "*That's* what you think of my beliefs; of the hours and days I spend – whilst running a business as well – trying to ensure that the innocents of this world have something to live for. Thank you very much for making your feelings clear. I had no idea you thought I was such a waste of time."

"The *innocents*! This has nothing to do with the *innocents*. They are the ones I'm trying to *protect*."

Mags got up from her chair.

"Do you know what I think," she said. "I think you wish it had been you on that street with that gun. Perhaps you should never have given it up; perhaps that's what you were put on this earth to do!"

He watched her leave the room, thinking she was probably right.

CHAPTER 5

The following morning – Wednesday – just after 7.30 am, during her first routine check of the day, Internal Investigative Assistant Vicky Barrowclough noticed that a name had appeared on her PC screen that should not have been there. She printed off the relevant information and placed it straight away in pole position on her boss's desk.

★

Tom entered the kitchen where he found Mags already dressed and seated at the large central island unit which was designed as an all-round breakfast bar. Tom sat down across from her.

"Morning," he offered.

There was no reply to break the frosty silence.

"You must have been up early," he ventured further.

She glared at him with fierce eyes but said nothing.

"Come on, Mags," he said, with a little whine. "I think you're over-reacting to this. Look, I know there's still a lot… "

"Over-reacting!" she spluttered. "Do you mean over-reacting to the biggest over-reaction in the history of civilisation as we know it?"

"Look, Mags. I know we are on a subject here where we have radically different views. Your opposition to just about everything I stand for is legend in the corridors of power at Westminster. You've never tried to keep it a secret from anyone. We always have had those differences, even before we were married, so there's nothing new here. But, for Heaven's sake, what was all that about last night? I shared my ideas with you because I genuinely respect your opinions.

I like to get to a balanced perspective and you always pick up on the things I need to consider… " He lost his thread as she continued to glower at him. "I wish to God I hadn't mentioned it."

"Really?" said Mags. "Because I'm glad you did. It's always best to find out what sort of a person you're living with, even though it might turn out to be a major disappointment."

"Right," said Tom. "I have to meet with a lot of rational, fully-hinged people today, and this is no preparation for that sort of thing. So I'll leave you to wallow in your uncomplicated, self-righteous idealism. Mind you don't drown. See you tomorrow night."

He walked from the room.

★

Tom's constituency headquarters was a single storey prefabricated building on Westbourne Avenue in Marlburgh, East London, just a short distance from the Cullen Field Estate. The premises comprised a reception area cum waiting room leading through to a large inner office accommodating ten workstations and a wall full of filing cabinets, with four smaller rooms off it down one side. The two end rooms of the four were the offices of Tom and Grace Goody. The middle two were set up as small meeting rooms with a folding partition separating them which could be pulled aside to provide a single larger one.

Grace entered Tom's office and sat down at his invitation on one of two leather wing chairs, positioned at ninety degrees to each other, close to and facing one of the windows. Tom was seated in the other chair and was annoyed that he was unable to stop himself looking as she crossed her beautiful legs, leaving enough of them visible to cause him to hesitate over his first few words.

"Er… you know when we visited Cullen Field Estate a few days ago?"

Grace was a stunning-looking woman. Tall and elegant, she almost invariably wore the uniform of her position, formal suits – usually with a skirt, rather than trousers – which were close fitting without being body-hugging, but clearly displayed her slim and rounded figure. Her rich brown hair was very simply pulled straight back from her face in a tight bun, sometimes a ponytail, and she wore rather heavy-rimmed glasses. She was thirty-nine years old – the same age as Mags.

"Yes, I can just about remember it," she said, smiling. "Wasn't that the visit after which you decided to change the world by ridding it of everyone you didn't like?"

"That's the one," said Tom, smiling back. "Though not exactly everyone," he added. "Andrew's safe – for the moment."

"And me?"

"Oh, you're way down the list; I might never get to you. Anyway, I've had some constructive feedback from my two bosses. Actually, more *destructive* from the one at home."

"Don't tell me you're surprised," said Grace. "It might not have been the best idea at this stage to share your ideas with her. Not while you're still in the process of formulating them, I mean."

"You're right – again," he said, in mock exasperation. "The thing with Mags, though, is that she does come up with objections that need addressing. She's really useful like that."

"Well, I'm sure she'll be pleased that you think she's useful," said Grace, still smiling.

"You know what I mean… " He leant back, as if suddenly not sure of himself.

"Look, Grace, all the stuff we talked about after the visit – you know, trying to achieve for the people what this one guy pulled off in about ten minutes; new system of justice to give us extra powers, etcetera, etcetera – it *is* all a bit extreme, isn't it? You know, put together in the excitement of the moment and all that. Now we're sort of calm and detached, what do you *really* think?"

"There's no need to put that emphasis on 'really' you know," she said, genuinely affronted. "I'll only ever give you one opinion, and that will always be what I *really* think."

"I know that, Grace. What I meant to ask is do you think this is a step too far?"

"No, I don't. The biggest question we can expect to have to answer will be 'is it fair?' and we'll be able to stand up and shout 'yes!' to that one. If we lay out the rules beforehand, and everyone understands them, and it's only going to affect the ones who choose to ignore them… Who can argue?"

"Thanks, Grace. That's what I hoped – and expected – you to

say. Actually, I've decided I'm going to do another tour of the estate this afternoon and see if everybody is still ecstatic with life. I'll just take Gerry and Mick, and get going straight away – kiss a few babies, open a couple of supermarkets. Now, unless you particularly want to come – in which case, of course, you're very welcome – I was planning to go on my own, except for the men in black. I just want this to be low key and unexpected. You know, to get a spontaneous reaction."

"I think that's a good idea," said Grace. "And I'm sure I might find something to gainfully occupy me in the meantime."

"Great, can we get together later, say, five o'clock?"

"Right."

She uncrossed her legs and stood up. This time the movement went unobserved, but only because her boss had very deliberately looked away.

"Thanks again, Grace. See you later."

★

Fred, having printed off his extra copies of the debate notice, had no trouble persuading the local library, the main supermarket, the college and the leisure centre to display them. He asked the person he met at each place if they would mind trying to get a feel as to how many were likely to go, suggesting they placed a form next to the notice for people to sign if they planned to attend.

★

At 11.30 am, Captain Peter Drake entered Riverside South, Tower 2 on Canary Wharf, where Germaine and Rolland's Investment Managers occupied the whole of the twenty-fifth floor. The Captain was slim, medium height and immaculately dressed in a light blue suit and blue and white striped shirt. His perfectly-knotted tie was a reminder of his days as a promising all-rounder at Surrey County Cricket Club. He was sandy-haired and clean-shaven except for a pencil-thin moustache. He took the security lift down to the lower basement. The first thing he noticed was a printed sheet on his desk which someone had leant up against his PC screen to make sure he didn't miss it. He read it quickly and stepped out into the main office.

"Vicky!"

Corporal Barrowclough had been waiting for the summons and rose from her desk to join him straight away. Vicky was almost as tall as the Captain in her two-inch heels; she was shapely – if not exactly slim – and attractive, with a round pleasant face and naturally-curly dark-brown hair which she wore long and loose onto her shoulders.

"Morning, sir."

"Morning, Vicky. This looks exciting."

"Could be, sir. I'd have waited until I had more, but it's Page One and it's linked to the recent Cullen Field incident which, as you know, is attracting a lot of attention. Thought I'd better raise it straight away."

"Source of the TIE?"

"Usual, sir. National Police Database. I picked it up this morning at seven-thirty from the daily dump. I'll say it again, sir, but direct access or even a twice-daily download would help a lot to keep on top of these things. We could have had this as early as midday yesterday."

"Point taken – again, Corporal, and I have raised it. Do we know why the name came up?"

"No, sir, not yet."

"Early ideas?"

"Could be a nominal, sir. It's not a common name but I've found twelve other matches. I'm halfway through checking them and nothing conclusive's come up. Still trying to find a link."

"Okay, thanks, Vicky. But keep right on top of this one. If you have to go deeper than the NPD, we can get any access code you need. Because if this is an actual, and not a nominal, then we sure as hell have one big problem."

"Yes, sir. That's what I was thinking."

★

David and Jo entered the premises of Blount of Hammersmith at 2.00 pm that same afternoon and rang the bell on the reception counter. A thin middle-aged man in a smart grey suit, white shirt and black tie came through to meet them.

"Chief Inspector Gerrard?"

"Mr Blount? This is Detective Sergeant Cottrell. Thank you for seeing us."

Henry Blount led them through to his office at the rear of the building and waved them to be seated. His expression seemed immovably mournful, as if this was a prerequisite of his profession.

"As you know," said David, "we're here to find out some details about Mrs Alma Deverall's funeral. We understand you handled this some weeks back. She was known at the time as Alma Coleridge."

"Yes, that's right, Chief Inspector, although the gentleman did make sure the headstone included her married name. A bit confusing really. Can I ask why you are interested in this burial?"

"Well actually, it's the person who notified you of the death that we're interested in," said David. "Presumably the gentleman you just mentioned."

Mr Blount turned to his PC and clicked onto a document.

"A Mr Alex Anderson, her carer."

Jo wrote down the name on her pad.

"Have you any details about this man?" asked David. "An address? Contact number?"

Mr Blount scrolled down the screen.

"No, nothing other than the address of the deceased and the phone number of that apartment. She wasn't the owner, apparently; she was there on a short-term lease."

"Can you describe Mr Anderson?" asked Jo.

"Tall, slim, short dark hair: very well dressed and nicely spoken. Genuinely upset by Mrs Coleridge's death. He seemed very fond of her."

"Did he have a beard or stubble or anything?"

"No, clean shaven."

"Accent?"

"Home Counties at a guess. Hardly any at all really."

Jo turned back a couple of pages in her notebook.

"Mrs Deverall – Coleridge – died on the 25th of April and was buried on the 28th. Is that right?"

Yes, that's right," said Mr Blount, consulting his screen.

"Isn't that rather quick for a suicide? Wouldn't you have expected a longer period in between? For a post mortem, for example."

"Yes, normally, but there were no suspicious circumstances. Apparently there had been two previous suicide attempts, and Mr Anderson wanted to go ahead as quickly as possible."

"And who attended the funeral?" asked David.

"Well, only Mr Anderson himself, apart from the bearers and myself, of course. He said that Mrs Coleridge had no living relatives and he knew of no close friends."

"So he was the only one at the graveside?"

"Apart from my own people, yes."

Jo checked her notes again.

"Who paid for the funeral, Mr Blount?" she asked. "And how were you reimbursed?"

"Mr Anderson paid, and in cash. It was a very inexpensive affair," he added with his first genuine display of sadness. "He said Mrs Coleridge always kept a large amount of cash around in the apartment – as many elderly people do, of course. He used some of it to pay for the funeral on the advice of the executors of the will."

"Do you know who the executors are?" asked David.

He clicked onto a few more files but shook his head.

"No information. I'm sorry."

"That's fine, you've been really helpful. Many thanks."

"And now you'd like to see the grave, I believe."

"Yes, if it's not too much trouble. And the address where you attended the deceased, please. Do you have the owner's name?"

"No, I'm sorry."

★

Jo read aloud from the inscription,

> "Rest in Peace
> Alma Elizabeth Deverall, nee Coleridge
> Devoted Wife of Maxwell John Deverall
> Loving Mother of John Alexander Deverall.
> Died 25th April… "

They stood in silence for half a minute or so, before they walked carefully round the headstone, in front of which there was laid a small bunch of flowers – relatively fresh – and examined the ground between it and the pathway. In spite of the ground being soft, there was no sign of any footprints.

"Okay, let's get the SOCO team down here and give Mrs D some company for a few hours. Might as well get them going straight away. I'll pay a visit to her last-but-one resting place. You stay and brief the gang, then get a lift down there. "

"Yes, sir," said Jo, reaching for her mobile.

★

David pulled up in front of the large, Edwardian, three-story terraced house which was 23 Darlington Road and pressed the button at the side of the front door for Apartment B.

Alan Venables was in his mid thirties, medium height, medium build, medium everything except his tan, which was very prominent and accentuated by a mass of blond hair which was almost shoulder length. He was dressed in old jeans and a loose-fitting sweatshirt. Any hopes David harboured of this being the man they sought were dashed the moment he opened the door.

"You're lucky to catch me in, Chief Inspector. I'm working from home today. How can I help you?"

"We're following up on the death of a lady who you knew as Mrs Coleridge. I am right in saying this is where she died?"

"Yes, that's right." Alan Venables looked suddenly anxious. "But I wasn't here at the time. I was in Dubai."

"And very nice, too, Mr Venables. There's really nothing for you to worry about, but could I have a look round the place, please? And then I just need a few minutes of your time."

Alan took him through the apartment, which was a galaxy away from the accommodation in St George's Close. As they sat down in the spacious lounge after the brief tour, the buzzer sounded.

"That will be my sergeant, I expect," said David. "Could you tell us about the tenancy, Mr Venables?" he asked, when Jo had joined them.

"Well, the place was taken by Mrs Coleridge on a short term lease effective from the middle of October last year when I started a three-month expat assignment to Dubai. She paid me the full rental in advance. My assignment was extended by three months and she wanted to stay on, so she made a further payment, again for the whole period in advance."

"And how did Mrs Coleridge come to take the flat, Mr Venables?" asked Jo.

"It was very simple," he replied, "and please call me Alan. I got the nod from my boss that I was going on this expat deal and I thought I'd try to let the apartment while I was away. I think it's better not to have a place standing empty for too long these days, don't you? So I just banged an ad in the local paper and on lettings.com to see what happened. I was dead lucky, because I was due to leave within a fortnight of placing the ad and this guy Anderson got in touch just a few days before I went. If I hadn't got someone right away I would have had to leave it empty anyway. That's it really. He said he was acting on behalf of this lady – Mrs Coleridge – and thought it would be perfect for her.

"Anyway, she came to look round, loved it and, as I said, paid the full three months in advance and moved in the day I left. I didn't ask her to pay the lot up front, but she said she'd rather not bother with monthly transfers."

"And how did she pay?" asked David.

"By cheque. It cleared the day before I left the country."

"Could I ask how much you asked for the apartment?"

"Actually, I didn't get chance to ask," said Alan, smiling. "I'd told this guy the reason I was letting the flat before the subject of cost came up. So he offered me a thousand a month, which is around a third of what it's worth. I laughed at first, thinking he was taking the piss; until he pointed out that I had less than a hundred hours to get someone else. He was a shrewd bugger, I'll give him that. Anyway, it was great for me, to be honest – one elderly person occupying the place, and it was all profit anyway. The company were paying all expenses abroad and what with no income tax to pay over there – this was the icing on the cake really. So I agreed and we shook on it."

"And what about other charges – utilities and such?"

"The rent covered all those costs. So council tax, heating, and the like went out as direct debits from my account as normal while I was away. It didn't leave hardly anything for me, but the main benefit was that I got my house-sitter."

"How was the additional three months' rent paid?" asked Jo.

"By bank transfer this time," Alan replied. "I was out of the country, of course, so a cheque was no good to me. I sent her my account details and she arranged the transfer. No problem."

"I will need to check these transactions just to get details of her bank, account number, etcetera," said David. "I'll need your permission to do that. Is that okay?"

"Yes, of course," said Alan. "Look, I know you probably can't tell me much, but is Mrs Coleridge's death suspicious or what? I heard it was definitely suicide. Has something new turned up?"

"No, nothing like that, Mr Venables – Alan," said David, "it's just that we have her on our records as Mrs Deverall. But we now know that her maiden name was Coleridge, so we're just tying up loose ends. By the way, how did you find out about her death?"

"I phoned on the day that she was due to leave just to wish her luck and to thank her for being a good tenant, and this Anderson guy answered the phone and told me what had happened. By the time I got back everything was taken care of. It was a bit spooky to tell you the truth. There was no evidence of anyone ever being there."

"And the man who set all this up, can you describe him?"

Alan thought for a moment.

"Tall, slim, dark hair, good-looking guy, actually. Well spoken, good clothes… the sort you don't mind doing business with, even if he gently gets one over on you." He smiled.

David stood up, extending his hand.

"Thank you very much, Alan. You've been extremely helpful. We'll let ourselves out downstairs."

They reached the entrance foyer.

"How did you get here?" asked David.

"Rob dropped me off."

"Good, we can get straight back to Parkside, then, and go through… Jo?"

Jo was staring at a large vase of flowers on a table beside the door.

"Alma Deverall died nearly five weeks ago, right, and was buried three days later? But those flowers on the grave were fresh; can't have been there more than couple of days. So somebody just might be visiting the grave on a regular basis."

"And the only person at the funeral was Mr Anderson," said David. "God, talk about the bleeding obvious. I'll drive, you get on to Rob."

★

Tom Brown's second trip to the estate only served to reinforce his first impression – that the community had been socially regenerated by a simple act of violence carried out, it seemed, by a single person; the 'Pied Piper', as one resident called him – getting rid of the rats so the townsfolk could come out to play.

His visit, however, was soon interrupted by the appearance of the local press who had obviously been alerted to his presence. It was still low key, but not what he wanted.

"Why are you here again, Mr Brown? Are you still sticking by what you said on your last visit?" Tom recognised Tony Dobson, a local reporter whose ambition to date had comfortably out-stripped his integrity. The reporter was in his late twenties, medium height and slim. He was good-looking with strong features, spoiled somewhat by their always displaying a look of either cynicism or outright disbelief.

"And what exactly do you think I said on my last visit?" Tom pushed back, aware that a different word used could be extrapolated into a different message.

"You said that you empathised with the residents in their support of the man who carried out the killings."

"I think you are misquoting me in the interests of controversy – *again* – Mr Dobson," he replied, aware that he was surrounded by people who were just as interested in his responses as was the reporter. "However, to answer your first question, I am here to talk to my constituents about *any* issue they would like to discuss. There is more than one thing going on in the world, you know."

"And my second question?"

"Just remind me what it was again," asked Tom, playing for time.

"Are you still sticking by… ?"

"Oh yes. Let me say this slowly, Mr Dobson, so there's no confusion this time. I am aware that these good people feel a sense of relief at the removal of a threat to their security and safety. I fully understand this and definitely do empathise with that feeling." He looked round, beaming at the crowd. "Never have I seen such a sea of smiling faces and I am realistic enough to know that the appearance of their Member of Parliament is not going to create that sort of effect."

He was rewarded with laughter all round, and one elderly lady shouted, "You can come round and appear to me any time, Tom," generating further laughter.

"Now you all heard her say that, didn't you?" Tom addressed the crowd in general, feeding off the positive atmosphere, and clearly annoying Tony Dobson. More laughter. "What's your name, my dear, so I can find out where you live?"

"Annie Berryman," the lady replied, "and you don't need to find out, I'll write down my address for you."

There were whistles, whoops and laughter from the crowd. Tom laughed along with them, then gradually raised his hands, appealing for silence.

"But there is a serious issue here. If we condone the act which removed this threat then we substitute one problem with another. In fact we would get the same problem back with different faces – and we would deserve to."

His audience was now hushed, but still positive, evidenced by the nodding of heads throughout the crowd. He addressed the reporter personally, a spontaneous reconciliation borne out of the general good feeling he was getting as feedback.

"It's a delicate point, Tony," he said, the reporter nodding in response to the use of his first name. "On the one hand, you cannot but feel happy for the people whose lives have been turned around by what has happened. But on the other hand, we must condemn the act itself. The challenge that we face, as your elected representatives, is to create this same effect, but within the boundaries of law and order. And we need to do something different from what we are doing now to bring that about." Still looking at the reporter, he added, "Thank you for your questions, Tony."

This brief impromptu speech drew applause all round, including from the reporter himself, who raised his hands above his head to ensure Tom could be seen him clapping along with the rest.

Tom checked his watch, saw that it was 4.30 and remembered

his meeting with Grace. He walked back to the library car park, where they had left their vehicle, followed by his two security attendants and a small group who had dogged his every step since he arrived. His final calling point was the library itself, where he chatted and joked with a couple of the librarians and a few customers. As he turned to leave he saw the notice.

"Justice or Law," he read aloud, and then went on to read the details of the proposed meeting.

"Have you got a copy of this?" he asked the librarian.

"I can take a copy for you," she replied, removing it from its blue-tack support and rushing across to the photocopier as if concerned that he might change his mind.

"Thank you," he said, taking the copy and bestowing on her his biggest smile of the day. "Goodbye, everyone."

★

Grace was working in her office when he got back. Hers was an exact mirror image of his own – same size, same desk and tilt-and-swivel, same arrangement of chairs and cabinets, and the same two windows at right-angles to each other on the outside walls. The rest of the staff had left for the day, and she had kicked off her shoes and draped her jacket round the back of one of the wing chairs facing out over the rear garden.

"We won't share our preparation schedule with Andrew," he said. "He wants me to soft-pedal for the time being, pending the outcome of the investigation. The problem is, with the election in less than eighteen months, we don't have any time to spare in getting something radical onto the agenda and into people's minds."

"I hope you're not intending to use the word 'radical' to describe this, especially with the general public. I think that might be unwise. And you would expect Andrew to be a bit cautious at this stage, wouldn't you? After all, if it turns out this has been a contract killing by another gang who are just waiting to move in, 'Cullen Field – Dream Haven' could be a very short-lived phenomenon."

"Why do I always feel that you're telling me off, Grace?" said Tom.

"I'm just offering a few words of caution – all well-intended, as always. You're the boss; you don't have to take any notice of them," she replied.

He showed her the notice about the debate.

"This is really good timing," he said, "because it gives us a chance to quantify people's views using this group as a sample. It would certainly be useful to pick up the sort of words they are using so we can build on those. I thought I might get a couple of the guys to dig around a bit and try to find out how many are likely to be going, and from where. I mean whether it's just the villagers or if many from the estate are planning to attend."

"How will we find out?" asked Grace.

"Well, at the library they had a list next to the notice for people to sign if they intend to go – it had quite a lot of names on already. I assume there are other notices around the estate, and if they have the same arrangement we could get a good idea."

"To what end, exactly?"

"Well, I had considered going along myself if it was worth it," he offered. "I mean if there was a big enough attendance… "

"I'm not sure that's a very good idea," said Grace. "For a start… "

"Good," he interrupted, "because having considered it, I decided against it. But I do think someone should go. What are you doing next Wednesday, Grace?"

"Are you serious?"

"Yes," said Tom, "about somebody going anyway. I thought you would be lower profile than me."

"Don't forget I did the first tour with you," she said. "Talking to residents, picture in paper and all that. I know I'm not in your celebrity league, but *someone* might recognise me."

"I'm sure they will, Grace. You're a very memorable presence, but would that matter? Anyway, I'm sure you could wear some sort of disguise," he said, with a very wide smile this time.

"Oh, yes," she said, "I've got a canary suit at home I once wore at a hen party. I could go in that."

"*You* went to a hen party in a *canary* suit?" exclaimed Tom.

"It was many years ago," said Grace, seeming to regret that she had shared such a personal secret with him. "If you think I should go, then I will, of course," she added, getting quickly back to business.

"That's not how it works, Grace, and you know it. I'm asking you if you think it's a good idea and whether you feel okay about going. You don't *have* to do it. I won't sulk if you don't."

"No, that should be okay," she said. "Bet it's a real eye-opener, in fact."

"Which is exactly the reason for going," he said. "Settled then. Thanks, Grace." He looked at his watch. "Right. Chairing a meeting in exactly one hour at local council office. That just gives me time to boil an egg and change into my chairing-a-council-meeting suit – no tie tonight, I think – decisions, decisions! – then Westminster Ho! tomorrow, for a full day preparing for the Inner City budget fiasco. Christ, it was so much more relaxing in the Marines."

★

It took David and Jo less than ten minutes to get from Darlington Road to the cemetery. Even so, by the time they arrived the site had been cleared and restored with only the senior officer remaining to check with them about when they might be recalled.

"Not sure yet, Rob," said Jo. "Could be a day, a week, who knows?"

"Well, from our point of view – I don't have to say it, but I will – the sooner the better."

"Understood," she said, "and thanks for a great job." She looked around the site; there was absolutely no sign that the SOCOs had been there at all.

David checked his watch. "Omar should be setting off about now with our lot for the surveillance team. Firearms should get here about the same time. We'll do the briefing away from the buildings so we don't attract attention. Then we should be able to get the first shift started within a couple of hours. Meanwhile, I'll leave you to speak to Mr Croft. I understand he looks a bit like Brad Pitt."

"I'll get on it right away," said Jo.

Jeremy Croft, the site manager, turned out to be a couple of inches shorter than Jo, very thin and with wispy grey hair combed straight back and stuck to his head with some sort of gel. Jo guessed he was in his mid-fifties. He was eager to help and his bright eyes showed rapt attention as they sat in his office while Jo explained their presence.

"We've received a tip-off, Mr Croft," she lied, "about a serial vandal in this area who is targeting graveyards. There seems to be a pattern which would put yours as the likely next site for his attention."

"Oh, dear," said Mr Croft, "I'm surprised I haven't heard about it at the area meetings. How strange no-one mentioned it... "

"Yes, well, perhaps you can ask why at the next meeting. In the meantime, we would like to set up a round-the-clock watch. Is there anywhere you could accommodate two officers without them getting in your way and attracting too much attention?"

He thought for a moment.

"Well, there's an office we could free up, I suppose. Let me show you."

They walked back to the foyer and he indicated a small room off it close to the outer door.

"This would be perfect, Mr Croft," said Jo. "Thank you, so much. We'll try not to be a nuisance."

She would do Mr Croft the courtesy of telling him the truth at a later date, she decided, when it was all over. For the time being it was better for him to have a much less alarming explanation for his staff as to why the building was to be occupied by police until further notice.

★

"On our way, sir. ETA in fifty minutes."

Omar Shakhir spoke into the hands-free from the unmarked police car.

"Good who have we got?" asked David.

"Baxter, Drury, Wheeler and, last but not least... "

"Yes, thank you DC Shakhir. Stop trying to build up your part. See you soon."

★

Twenty people stood round a grave in the corner of the cemetery grounds furthest away from the chapel buildings, heads bowed like a group of mourners. They comprised David and Jo, the four detective constables from Parkside, and fourteen officers from the Special Firearms Unit.

"So, briefly, one last time," said David. "Two teams of nine each working twelve hour shifts. Each team comprising two DCs stationed in the chapel, working as spotters; and seven SFOs in two vehicles, one on the main road near the gates and one on the street down the side of the grounds. We've got the length of railing removed, Jo?"

"Yes, sir, and tape across the gap to look like it's in the process of being replaced. We might have to rethink that if it goes on any length of time."

"Okay. That's for cemetery working hours, of course. I'll leave you to decide if you want to move one or more SFOs into the chapel after the staff leave. And remember – as if you wouldn't – if this is the guy we're looking for, based on what he did, he's extremely dangerous. No heroics, please. Any questions?"

No one had.

"Another thing, and this is for the DCs. Remember, you are here as spotters only and in the event of a strike, you stay out of sight until the suspect is immobilised. Understood? I'm looking at you, Calamity Jane," he said, addressing DC Baxter. "You do understand the expression 'no heroics' I assume?"

"Sure do, Sheriff," said Catherine, making everyone laugh and easing the tension. David smiled and continued.

"You will, of course, need to exercise maximum discretion if he turns up in daylight when there are a lot of people around. In that situation the on-site pair in the chapel will need to advise the unit of the situation and let them decide. Needless to say, optimum caution. Police Complaints have enough work to be going on with already."

The first surveillance shift was in place by 6.00 pm. The office – from which two DCs would maintain their watch – was perfectly sited so that both the headstone and the cemetery gates, which were permanently open, were clearly visible. The entrance to the cemetery was from a semi-residential road which also hosted a few restaurants and small bars, and which had been widened to incorporate parking spaces for both residents and customers. The Chapel of Rest and other buildings formed a small complex about fifty yards inside the gates at the end of a gravel drive.

Detective Constables Catherine Baxter and Geoff Drury settled to wait. They knew this could be a complete waste of time; and, even if it wasn't, it could be days or weeks before the man might show again. Or they could be very lucky…

★

The Dog and Duck public house dated back to when Meadow Village was first established over 250 years ago. The double front doors opened directly into the main bar which was the extent of the original hostelry. Since then it had been tastefully and aesthetically extended, with the addition of a smaller bar at the rear and a large dining room to the right. The main bar now incorporated a 'snug' which was generally kept empty for meetings and small parties and which Jed Smithers, the landlord, referred to grandly as his Corporate Entertaining Suite. There were open fireplaces in both bars and the dining room and the place retained its late eighteenth century feel throughout.

That evening the main bar was buzzing with anticipation.

"Much better than no interest at all," said George. "Just run through the list again, Fred, slowly this time so we can actually absorb it."

Fred sighed and read from the sheet in front of him. He was unusually tall for someone in his mid-seventies, slim and upright and strikingly handsome in his way. He was a great favourite within the group, with a permanent twinkle in his eye and usually a joke for every occasion. But he was showing clear signs of anxiety over the escalation of the event.

"Forty-seven at the library; three at the leisure centre; seventeen at the supermarket; twenty-eight actual signatories at the college plus the Head of Sociology is bringing all his final year students along. That's another twenty-three including himself."

"So," said Clive, who was adding up the numbers on his mobile's calculator, "if we assume all ninety-seven of us attend, that's over two hundred already."

"But this isn't what we wanted," said Fred. "We've got ourselves in this situation by accident. It was just an idea for a different 3AF meeting, not a national referendum. Where are we going to hold it? Do we get a marquee?"

"I suggest we contact the council office and ask if they have anything available that can accommodate, say, three hundred people," said George. "They must have some big conference rooms or lecture theatres we could use."

"What about Wembley Stadium?" said Clive. "We might be being optimistic thinking we're only going to get three hundred. Or should that be pessimistic?"

"OK," said George, "let's say five hundred. If we get more than that and some people can't get in, I think we can justifiably say we did our best. That will be over five times our usual attendance."

"Do you still want me to chair it?" asked Fred. "Only I thought it would just be the usual crowd."

"Really?" said George, with a knowing smile. "Can anybody remember who it was who suggested we invite people from the estate? All together… " He raised his arms to conduct the collective response.

"Fred Dawson!" they said in unison, laughing.

"Fair point," said Fred, and the twinkle returned. "I'll do it."

★

Tom scored a few welcome points with Mags by opting out of a function at Westminster to attend Katey's parents' evening. Bishop Adcock High was a small independent school set in large, well-tended gardens just over a mile's walk from Etherington Place through a leafy lane and along a paved pathway, crossing a couple of wild flower meadows. It was the perfect evening for such a walk; warm and still, with the sinking sun picking out the colours amidst the lush green.

He took Mags's hand as they walked home and although she did not exactly reciprocate his grip, she made no effort to pull away. They were joined by one of Katey's school friends, a tall, good-looking Kenyan boy, and the two of them walked behind, laughing and talking conspiratorially in low voices. Tom was a little agitated by this intrusion into what he regarded as a family affair.

"Listen," said Mags, "the only reason she didn't insist we drove here tonight was so that she could walk back with him. She can't ignore her friends, just because she's with us."

"No, of course not," Tom nodded and smiled at her. They

walked on in silence for a couple of minutes. "How old is he, anyway?"

"Sixteen," answered Mags.

"Sixteen!" said Tom, a little too loudly and then whispered, "In the same year as Jack?"

"No, the year below, but Jack knows him; says he's a really good kid."

"Even so, he's a bit old for her, isn't he?"

"He's just a friend," said Mags. "She's not mentioned anything about marrying him yet."

Tom turned to her wide-eyed.

"Just a joke," said Mags, smiling quite warmly now. "Don't worry. It's only the same age difference as you and me, after all."

"Yes, but that's different," said Tom.

"Oh, of course, it would be," replied Mags, now grinning broadly. The boy left them just before they reached home, shouting, "Good night, Mr Brown! Good night, Mrs T!"

"Goodnight, Jason," said Mags.

"Jason, eh? Mrs T?" said Tom. "Is he a regular visitor, then?"

"He quite often walks home with Katey, and he's popped in for a chat a couple of times," said Mags. "Don't worry," she said again, still smiling, "they're just school friends."

And this time she squeezed his hand.

"Right, who fancies a coffee?" asked Tom when they arrived home.

"I'll do it," said Katey. "Three coffees?" She went through to the kitchen. Tom looked at Mags wide-eyed in amazement.

"You've got Jason to thank for that," she said. "He always puts her in a good mood." Katey followed them through into the huge rear living room a few minutes later with three steaming mugs on a tray. Their daughter, at fourteen, was tall and slim and already had the face and figure of a young woman – a beautiful young woman – although she had managed to retain her teenager's scowl. Her hair was almost white blonde, long and straight.

"Well," said Mags, "we're really pleased you're doing well, Katey. If you want to make us feel absolutely ecstatic, it seems you just have to concentrate more and work harder, according to Mrs Metcalfe… "

"*And* Mrs Latham, *and* Mr Hartson, *and...* " Tom added, with a smile, counting on his fingers. Katey held up her hands in a gesture which exactly mimicked one of her father's.

"Yes, I know; they all say the same. But the point is, if you're naturally brilliant, you're going to do okay anyway. It's not like you have to cling to every word every teacher says."

Tom shook his head, still smiling. "That's true, of course, but life is so unfair to brilliant people. It treats them the same as *ordinary* people up to a certain age, which means they are judged on trivia like exam results and dissertation reports and the like. I know it's frustrating for a true genius but... " He shrugged and spread his arms.

"Yes, okay, point taken. Anyway, Jason says I should try harder as well."

"Well, there you are, then," said Mags, jumping in before Tom had time to say anything. "It must be right. We're all agreed then?"

"I suppose... " said Katey. "Anyway, Dad," she went on, brightly, "I know you're mad busy, what with the usual stuff and this Cullen Field thing. It was really great you coming tonight."

"Of course I was going to come, Princess," he said. "It's a matter of priorities, and when have you ever been lower than number one?"

She screwed up her face to think.

"Well... the last three parents' evenings, for a start."

"Point taken," said Tom, holding up his hands in the familiar gesture of surrender.

"Anyway, I bet you only came because you know all the girls fancy you," said Katey, smiling accusingly.

"Katey!" said Mags, pretending to be shocked. "That's not true, is it?"

"Of course not," said Tom. "Ninety percent perhaps, but surely not all of them."

CHAPTER 6

On the second day of the stake-out, soon after darkness had fallen, the figure turned in through the gates from the road and walked slowly down the driveway. He carried a small bunch of flowers and was wearing a long dark raincoat, ankle high boots and an army-style cap in standard DPM camouflage colours, which he removed soon after passing through the gates. He stopped briefly in front of the Chapel of Rest and looked round, before walking down the path to the left until he was opposite the headstone. He stepped over to it, carefully standing on the raised edges around the stone slabs marking the graves between the path and the one he had come to visit. He stooped down, and removed the bunch of flowers from the grave, putting them to one side before replacing them with the fresh ones. From the office in the chapel, Catherine, Geoff and Jocky McLean, one of the SFOs, watched him stand up slowly and look round again.

Jocky was already on the radio speaking to his two colleagues in the car near the gates and the four in the van on the side street.

The man was looking at the headstone again and appeared to be totally engrossed in it. They watched the blue car with lights extinguished crawl silently along the road towards the gates. Moving out of the office to the exterior door of the foyer, Jocky checked the semi-automatic Heckler & Koch MP5 and slipped off the safety. Catherine was at the outer door, ready to open it. Jocky's radio sounded.

"One in position; ready to go."

"Copy; wait for go," said Jocky.

"Two in position; ready to go."

Catherine turned the handle.

"Okay – *go to strike!*"

She pulled open the door and Jocky raced through it running silently and low towards the man. As he closed in on him, the figure whirled round, his right arm suddenly extended, pistol in hand and pointed directly at him. Jocky switched on the spotter light on his weapon prompting the same action from the six other officers converging on their target. The night was suddenly filled with roaring voices and beams of light.

"Police!

"Drop the gun!"

"Drop it now!"

"Get down!"

"On your face!"

"Now! Get down!"

The man spread his arms and released his grip on the pistol butt allowing the weapon to swing and hang from his finger by the trigger guard.

"Drop the gun!"

"Get down!"

"Face down!"

"On the ground!"

"Now!"

He let the gun fall and dropped to his knees.

They had reached him by now and were pushing him onto his face across the grave; pulling his arms roughly behind him, two holding him down, one applying cuffs, another searching him.

In less than a minute it was over and they pulled him to his feet, turned him and marched him over to the chapel, where Catherine and Geoff were waiting.

"Mr Alex Anderson?" said Catherine.

"It's a long story," replied the man.

They could see he had been crying.

★

Back at Parkside, Mr Alex Anderson was relaxed and courteous and cooperated fully with their scanning his fingerprints, taking a sample for DNA testing and taking the usual set of photographs. They removed his belt and boot laces, and placed them along with his other personal items in a labelled plastic bag. Unusually, he carried no wallet and no other form of identification. He had with him only a set of house keys, having apparently walked to the cemetery.

In the small interview room at Parkside Police Station. Jo switched on the recorders and stated the time, date and names of those present in the room.

"Mr Anderson – that is your real name, isn't it?" David began.

"Yes."

"You have the right to legal representation. If you wish to make a call, or we can arrange… "

"No, thank you. I'll wait to see what this is about first."

"Very well," said David. "We have been looking into the disappearance of a Mrs Alma Deverall since her previous address went up for sale without her returning to it after an extended period of absence. Her neighbours were concerned that something may have happened to her. We now know, sadly, that they were justified in their concern and we are trying to piece together the last six months of her life. From what we know already, you were very much involved with her during that period."

The man nodded.

"Would you mind filling in the gaps for us?"

"Yes, certainly. There's no mystery. I am a full-time carer with Social Services. I was assigned to Mrs Deverall's case last year following her second attempt to take her own life. I visited her once a week, always in the evening. She preferred that time because that was the part of the day when she felt most vulnerable from those bastards on the estate. They were the ones that had caused her to try to kill herself. She said at least one evening a week she would feel safe. It's appalling, isn't it, that a gentle old lady should live in fear like that?"

"You say there's no mystery, Mr Anderson. Then can you explain why Social Services have no record of a carer being assigned to Mrs Deverall? And, in fact, don't appear to employ anyone called Alex Anderson. "

The man gave a brief laugh.

"I can't explain it, but it doesn't surprise me in the least when you see the extent of some of the other administrative cock-ups in the organisation… "

"Really?" put in Jo. "I've always found them very efficient when I've had to deal with them."

"Well, perhaps they make a special effort when they're dealing with the police."

"Oh, they did, Mr Anderson, when we asked them about the carer and about your employment with them. They spent a lot of time checking."

The man hesitated for just a moment.

"Well, as I say, I can't explain it. There are other people who can confirm it, though. I know Alma told the lady next door, if you want to check with her."

"We already have, Mr Anderson."

"And… ?"

"Tell us about Mrs Deverall leaving the estate," asked David.

"Well, she was still anxious and stressed with it all in between my visits and asked if I could help her find somewhere to stay for a while until she felt better. That was last October and it was coming up to the time of year when she felt most at risk – you know, when it gets dark early during the winter months."

"A little outside your remit, I would have thought."

"Way outside, but she'd come to regard me as a friend – even after just a few visits – and there was no-one else for her to ask."

"So what did you do?"

"I looked on a few websites and this apartment sort of jumped out at me. A three month tenancy, fantastic accommodation and – I figured – the chance of a really good deal. I got in touch with the guy and did the business. Mrs Deverall loved it."

"Hammersmith was a bit out of the way, wasn't it? A lot different from what she was used to."

"Oh, you're familiar with the apartment, are you? Well, that's exactly what I said to her when she said she'd take it. I really thought she'd say no. But that was the reason she *did* want it. Because it *was* a complete change, geographically and… socially, I guess. I think she saw it as a bit of an adventure."

"And was she happy there?" Jo again.

"Absolutely. I was taken off the case – naturally – when she moved, although I know she still thought of me as her carer. But yes, she recovered her health and spirits, and the tenancy was extended by three months, which was a massive bonus."

"Did you see her a lot while she was there?"

"Two or three times a week. I used to know the area very well, so it was a good excuse to go back."

"So what happened when the tenancy came to an end?"

The man's expression changed abruptly with the question, as if a dark cloud had passed over his face. His voice was hesitant and soft and he seemed temporarily to lose his composure.

"Well, it all went wrong," he said, after a long pause. "She became anxious again at the prospect of returning to the estate. Her mood dipped and she got very depressed. I asked her if she'd like me to find her some new alternative accommodation. But she said no; and then she rallied and I thought she was okay again. The next day, two days before she was due to leave, I found her... dead." He had to force the word out.

No-one spoke for a long time.

"I guess you know the rest," he said. "I've visited the grave quite a few times since. There was no-one but me at her funeral. I had no idea who to contact – she had no husband and her son was killed a few years ago – so I was all she had really. She was a nice lady, a brave lady. She deserved so much more." They both noticed a slight, but definite, break in his voice. "It's ironic, isn't it," he went on, "that the main reasons for her taking her own life were removed three weeks after she died – the fucking Bradys! Sorry, ma'am," he added, directing the apology at Jo.

"It's late," said David, looking at his watch and noting that it was nearly midnight. "We will need to talk to you some more, Mr Anderson, but we can do that in the morning."

"Am I being charged with something?" asked the man. "If not, why can't I go?"

"As I say", replied David, "we need to ask you a few more questions."

"Such as?" asked the man.

"Well, there's the issue with the carer record. I hear what you say about admin cock-ups, we have them here as well, but this was a police enquiry and, as you suggested yourself, people tend to dig very deep to provide us with the correct information in those circumstances. So I am not entirely satisfied with your theory about that. And then there is the small issue of your threatening a police officer with a firearm."

"It wasn't even loaded, for God's sake, and I don't think you can say I threatened him… "

"The officer wasn't to know it wasn't loaded, Mr Anderson. And we can spend all night talking semantics, but pointing a gun at someone's head – in my book – is threatening them."

"Okay," said the man, "but Christ! When someone runs straight at you at night in a graveyard screaming like a banshee… it was a reflex action, I guess."

"One that could have got you killed," said Jo. "And I assume you are aware that the courts are required to give an automatic five year sentence for anyone illegally in possession of a firearm."

"Look, I do have a license for the gun and pistol-shooting's a hobby of mine. I'm very good at it, in fact, and if you want a demonstration, then take me to your shooting range and I promise I will amaze you. If you are just going to charge me with carrying a weapon, then I plead guilty. Can't I go home and come back to the station in the morning?"

"I'm afraid not, Mr Anderson," said David. "You mentioned the Bradys; well I have to tell you that the search for Mrs Deverall was directly linked to our investigations into their murder. And we shall be checking your gun against the bullets found at the scene of the crime.

"Good," said the man. "If it all hinges on that, I can't wait for the results."

"Actually, I'm surprised that you haven't asked why we had armed police waiting for you at the cemetery, Mr Anderson. It's almost as if you know why… "

"Well, I haven't watched much television recently, Chief Inspector, but I seem to remember that in cases like this, it's usually the police who ask the questions. I guess I just went along with the accepted protocol."

"You see, we believe," went on David, ignoring the remark, "that there is possibly a link between the killings and Mrs Deverall's suicide – an act of revenge on her behalf. You knew they called her

Deverall, didn't you, Mr Anderson? Yet you gave her name as Coleridge both to Mr Venables and to the undertaker. Why was that?"

"Mrs Deverall was worried that she might get into trouble if the council found out that she had rented another place while she was still in council property. I told her there wouldn't be a problem, but you know what elderly people are like, once they get something into their heads. So I suggested she used her maiden name for the tenancy agreement. It then seemed obvious to give that name to the undertaker as well, but I did make sure both her names were on the headstone."

"Yes, that's another thing," said David. "Did she talk about her husband much?"

"No, apparently he died when they were both in their forties."

"Yet she told you his name, including his middle name. And the full name of her son as well. They were on the headstone."

"Yes, she did. I can't remember how that came up in conversation."

David paused for a few moments.

"I think we should call it a day – or night – Mr Anderson," he said, with finality this time. "We shall be holding you overnight. It's not my intention to charge you, but if you want, I can do – with possession of a firearm and threatening a police officer. When we resume in the morning, I suggest you get in touch with your lawyer. I think we should then go over again what we've covered tonight so there is no misunderstanding and then take it on from there. Thank you for your cooperation so far."

The man said nothing.

"Interview finished at 12:13 am," said Jo to the digital recorders, and switched them both off. "Good night, Mr Anderson," she added, as the two officers rose. The police constable standing behind them opened the door and they left the room.

CHAPTER 7

The following morning, Peter Drake heard the news item on his personal radio, crushed in a carriage on the Docklands Light Railway on his way to work…

"Police investigating the murder of three brothers, Jimmy, Kevin and Karl Brady, in the Cullen Field area of Marlburgh, East London, have issued a statement that a man was detained yesterday evening and is helping them with their enquiries. Detective Chief Inspector David Gerrard, the officer in charge of the investigation, said that no charges have been made and that this line of enquiry is at an early stage."

By the time he got to the office at a few minutes after 8.00 am, he had set in motion the 'wiping' of one of their apartments. He had also called the Brigadier's PA. Vicky was already at her desk when he arrived. As usual, she had beaten him in by over half an hour.

"How do you manage to get in so early?" he asked. "Do you live here?"

"No, sir. But I didn't join the army to work nine-to-five; so I thought I'd work seven-to-seven instead."

"I wish I hadn't asked," he said. "I don't suppose you heard the news this morning, did you?"

"Do you mean all of it, sir, or did you have a particular item in mind?"

"You *are* on form today," he gave a brief laugh, "but actually this is no joking matter. I meant the news item about the arrest in the Cullen Field case."

"No, I didn't hear that," she said, suddenly very serious. "Did they say who it was?"

"No. Was there anything on the download from NPD?"

"Nothing, sir. No mention of Page One."

"That's good, of course, but I think it's time to tell the big guy. I've set up a meeting with him that should be starting… " he looked at his watch, "… right now."

That same second the door opened and a large, barrel-shaped man with a very red face, sporting a huge moustache and wearing a loud-checked three-piece suit, marched into the room. He looked every inch the archetypal senior officer from an Ealing comedy.

"Sir!" said Peter and Vicky together, standing to attention and saluting.

"At ease," said Brigadier Barry Henshaw. "What's all this about, chaps? Eight-fifteen? Not had my second cuppa yet. Better be good."

He lowered himself into one of the wing chairs next to Peter's desk, his considerable bulk barely fitting between the arms, and waved his two subordinates to be seated. Peter's office was a good size and well furnished with comfortable chairs and smart cabinets and tables. What spoilt the overall effect was his desk, which was purely functional with two PC monitor screens, four rather old-fashioned-looking phones and an attendant mass of cables, along with a huge angle-poise lamp which was unmanageable and never used.

"I'm afraid it's not good, sir," said Peter. "It's bad, in fact – or most probably bad. We've been following up a True Identity Event on Phoenix Agent One. I've asked Corporal Barrowclough to join us because she has been pulling the data together."

"Okay, let's hear it then, Corporal," he said, turning to Vicky.

She took the Brigadier very quickly through what they had so far with Peter adding the latest news about the arrest the previous evening, which had prompted his calling the meeting.

"Conclusions?" asked the Brigadier.

"Well, based on the facts, *in*conclusive, sir. We could have just a nominal," said Peter. "But gut-feel it's an actual and worst case he's spilled already. That's highly unlikely, though. My expectation is that he'll play for time until we can exorcise. I don't know what name he's using but I'm certain it won't be ours yet."

"Highly unlikely, you say?" repeated the Brigadier. "About as highly unlikely as his going off-programme?"

"I take your point, sir," said Peter. "What do you think?"

"Do the wipe right away – that's the first thing... "

"Already under way, sir."

"Good, and get everything in place to exorcise, because this looks like a cast-iron actual to me," he said, squeezing out of the chair and standing up. The others immediately got to their feet.

"He's the best we have, sir," said Peter.

"*Was* the best; not any more it seems."

"Yes, sir."

"Thank you, Corporal," he said, nodding to Vicky, and, after returning their salutes, he spun on his heel and marched from the room. Vicky sat back in her chair looking miserable.

"What a pity," she said, with a sigh. "He's the best-looking as well."

A phone on Peter's desk rang and he dived for the handset as if a second ring would cause the world to end.

"Yes?"

"Wipe completed."

"Excellent. Report, please, Jim." He pressed the speaker button so Vicky could hear.

"CCTV monitors and cameras removed; all alarms removed except one domestic external; keypad entries to all rooms removed and replaced by traditional locks and bolts."

"PCs?"

"Removed and substituted with work PC, plus printer, fax and hard-drive with client lists, investment plans, performance data – all the usual stuff."

"Handguns?"

"Four replaced, like for like. There'll be no fingerprints, of course, but that would be consistent with an enthusiast, who'd clean them thoroughly after use anyway."

"How long, Jim?"

"Twenty-eight minutes twelve seconds, sir. Over two minutes outside our record, but not bad."

"More than not bad, Jim; bloody brilliant. Well done to you and the guys."

"Thank you, sir."

★

"So," said David Gerrard. "You've had time to sleep on it. What do you think of our friend's account so far?"

They were back in David's office again. It was less than seven hours since he had briefed the Press Officer the previous night before going home. He looked weary and dishevelled and was as yet unshaven. By contrast, Jo looked her usual immaculate self in a dark blue trouser suit and cream shirt, her hair hanging loose and natural.

"A lot of it holds water," she said, "but I don't believe that about an admin cock-up at the Social Services. I don't believe he's an official carer. Cathy says when the guy approached him in the cemetery, she didn't actually see him go for his gun; it was suddenly there in his hand. In fact, she reckons if it had been loaded he could probably have taken him out – if he'd wanted to – before he'd have had chance to fire. It doesn't fit the profile of your average health worker, multi-skilled though I'm sure they have to be."

"But it does fit the profile of a clinical killer, doesn't it?"

"Yes, it does. And she also said that when she asked if he was Alex Anderson, he said, 'it's a long story'. I've no idea what he meant by that. If he's not using his real name, of course, that might explain why he wasn't carrying anything which would confirm his identity – no credit cards, nothing with a name on it. And the name itself – a bit of a coincidence – Alex Anderson."

David sat back in thought for a few minutes, rapidly clicking the point of his pen in and out.

"Anything else?" he asked.

"Well, yes. How do you think Mrs D came to be able to afford a flat in Hammersmith – even at a knock-down price – in addition to her place in Cullen Field? Or even without her place in Cullen Field, come to think of it? It cost her six grand altogether."

"Yes, I thought of that, too," said David. "She probably got a good pay-out from the army when her son died, and she may even have had him insured privately – although that's less likely, given his occupation. That would also explain why she paid the lot up front. It would just mean writing a single cheque from a savings or investment account, rather than setting up a standing order or DD. But let's not lose that thought."

Geoff Drury entered the room carrying a sheet of paper and a transparent plastic wallet containing a firearm, both of which he placed on the desk in front of the Chief Inspector.

"Report on the gun," he said. "Not the one used to kill the Bradys. Same 9mm, but the signature on the bullets didn't match."

David was indifferent to the news.

"No surprises," he said. "Anyone carrying out contract or revenge killings would, no doubt, have more than one weapon, so it doesn't tell us anything. Jo, can you set up for us to start talking to him again in about an hour, let's say nine-thirty. And get him to make a phone call or something. He's not been charged; he can call who he likes. I don't want any technicalities to get in the way if we take this further. Oh, and Geoff, set up an ID parade for mid-afternoon; get the landlord of the Wild Boar to look him over." DC Drury left the room. "And now, Detective Sergeant, I'll get a shave and see if I can make myself look a tenth as respectable as you do."

★

One of the phones rang in Peter Drake's office at 8.45 am. He clicked in the loud speaker button but said nothing, just listened to the message.

"Hi, just to let you know I won't be able to make it this morning. But someone needs to take care of the stuff on page one. I suggest the best way would be to delete it and arrange for cover as soon as possible. See you as soon as I can get away."

The caller rang off. Peter shook his head and clicked the button out again. Then he picked up another phone.

"Actual confirmed," he said. "Exorcise."

★

This time, sitting across the table from them in the interview room, next to the prisoner, was a very large man with a prominent stomach in a crumpled, albeit expensive, grey pinstriped suit, white shirt and grey tie. His face was round and ruddy and what hair he had was parted low on one side and stuck to his head in a classic comb-over.

The room itself was reasonably large and not unfriendly, with a carpet and comfortable chairs, and brightly lit by a number of spotlights set into the ceiling panels. On the wall next to the table where they sat was a large mirror which, from the other side, was a window.

Jo switched on the recorders. "Interview started at nine-thirty," she said. "Present, Mr Alex Anderson, Mr Clive Granville – solicitor, Detective Chief Inspector David Gerrard and Detective Sergeant Jo Cottrell. Also in attendance, Constable Simon Long."

For the second time in the space of twelve hours, they listened to the man tell his story.

"You need to know," he began, "that I am *not* Alex Anderson, a carer with Social Services. My name is James Philip Lorimar; I am an Investment Manager with a company called Germaine and Rolland."

David's eyes blazed.

"Are you saying that you sat in that chair last night and told us a pack of lies until after midnight?"

"No, I'm not," said Lorimar. "The story was correct, but I withheld my true identity."

"Please don't try to be funny with me, Mr... Whoever. I don't fair well without a good night's sleep at the best of times. Now just tell us the real story."

"As I said, I am currently employed as an Investment Manager at Germaine and Rolland on Canary Wharf. I joined them three years ago as an Analyst prior to which I was in active service in Afghanistan where I was a close friend of John Deverall, Alma's only son."

"This will check out, won't it?" asked David. "I am not in the mood for any more works of fiction."

"I promise you it will – and all that follows. We – John and I – were both in the SAS operating as lead marksmen – snipers – out of Bagram. On our way back from a hit, our patrol was involved in an explosion and John was fatally wounded. Before he died, he told me about his mother; how he had had a major falling-out with her over his role in the war. She was horrified that he was, as he said she put it 'a hired killer shooting people who were looking the other way'. They had an enormous row and she completely disowned him; he hadn't seen her for well over a year.

"It was clear that the knowledge that he would never be able to make it up with her was more upsetting for him than the closeness of his own death. He made me promise, just minutes before he died, that I would check that she was alright and keep an eye on her."

He faltered briefly in his story.

"Go on," said Jo.

"To my shame," he said, "I left the Special Forces shortly after John's death, but it was well over two years before I visited her. It wasn't like I was at the other end of the world, either. So no excuses – I just simply never got round to it."

"But you did eventually go to see her?" asked Jo.

"Yes. I actually visited the estate on several occasions before meeting her and, I tell you, it was a real eye-opener. God knows how you can let people like that get away with it." His demeanour changed quite dramatically, just like the previous evening, when he got on to this subject. "They really hounded her. I had a couple of skirmishes with the bastards myself." He paused a few moments to regain his composure. "But it was a while before I actually went to see her. I wasn't quite sure how to break the ice, but in the end I just knocked on her door and introduced myself. She seemed really pleased to meet me – because of John, of course. I told her how much he regretted their quarrelling and she cried a lot. Then I went back to see her about once a week after that."

"Why did she tell the neighbours that you were a carer?" said Jo. "Why didn't she just tell them the truth?"

The man laughed. "I said everyone would think she had a toy boy, and she got quite serious as if she was really worried that they would. So, jokingly, I said, 'Okay, just tell them I'm from Social Services' and apparently she did. So that's what we told everybody. She seemed more comfortable with that."

"And then?" asked David.

"The rest of the story's the same as before. I made up a name for the carer for when I did things like paying the rent and collecting her pension, and I gave the same name to the undertaker when Mrs Deverall died just to keep the separate identity. It was based on John's middle name – Alexander. I just split it up and added 'son' – Alex Anderson. It was sort of symbolic and Alma seemed to take some comfort in that."

He paused, as if waiting for any more questions. David and Jo were silent.

"About the gun," he continued. "I guess old habits die hard. I know I shouldn't carry it, but frankly, once I started going onto that estate, it seemed like a good idea anyway. But I never have it loaded and I'd only ever use it to frighten, certainly not to kill."

"Where were you on the evening of Saturday, 7th of May, Mr Lorimar?" asked David.

The man smiled. "Saturday evening, let me see. Usual riotous weekend stuff, I expect. Concert on BBC2, followed by *Casualty* on one, then news and *Match of the Day*. Except was that after the end of the season? If so, probably reading or listening to CDs – or both."

"How can you be that sure? Are you trying to tell us you do the same every Saturday? I'm afraid I don't believe you."

"Just about every night, Chief Inspector, not just every Saturday night."

"A bit different from the excitement and camaraderie of conflict. Is that normal for someone leaving the Special Forces?"

"It is for people in my line of work. Snipers are notorious loners, anyone will tell you that. We're seen as sort of vermin in the forces, even by our own side. Not really cricket, is it, shooting people who are looking the other way, as Alma put it? Until, of course, they're pinned down somewhere and suddenly we get the call and we're heroes when we get them out. Then as soon as it's over, we're back to being scum again."

"I see," said David, "So what do you do for relaxation? You're not a sniper now; I can't believe your colleagues at Germaine hold that against you."

"No, of course not, but it's just what you become. I do go out for a drink with them occasionally, most often on a Friday after work. And I go four or five times a week to the gun club. Quite a number of ex-service people are members there."

"Except they won't talk to you, I expect, because of what you did."

"Actually, I forgot to share that detail with them."

"So coming back to the Saturday in question, is there anyone who can corroborate your story, Mr Lorimar? Someone who will confirm that you were there? A companion, for example; who lives with you and enjoys the same TV programmes?"

"No, no-one. But you'll find that's the same every night, Chief Inspector."

David remained silent and the man sat back. His solicitor nodded wisely in silent support.

"That's a great story, Mr Lorimar," said David. "I am right in calling you Mr Lorimar, am I? You don't have any other names up your sleeve?"

The man smiled and nodded. "No, Lorimar it is."

"But what I can't understand is why you gave us all that crap last night about Mr Anderson. All this would sound fine if it wasn't for the fact that, twelve hours ago, you sat in that same chair and lied through your teeth!" His voice was rising. "So, come on, Mr Lorimar-hyphen-Anderson, why not complete the tale for us and tell us how you exterminated the Brady boys, rather than hold it back for the next episode when you reveal that you're actually Spider Man in a baseball cap!"

He could sense, with some satisfaction, that Clive Granville was bristling at the man's side.

"Chief Inspector!" he began, voice raised with indignation on behalf of his client. "I really don't think… "

The man interrupted him,

"I don't know why I told you what I did last night," said the man, very calmly and clearly unfazed by the rising anger of the DCI. "Ever since I started visiting Mrs Deverall, I've been playing the part of her carer in different situations, so I guess it just felt natural to keep doing it. It was clearly wrong of me. But apart from that, what I've told you on both occasions is true except for the reason why I got in touch with her in the first place. It wasn't because of the Social Services, it was because of a favour to a dead friend. And bear in mind, I had no idea when you collared me last night in the cemetery that it was anything to do with a murder. I had nothing to do with the death of those people and I don't want any complications. What you've heard today is true."

"Have you ever been with the army in Northern Ireland, Mr Anderson?" asked David.

"Lorimar," the man corrected him. "Yes, I did have a spell there; that's where I first met John Deverall, in fact. Why?"

"Had you ever met Mrs Deverall before?"

"No, I told you, the first time I met her was about nine months ago."

"And how close a friend was John Deverall?"

"Pretty close. Well, as close as anyone else in the circumstances. You get thrown together – it's not like you clock off and go home every night, you know. You're with people 24/7. So you're going to get close to the guys in your outfit, aren't you?"

"Would you say closer than you were to other soldiers in your outfit?"

"Yes, probably, because of the specialist work we did. There were just the two of us doing that in our squad. As I said, a lot of the guys don't really approve of what we do, so snipers do tend to stick together."

"What are the names of your parents, Mr… " he pretended to check his notes "… Lorimar."

"Chief Inspector," interrupted the solicitor, "my client has fully cooperated in giving a complete version of his story; he has, in my view, satisfactorily answered your questions; and he clearly regrets giving you false information last night. You don't have anything to link him with these killings, and because you don't, you seem now to be asking him almost random questions."

David listened politely to the solicitor's comments. "Nevertheless, Mr Granville, I'd like your client to answer the question. You can hardly claim it's difficult or incriminating. So, what are the names of your parents – their full names?"

"*Were* the names," the man corrected. "They are both dead. James Allan Lorimar and Alice May Lorimar."

"Did John Deverall know their names, do you think?"

"I've no idea. Why?" The man, who had been totally relaxed throughout, now seemed confused and a little uncomfortable.

"Yes, where is this going?" asked Clive Granville.

"Because I'm still having difficulty in understanding how you came to know the full names of both John Deverall's parents, particularly his father, and – more to the point – why you don't remember how you know."

"I really don't see the relevance in this," said the solicitor.

"I'm not sure of the relevance myself, yet. But put yourself in my position," said David, looking at a point in space between the two men opposite. "A man deliberately draws attention to himself in a crowded pub, openly challenges the three most feared toe-rags on a very tough estate, lures them away from habitation and executes them. Motive for the killings is almost certainly revenge. Now I'm sure you're aware of an important statistic associated with crimes like this, which is, the best chance of solving them is within the first forty-eight hours. After that, it becomes exponentially more difficult.

"Well, nearly two weeks have passed now and I am under enormous pressure to come up with a result in one of the most dramatic and highly publicised murder cases in recent years. And, based on that aforementioned statistic, it's not looking too promising. Or it wasn't!" He paused. "Then suddenly, we have a person," he continued, indicating the prisoner, and turning his eyes to look directly at him, "who carries a gun, is an expert marksman, befriends a victim of the Bradys, and sees her take her own life rather than go back to face them. A man, in fact, who seems to have several identities. You do see where I'm going with this, don't you?"

No-one immediately volunteered to fill the silence that followed. Eventually, it was the solicitor who spoke, politely this time.

"Chief Inspector, would it be possible if I could have a private word with my client?"

"Interview suspended at 10:23 am," said David, by way of an answer, stopping the two recorders. "Let's reconvene after lunch at, let's say, one o'clock.

★

Jo stopped off in the Operations room to brief the team while David went through to his office where his boss, Detective Superintendent Allan Pickford, was waiting for him. Alan was a little over six feet tall, slim and straight-backed, with an almost military posture. His face seemed to be fixed in a permanent frown, which was a contradiction to his friendly and supportive management style. He introduced Jane Duncan of the CPS, who was waiting with him.

"I thought it would be useful if Jane sat in while we review where we are," said Alan. "I trust you have no objection."

"None at all. Morning, Jane."

"Morning, David."

"Do carry on then," said Allan, waving Jane to one of the chairs in front of David's desk and then leaning against the wall.

"Well," said David, "he's changed his story this morning – or his identity, as he put it. He's now claiming to be an Investment Manager called James Lorimar with – would you believe – a history of sniping for the SAS. I'm sure we'll quickly confirm a lot of his story: address, occupation, army record, date of birth and such. Jo's getting people on to that right now and I have a feeling that's all going to check out. But the very nature of the killings clearly points to someone like him – the precise headshots, I mean. Oh, and he hasn't got an alibi for the night of the killings, but it seems he hasn't got one for any night. Very much a loner, he says – we're checking if that's true as well."

Jo entered the room and sat down on the vacant chair, nodding to Jane.

"What doesn't hang together at all for me is the motive. It's hard to believe that someone fit and well, prime of life, with a good job and God knows what else going for him, should take it on himself to avenge someone in that way; someone he's known for less than a year. Especially now she's beyond help, anyway."

"So either," said Jo, "he didn't do it, or he's closer to Mrs Deverall than he's saying."

"Or," put in the Superintendent, "he simply felt he *had* to do it, because of the promise he'd made and the fact that he hadn't kept that promise for so long."

David nodded and then turned to Jo.

"Something you said just then, about perhaps he was closer to Mrs D than he says. If this man had been, say, her nephew, we'd be close to charging him right now, wouldn't we?"

He paused for a few moments.

"Jo, get someone to check out the military records for John Deverall as well as James Lorimar. In particular, for the time they were together in Northern Ireland and, later, from the time they became snipers in Afghanistan up to when Deverall was killed. Can you also get me a list of all the soldiers in their unit at the time of his death? Check if any of them have left the army since then and, if so, where they are living. I'd like to talk to somebody who knew these two men."

"What about an ID parade with the landlord of the Wild Boar?" asked Allan.

"Arranged for this afternoon," said David.

"Good," said his boss. "Jane, any comments?"

"Well, what you've implied, David, is absolutely right. We have nothing but circumstantial so far – compelling, but circumstantial all the same. Nothing that would point conclusively to his guilt. That situation would, in theory, change after the ID parade if he gets picked out. But even then I wouldn't be all that confident that the landlord wouldn't be persuaded in court to change his mind, or at least say he's not sure. He might even feel he needed to do it for his own protection. They're not exactly baying for the killer's blood out there – more for his knighthood! Given that we've been on it for two weeks – and bearing in mind the public mood – we have to get it right. We need more. As I know you know," she added.

"Agreed," said David. "I'd love to know what Granville's telling him right now. I guess we'll soon find out."

Allan and Jane left the office.

"Right, Jo. Can you get the team digging up those army guys right away, then we'll go back in."

★

Tom rose to his feet amid groans from the government benches and an air of almost mischievous expectancy on his own side of the House.

"Mr Speaker, would the Right Honourable Gentlemen, the Home Secretary, care to expand on the distribution of the additional £2.5 billion ear-marked for the next phase of redevelopment? And in particular, on what basis has £1 billion of this vast amount been allocated to the establishment of *more* leisure centres and clubs? He said – and I think these were his exact words – 'the *initial* phase would provide enough facilities of this kind to enable every person between the ages of twelve and eighteen to become members if they wished'. Has he simply not counted the number of people accurately – I know at that time of life they tend not to keep very still – or did he hugely underestimate the cost of establishing these facilities in Phase 1?

"And if it is neither of these reasons, then I have great difficulty in understanding why, with figures showing a twenty-five percent success rate with these centres, they do not, overall, have three-quarters capacity still available. In which case, why is he proposing to build more?"

There were the usual cries of "Hear, hear!" from around him and predictable gasps of implied disbelief at his ignorance from the benches opposite. The Home Secretary, Mr Gerald Portman, got slowly to his feet, shaking his head with an indulgent sigh.

"Mr Speaker, the Right Honourable Gentleman's ability to remember verbatim snippets from history in order to quote them out of context at a later date is already legendary. It must be a source of much frustration for him that such a rare skill has no use whatsoever in the real world. And although I believe he has made his best stab at the mathematics of the situation, he would be well advised to leave numbers alone and stick to words – of which he always seems to have a surfeit for what he has to say."

There was standard, exaggerated laughter from the government benches, and even a small smile from Andrew Donald.

"Firstly, I would like to provide him with a little guidance in interpreting the facts correctly. The twenty-five percent success rate which has been quoted now for some time and which, until a few moments ago, I assumed everyone understood, applies to the reduction in street crime and social disturbance in the areas where such facilities have been introduced. It does *not* reflect the percentage of twelve to eighteen year-olds who are members of these erstwhile establishments. Is everyone clear on that so far? Or perhaps the question should be 'is everyone except the Right Honourable Member for Princes and Marlburgh clear on that?'"

He peered round the chamber over the top of his glasses like a headmaster imparting some complex message at a school assembly. There was laughter again from the government benches as Tom Brown rose to his feet. The Home Secretary sat down.

"Mr Speaker, I thank the Right Honourable Gentleman for his brief seminar on statistics. Let me rephrase the question then. If the twenty-five percent improvement has been the result of providing these facilities for a hundred percent of the targeted population – and that link has been made by the government, not the Opposition – isn't that a very poor return on investment? In which case, how can he possibly believe that the solution for addressing the remainder of the problem is to introduce *more* of these? Perhaps it was remiss of me to assume that there is any measurable relationship between the amount of money poured into these centres and the reduction in street crime. In which case, I apologise for wasting his time.

"And before he responds, let me put that £1 billion into some easily recognisable context. It equates to one-tenth of the total government spend on policing for this year. It seems to me that increasing *that* spend by the same amount would have a greater and more direct impact on the issue than using it to produce more spare capacity."

There were more cheers from the Opposition benches as the Home Secretary rose again, this time more quickly. Whilst he gathered himself for the fray, Andrew Donald turned in his seat to speak briefly to Tom who was sitting immediately behind him. The Home Secretary began, speaking not directly to the questioner or even the Opposition generally, but to his own Front and Back benchers.

"Mr Speaker, we have to believe that the Right Honourable Gentleman is well-meaning in his comments. We know that he is a great advocate of law and order, in spite of what one has read about him recently, and… "

There was uproar on the Opposition benches. Most of the members were on their feet with cries of "Shame!" and "Cheap!" A notable exception to this demonstration of solidarity was Andrew, who sat quietly shaking his head, catching Ellen Gormley's eye across the House. The Prime Minister shrugged back at him.

"Order! Order!" the Speaker shouted and the furore subsided.

"As I was saying," continued the Home Secretary. "I am sure his motives are genuine, but he continues to demonstrate a naivety which exposes a weakness in the pursuit of his goals. I ask the House to accept, in the interest of expediency in this debate, that direct statistical relationships are not always conveniently available to link related facts. The simple truth – I repeat – is that where leisure centres and clubs have been introduced and *embraced* by the target section of the community, street crime has fallen by a quarter – that is an irrefutable fact; I don't think anyone has ever challenged that from either side of the House. We believe that further investment will continue this trend. This money will be spent on introducing more specialist clubs, for pursuits such as climbing, cycling, and other sporting activities, and improving facilities in existing ones. And we shall be focusing our efforts on the Frequent Serious Incident Areas – the FSIAs. *In addition* to this figure, the balance of £1.5 billion will include a generous amount to be managed by local authorities to arrange special functions such as trips, concerts and other public meeting events designed to bring together different groups within communities. *That* is where the money will be spent."

The Home Secretary sat down to cries of support from his own party. There was silence on the Opposition side. Tom did not move but the Shadow Home Secretary, Jackie Hewlett, rose to her feet.

*

"His CV checks out okay. Army record runs almost parallel to the late Mr Deverall's from their time together in Northern Ireland right up to the time of Deverall's death. Germaine and Rolland verify start date and current job title. His boss also confirmed that he's a very private person – keeps himself to himself, doesn't mix much. Omar is checking the gun club tonight regarding his membership. Given all the above, we'd expect that to be okay as well. Oh, and the warrant to search his premises has come through."

Jo handed David a sheet with three names and addresses on it. "Catherine got the details of members of his unit. They won't release information on those still in the forces, but these three have left since Deverall's death."

"All in the North West," said David, reading the sheet. "Two in Greater Manchester and one in Pretherby, Lancashire. Never heard of Pretherby,"

"That one was invalided out shortly after the incident, though there's nothing to say whether or not it was a result of it."

"If we needed to, could we do three visits in one trip?"

"We'd be hard pressed to do all three in the… " Jo looked at her watch and calculated "… seventeen-and-a-half hours we've got left before we need to charge or release him. We could probably get to the first one by seven tonight if we could justify a chopper. Second one by, say, nine, and then it's around one-and-a-half hours in a very fast car to Pretherby."

"That's fantastic, Jo," said David, wide-eyed in admiration. "How the hell do you know all that?"

"Not me, sir. Little diddy Baxter checked all this out when she got the addresses. Even so, I think it's optimistic to say the least. We may have to release him and bring him back. Unless you really intend doing him for threatening behaviour."

"Or benefit fraud," said David. "He hasn't informed the DWP about Alma's death yet." Jo raised her eyebrows. "Just a joke, Detective Sergeant, anyway, I'm pretty sure we could get an extension if we needed to. But let's see if we can get these guys on the phone and ask each of them, firstly, can they confirm they were with the unit during the period concerned. Secondly, did they know John Deverall and James Lorimar? I'd like you personally to make contact, Jo. Do we have phone numbers for all three?" She nodded, pointing to the sheet. "Good, then can you do that now, and get back to me within the hour?" He thought for a moment, checking his watch. "Five past four. I guess we'll be lucky to get them within that time, come to think of it; they'll probably be at work or on their way home."

"I'll do my best."

She left the office.

Twenty minutes later she was back.

"Got all three, sir," she said, looking very pleased with herself. "Two on mobiles – at work, like you said – and one at home. He's the one who was discharged due to incapacity, the one in Pretherby. Really interesting this – all three remembered Deverall; not one had heard of Lorimar. They all knew of Deverall's death, and one of them – the one who was injured – he was actually there when it happened – used the phrase 'blown to pieces'. When I asked him did that mean he had been killed instantly, he said 'probably the most instantly anyone's ever been killed.' It doesn't sound like he had much time to make a dramatic death-bed speech."

"Right," said David, with some relish.

★

Grace took Tom's call at a little after 5.00 pm.

"Hello, this is Goody," she said, as usual.

"Have you got anything for me?"

"You're late phoning," she said, annoyed at the abruptness of his manner. "Such as what?"

"You know what, Grace! About the debate?"

"It looks like it's going to be big," she said. "Up to now they have over three hundred people signed up to go from the estate alone. They've stopped asking people to put their names down at three of the places where the notices are. And apparently the 3AF secretary is trying to move the debate to the council offices, because everyone in the village is planning to attend as well. Anyway, it's probably going to be at the Lecture Room in the Town Hall – seats around six-fifty theatre-style. They're talking about cancelling a concert to accommodate it."

"I wish it was one of Portman's newly-fucking-funded concerts!"

"I beg your pardon! Please don't use that language with me!" snapped Grace. "What on earth is the matter?"

"Sorry, Grace," he said. "You're right, that wasn't necessary. Is it okay to say 'bloody' though? Because I've had it today with bloody Donald and bloody Hewlett. And I've got to stay over for a review meeting with them both first thing in the morning. Saturday, for God's sake! There goes the surgery again – or some of it. I'll tell you about it when – or if – I see you next week. That's assuming I'm not suspended!"

"Can't wait," said Grace. "And bloody Portman?"

"Not him, he's okay," said Tom. "I thought he was bloody good, in fact, though he didn't do me any favours. Any reaction on the streets to the arrest?"

"Total dismay, it seems. Everyone's hoping it's not the man."

"Good," said Tom. Then, after a pause, "I think so, anyway."

After ending the call, he phoned Mags.

"Hi, sorry but I'm afraid I'm stuck here tonight. Got a meeting with… "

"Okay," she cut in, her voice expressionless.

"So I'll see you tomorrow after the surgery. Should be back there around… "

"Right."

"Shame, because I thought we could…"

"Bye."

She ended the call, mentally erasing, he suspected, the points he had gained for the parents' evening.

★

"They're checking out guys in the same unit around the time of Deverall's death. I'm worried that if they talk to these people it's all going to kick off." Vicky Barrowclough was alerting her boss to the police's further probing for details concerning James Lorimar.

"That's something we didn't anticipate; something we need to put right," said Peter. "We have to get to Lorimar fast. I think our man may have to sacrifice himself for the greater good. Pull Granville in for briefing. Let's hope we're not too late. By the way, what's the investigating officer's name again? They mentioned it on the news."

"Detective Chief Inspector David Gerrard," said Vicky, handing him a sheet of paper.

"He's a sharp bastard, I'll give him that," said Peter. "Might be an idea to get the name and contact details for his Chief Constable as well."

"It's on there," said Vicky, pointing to the sheet of paper. "Heather Rayburn; and those are her three contact numbers – office reception, direct line and mobile."

Peter smiled. "Thanks, Corporal. You don't need me at all really, do you?"

★

"Well, I hardly expected anything else," David Gerrard had just been told that the landlord of the Wild Boar had failed to pick out James Lorimar at the identity parade. "They'd probably lynch him if they thought he'd helped us catch their hero." He looked at his watch for the twentieth time. "Where the bloody hell is Granville? And what could be more important than representing Pinocchio in there?"

"I don't know, but he shot off at a rate of knots," said Jo.

Geoff Drury knocked on David's door. He waved him inside.

"Solicitor's back, sir. Says he's ready when you are."

David looked across at Jo, eyes wide. "Ready when you are," he repeated, checking for the twenty-first time. "Seven o'clock. *We've* been ready for six bloody hours." They rose to leave. "I tell you, Jo, sometimes – like right now – I think I'd like to go down in history as the first DCI ever to beat a solicitor to death during an interview."

Jo laughed. "Well, before you do that, sir, let me check the records. I find it hard to believe it's never happened before."

David switched on the recording machines in the interview room and stated the names of those present. He also made a point of stating the time very loudly.

"Before we go any further," Clive Granville took the two officers by surprise before they could start, "my client would like to make a final statement."

"What, *another* final statement?" asked David. "Oh, I can hardly wait! Who are you this time, Billy the Kid?"

"My client, Mr Lorimar," said the solicitor, emphasising the name, "simply wishes to add to his last statement – to complete it, in effect."

David sat back in his chair.

"Over to you, Detective Sergeant," he said. "I don't think I can handle another layer of complexity."

"Please go ahead," said Jo, while David sighed loudly and fidgeted in his seat. "And please, Mr Lorimar, do try to finish the story this time," she added, smiling gently, like someone encouraging a reluctant child to drink his milk.

"My last statement," began the man, "stands as made, but, as Mr Granville says, I wish to complete the picture. Following the death of Mrs Deverall I got very depressed – overcome by guilt, you might say. I felt I had let both John and his mother down badly. If I had been more proactive and assertive when the tenancy in Hammersmith ran out and had found her another place, instead of putting the decision on to her, then... well, who knows? The fact is, I didn't and as a result of that... she's dead." His voice showed signs of breaking again as he spoke the last two words.

"During the week following the funeral I went back onto the

estate every night. I watched those Brady bastards out there stirring things up all the time – all over the place. They had this army of young kids who I reckon would walk through walls for them; they never got their own hands dirty. Fires, beatings, vandalism, drug-dealing, and three stabbings – all in those few days. And not one person daring to come out of their house to confront them, or even try to reason or plead with them. Hundreds of people running scared – or rather, hiding scared. It must be like the blitz, except that the enemy is just a few feet away in the streets and actually lives next door. What sort of a fucking life is that?" he shouted across at the officers. "Sorry, ma'am," he apologised again.

"So what did you decide to do?" asked Jo.

"Get rid of them," the man replied. David sat bolt upright in his chair.

"And how did you propose to do that?" asked Jo, before he could grab the reins again.

"Just take a guess, Detective Sergeant," said the man, with gentle sarcasm.

The two police officers were temporarily taken aback. They looked expectantly at the solicitor, who returned their looks calmly, raising his eyebrows as if to invite a question.

Jo accepted his invitation. "Mr Granville, are you entirely comfortable with your client's… position?"

"It is my client's expressed wish to make this statement," he replied. "I have alerted him as to the implications of his admitting those *intentions* and advised him to consider his position carefully, but he is insistent that he wants to say this. And… he is choosing his words judiciously."

In fact, James Lorimar had already chosen all the words he was intending to use; he had nothing more to say.

★

David walked out of the front doors of Parkside Police Station and down the two steps to street level. He placed the single A4 sheet on the stand and looked around at the gathered mass of reporters and TV cameras. The crowd fell silent.

"Detective Chief Inspector David Gerrard, investigating officer," he introduced himself. "I wish to make a statement regarding the ongoing investigation into the deaths of three men in the Cullen Field area two weeks ago. At 8:35 pm today, Mr James Lorimar, a forty-one-year-old Investment Manager, was charged with the murder of Jimmy, Kevin and Karl Brady on the 7th of May this year. The charge was made after due consultation with the Crown Prosecutor. As of now, we are not looking for anyone else in connection with this incident.

"That is all I am able to tell you at this point in time. We will release further details as and when appropriate. As a consequence, I am not able to take any questions. Thank you."

The questions came in a torrent, anyway, as David turned away and walked back into the building, ignoring them all.

CHAPTER 8

At 7.30 am on Saturday morning the G4 vehicle arrived at Parkside, along with two police cars, to pick up the prisoner for the short journey to Marlburgh Central Magistrates Court. James Lorimar was taken from the police holding cells in through the rear doors of the vehicle and secured in his seat inside. By 7.50 am, he was being provided with a light breakfast in his new accommodation in the secure basement area of the court building.

At 9.00am prompt, the same two security officers who had delivered him just over an hour ago, escorted him into the Perspex cubicle in the courtroom to face the three presiding magistrates, seated in a line in front of him. Also present were Clive Granville, his solicitor, Jane Duncan of the Crown Prosecution Service and DS Jo Cottrell. There was no media presence; no-one seemed to have had time to make the connection between the police statement from Parkside and the next sitting of the local magistrate.

The middle of the three magistrates was a handsome, fifty-something blonde woman dressed formally in a pale blue suit with a cream shirt and loosely-fastened tie striped with both colours. Her two colleagues flanking her were male, in their early forties, and dressed smartly in dark business suits.

The woman spoke to the prisoner.

"Could you please state your name and address?"

"James Philip Lorimar; 18 Barrington Mansions, Hammersmith."

"Thank you." She turned to Jane.

"Ms Duncan, would you speak for the Crown, please?"

"Yes, ma'am. The defendant is accused of the killing of three brothers in the Cullen Field area in May. We have evidence which –"

Clive Granville rose to his feet.

"If I may interrupt, ma'am, with apologies to Ms Duncan. If it would expedite the process, I can confirm that we shall not be requesting bail for Mr Lorimar."

The other two magistrates leant in so all three could confer. They spoke for less than a minute then settled back in their seats

"Is Mr Lorimar intending to enter a plea?" asked the woman magistrate.

"No, ma'am."

There was more conferring, this time for an even shorter time.

"Very well, the decision of this court is that Mr Lorimar be remanded in custody pending trial at Crown Court, the date and venue to be set within twenty-four hours of this hearing. You may take the prisoner away."

James Lorimar was escorted from the box and taken back to the court cells to await his onward journey.

★

When Tom finally arrived at his constituency office at 10.50 am that morning, the press – having picked up on the previous evening's statement – had already gathered in substantial numbers in front of the building. He was not in the greatest of moods. Traffic accidents and roadworks had more than doubled the time it would normally have taken him to make the journey from SW1 to Marlburgh on a Saturday morning. He pulled into the small parking area at the side of the building and got out of the car.

"Mr Brown. What are your feelings this morning on hearing the news of the arrest?" The reporter was a small attractive woman with straight blonde hair, wearing a short blue dress and white jacket. She smiled sweetly at him as she stood at his side so that the TV camera could get them both in shot.

"Well, if this man *is* the perpetrator of this crime," said Tom, addressing the crowd in general, "then obviously I'm pleased that he has finally been found and I congratulate the police on what, hopefully, will be the resolution of a very difficult case."

"You have said more than once that you have sympathy with the residents of Cullen Field, and have admitted that this man has done them a favour. Are you not a little saddened that he is likely to receive a long custodial sentence for what in effect is just a good deed?"

"Well, firstly," said Tom, "we do not know yet if this is the man who committed the crime, so let's not get ahead of ourselves by speculating about a sentence. Also, we have no idea at this stage *why* the killer – whoever he is – carried out this crime. What we do know, is that it was to the benefit of the community. But we should be wary of assuming that this is why he did it; of making him a hero before we know his personal motivation for the act."

"But if he *did* do it specifically for the benefit of one, or some, or all of the community… " Someone else called out the question from the back of the crowd.

"It would be unfortunate if this person carried out the crime because he felt it was his only recourse to justice. That is why I have said, on several occasions, we must have in place a means of addressing this sort of issue within the law. To do that, we need to review our current practices and, if necessary, take some serious decisions about the way we approach the problem of intimidation and violence on our streets.

"Now if you'll excuse me, I have a number of meetings scheduled which I must get to right away. Thank you." He treated the woman to a friendly smile before going inside.

The reporters turned away, some to get to their next story, some to remain for further comments when he left later. Tom went straight to his office, saying his usual breezy 'good morning' to his PA, Jenny Britani, on the way. He checked his watch – 11.00 am. Better late…

Grace popped her head round the door. She was wearing one of her 'dress-down-Saturday' outfits, as Tom liked to call them. A short yellow flared dress, low cut and belted at the waist, and black leggings. Her hair was free of constraints and fell naturally and lush onto her shoulders. The dark-rimmed glasses had been discarded in favour of contact lenses.

"Good morning."

"Good morning. What are you doing here?" he asked, feeling suddenly better.

"I work here," she said, and then read from a small post-it note stuck on the palm of her hand, "Message from Mr George Holland – about you chairing a meeting or something. He phoned just after nine o'clock – when you *should* have been here. Here's the number." She placed the note on his desk in front of him.

"George Holland," said Tom. "That name rings a bell… "

"Chairman of the 3AF in Meadow Village. The group that are doing the debate."

"And is that the meeting he wants me to chair?"

"He didn't say; just asked for you to phone him. But it seems likely, don't you think?"

"Mmmm… yes, I guess it must be. If it is, what do you think? Should I do it?"

"I think it could be a good thing," said Grace. "It would mean you'd have to be absolutely neutral, of course, assuming that you're actually capable of that," she added, with a critical smile.

"Don't you start on me as well," said Tom. "Andrew had a real go this morning after that exchange in the House yesterday. Do you know what his opening gambit was? 'You're not in the bloody Marines now, Tom. You don't have to take spontaneous decisions on the ground when the official chain of command is clearly visible and sitting right in front of you!'"

The sudden tinkling of very girlish laughter took him by surprise. He raised his eyebrows at her.

"Well, that's a reaction I've never been able to squeeze out of you," he said. "I must get Andrew to chastise me more often. I'll get you a ringside seat next time."

"I've absolutely no sympathy," said Grace, recovering her poise but still smiling at him. "I'm not sure how he could have put it any more plainly to you beforehand – if what you told me was true – that he didn't want you challenging the government over their public disorder record."

"I wasn't challenging their record – I was challenging their budget for further funding."

"Well, I watched you on last night's *House Calls* and I have to say, I couldn't tell the difference."

"Well, it must have been very badly edited," said Tom, dismissively. "Because it wasn't like that at all. And now, Ms Goody, if you're through giving me my weekly appraisal, would you please wheel in the first victim."

She left the office, stopping briefly in the doorway.

"Hey, I've just thought of something. I spent all last night washing and pressing my canary suit. I suppose that was a waste of time if you're chairing the debate."

"That's politics," he called after her, enjoying the mental image of Grace in her fancy dress and reflecting on the rare unguarded moment when she had let the information slip. No-one knew anything about Grace's life outside her work. There was never any mention of a partner, male or female, and given the amount of time she spent at her job, and her availability at short notice at all hours on any day, it seemed unlikely that one existed. It was rumoured that in the past she had experienced a deep emotional trauma which had caused her to build a defensive wall around herself. But it was only a rumour, like the one about her having a long-term – albeit unspecified – working relationship with Andrew Donald.

As Tom prepared to start his first constituent meeting, he couldn't help but feel slightly privileged that she had chosen to step out of character to share that small private secret with him.

Four hours later he phoned George Holland.

★

"*Six weeks!*" Jo's eyes were wide in disbelief.

"That's right; that's what Jane said."

"But that's about – what – a tenth of the time I would have expected."

"Well, they are trying to reduce the period between charging and trial… "

"Yes, but even so, *six weeks!*"

"It's not going to get any longer just by you repeating it over and over," said David, laughing.

"And was Jane okay with that?"

"Yes, she seemed pretty relaxed… "

"But why?"

"Why was she relaxed?"

"No, you know what I mean. Why such a short time?"

"I don't know. All Jane would say is that they want our man off the radar as soon as possible. Seems he's just too high profile."

"In which case, why the Old Bailey?"

"No idea. Just add it to the list of things I can't work out. Anyway, Detective Sergeant, here's to a result at last – as far as it goes."

They raised their glasses and took a celebratory sip of their drinks. David Gerrard looked pensively out of the window of the Dog and Duck. After the drama of the past few days they had decided to take time out from the familiar surroundings of Parkside. They were seated in the main bar area, overlooking Settlement Lane at the point where it became Main Street. The place was filling up and the atmosphere was friendly and relaxed. The venue had been Jo's suggestion, after visiting the library on the estate the previous day and seeing the notice about the debate. It was the first time either of them had been in the pub.

"Because there's still a lot of stuff I don't get," David went on. "His confession doesn't go anywhere near answering all the questions. Here's a few that really bother me." He leant across the table towards Jo, speaking softly and counting them on his fingers.

"One – how come he knew the names, especially the middle names, of Deverall's parents? I don't know why, but that's kept me awake the last few nights. Two – why did he take such care not to leave a trail to Mrs Deverall when she moved? All that stuff about cash and her maiden name – totally unnecessary. Three – how come not one of those guys from the same unit, who all knew Deverall, had ever heard of him? Four – if Deverall was killed instantly, what was all that crap about a dying request? Five – assuming he's the one responsible for vacating the property – letter to the council with forged signature – why did he wait until after he'd killed the Bradys to do it? Why not immediately after Alma's death? Six – why did he confess when he did, and, seven – what the hell was his lawyer doing sitting there contemplating his bloody navel while he was doing it?"

"Well, he didn't actually confess, did he, sir, even though it was sufficient for the CPS? I think he said just enough to stop us pursuing the answers to those questions."

"That's right. Like someone had a word with Granville and told him to advise his client to give us at least enough to bring a charge.

Even if he did do that, if I was Lorimar, I'd have told him where to shove his advice and got another lawyer."

"The thing is," said Jo, "all this doesn't really matter now in the process of law. Getting answers to these questions would have been critical without that clear statement of intent, but now they're academic, I guess, unless he chooses to retract it?"

"Academic as far as the law is concerned," he agreed, "but more than that in terms of good policing. I believe we need to understand this, even if we don't need the facts to close the case. I don't believe we've finished the job; we've had it taken off us, and we need to know why. The guys have worked really hard in the course of this investigation; we owe it to *them* to tie up the loose ends."

"But when are we going to do that, sir?" she asked.

David sighed and leant back in his chair.

"You're right. We'd need to take this on almost as a personal thing. It's not on the official radar any more, and, to be honest, I don't even know whether the guys will be all that bothered anyway. They'll be in no doubt they've done their job. They've caught the bad guy – well, the guy who did the murders – and that was what we asked them to do." He brightened a little, half joking, "We could even argue that he gave in because he realised we were so good, there was no point in trying to hold out; we'd get him anyway. And who's to say that's not the truth. I mean, we're a bloody good team, aren't we?"

"We sure are, coach," said Jo, laughing. "And I like that – 'we're so good, there was no point in trying to hold out; we'd get him anyway'. I'm conceited enough to believe that."

"Anyway, I'm hungry. Let's order that Sunday roast before they run out of Yorkshire puddings."

★

When Tom Brown stepped out of the taxi at the same venue two days later, he was greeted at the front door by George Holland and a large, sixty-something gentleman in light grey trousers and wearing a double-breasted blazer over a cream shirt and a blue and yellow striped tie, which Tom assumed was old-school or cricket-club. His ruddy face, huge moustache and military bearing shouted ex-RAF. George introduced himself and Arnold Danby.

"Thank you for coming, Mr Brown. There's a crowd in there wanting to meet you, but we'll get quickly through the pleasantries and down to business. I know you're a busy man and… "

Tom held up his hand.

"It's Tom, not Mr Brown, George, and the only thing I'm busy with tonight is a couple of pints and a chat to you good people about what's happening tomorrow. Everything else is off limits for the next few hours."

They went inside and Tom met with the other customers in the pub, most of which were members of the 3AF. After furnishing themselves with a pint each of Thwaites 'Lancaster Bomber' – the landlord's 'guest ale' of the week in deference to the Squadron Leader's visit – George, Fred, and Arnold adjourned with Tom to the snug which the landlord had reserved for their meeting.

"You were in the military yourself, Tom?" said Arnold, briefly high-jacking the agenda.

"That's right. Started in the army at seventeen, three years later transferred into the Marines, then finally the SBS. I left around six years ago after eighteen years in total. I can't imagine I'll last that long in politics."

"Seventeen?" said Arnold. "You started at seventeen? I would have thought you'd have gone a different route – you know, through college, commission and all that. Especially with your father being who he is."

"Why, who is your father, Tom?" asked Fred.

"General Sir Richard Tomlinson-Brown," Arnold answered for him.

"And he was the reason," said Tom. "It was my tilt at parental authority. That's what everybody expected me to do – get a commission – father's footsteps and all that. So instead, I enlisted at the earliest possible opportunity right at the bottom and changed my name to plain Tom Brown. I just couldn't stand the thought of being constantly compared with – and coming up short against – the good General – or Lieutenant-General as he was then."

"How did he feel about that?" asked George.

"Well, publicly, he supported the decision, but in private he told me exactly what he thought of it. Caused some problems between us at the time but we're friends again now. And speaking for myself, I've never once regretted the decision."

"I'm not surprised considering what you achieved," said Arnold. "Why did you leave, by the way?"

"Well, when I reached the rank of Colonel, I had to swap the firing line for a desk, so I thought I might as well have a desk nearer home."

"Anyway," said Arnold, getting to his feet, "I'm afraid I've deflected you from your purpose, George. I'm a gate-crasher, Tom. I'm not part of the group. Leaving tomorrow; sorry I can't make the debate."

"Arnold gave an amazing talk on the Falklands conflict at last week's meeting and decided to stay on for a few days here at the Dog," said George.

Tom stood and shook Arnold's hand. "Perhaps you can give me a private hearing of that speech some time, Squadron Leader. I'd love to swap a few stories."

Arnold left the snug and they got down to business.

★

Tom arrived at the council offices at 6.30 pm and was met by George, who showed him to the Lecture Theatre where the debate was scheduled to start in an hour's time. As people settled into their seats and the sound and lighting engineers carried out their final checks, Tom spent the last few minutes on the floor above in the Banqueting Suite with people who would be watching the event on two large screens.

"Actually," he joked, pointing to one of the screens, "my only reason for coming up here is to let you see me in the flesh so you can say things like, 'well the camera certainly doesn't do him justice'. Which is only the truth, after all."

Someone shouted from the back of the room. "You look good to me in the flesh *and* on TV, Tom!"

"Annie Berryman!" he exclaimed, "Are you stalking me? I do hope so."

There was laughter all round, then the announcement was made that the debate would start in five minutes and would the audience take their seats and the officials their places on the platform.

Around 1,600 people turned up to attend the function. By allowing nearly 300 to stand around the back of the two rooms of the suite and using every available seat in the Lecture Theatre, including those normally left vacant because of line-of-sight problems with the stage, they managed to accommodate all of them.

Tom, George, and a rather white-faced Fred Dawson, took their seats on the stage, the last of these attempting to hide behind the decanter of iced water in front of him. The council had generously provided a professional Master of Ceremonies from their own resources, who banged his gavel loudly on the baize-covered trestle table, perhaps a little over-zealously for the good of its fragile construction.

"Ladies and gentlemen!" he bellowed. "Please put your hands together for your Member of Parliament, *Mister... Tom... Brown!*"

Tom raised his hand to acknowledge the enthusiastic response to the MC's announcement, mouthing the words 'thank you' around the room, and at the camera conveying the images to the Banqueting Suite, as the applause was sustained effortlessly for nearly a minute.

"Ladies and gentlemen," he boomed, in his well practiced House of Commons voice. "Welcome to what I am sure will prove to be one of the most interesting and stimulating evenings any of us will have experienced. I thank you all for your attendance – we have around sixteen hundred people in this building – which is amazing – and hopefully all are here to listen to our debate. If any of you have been in hiding for the last week and have turned up for the Ivory Tower concert, then my apologies, but I can tell you that they will be playing at Croydon Civic Hall next Thursday. So you can catch them there and then."

There was laughter all round the theatre, and also in the Banqueting Suite.

"Seriously," Tom went on, "we must apologise to Ivory Tower for postponing their concert and thank them for their cooperation in agreeing to do so.

"I don't want to delay the start of the debate any more than necessary, but I feel we need to agree a few house rules, given the unusual circumstances that have brought us together tonight. Let me make just a few remarks about the process of the debate.

"Firstly, this is not a public debate, as such. This has been arranged by the local branch of the Third Age Forum – or 3AF as it is more normally referred to. And just in case – like me, until recently – you are not fully aware of what the 3AF is and does, it is a national network established for the purpose of sharing information and promoting learning in retirement. It boasts a membership of around half a million countrywide; it is managed and maintained by volunteers and funded through charitable donations. The two main officials of the Meadow Village branch are with me on stage tonight. On my left," and he half-turned to smile at him, "is Mr George Holland, President of the group, who will be proposing the motion; and on my right," turning again, "Mr Fred Dawson, Secretary, who will oppose it. I think we should all express our appreciation for their generosity in extending invitations to attend to so many people, and their efforts, along with other members of the branch, in making it happen."

With Tom leading there was enthusiastic applause again from all present.

"I'd particularly like to thank them for asking *me* along. I spend a lot of my time in a room with up to this many people in it, but only around half of them are ever smiling at the same time!"

Laughter again.

"I would like to welcome the ladies and gentlemen of the press who are here tonight representing both the local and national media. And I'd ask that they respect the process of the debate by listening and reporting rather than participating. No-one in this room – and I repeat, *no-one* – is here this evening to provide official comments relating to the subject under discussion.

"The rules of the meeting are simple, but for those who have never attended a formal debate before, let me outline the procedure. The motion before us tonight is," and he referred to his notes, "'Extreme action by an individual or individuals, which may result in the permanent removal of another individual or individuals, is justified in circumstances where this results in an overwhelming benefit to the community at large, even in the case where such extreme action is outside the law.'

"Mr Holland – George – will propose the motion by adding his supporting remarks to that point of view. Mr Dawson – Fred – will then oppose the motion by pointing out what he feels are the negative aspects. After they have completed their formal inputs to the meeting, anyone in the room will be entitled to say their piece for or against the motion. I only ask that you raise your hand to indicate your intention to speak rather than shouting out. I will then decide which speaker next has the floor – or should I say – the microphone. There are four people – all raise your mikes, please – two in each of the aisles who will hand you a microphone so we can all hear you. And all remarks should be addressed to the chair – that's me. And if you want to do it very professionally, then you should start your contribution by saying, 'Mr Chairman'. However," and he smiled again at the audience and camera, "I won't be offended if you miss that bit out.

"At the end of the session," he continued, "which is timed for ninety minutes – until around nine-fifteen – by which time I hope we will have given everyone who wishes to speak the chance to do so, we shall have a show of hands – in here and in the Banqueting Suite – for and against the motion. All clear? – Good.

"Just one last, and very important, point. The motion has been carefully and deliberately worded in general terms. We are not here to discuss what has happened recently in Cullen Field. The issue is much wider than that, and I must ask you to ensure that any remarks you have are consistent with the motion and are not related to that very specific event. The two issues are clearly linked – it would be nonsense for me to pretend they were not. But it is imperative that we stick to the subject as clearly stated for us by Mr Holland and his group. Is everyone very clear about that?"

He could see 600 or so nodding heads. He had done what he could up to now. He turned to George.

"Mr Holland… George… "

The debate began.

★

George had the *Daily Telegraph* delivered to his house Monday to Saturday each week. As he sat down for breakfast the following day, he picked up Thursday's offering and read the account of the meeting, which had made the front page despite its late conclusion.

He then re-read, twice, the parts of the article which gave details and comments on his own contribution. It was like reading about somebody else, he thought, a close acquaintance perhaps, but surely not himself.

Irene had been reading the article over his shoulder. The actual result of the voting was presented in a small table on page two.

"'Number of attendees; 1,612'," she read. "'Votes for the motion; 1,503 – ninety-three percent. Against; 109 – seven percent I'll tell you what, that was a hundred very brave people given the mood in there, don't you think?"

"I know. I felt really sorry for Fred when they booed him at the beginning after he'd opposed the motion."

"I thought Tom did a great job in rescuing him, though. In fact, he was brilliant all night, wasn't he?"

"Yes, and he's happily married to a very beautiful woman," said George with a teasing smile. "So you'd best resign yourself to making do with me."

Irene laughed. "Oh, I don't mind that so much. You're obviously going to be more famous than him very soon. By the way," she added, "there's an editorial piece inside."

"Tell you what, you read that first," he said, standing up. "I'm just going down to the shop."

"Before your breakfast?"

"I'll have it when I get back; I won't be long."

He was still putting on his jacket as he left the house.

As he approached the shop he could see about a dozen or so people talking excitedly outside. They all turned to greet him with wide smiles and cheerful greetings. Fred affected a low bow, and muttered, deferentially, "Your Highness." Everyone laughed. There was a lot of back-slapping and mutual congratulations.

"Look at this lot," said Clive, pointing to a pile of papers on the wooden bench in front of the shop. He picked up a copy of the *Daily Mail,* holding it up for George to see. "'The Meek *Shall* Inherit the Earth'," he read from the headline, "and it goes on to say what a thoroughly splendid lot of chaps we are. 'We Need Vigilantes!'" he read from the *Daily Mirror.* "Nice and subtle, as always. I don't like this one as much, though; it's all about you and Fred… "

They all laughed.

"It's unbelievable, isn't it?" said George. "Front page on just about every one. That means it was seen as one of the two or three biggest stories of the day."

"It's not over, either, George," said Fred, "you've got all those other lectures to do at the other Forum branches."

"Other lectures?" asked Emily Burton. "What other lectures?"

"Haven't you heard, Em?" said Fred, "George is spreading the word around the country. We're having 'Tour of Holland' tee-shirts printed."

"God, I'd completely forgotten," said George. "Sounds like a good excuse for doing something to settle my nerves. Let's get together in the Dog at lunchtime. My shout!"

★

A similar collection of dailies were spread across Andrew's desk. He, Tom and Grace were dipping into them.

"I'll tell you what," said Tom, "I've never had to work so hard in my life."

"But you managed to stay out of trouble," said Grace with a smile. "No taking sides, no breaks with neutrality. And you've got yourself a very big fan." She picked up *The Times* and read aloud. "'If the revolution is to happen, there can be few, if any, more qualified to lead it than Mr Tom Brown, the Member of Parliament representing the residents of Cullen Field, and the chairman of last night's debate. His record to date speaks volumes in support of that. He is someone who earlier in his life shunned an open door to a privileged position in order to fight his way there from the very bottom of the pile. A man who leads by example, with an effortless style and ability to communicate and empathise at all levels; he is exactly what this country needs in its political vanguard, whatever the issues and challenges. I believe, along with – I suspect – all of the people present last night, that this man really can put the 'Great' back in front of Britain and banish that particular cliché for ever'."

She looked up at Tom and raised her eyebrows. "You will *never* guess who wrote that."

"Sounds like it might have been you, Tom," said Andrew, with not a trace of humour.

"Tell me," Tom asked Grace.

"Tony Dobson. I thought you two weren't exactly best friends."

"You've not been crossing palms, have you, Tom?" asked Andrew.

Tom ignored him, speaking to Grace again.

"We certainly weren't, and I can't think why we still aren't."

"This one says it for me," said Andrew, reading from the *Guardian*'s 'Comments' page. "'Although the debate may have been passionate and momentous for the participants, in no way can this be regarded as a meaningful sample of the population from whose collective viewpoint any conclusions can be extrapolated to represent national opinion. Those involved were too close to the recent action to be even remotely objective in formulating their views on the wider issue. So, headline-grabbing though the whole exercise has been, it is little better than worthless in pointing the way forward.'"

Tom shrugged. "Well, I agree with one thing. It was certainly passionate."

CHAPTER 9

David Gerrard pulled off the M6 into the motorway services at Charnock Richard. After visiting the men's room and picking up a pack of sandwiches, he settled into the driver's seat for a welcome rest.

He studied his road atlas, all too aware that he was now approaching what he regarded as the 'really difficult bit' – a combination of unknown territory and off-motorway driving. He knew the sat-nav would take him to the doorstep of his final destination, but he always needed to check the route on the map for his personal comfort.

He had been driving for just over three hours and had decided two hours ago that this was not the best way to spend the first day's holiday he'd had for four months. Not only that, but he had kept the purpose of his trip a secret from both his boss and his second in command, and he was wishing now that he had at least told Jo of where he was going. And not for the first time during the journey he wondered why he was doing this within two days of Lorimar's trial when he'd had six-and-a-half weeks to do it before now. Perhaps it would be worth it; perhaps he would sleep better after today.

He worked out the remainder of his route, along the M65 – which he never knew existed – on to the A666, then the A59, to the small Lancashire town of Pretherby. He turned on the ignition, tapped the sat-nav screen with his left forefinger, an action as automatic as taking off the handbrake, and pulled out of the services at just ten minutes before noon.

He arrived at the home of ex-Corporal Michael Hanson one hour later, a neat terraced house in an attractive row rising up a hill and overlooking wild moorland. The door was opened by his mother who showed him through to where her son was sitting watching the television from his wheelchair.

Ninety minutes later he left the house feeling that his curiosity and secrecy had been fully vindicated, and started the long drive back home.

★

It was after 6.00 pm when he arrived back at Parkside. Jo was still at her desk.

"I thought you were on holiday," she said. "We can manage without you for a day, you know."

"Come in here, Jo," he said, walking past her into his office.

Jo followed him, curious to know why he seemed to be in such a state of excitement.

"Well," she said. "I hope this is good. I usually sneak off *early* when you're not here." She looked very deliberately at her watch.

"Literally two minutes," said David. "Please, take a seat."

He walked back past Jo and shut his office door which she had optimistically left open. He sat down and beamed across his desk at her.

"That man is not James Lorimar," he said.

"Really. Who is he then?"

"Well, I don't know actually," he said, instantly deflated. "But I do know it's not Lorimar – or I'm pretty sure it isn't."

"Not absolutely sure, then?" asked Jo, leaning back in her chair.

"God, Jo, I didn't expect you to punch the air or anything, but you could sound a bit more interested. I've driven about eight thousand miles today to check this out."

Jo leant forward again putting her elbows halfway across his desk and opening her eyes as wide as she could in mock astonishment.

"Wow! That's amazing!" Then she laughed. "You haven't been to Pretherby, by any chance?"

"How did you know that?" he asked.

"I'm a detective," she said.

"You're too bloody smart for your own good, I know that," he said. "The point is, what do we do about it?"

"Well, do we need to do anything? We're certain we've got our killer, aren't we, and even if Lorimar's not the name on his birth certificate, lots of people change their names for all sorts of reasons. It's not like he's changed it after the killings to avoid getting caught. What exactly happened today?"

"I talked to Mike Hanson and he confirmed the details of the incident that Lorimar described when Deverall was killed. That's when he got injured himself. Mike said that Deverall had gone on a bit ahead of the main party to check if the way was clear; he disappeared round a rock – then the explosion. They stayed back for a minute or so and then he – Hanson – went on round the rock. He said there was hardly anything left of Deverall. He doesn't remember anything after that until he woke up in hospital with both legs missing. Apparently there was a second explosion; he nearly died himself, poor sod. Might have been better if he had. But he did say there was no-one there called Lorimar."

"Did you show him the photo?"

"Yes, that was weird, actually. He had been okay up to then, except a bit shaky when he was describing the first explosion, but when I showed him the photo of Lorimar, he got really upset. He said something like – 'what are you showing me that for – that's not him.' Then he started crying and I had to get his mother to calm him down. He recovered fairly quickly, but I didn't want to push it again. I left soon after that."

"But if most of the details of the incident check out," said Jo, "then Lorimar *must* have been there, mustn't he? Perhaps he was just a very low profile guy who didn't get noticed in a crowd. Unless someone else told him about it and he's just acting out a sort of weird fantasy – that would explain why he got it wrong about Deverall dying instantly."

David remained silent, taking on board Jo's comments.

"Or," she went on, "it could be that Deverall had told him all this about his mum before the time he was killed, and Lorimar just invented the thing about the death-bed promise to make it look better for him. But, I mean, on the one hand we've got three people who we'd expect to remember him but who say they don't; on the other hand we've got a history that checks out with current employer, his army record… "

David held up his hand to stop her.

"Sorry, Jo, but I thought you were with me on this one. I understood that after you spoke on the phone to those three guys we both agreed there was something fishy about his statement."

"We did, but that was weeks ago and to be honest, I've not really thought about it recently. We've picked up two big cases since then. I didn't realise you were still bothered about it either. I admit, from what you've just told me, there's a chance he isn't who he says he is, but why would he confess – or *nearly* confess – to a murder but not give his real name? Surely if you're going to lie, you give your correct name and say that you haven't done it; not the other way round. The question is, have we got the guy who killed the Bradys? If we have, a lot of the other stuff becomes sort of insignificant, doesn't it? Or am I missing something really obvious?"

David did not answer for a moment. Then he shook his head and sighed.

"I don't know, Jo, but what I do know – know for certain – is that we don't have the whole truth. I'm not clear what the process of law is if we convict somebody of murder and then find out afterwards that he's not who he says he is. Does he get off on a technicality, do you think? I've never heard the like before, but perhaps this guy knows something we don't. And you could be right. It seems he is definitely a loner, so he might have been really low profile compared to the other guys. Perhaps if I'd shown this photograph to either of the other two, they'd have said, 'Oh, yes, that's old silent Lorimar; clean forgot about him. We used to call him the Invisible Man.'"

He sighed again.

"Anyway, I'm on holiday, for God's sake." He stood up. "Let's get out of here."

★

The following evening, George entered the lecture hall at the Business Centre in the Whitewell Commercial Park in Croydon at 7.20 pm, just a few minutes before he was due to be introduced by Henry Moorcroft, the national President of the 3AF. The rows of tiered seats were completely full, with a large number of people standing at the back of the room. George estimated there were 600 to 700 people in the audience.

As he stood to acknowledge the applause after the President's opening words, he checked his one cue card, which contained two quotes he was proposing to use.

"Thank you, Mr President, for that wonderful introduction," he said, smiling at his host and then around the room. "I hardly recognised the person you were talking about. And thank you for inviting me here this evening. I see a couple of familiar faces out there. My wife, Irene, who is here to make sure I'm doing what I say I'm doing. And Mr Tony Dobson, who has been with me at all eight of the previous meetings over the past five weeks, including the first one at our local branch. So far he's always managed to stay awake right to the end, and his reporting of my speeches in such detail and with such an impressive circulation, has meant that I've had to change them every time."

There was laughter around the room, and Tony smiled and nodded his appreciation at the mention of his name.

"We come together this evening to – I quote – '… consider one of the most important issues facing communities in the first quarter of the twenty-first century'. And that issue is whether the pursuit of justice is more important than compliance with the law. However, in all the meetings I have had so far with members of our organisation, in all parts of the country, that general question has been redefined as a much more specific one. Because if it were not for the dramatic events of eight weeks ago on the Cullen Field Estate in East London, we would not be here in this room tonight. What that terrifying incident has catalysed, particularly within *our* peer group in society" – he spread his arms to collectively embrace the people in the room – "is a fundamental appraisal of how we manage unlawful, disruptive and intimidating behaviour in today's communities. And the question, 'Justice or Law', which has been the banner headline of this series of lectures, is no more than a loose, all-purpose derivative of that much more fundamental concern.

"Tomorrow, James Lorimar will be presented in court for the start of his trial. We do not know anything factual about this person, apart from his name, his occupation and his age. No photographs of him have been produced, nor details of his life and family background released. But it's what people *think* about him that makes this man already remarkable. I am not proposing to spend any time with you discussing whether Mr Lorimar, if he *did* commit this crime, is a hero or a villain. Each of you will have made up your mind on that by now. But whichever he is, I can tell you with absolute certainty that he has enriched the lives of a whole community by one single dramatic act of seemingly premeditated violence.

"And the reason I can tell you that with absolute certainty is that I am part of that community – at least I am now. We were separate communities before – an allegedly brutal estate, and a gentle geriatric village. Now we are happily married and probably still on honeymoon. I anticipate that the parties to this marriage will have their differences in the future, as in all such partnerships, but I believe that the bond between us is already strong enough to allow us to do so without spite and subsequent vendetta. One result of this solitary act has been the gelling of two substantially diverse groups of people into a single entity.

"But the main over-riding benefit has been the freeing of the population from their previous virtual imprisonment. And to my surprise – and that of everyone in Meadow Village – the Cullen Field estate with its appalling reputation was full of people exactly like us. Ordinary, unassuming people who just wanted a normal quiet life. As Tom Brown put it, 'the challenge that we face, as your elected representatives, is to create this same effect, but within the boundaries of law and order. And we' – meaning Parliament – 'need to do something different from what we are doing now to bring about this change.' Tony was there when he spoke those words" – he gestured towards the journalist – "and he reported them, in fact. Mr Brown was speaking to the people on the estate a few days after the killings and I know they took his words on board as a genuine commitment.

"So what was it, in simple terms, that this person did which has made such a difference? If we are to believe the accounts of the witnesses to the prelude of this crime, he identified the problem, singled out those responsible – very deliberately and publicly – then, having selected them, he removed them – permanently. And that last word is the crux of it all – *"Permanently!"*

George banged his fist heavily on the table in front of him as he said the last word, his first show of real passion in the whole of his nine appearances. He appeared to be taken a little bit by surprise himself, as were the audience, the whole of which seemed to jump slightly, as a single object, in their seats.

"I have always been a champion of the death penalty. It makes perfect sense to me that, if a person chooses to take another one's life, they should expect no less than reciprocal treatment if he or she be caught. The finality of these consequences, I would argue, being a greater deterrent than a period of imprisonment – often disproportionately brief – after which the killer can emerge, still relatively young in many cases, to take the plaudits of his peers. The doomed Antisocial Behaviour Orders, mercifully discontinued some years ago, demonstrated the weakness – the idiocy, in fact – of a system whereby people who set out to create mayhem and fear are presented with a badge for doing so. The ASBO was, in effect, an achievement award, just like a swimming certificate. Ridiculous! Youngsters in many areas, as many of us will remember, were being shunned or actually attacked for not having succeeded in getting one.

"Such a structure of recognition, however, only works if you are able to display your trophy at some stage – immediately, if it's an ASBO, or later, if it's a prison sentence. Take away that opportunity and the trophy is irrelevant. If the reward for such crimes is permanent removal from the society whose laws and principles the perpetrators choose to reject, then such exploits become acts of self-destruction, rather than an investment, the return on which will be some kind of sick notoriety in the future.

"Removing people permanently from society as a proposed solution is not new; it is too simple and obvious to be regarded as innovative in any way. It already happens, but only in very exceptional cases and for the severest of crimes. But somehow it now seems to have more substance. Previously the whole concept was untested, in terms of both the treatment and the subsequent health of the patient. What we've now had is at least a peek at the latter. If you remove an irritation which is infecting the whole body, then the process of healing can be spectacularly fast. It can be argued – and indeed a large portion of the press has argued – that it is dangerous to use the example of this one incident on this one estate to draw any conclusions of statistical relevance. They are absolutely correct in making everyone aware of that. However, it is the best indicator we have with which to consider the way forward.

"The government has done conspicuously well over the past five years or so in putting in place every conceivable facility and opportunity for these gangs to pursue alternatives to their antisocial behaviour. It deserves our praise and thanks for those efforts, and a significant proportion of its target group have responded by giving up the streets. I also applaud those who have made that life change, because many will have done so whilst facing the might of peer pressure which I believe is the single most powerful shaper of behaviour in our society today. But what of the rest? Those who continue to ignore these opportunities in order to inflict a climate of social terror on their immediate neighbours and other residential areas. Those, in effect, who have no ambition or intention of being part of community life.

"The government are proposing to further invest in order to make more facilities available. I am sure that much cleverer men and women than me have decided that is the right thing to do. And, for all our sakes, I hope they're right. However, I personally doubt it, because I think they are addressing the wrong problem. On the evidence of the thousands of comments made to me over the past few weeks, what we want to know is what they intend to do about those who will *not* – not *ever* – change their behaviour."

The applause was spontaneous and energetic. Several members of the press, though not joining in, nodded in agreement.

"It's interesting, isn't it, that these debates and discussions always seem to centre around what we should be doing for these thugs, these vandals, these low-lifes; what we need to put in place for *them,* how much we can afford to spend on *them.* What someone should be addressing is what they can do for *us.* The people who never do anything wrong; the ones who live within the law; the vast majority of nice, friendly people. Well, for a start, they can separate us from the others! Or, more accurately, keep the others away from us – *permanently!*"

When the applause died down, he played his highest trump card.

"If we – the section of the public represented by the age profile of the 3AF – have a mind to, I believe we can bring about that change in policy which will address *our* issues and *our* concerns. We are, by a considerable margin, the single largest category of voters in the electorate, and, if we can devise a mechanism – a process – for concerting our efforts, our opinions, *and* our votes, I reckon we can do just about anything we like!"

★

By 9.30 am, there were several hundred people already jostling for position along Old Bailey, the road which played host to – and shared its name with – the Central Criminal Court. The police had been expecting a large turnout to witness the arrival of James Lorimar, but were taken by surprise by the timing and size of the initial crowd.

By 10.30 they were struggling to maintain a clear passage for the arrival of the police security vehicle bringing the prisoner to court, and the massive media presence was having difficulty finding prime positions to record and relay the event. Additional police, arriving in half a dozen personnel carriers, were forced to disembark on Ludgate Hill, a quarter of a mile from the court and, without wishing to administer a heavy hand to an excitable but peaceful gathering, simply placed themselves along the roadside to gently restrain the crowd which, by 10.55, had spread a half mile back along the approach route to the court. The whole scene was more reminiscent of a Royal Wedding.

This comparison was reinforced by the hundreds of banners and placards held aloft as the vehicle bearing James Lorimar finally reached the outliers in the crowd. Proclamations, ranging from the simple 'Free James Lorimar' to the more subtle 'Sir James Lorimar – Street Cleaner' and the tabloidish 'Lorimarvellous!', were brandished with passionate enthusiasm as the eager press turned cameras and camcorders on them to capture the mood.

Their focus of attention quickly switched as the small cavalcade stopped in front of the court building. The cries reached nearly fever pitch as the rear doors of the main vehicle were opened and they caught their first glimpse of the man they had come to support. James Lorimar, handcuffed to a very large policeman, was wearing his now-famous black baseball cap, but there was no attempt at further concealing his face; no dramatic head-covering to frustrate the assembly. This seemed to establish an immediate bond between him and the onlookers and there were shouts of "We're with you, James!" and "We're all on your side!" A member of one group shouted out the words adorning the banner they were holding high above their heads – "Come and live on our street, James!" Lorimar turned and smiled at the crowd as he entered the building in a strobe-fest of flashing cameras.

As he disappeared from view, a small section of the crowd began to chant his name, like a goal scorer in an important football match.

"Lor–i–mar! Lor-i-mar!"

The chant was picked up by those closest to them in the mass of people, and then spread along the length of the road and beyond, engulfing all present in the display of solidarity. The TV reporters speaking into camera had to shout loudly to get the message back to their viewers, but were clearly enjoying being part of the event. No-one on Old Bailey itself showed any sign of leaving immediately and the chant continued. After ten minutes or so, the noise died down and people drifted off until the road was clear except for the remnants of a media presence and the usual traffic of court officials and prison vans arriving and departing.

★

Tom Brown, along with half the country, was watching the TV coverage of the event with a number of his staff in one of the meeting rooms at his constituency office on Westbourne Avenue. He was relishing the atmosphere of the event and mentally assessing how he would use this collective mood in his own crusade. Following his delight at reading the newspaper accounts of George Holland's exploits of the previous evening, this was a very thick layer of icing on his cake. He was wondering, in fact, whether he would have to do anything himself to make his proposals a reality, whilst he had two high profile people bending the population's will with such apparent ease.

Then, as the man turned to the crowd just prior to entering the building and the camera zoomed in on his face, he shot forward in his chair as if in an attempt to further enlarge the image. Although he said nothing, everyone in the room could sense his feeling of shock. Tom recovered himself quickly and leant back in his seat, seemingly relaxed again. All returned to watching the screen without making comment.

★

At a few minutes past 12.30 pm, the Hollands drove in to Meadow Village. Immediately on arriving home, their house phone rang. It was Henry Moorcroft, following up on his meeting with George that morning.

"I spoke to my contact at the DWP, George. He can't give a definitive answer, only an opinion, but he's pretty well informed. I'm afraid he thinks they're unlikely to agree to your using the REP database."

"Why's that, do you think?"

"Well, he said it was because the request is a personal one and not directly linked to your being a member of the 3AF."

"But the initiative has come directly out of the meetings of nine different branches. Surely… "

"I agree in principle, George, and as I said, that's not official, just his opinion. If they ask for *my* opinion, I'll certainly support your request. That's all I can do."

"Okay, thanks, Henry. I really do appreciate your help with this. We'll keep our fingers crossed. And thanks for your hospitality yesterday."

"No thanks necessary, George. It was an absolute pleasure."

George ended the call then picked up the phone again. His call was answered immediately.

"Hi, George."

"Hi, Tom. Look, I'm hoping to do a mail-out to everyone on the REP to ascertain whether the vote at the debate and the reaction at these other meetings is representative of the wider population."

"Just let me stop you there, George. Remind me what the REP is."

"It's the Register of Eligible Persons. The DWP's list of people who have retired or are working after state retirement age in the

UK. 'Registered', in this context, means that the individual, on retirement or reaching the qualifying age, has subscribed to the government's home PC scheme, at which time they are automatically added to the national database."

"Right, got it," said Tom. "And from then on all communication from the DWP and such is done via email and all information posted on a special website. So you're planning to use it for your mail-out?"

"It's the only way it can be done to reach that population. There are about sixteen million targets. But I've just got a message that I'll probably be denied use of the database. I thought you should be aware that certain forces in the government may try to block a legitimate use of the facility because of potential pressure on their policies."

Tom laughed.

"Thanks for the heads-up, George. You're really getting the hang of this political thing, aren't you? Well, without wanting to sound too overconfident, I suggest you start working on the format and content of the questionnaire right now and leave me to oil the machinery if necessary. I think it's a great idea. And by the way, many congratulations on your speech last night. Tony emailed me a copy about three o'clock in the morning, although I have to admit to not reading it until after six-thirty. Lazy sods, we politicians, you know. Come to think of it, it wouldn't harm you having a quiet word with Tony about your survey. And I trust you *not* to tell him it was my idea."

"Yes, I'm sure he'd love that. I'll do it – and your secret's safe with me."

"And then I reckon you and Irene deserve a holiday after all this. You could work on your questionnaire on a beach somewhere, I'm sure."

"If I mention a holiday to Irene, she'll have me climbing Ben Nevis or something. She doesn't do relaxation very well."

"Even better; it must be boring in those bivouacs if you don't have anything to do. The survey will come on leaps and bounds."

George laughed.

"Perhaps we will have a holiday. In fact, we'll definitely do it. Yes, definitely."

As Tom ended the call, Grace walked into his office.

"Do you mind telling me what that was about in there?" she asked. "You looked like you'd seen a ghost."

"No fooling you, eh, Grace," he replied. "It's just that I could have sworn I recognised the guy when he turned to the camera. Someone I knew really well, in fact. Anyway, he died some years ago, so obviously it's not him. But, yes, I guess you could say that for a moment I thought I'd seen a ghost."

"No doubt we'll find out a lot about our mystery avenger during the course of the next few days," said Grace, "but I shouldn't count on his having come back from the dead to do his good deed."

"Did you see the news and the papers this morning on George's speech?" he asked. "There is such a force at work out there, Grace; we had just better be ready to align ourselves with it before it flattens us. We have to grasp the nettle and run with it."

Grace nodded, smiling.

"It might help if we didn't mix our metaphors on the way," she said."

"And, I just got a call from George himself. He's planning an electronic mail-out to the registered retirement listing. Do you know that list represents forty percent of the electorate and over *fifty* percent of those who actually vote? Well that's not a bad start if he's suggesting some sort of alliance for pushing through some reforms. And, another thing… "

"Just hold on," Grace interrupted. "We're on dangerous ground here – or at the very least we're getting ahead of ourselves. If we're talking about fighting an election, which is the only time when those electoral figures mean anything, we're a long way from integrating your proposals into a credible manifesto. I don't want to risk the might of your anger by bringing reality into the discussion, but we haven't got near to discussing with Andrew and Reggie how the funding is going to work."

"Well, thanks for jumping in like that, Grace," said Tom. "I apologise for going on about probably the most exciting prospect for change this century, and omitting to mention the riveting topic of finance… "

"It's all very well getting huffy… " began Grace.

"Huffy?" interrupted Tom. "What the hell's 'huffy'? I wouldn't have a clue how to get huffy!"

They both laughed and relaxed.

"What I mean," said Grace, "is that before we charge into the public arena with promises of huge changes, we need to be absolutely sure we can deliver. Something's got to pay for it in the short-term even if you're right about long-term savings or cost-neutrality. But we haven't got anywhere near to a conclusion on that."

"Just imagine though," said Tom, "what would happen if we made the promises riding on the back of this wave of demand for change. Once the promise is out there, we would *have* to deliver."

"You're not seriously suggesting we hold our own Party to ransom?" Grace was open-mouthed. "There are already massive demands on the NHS and Social Services for more money to support the same cross-section of voters that you're pinning your hopes on. Are they going to vote for money being diverted from essential services to protect what is, let's be accurate about this, a small minority of people who are likely to meet with harm in the future?"

"I know what you're saying, Grace, about the high maintenance cost of this group of people, but you are missing the point with that last statement. It's only a small number who would be affected as things stand because they all stay away from places where they should have every right to go without worrying about it. And this is not just for the retired population; think about the Cullen Field residents, how their lives have changed. What proportion of them are retired do you think? Ten percent? Probably nearer five. Let me tell you what I think is going to happen, Grace. And if I'm right, I'll say 'I told you so', and if I'm wrong, I want you to promise you won't say anything. Okay?"

Grace smiled. "Okay."

"James Lorimar will be convicted of murder and there'll be a massive campaign to free him. It will be country-wide, not just in Marlburgh. They'll know that it won't happen, of course, so there'll be a demand for a change to the system along the lines of 'justice before law' or something like that. There's enough evidence out there already to make that a certainty. And what that means is that they will want people to have the right to take the law into their own hands – or administer justice outside the law – where they feel it is necessary.

"In other words, the legalising, or at least condoning, of vigilantism. And there'll be such a groundswell of feeling that when we get the next Cullen Field type of incident, and then the next, and continue to put the avengers away, it'll get more and more difficult to contain the public's anger. *Un-less,*" he said, drawing out the word, "we convince them that we'll do the job for them. *We'll* identify the bad guys, *we'll* single them out; *we'll* make sure they'll never come back. No more bloody pussy-footing around with sick cowboys – let's start calling them baddies again!"

Grace was smiling wider as his fervour gained momentum. It made him aware that he was getting carried away and repeating what he'd said to her a dozen times before. He stopped; then seemed to think of something else and rose from his chair.

"Oh yes, and at the same time, good old George will become Chief Shop Steward of the… " he paused to work it out "… NUWF – the National Union of Wrinkled Folk – and he'll lead protest marches to London from as far a field as Eastbourne and Ashford and the deafening sounds of zimmer and wheelchair on tarmac will reverberate around the world, and civilisation as we know it will cease to exist!"

He was striding round the office, staring ahead with demonic eyes and repeatedly pointing into the air to emphasise each point. Grace was laughing more than he had ever heard her laugh before, with that same girly tinkle. He stopped in front of her and wagged his finger in her face.

"You can laugh, Miss Two-Shoes, but when I rule the world, then you'd better watch out!"

"I can't wait," said Grace, struggling to put on a serious face. "A bit of discipline never did anybody any harm."

They looked at each other for a long moment in silence. Tom sat back down in his chair still holding Grace's eyes with his.

"I'll remember you said that," he said.

"I'll remind you if you don't," she smiled back.

CHAPTER 10

The trial of James Lorimar was to be disproportionately short in relation to its lasting impact outside the court. It did, however, include the drama of a faltering start and a breathtaking conclusion.

The most senior permanent judge at the Central Criminal Court, with the title of Recorder of London, was presiding in the new show-piece courtroom in which the public gallery had been extended to more than three times its original capacity. It could now accommodate up to 100 observers, and every seat was taken. As the courtroom settled, the Honourable Justice Owen Templar QC made a direct appeal to the public gallery. He was a man of medium height and build, made to look larger by the uniform of his office, which ebbed and flowed with his embellished theatrical movements. His features were sharp and distinguished, with bushy white eyebrows which at first sight looked like an extension of his wig. A rimless pair of glasses perched on the end of his nose.

"I am aware," he said, in a voice which was disproportionately loud for his size, "of the depth of interest in this case throughout the country and the heightened feelings it has stimulated in many people. The presence of so many onlookers outside the court this morning is evidence of that, and the number of people intent on observing this event who have failed to gain access to the public gallery today is unprecedented in my experience. However, I must insist that those privileged to be sitting in witness of the due process of law in this courtroom be good enough to respect their role as silent observers. The defendant will be treated in exactly the same way as any other in his position with no regard for the amount of attention he has attracted outside this court. I am sure I can depend on your cooperation, but in the event that I am proved wrong in that assumption, I will have no hesitation in quickly removing any transgressor from the room."

There was a respectful nodding from the gallery and people leant forward in their seats in anticipation of the judicial vehicle slipping smoothly into gear. They did not have to wait long for the first stutter of the engine.

The Clerk of the Court began to read the charge.

The Defence Counsel rose to his feet. Dean Calvert was tall, slim and good-looking, but whereas his appearance and posture radiated confidence, he seemed a little hesitant and his face was slightly flushed.

"M'lord, if it pleases the court, before my client is asked to respond to the charge, he respectfully requests that he may make his plea against an alternative charge; that of 'justifiable homicide'."

Justice Templar took a long time in responding, dragging out the counsel's discomfort.

"Why on earth should that 'please the court', as you put it, Mr Calvert? I am sure you are aware – or certainly should be – that such a plea is preferentially available only to members of the police and armed forces in cases where they deem in mitigation that their sworn duty requires such action. How can that possibly apply to the defendant?"

"Mr Lorimar has requested that his case be viewed in such a way, because he acted selflessly on behalf of a community rather than for his own ends. My client believes that, although he received no direct order to carry out the deed, he was driven by the same motives as the aforementioned agencies of law and national security."

Forgetting, or ignoring, the judge's plea for quiet surveillance, a low muttering spread around the higher tiers of the room.

At this very early stage of the proceedings, the judge showed clear signs of irritation, which he made no attempt to conceal from the packed gallery. He looked sternly around them like a teacher rudely interrupted by a restless class of pupils. A hush returned, and Justice Templar directed his attention back to the Defence Counsel.

"Could you please approach the bench, Mr Calvert, and you too,

Ms Cartwright," turning also to the Prosecution Counsel. Penny Cartwright was almost a head shorter than her opponent and had a rather overly-rounded figure. The large expressive eyes in her pretty, heart-shaped face opened even wider at the summons.

The two counsels duly stood before the judge, who spoke quietly to them, his comments beyond the hearing of the gallery.

"Mr Calvert, I think it is in the interest of public confidence in a system which has already taken a battering as a result of this gentleman's actions, that we avoid any attempts at turning this into a sort of cabaret. You are well aware of the rules relating to a plea of justifiable homicide and did not need me to publicly define them for the benefit of the press. I am sure they will derive some interesting headlines from our little exchange, but let us not assist them any further in doing their job. If you require a brief time out with your client to explain the simplicity of choice regarding his plea, then I will allow it; in fact, I insist on it. But I will not tolerate any more semantic trickery, Mr Calvert. Do I make myself clear?"

"Yes, m'lord." Dean Calvert nodded, respectfully.

"And you, too, Ms Cartwright?"

"Yes, m'lord," said Penny Cartwright.

The two counsels, both duly admonished, and one silently indignant, returned to their respective positions in court.

"Court will adjourn for thirty minutes," boomed the judge.

"All rise!" The Clerk of the Court.

Justice Templar glided from the room, as the galley became instantly animated and the prisoner was led from the dock to meet with his counsel.

Exactly thirty minutes later, with the accused back in place and all officials in readiness, the judge returned and the court stood again at the prompting of the Clerk. When everyone was settled and duly hushed by his sweeping glare, which seemed to dare anyone to make a noise, he turned again to the Defence Counsel.

"Mr Calvert, have you apprised your client of his very short list of options in responding to the eagerly awaited question?"

"Yes, m'lord."

"Then let us put it to the test." He turned to the Clerk of the Court.

"Proceed."

"James Philip Lorimar, you are charged that on the 7th of May this year, you did wilfully and deliberately shoot to death James Anthony Brady. Do you plead Guilty or Not Guilty?"

The atmosphere in the courtroom was electric. There was no sound at all, but an almost tangible feeling of eager expectancy, which was quickly heightened by the lack of any response from the defendant. After several moments, he turned to his counsel and beckoned him across. Dean Calvert went hurriedly to him and Lorimar bent forward to whisper in his ear. Justice Templar was losing patience; after three quarters of an hour in court, he had failed to extract a plea from the prisoner.

"Am I missing something here?" he said, to the court in general. "Could the Counsel for the Defence perhaps assist me in getting past this normally straightforward and brief stage in the proceedings?"

"Our apologies, m'lord, but my client wishes to know why he has not been asked to plead to all three killings when, I think it is safe to assume, even at this delicate judicial stage, that they were perpetrated simultaneously by the same party, be it by my client, or by person or persons unknown. Also, he points out, that the original charge shortly following his arrest was the killing of all three victims."

Owen Templar held the barrister's eyes for a full ten seconds before the latter dropped his gaze to the papers in his hand.

"Please approach the bench again, Mr Calvert," he said in a loud, almost threatening, whisper. "You too, Ms Cartwright."

They stood before him like naughty children. Again he spoke softly to them but this time he seemed less concerned as to whether their conversation could be heard or not.

"Tell me, have you two met prior to your arriving in court today?" he asked.

The two counsels looked at each other in puzzlement before responding.

"Of course, m'lord."

"Yes, m'lord."

"And what did you talk about – when you met previously?"

"I'm sorry," said Penny. "I'm afraid I don't understand what… "

The judge interrupted, now lowering his voice.

"The weather, perhaps? The appalling state of the motorways?

You see, what I would have *expected* you to talk about were certain aspects of what I personally think is an extremely important case. I am led to believe, in fact, by an even wiser person than me, if you can even dream that such an entity exists, that it is unprecedented in terms of its high profile. Do you not agree that this case warrants that description?"

"Of course, m'lord," replied Penny. "We are privileged to be… "

"Then how can it reasonably be that you, Ms Cartwright, have not seen fit to let Defence Counsel know in advance the precise extent of the charge that you are bringing against this man?"

"Well, m'lord… "

"And, you, Mr Calvert. Why did you not ensure that you had all the information to pass on to your client?"

The Defence Counsel did not attempt to answer the question, but asked one of his own.

"Might we have another word with you in private, m'lord? I do not believe it should be necessary for another adjournment, and I do feel that if the simple issue of the precise charge is resolved, my client will fully cooperate in the expedition of this case."

"I do hope so," said the judge. "He seems more interested in exhibition than expedition right now. Very well, fifteen minutes."

The judge explained that there would be a brief pause in the proceedings but charged everyone to remain quietly in their seats.

Away from the court, and with a gallantry which surprised his opponent, Dean Calvert attempted to mollify Judge Templar.

"I sincerely apologise, sir, for my client's response to the charge and for any confusion over the specific wording. Penny is blameless in this; she did inform me that he would be charged with the one killing and I passed that on to Mr Lorimar. In the absence of his making any objection – or even comment – at the time, I assumed he had accepted this. I believe he will plead guilty to a charge which includes all three killings, and I request that the charge be revised to reflect this. If Penny agrees."

"Well, Penny?" asked the judge. "I'm not sure why he should be charged with just one under the circumstances, anyway. It's like going back in time twelve years to before the abrogation of double jeopardy. Why exactly did you choose to do that?"

"Because we have no hard evidence, as such. Not even a signed statement from Lorimar. Just information he imparted at an interview, and he said nothing at all after he was cautioned. He could change his mind now about his intention to get rid of the brothers, and I'm not sure what we could do other than pile up circumstantial evidence. To get a conviction from a jury for *this* man I think we'd need more than that. And if we couldn't get 'fresh and viable' new evidence – as the manual puts it – then it gave us a chance to get a different slant on what we *have* got to bring a further… "

"But he's obviously going to plead guilty," said the judge, interrupting and not even bothering to consult Dean Calvert. "He virtually did when he asked for justifiable homicide. He can't suddenly decide he didn't kill them just because we won't change the words."

"True, sir," said Penny, "but I certainly wasn't convinced of that *before* the trial started. And I thought it would be easier to bring that second case, if necessary, using that circumstantial evidence again if… "

"Yes, I do take your point, but it's just confused everybody. God knows, we look like we don't know what the hell we're doing out there. And looks *don't* deceive on this occasion. Now please. Let's get our act together."

He turned to the Prosecuting Counsel.

"Penny, you will change the charge to include all three victims, right?"

Without waiting for a reply, he turned to Dean Calvert.

"Dean, is Lorimar going to plead guilty – you do have some inkling, don't you?"

"Yes, sir – definitely."

"Definitely you have some inkling or definitely he's going to plead guilty?"

"Both, sir."

Owen Templar smiled to himself.

"Then what?"

"Sir?"

"Well, that can't be it, surely. We have an audience to satisfy. Somehow I can't believe he says 'guilty, m'lord' and I say – 'you're a bad boy and I'm putting you away.' What else?"

"I'll make a plea in mitigation and with your permission, sir, I'd like to call some witnesses to support that plea, as well as questioning the accused himself. I know this is a little unusual – I admit these are not technically character witnesses – but there are precedents… "

"Okay, that will keep the show on the road, but to what end, Dean? I have to impose a mandatory life sentence – I assume he is going to plead guilty to murder. He's not claiming manslaughter, is he, for God's sake? I've seen Prosecution's Exhibits A, B and C – the photos of the three clean head shots. Or self-defence? Mind you, nothing would surprise me today," he added, half to himself. "The only mitigation can be what happened before the day of the killing, and that only reinforces premeditation."

"Nevertheless, sir, there is still the subject of parole. And if I could be so bold, I believe an out-and-out condemnation of this man as a cold-blooded killer may be perceived as showing a lack of sensitivity and empathy with the mass of people who have been touched by his act. And should you agree with that point, sir, you will need some evidence to support any conciliatory remarks you choose to make. So with your permission… "

Justice Templar smiled to himself at the Defence Counsel's gentle prompting, laden with respect, but very much to the point.

"Very well. Penny, were you aware of this? Are you okay with it?"

"I was aware of Dean's intentions in the event of a guilty plea, and I've no objection," said Penny. "It goes without saying that I reserve the right to cross-examine anyone Dean calls to the stand."

"Right. And that's it?"

"I believe my client will ask to make a statement from the stand," said Dean. "He has asked if he can make this *after* sentencing. I have informed him that his only opportunity will be just before you pass sentence."

"Well, you can always ask. It's unprecedented, but so is everything until it happens the first time. Let's get back in there."

The court stood again as the judge and two counsels returned.

"Shall we try again, Mr Calvert? Strike three!"

He nodded to the Clerk who restated the charge including the names of all three victims. This time, the accused's hesitation was for effect only, and very brief.

"Guilty, m'lord."

The courtroom erupted in an explosion of shouts and cheers as people sprang to their feet. Owen Templar shouted for order as both counsels turned to the gallery with gestures for calm. Within a minute people were seated again and a tense stability had returned to the proceedings. The judge repeated his earlier warning to the gallery, but this time more out of procedural protocol than with any real threat.

"I ask you, again, to observe the rules of this court by remaining silent. You are not participants in this process, but observers. You are welcome to be present here in that capacity but, as I stated earlier, I will not tolerate people overstepping the very distinct boundary of their involvement. Thank you."

With the plea of guilty, several people entered the courtroom who had been waiting to be called as prosecution witnesses. These included DCI David Gerrard and DS Jo Cottrell who sat down together a few rows behind the Prosecution Counsel.

When all the newcomers were seated, the judge turned to the Defence Counsel, opening his arms in a gesture of invitation for him to speak.

"Thank you, m'lord," said Dean. "I wish to make a plea in mitigation on behalf of my client."

"Really," said the judge.

"Yes, m'lord."

Dean cleared his throat with some drama and addressed the courtroom generally, moving his eyes to all areas to include everyone.

"You see before you a man who has experienced much violence in his lifetime. During a military career spanning one quarter of a century, he has seen service in Northern Ireland, as a teenager, and later, in the special forces, in Iraq, Africa and Afghanistan. This man has put himself at risk in three different continents for the benefit of others with no thought for his own safety – his own life, even. Our country has required him – *ordered* him – to carry out such acts on behalf of the people in this room, people whose lives are safer and more secure as a result of his unquestioning fulfilment of these duties."

There were mumbles of agreement and support and some gentle hand-clapping from the public gallery. It quickly subsided without the judge's prompting.

"It is against this background and in the context of his alleged crime that…"

"Not 'alleged' any more, Mr Calvert," interrupted the judge.

"Thank you, m'lord, for pointing out that technicality," said Dean, stiffly. "As I was saying, it is against this background and in the context of his crime that we must judge him. I ask you to consider the frustration of such a man, trained to act, selflessly, for the benefit of the good citizens of this country, finding himself in a situation, threatened with his own life, but with the opportunity, as he saw it, to put right a situation which had brought distress and fear to so many innocent people.

"It is my intention to present a clear picture of the events leading up to, and during, that evening. Because I believe that the provocation faced by James Lorimar at the time, and his previous knowledge of the nature of the three brothers and their heinous acts of local terrorism, are enough to understand, if not condone, his actions. And I believe it is imperative that this should be understood before deciding this man's future. In order to present this picture as objectively as possible, m'lord, I would ask the indulgence of the court in allowing my calling a number of witnesses to set the scene and to recount the story of that fateful evening."

The judge nodded grandly and benignly, as if bestowing an enormous favour.

"Thank you, m'lord. Call Lucille Ambrose!"

Lucille took the stand.

"Mrs Ambrose, you live at Number 11, St George's Close, on the Cullen Field Estate, is that right?" asked Dean.

"Yes, that's right."

"And you and your husband were a Mrs Alma Deverall's next-door neighbour for how long?"

"About ten years."

"And could you describe to the court the problems this elderly lady encountered from the gangs on the estate?"

"Yes, well, a couple of years ago, she reported some lads setting fire to a car on Kingdom Road. They must have seen her watching or found out, because they gave her lots of grief after that. I mean we all got shouted at and jostled and such at times, but this was really personal."

"What exactly did they do?"

"They wrote really bad words all over her walls and front door, and put dog… you know… stuff through the letter-box. And they smashed in the front door a few times as well. Poor woman. She was beside herself." Lucille's voice was trembling a little.

"She must have been. How did she react to that?"

"She tried to do herself in – twice."

There were some gasps from the public gallery followed by whispered conversations.

"Did she not call the police?"

"No, she thought that would make it worse."

Dean looked around the courtroom with raised eyebrows to reinforce the information. He turned back to Lucille.

"And you believe it was the three brothers who were responsible for this cruel harassment of Mrs Deverall?" asked Dean. Penny let it go; they were only talking mitigation, not proof.

"Well, I didn't actually see them doing anything, but there again, they never did do anything themselves. They just got others to do stuff for them."

"Quite. Mrs Ambrose, tell us about the man who came to the house to visit her."

"It was around last September, this man – she said he was a carer – started calling round, about once a week, it was, in the evening. He seemed to cheer her up no end. We could hear them next door laughing for lots of the time he was there. And then a few weeks later – in October I think – she said she was leaving to stay with friends for a while."

"And the man who visited Mrs Deverall; do you see him in the courtroom today?"

She glanced across at James Lorimar.

"Well, in all honesty, like I told the lady detective, I never did see him closely, let alone meet him. I couldn't really say for certain that it was the gentleman over there."

"I should like to state for the benefit of the court, that the man Mrs Ambrose described was indeed the defendant, James Lorimar. Thank you, Mrs Ambrose; no further questions."

Lucille's evidence was accepted without question by the judge and with no cross examination by Penny Cartwright.

"So here was a case," said Dean, in summary, as Lucille left the stand, "of an elderly lady whose life had been made, literally, unbearable. And who was saved by the actions of her carer. Whether we accept that the man was her 'carer' in the occupational meaning of the word, there can be no doubt that 'carer' certainly described him in its literal sense."

Dean Calvert next called Alan Venables to the stand.

"Mr Venables is the owner of the apartment, where," he stated with emphatic emotion, "this unfortunate lady would ultimately take her own life."

As Alan Venables took the stand, nodding in recognition to the defendant, who returned the greeting in kind, Judge Templar addressed the Defence Counsel.

"Mr Calvert, I am sure we will hear an accurate, perhaps even interesting, description of the circumstances relating to this Mrs Deverall's occupation of this gentleman's property, but can you enlighten me as to how this is relevant to the sentence I am required to pass on the prisoner?"

"If it pleases, m'lord, I am keen to demonstrate the level of support and attention Mr Lorimar extended to this lady, who, as we shall see as the account unfolds, chose to end her life whilst, in effect, still under his care. My view is that you might feel, as I do, that this may have contributed significantly to the action he took. I think the time taken to consider this will be justified, and thanks to the prisoner's guilty plea, the case proceedings will still prove to be a relatively short notwithstanding."

"Very well. Please proceed, but let us not drag this out simply to fill the time that may have been saved, as you put it."

Dean turned to Alan Venables.

"Mr Venables, I understand you live at 23B Darlington Road, Hammersmith?"

"Yes, that's right."

"And is that the address where Mrs Deverall lived in the months leading up to her death?"

"Yes, it is."

"Please tell the court how she came to take up a short-term tenancy in your apartment."

"Certainly. Last October I left the country for a three-month expatriate assignment, and advertised the place for rental for that period. Mr Lorimar replied to the ad and Mrs Deverall came along to look at it. She liked it and paid me the three months rent in advance. Actually, I knew her as Mrs Coleridge at the time and Mr Lorimar as Mr Anderson."

Dean Calvert jumped in quickly.

"Yes, thank you, Mr Venables, that has all been cleared up now. But please tell us, when did you return from your assignment?"

"The middle of April, as it turned out. It got extended for a further three months, and Mrs Deverall stayed on."

"So that was a period of six months in total. Very briefly, how would you summarise Mr Lorimar's role in all these arrangements?"

"He made it all happen. He answered the ad, sorted out the money side of things and... well, he was still there when I phoned and discovered Mrs Deverall had taken her own life." He looked down and his eyes clouded over. "Such a shame," he added.

Alan Venables stepped down and Dean called Henry Blount to the stand. The judge sighed very loudly and raised his eyebrows at the Defence counsel. Dean pretended not to notice and continued.

"Mr Blount, you are the proprietor of Blount of Hammersmith, Undertakers, are you not?"

"Funeral Directors," he corrected.

"My apologies; Funeral Directors. You were called to 23B Darlington Road to attend Mrs Deverall shortly after she had taken her own life?"

"That is correct."

"Could you please describe for the court Mr Lorimar's involvement on that day and subsequently?"

"Well, quite simply, he took charge of everything, informed all the appropriate people, paid the fees, decided on the gravestone, where she should be buried – as I say, everything. No-one else was involved."

"And why was that?"

"Well, apparently Mrs Deverall didn't have any living relatives or close friends. In fact, Mr Lorimar was the only mourner at the funeral."

"Thank you, Mr Blount, no further questions." He sat down.

Penny Cartwright got to her feet.

"Mr Blount, you said *apparently* the deceased had no family or friends. And the funeral took place just three days after the death. Is it not rather strange that more of an attempt wasn't made to find any possible contacts before rushing it through so quickly?"

"Don't bother to answer that, Mr Blount." Owen Templar stepped in and turned to Penny. "I can't begin to imagine how such information will assist me in my deliberations, Ms Cartwright."

He turned back to Dean Calvert again.

"Is that all, Mr Calvert?"

"For this witness, m'lord, yes. Thank you, Mr Blount. I should like to call two more witnesses who will assist in recounting the events of the evening in question. Perhaps this, allowing for any Prosecution Counsel's questions, may take us a further hour or so…" He paused, enquiringly.

"Very well, as Mr Calvert strongly and not very subtly hints, this may be an appropriate time to recess for lunch. Please all be back in your places by two-thirty sharp."

"All rise!" The Clerk of the Court.

★

At 2.30 prompt, the Honourable Justice Owen Templar returned to his courtroom where everyone was in readiness for the start of the afternoon session.

"Proceed, Mr Calvert, and let us please tell the story as economically as possible with the words at our disposal."

Dean Calvert looked at the judge a little startled and with a slightly hurt expression.

"Call Mr Maxwell Jordan," he announced.

The landlord of the Wild Boar Inn took the stand and the oath.

"Mr Jordan," said Dean, "no doubt you recall the evening of the 7th of May when Mr Lorimar entered your public house?"

"Yes, sir."

"Please describe what happened."

"Well, I was having an argument with the Bradys over payment for drinks – they seemed to think they were different, like they should get the stuff free. And this guy came in… " he nodded towards Lorimar "… and sat right next to them at the bar. Ordered a triple Jameson's. Everything was okay at first, until he accidentally spilt Kevin's pint all over him. Then it kicked off, Kevin grabbed him, I tried to calm him down, and the guy offered to pay for some more drinks and a new shirt for Kevin." He paused and looked across again at the man in the dock.

"Yes, and then what?" Dean prompted.

"He gave Jimmy Brady two hundred quid – Jimmy insisted he bought drinks for everybody. I told him he didn't need to but he said it was okay. And then he got up to go and they said they'd give him five seconds start, I think it was. So he pushed them over and ran out. They got up and ran after him. That was it. He just wanted to get away, avoid any trouble."

Penny Cartwright rose to question him when the Defence had finished.

"Mr Jordan, you seem to remember a lot about what happened that evening in very precise detail. Am I right in saying that when you were asked to pick out this man at an identity parade less than two weeks after the event, you *said* you didn't recognise him?"

"Yes, sir – ma'am."

"Why is that, do you think? Was it perhaps that you did recognise him, but didn't want him to be charged?"

"Definitely not. I just didn't recognise him. He had his cap pulled right down and… "

"But you are certain this is the man now?"

"Well, yes. I mean, I *know* it's him, don't I? That's why he's here, isn't it? No point in saying it might not be him now, is there?"

"Quite. The story you've just told is of a man who, in effect, was a victim of physical harassment in your pub on that night. You depict him as an innocent in all of this. Don't you think, knowing what we know now, that he was fully in control of what was going on all the time he was in the Wild Boar? That he engineered the whole thing – spilling the drink, for example. And that, for all he knew, the three people he had chosen to kill were unarmed. Isn't all that true, Mr Jordan?"

"No, he just came in for a quiet drink and… "

"I don't think so!" said Penny, sitting down.

There was some laughter around the court. Even the Counsel

for the Defence looked a little embarrassed at his witness's attempt to whitewash the incident. He got to his feet quickly.

"Thank you, Mr Jordan."

As the landlord left the witness box he glanced across again at the defendant who returned his look with a nod of recognition.

The judge waited until he had left the courtroom and addressed his next remark to Dean.

"Mr Calvert, could you explain the purpose of this course of questioning. Given your attempts so far to depict Mr Lorimar as a man on a mission, driven by circumstances to carry out this crime – to which he has pleaded guilty – I am not sure why you would want to imply that his actions were due to provocation on the evening of the incident itself. Is it too big an assumption for us to accept that the very reason for his being in the Wild Boar public house at that time was because he knew his intended victims were there? This, in fact, would be totally consistent with the case you have been building so far."

"Yes, m'lord. Perhaps I over-elaborate, for which I apologise if it impedes the progress of this case. My purpose in calling the last witness was really just to confirm the type of individuals Mr Lorimar had set himself against. Even accepting his motives for being in the public house that evening, the unprovoked aggression he experienced would scarcely have deflected him from his intended course of action and could only have hardened his resolve."

"I understand your point, Mr Calvert… "

"Thank you, m'lord."

"… although that does not necessarily mean that I agree with it. I recall you said you had two more witnesses. In the light of what I think we just agreed, is it still relevant to call the final one?"

"I particularly think so, m'lord, as this has been very delicately arranged and involves one of the very last people to see the victims alive and at the scene of their demise."

"Very well; do continue."

"Thank you, m'lord. The next witness is a boy, fourteen years of age, who resides on the Cullen Field Estate. He was, by his own admission, a member of the Brady gang, but has agreed to give an account of the events of that evening up to what we believe was just a few minutes before the three men were killed. He has agreed to do this anonymously, for obvious reasons. Because of his age and the need to preserve his identity he will not, of course, actually be present in this courtroom. He is in a secure room within this building and we have an audio link with him. His voice will be electronically distorted, to ensure no possibility of accidental recognition. He is accompanied by his mother and a police officer. For the purpose of the court record, he will be referred to as Damian, although I emphasise that this is not one of his names – neither a forename nor a family name. Would you like me to proceed, m'lord, or would you like to address the witness prior to my questioning him?"

Whilst Dean was speaking, a technician was attaching a radio microphone to the lapel of his gown.

"I should like to speak with this young man first."

The technician moved across to the bench and placed a microphone on a small angled stand in front of the judge for him to speak into. Another technician at the back of the room activated it, and raised his hand to signal its readiness.

"Damian, can you hear me?"

There was a muffled noise from the invisible speakers of the courtroom PA system. This was followed by the sound of whispered prompting and then a stronger response.

"Yes."

"Yes, *m'lord*." Another prompt.

"Yes, m'lord."

"Firstly, Damian, let me thank you for coming here today to help us with this case. In a moment I will ask Mr Bradley, who is our Clerk of the Court, to ask you to take an oath. Do you know what that means?"

"Yes, I think so."

"Well, just to be absolutely clear, let me explain. You will be asked to promise to tell the truth in this court of law. You are bound by the same rules as the witnesses who have appeared in this courtroom, even though you are not actually here, and you must take this oath, on your holy book, in the knowledge that you yourself can be charged with an offence if you do not tell the truth. Do you understand, Damian?"

"Yes – m'lord."

"Excellent. I am now addressing the police officer in the room with you. Officer, do you have the book in question?"

"Yes, m'lord."

"Then, Mr Bradley… "

"Take the holy book in your hand, Damian, and read the words on the card the officer is holding in front of you."

There was a sound of whispering and shuffling, then, "I swear by Almighty God that the evidence I shall give will be the truth, the whole truth and nothing but the truth."

"Thank you, Damian," said Judge Templar. "Mr Calvert… "

During the whole of the proceedings up to that point, the public's eyes had been focused almost exclusively on the man in the dock. Although they were clearly absorbed by the questioning of the witnesses and the exchanges between judge and counsel, their collective gaze was fixed – almost transfixed – on James Lorimar. The man himself seemed totally relaxed but fully attentive throughout, his eyes switching quickly from speaker to speaker as each dialogue unfolded as if eager not to miss a single word, and to clearly grasp the meaning of each. To an experienced observer of human behaviour, like Detective Chief Inspector David Gerrard, it seemed as if the man was checking that everything was going to plan. As if he, rather than any of the officials, was controlling the proceedings. This notion was reinforced by a number of brief consultations, invariably prompted by the prisoner, with his counsel.

He also noted, with some amusement, that the gallery's intense concentration on the prisoner wavered significantly as Dean Calvert began to question Damian, and people started to look around the courtroom, as if searching for the source of the alien-sounding disembodied voice.

"Damian," Dean began, "let me first add my thanks for your attending court today. Can you confirm, please, that you are fourteen years of age… "

"Yes."

"… that you live on the Cullen Field Estate… "

"Yes."

"… and that at the time of the incident, you were a member of what was known as 'The Brady Gang'?"

There was a brief silence, followed by whispered encouragement from a female voice.

"Yes."

"Thank you, Damian. Could you explain, in your own words, what happened that evening, starting with the disturbance in Kingdom Road."

"Well, somebody set fire to these cars, like... then the police came and the fire guys and some of us – I mean, some of *them*... "

"It's alright, Damian," Dean interrupted, "you're not in trouble, but you are under oath, so just tell us exactly what happened."

"Okay, we had a go at the uniforms, then somebody threw something onto the road and – shit – we were all, like, fucking deaf and blind for a minute. Then it pissed down and suddenly Jimmy and the twins were there. They went to the pub and we just hung around outside, like we always do, in case something else was going off."

He seemed to run out of words. After a long silence, Dean prompted him again.

"Okay, that's great so far, Damian. What happened next?"

"Well about nine o'clock – or maybe it was ten o'clock – this dude runs out of the pub and away down the street. We'd seen him go in, like, a bit earlier. Then Jimmy and Kev and Karl came out and ran after him. We all went along with them and trapped him on Cullen Industrial Park down a dead-end street. Then Jimmy beat up Ahmed when he asked if we could stay."

"Why did you want to stay, Damian?" Dean asked.

"To see the action, like."

"What were you expecting to see, exactly?"

"We thought they were going to kill him."

There were gasps and cries from the public gallery. Penny Cartwright sprang to her feet.

"M'lord! There is no way this person – Damian – could know that. He... "

"Ms Cartwright," interrupted the judge, "I don't think that Damian is saying – or the Defence is implying – that he *knew* that was their intention. I think he has just said he wanted to stay to find out, but that is what he *thought* was going to happen. Carry on, Mr Calvert."

Dean addressed the room in general again.

"Why did you think that, Damian?"

"Think what?"

"That they were going to kill him."

"Don't know. Guess because that's why they told us to 'fuck off'. We figured they didn't want any witnesses so it must have been that."

"Did you expect it because you had seen them kill someone before?"

Penny was on her feet again.

"M'lord, merely an observation. Before you allow Damian to answer that question, should we be permitting this young person to possibly incriminate himself in other crimes, even as an accessory? There may even be implications for the future process of law should he refer to any cases currently under investigation or where charges have been made."

Owen Templar turned to Dean.

"Mr Calvert, what is the purpose of this last question? I think Damian has painted an intimidating enough picture in terms of the pursuit of the accused, and his verbatim recollection of how one of the victims dismissed the gang. You may feel on reflection that this is sufficient for the purposes of mitigation."

"I take my learned friend's point, m'lord, and withdraw the question," said Dean. "And I do agree that the picture Damian has drawn for us graphically depicts the vulnerability of Mr Lorimar's situation and the frame of mind of his would-be attackers. I am sure that if Damian believed the brothers intended to kill him, the thought would certainly have crossed Mr Lorimar's mind as well."

He spoke again to the witness.

"What did you do after Jimmy Brady had attacked the other boy?"

"We left. Everybody did."

"And what did the Bradys do next?"

"Don't know. They were going down the street towards this guy. Well, I do know what they did – they got themselves killed, didn't they?"

"Thank you, Damian. That was very helpful." He turned to the bench. "No further questions, m'lord, and that was my last witness."

"Any questions for Damian, Ms Cartwright?"

"No, m'lord."

"Then thank you again, Damian, for your assistance with this case. Mr Calvert, you indicated that you would be calling Mr Lorimar to the stand… "

There was a hum of expectation around the courtroom which the judge chose not to address with a reprimand, although he waited for it to subside before continuing.

"I assume you still wish to do this?"

"I do, m'lord."

"Well, it is now four-fifteen. It seems inappropriate to begin what could be a lengthy session at this time. Court is adjourned until eleven o'clock tomorrow morning."

The Clerk of the Court got to his feet.

"All rise."

★

David Gerrard and Jo Cottrell sat in the warm sunshine with their drinks outside the pub on Ludgate Hill. The Ye Olde London was a traditional English public house with a lively bar at ground level and a further extensive bar downstairs, plus an external courtyard popular with patrons for outside drinking and dining. The street frontage was mainly of leaded glass with the pub sign above in large gold letters on a bright red background. The half-dozen hanging baskets were a riot of colour at the very peak of their seasonal splendour.

"Bloody ironic isn't it," said David. "We do all that bloody work for the Prosecution and the Defence call all our bloody witnesses. We had all those guys lined up to convince people he'd carried out a brutal, pre-meditated murder, and the same ones all get to show what a really good bloke he is – and by answering the same questions, more or less. There's nothing normal about this case. And I tell you what; I reckon there'll be another twist to this tomorrow. I think that revelations await us."

"Such as what?" asked Jo.

"Well, we might find out who he is, for a start."

"You don't think," she whispered, her eyes darting theatrically from side to side as she spoke, "that he really *is* Pinocchio?"

"Listen, Detective hanging-by-a-thread-Sergeant Cottrell, it's the senior officer who takes the piss. Don't you watch any television?"

"Only wildlife programmes."

"Ah well, at least that explains why you don't understand human beings."

Jo spluttered. "And you do, of course? All of them."

"Just listen to the girl," said David, in mock exasperation. "You seem to be suffering from delusions of adequacy. What makes you think you can suddenly start treating me as an equal?"

"Well, for a start, I bought the drinks…"

"So?"

"… as I did the last time and the time before that. You'd be dehydrated if it wasn't for me… sir."

"You're right," he smiled, and then became serious again. "But you're *not* right to dismiss this thing about Lorimar's real identity."

"I'm not dismissing it, or saying you're wrong about him, sir. I'm just still not sure it's all that relevant."

"We'll see," said David, suddenly lost in his thoughts.

"Time to go?" asked Jo, not wishing to end up sitting in silence for minutes on end until he emerged from his meditation.

"Certainly not. My round," said David. "Never let it be said… "

★

Tom stayed at the constituency office for the rest of the day for his regular Thursday surgery, which started at 1.00 pm with a planned finish at 7.00 pm in the evening. Allowing fifteen minutes for each meeting, this made him available, in theory at least, to twenty-four of his constituents, and more if they attended in pairs or groups.

On this particular day, aside from a complaint about excessive litter on a pedestrian shopping street and another bemoaning the inadequacies of public transport in the area, everyone wanted to talk about the Lorimar trial. Twenty-one of the attendees were from the estate itself, with a variety of comments and questions. It was clear that the overwhelming view regarding the Bradys' incident was that the main victim was James Lorimar, a casualty of State incompetence.

He finished his last meeting at 7.45 pm, and rather than remain in Marlburgh, he decided to drive to London and spend the night at the apartment at Balmaha in SW1. His constituency home, the top floor of a large three-storey Edwardian detached house, was at the opposite end of Westbourne Avenue from his office – a few minutes' walk. It was well appointed, beautifully furnished and airy, with high ceilings and open fireplaces, and overlooked a small park – the same one which gave its name to Parkside police station. It was a quiet and friendly neighbourhood and he always felt relaxed and comfortable there.

However, the roads into the centre of London would be relatively quiet at this time of the evening compared to the morning's white-water experience of the A12, A11 and beyond. The alternative to that – a gentle twenty-minute stroll to work – was enough to persuade him to make the effort tonight.

Just after 10.00 pm, he parked his Audi R8 in his designated space in the basement car park and took the lift to the second floor apartment. Situated on Vauxhall Road, close – but not too close – to Westminster, this was Tom's favourite of their four residences. He sat for several minutes in front of the floor-to-ceiling windows in the huge semi-circular living area while he went quickly through the mail which had accumulated since his last visit. It was luxuriously furnished in a modern style with squared black leather chairs and sofas on a polished oak floor, and glass and chrome dining furniture and cabinets. The walls were plain white and hung with a selection of Mags's paintings.

After a while, he pulled on a fleece jacket, poured himself a very large Jack Daniels, then slid open the patio doors of the master bedroom and parked himself at the table on the triangular balcony overlooking the Thames. He sipped his drink and looked down the river past the Houses of Parliament to St Paul's and, beyond that, the towering office blocks of the City of London.

Then he took out his mobile and phoned Mags.

"So," he said, "what have you been doing with yourself while the cat's been away?"

She seemed pleased to hear his voice.

"Well," she said, "I've spent most of the evening at the Dilleys'. Angela enticed me round by saying there was some very important news I needed to hear. I should have known better."

"Even so, sounds exciting," said Tom. "What was it about? It's safe to tell me, I'm sitting down."

"Well," said Mags, half whispering, as if she was about to reveal a startling secret, "Jock is taking early retirement."

"No!" gasped Tom. "Oh, my God! Whatever next?"

"Perhaps I should have broken it to you a little more gently. Are you alright?"

"Yes, but I'm going to need a really stiff drink. Luckily I have one in my hand."

Mags laughed.

"So have I. What's yours?"

"JD."

"So's mine. Cheers."

"Cheers."

"Actually," said Mags, "I've already had a couple of glasses of champers with Ange. To celebrate the pending event."

"Celebrate? Well, from what I've heard about domestic life in retirement, I'm not sure it's something to look forward to with champagne. What did Jock McDilley have to say? Did he get a word in?"

"He wasn't there. He was in his den mounting butterflies."

"Mounting butterflies! The dirty pervert! I always suspected he had a very small dick; but, I mean, butterflies!"

Mags burst out laughing.

"That's very naughty," she chastised. "By the way, did you watch Lorimar arriving at the Old Bailey? God, it gave me such a shock. Just for a minute… "

"Yes, same here. Spitting image. It scared me half to death. Did you hear any of the trial on the radio?"

"No. Had a meeting this afternoon. Little Winton By-Pass Action Group. Better tell the filth to start dusting down their riot shields."

It was Tom's turn to laugh.

"Where are you, by the way?" she asked. "I can hear a lot of noise."

"SW1," he said. "On the balcony. Bloody freezing."

"You're back tomorrow evening?"

"Of course. Poets' day. Shouldn't be late."

"Good. See you then."

There was a lengthy pause, as if each was waiting for the other to end the call. Tom spoke first.

"Oh, Mags!"

"Yes?"

"Love you."

"Love you, too."

CHAPTER 11

Owen Templar arrived at the court at 10.00 am sharp the next morning. Like most people in employment, he always felt much better on a Friday than on any other working day. Today, the feeling would be short-lived. He was met in the doorway of his expansive office by his secretary, who was in the process of smoothing the creases out of the judge's robe as he entered.

"You have a visitor, sir," he said, in a conspiratorial whisper. "Lord Chief Justice."

Justice Templar rolled his eyes in response, as if a precious secret was shared by the two of them.

"Thank you, Billy."

Billy Wakeley was a little under medium height and slim to the point of thinness. His smiling friendly face looked impossibly young for someone in their mid-twenties. He wrapped the red robe carefully onto its padded hanger and hung it in its usual place on the back of the huge oak door, before leaving the room and closing it behind him.

Lord Charles Nicholson rose from his seat and extended his hand.

"Hello, Owen," he said. "How are you?"

"Fine thanks, Charlie, and you?"

"Very well, thank you. Bet you're enjoying all this limelight? With Lorimar, I mean."

Lord Charles was a large, well-built, distinguished looking man, in a grey pin-striped three-piece suit and bright yellow tie with matching handkerchief in the top pocket of his jacket.

"Just another case, Charlie," Owen replied with a wide smile. "You know me."

The two men sat down in the expensive Queen Anne chairs at either side of the Regency occasional table as Billy quietly opened the door again and pushed the tea trolley into the room.

"Knew you wouldn't mind, Owen, so I asked Billy to double up on the tea and biscuits."

"It's unlike you not to be queuing outside when the doors open for elevenses at your club, Charlie. The other members will suspect that the beer is off or something. This must be serious."

His visitor chuckled. Then he frowned and leant forward in his chair.

"Well, it is rather," he said.

★

Just before 11.00 am the small convoy repeated its journey of exactly twenty-four hours ago through the same crowds of on-lookers; same banners, same shouts, same emotional reception as James Lorimar stepped down from the back of the security van, like a king descending from his carriage.

He waved to the crowd, ratcheting up the volume of their cheering. People had been camped outside the Old Bailey, and along the road approaching it, for a couple of hours. It was reminiscent of the final day at Wimbledon; the queue for tickets for a pop concert; or the January sale at Harrods.

Inside the courtroom, the privileged hundred followers of the accused man who had gained entry to the public gallery settled excitedly in their seats feeling like a gathering of celebrities at 'An Audience with James Lorimar', With the order to "all rise" from the Clerk of the Court, they almost leapt to their feet as the judge entered the court, as if their own perceived haste might expedite the start of the proceedings.

He addressed the Defence.

"Mr Calvert, please… "

"I should like to take a small amount of the court's time, m'lord, to establish the relationship between Mr Lorimar and Mrs Deverall."

Judge Templar said nothing but opened his arms wide in a signal to proceed.

"Mr James Lorimar, would you please stand."

There was a burst of animation around the room with several people offering gentle applause as the prisoner rose to his feet.

"Very briefly, Mr Lorimar, please describe to the court how you came to know Mrs Deverall," said Dean.

"Yes, of course. I am currently an Investment Manager with Germaine and Rolland. Before that I was in the armed forces where I was a close friend of Mrs Deverall's only son. He was killed in action a few years ago, but before he died he asked me to look out for his mother, Alma, as he would not be around to do so any more.

"Alma and I became friends. We pretended I was her carer – it was our little secret – and when she became ill and depressed, I found her the apartment in Hammersmith – as you heard from Mr Venables – for a period of respite. As you have also heard, it was there she took her life just prior to the end of the tenancy, when she was due to return to the estate."

The calm control he had displayed throughout the trial, seemed to briefly leave him and for a fleeting moment he visibly slumped. He recovered immediately.

"Thank you, Mr Lorimar. No further questions from me, m'lord."

There was a ripple of disappointment around the public gallery.

"Ms Cartwright?" The judge turned to Penny. "Do you have any questions for the prisoner?"

"No, m'lord," she said.

"That will be all, Mr Lorimar. You may be seated." He turned again to the Defence Counsel. "Over to you, Mr Calvert."

"Thank you, m'lord," said Dean. "If it pleases the court, I would like to summarise this plea for mitigation before you pass sentence."

Justice Templar gave the slightest of nods. Dean gathered himself for his keynote speech, sweeping his right arm round in almost a full circle to have it stop, pointing, open-palmed, towards the dock.

"The man standing before you is a brave man… " He paused for effect. "The man standing before you is a good man… a *just* man. And yet, the man standing before you is a guilty man. Guilty of what? Guilty of rendering a form of justice consistent with that which he has been required to do for a quarter of a century in the defence of the freedom of this country and its allies. In law, this man is a criminal; in reality, he is a saviour, whose efforts have liberated a community from a lurking menace which plagued their every day's existence."

He paused again, this time receiving a gentle ripple of applause from the gallery. David Gerrard was thinking about the counsel's ill-chosen adjective. 'Lurking' was not how he would have chosen to describe the Bradys. 'In-your-face', he thought – in every sense of the expression – would have been much more suitable. Dean Calvert continued.

"We should not condone this act, nor praise it, nor rejoice in it. After all, the act of taking another human being's life goes against every instinct of law-abiding people. But we can perhaps *understand* it, and I believe we have before us a person who was driven by sadness and desperation to do something in recompense for the sorrow in losing a person whom he clearly cared for very much."

Again a ripple of applause, the judge glowering to silence it this time.

"And, m'lord, having taken such a decision, Mr Lorimar was clearly in no position to change his mind, faced with the wrath and venom of his intended victims. In the end, ironically, they left him no choice and, through their own evil intentions, sealed their fate. I respectfully request, m'lord, that you see this man as he is – as I said. A brave, good and just man, a criminal in law," – he paused for emphasis – "but a *victim* of his own high ideals."

The courtroom spontaneously erupted in shouts of support and appreciation. Justice Templar banged his fist onto the bench in front of him, in obvious anger and exasperation. His voice boomed across the room.

"We are nearing the end of these proceedings. That is the only reason why I will not be asking the attendants to clear this courtroom. Does everybody – I mean – *everybody* – understand?"

The room almost crashed into silence. People nodded; some actually said 'yes'; some even 'sorry'.

"Thank you, Mr Calvert, for your eloquent justification of the defendant's act of murder. Because, notwithstanding your comments, a simple act of murder is what it is. Premeditated and callous. It is an undisputed fact that Mr Lorimar has shown much courage in his chosen profession. In that context, I agree that the word brave may be justifiably applied to him. But not so, I believe, in the perpetration of this crime. In spite of the numerical odds against him, the three young men would have had little or no chance against someone with his training. In any case, I must carry out my obligatory duty. Ms Cartwright, do you have any comments before I pass sentence?"

"No, m'lord," she replied.

"And does the prisoner have anything to say for himself?" The question was asked wearily and mechanically to the court in general.

"Yes, m'lord. My client would like to make a statement from the dock."

"Please have him go ahead."

The prisoner stood and removed three folded A4 sheets – stapled together – from the inside pocket of his jacket. He unfolded them, cast his eyes for a few moments over the first sheet, then looked up and addressed the judge directly.

"First let me thank you, m'lord, for allowing me to speak today, and also for permitting Mr Calvert to spend so much of the court's time yesterday on my behalf in relating the mitigating circumstances leading up to the incident. However, I want to make it clear to everyone that my act of retribution was premeditated and carefully staged. I could not be more gratified by the way this one incident has served to unite those oppressed people of our communities and highlight the plight in which so many find themselves. That has been an enormous bonus and a great and necessary comfort to me.

"I say a necessary comfort, because it was certainly *not* my intention to get caught. Indeed, I did not *expect* to get caught, and my somewhat reluctant congratulations must go to Detective Chief Inspector David Gerrard and his team, for their tenacity and skill."

For one bizarre moment, David wondered whether he should get to his feet and bow to the gallery.

"The proceedings of the last two days have also demonstrated how fortunate we are in possessing such institutionalised integrity in our judicial system. No-one need fear when the machinery of the law is in such good hands – no-one, that is, except people like me. So we have laws to protect us, we have good, professional people to ensure we comply with these laws, and we have solid reliable systems in place to enable those people to deal with the likes of me when they do not comply. So what is wrong? Because something most certainly is!

"I quote from a statement made by ex-Squadron Leader Arnold Danby at a meeting of the Third Age Forum, just prior to my arrest. This quotation has been subsequently used by Mr George Holland and reported in the press.

"'… more important than the law is justice. It appears that, in the space of less than an hour, a single person, now being hunted as a triple murderer, and whose freedom – and, effectively, whose life – will end when he is caught, has put to rights something that all the agents of the law have abjectly failed to do for God knows how many years. Isn't it ironic that justice, it seems, has been done, and the law will now punish the person who achieved it.'

"I feel he captured the essence very concisely. However, I must take issue with one aspect of the squadron leader's words. He said '… something that all the agents of the law have *abjectly failed to do…* ' That part of his statement implies a level of incompetence on the part of those agents – the police, lawyers, barristers, judges. I do not believe that is true.

"*It is the law itself that is failing us!* Or more specifically that part of the law that dishes out justice. How can it be right that the likes of the Bradys and their disciples are allowed to roam the streets like a pride of hungry man-eaters, causing widespread distress and intimidation, whilst good people cower in fear behind their curtains in darkened rooms? And all this is going on when the police are *fully aware* of the sort of people they are and the sort of things they are doing. So why don't they put them away? Well, to do so we must rely on people with complete faith that their testimony will lead to these heathens' imprisonment. And how can they have that faith when so many attempts to imprison them fail on technicalities and trivial details – not cautioning them at the right time, incomplete paperwork, and witnesses trapped into saying what they don't really mean. And without faith in a guarantee of success, who with any sense would put themselves in a position where the likelihood is they will face retribution as this flawed system pours the antagonists back onto the streets.

"If I had any doubts before, then the reaction of the public to this whole issue has wiped them out. I now know for *certain* how our society needs to change – *must* change. It needs to focus on the good people, the nice people. It needs to care a lot less about those who *choose* not to be good and nice. We are all sensitive to the effects of poverty, parental guidance, local environment, peer pressure, etcetera. These are massive forces for shaping behaviour. But even in their extreme forms they are resistible forces. Carrots are fine in the first place for attempting to lead these disadvantaged people onto the path of righteousness. But when the carrots have failed, or have all been devoured with no discernable effect, then we must bring sticks to bear – heavy sticks, hurting sticks. Not gentle apologetic taps which do no more than induce sneers and mocking laughter. And after the carrots and the sticks – the most singularly effective measure of all – so obvious, and with a *guarantee* of success, but so radical very few even dare to mention, let alone propose, it. *Permanent separation and isolation!*

"And I don't mean life imprisonment as we have it now. Judges *are* able to put away people for good as the law stands now – a situation where justice and law may be perceived as being the same. But so many times, life imprisonment means a relatively short period weighed against a full life span of, say, eighty years, or perhaps fifty or sixty remaining years. But this is not the point anyway! Not at all! Such sentences are currently reserved for extreme cases of violence and murder, and for those involved in the planning and execution of acts of terrorism. And it is right that such people are excluded from our society; they have no place in a civilised world.

"But these are not the ones who plague so many lives day in, day out. People are not scared of going out for a walk around their neighbourhood streets in the evening for fear of being blown up by a suicide bomber, or brutally murdered by a psychopathic stranger lurking in the shadows. The chance of that happening is less than the likelihood of being killed by a slate falling from a roof as they pass. They stay at home to avoid the threats, hassle and intimidation heaped upon them by roving gangs seeking soft targets, whose success criteria is the look of fear on the faces of their randomly chosen prey.

"They need stopping. They need stopping permanently. Or at least they need to be placed where they can pursue their interests without the wholesale pain and anguish they cause the people who wish to live in peace. Let them kill; let them maim and wound and torment. And let us find a place where they can do this away from the world they reject, where they can inflict their misery on each other. Forget the specific crime; forget the need for proof; forget the requirement for witnesses and their subsequent protection and – quite often – their necessary isolation for their own safety. The question should not be – 'are they guilty or not guilty?' It should be 'would the world – society, community, define it as you wish – would it be better or not *without* these people in it?' If the answer is 'better', then it is the law's duty to make it so by removing them.

"This is a radical step. It would mean an enormous amount of parliamentary work, even if there was a will within the powers that be to address the nation's concerns so controversially. But the controversy is all in the means; the end is indisputable in its benefit. Unfortunately, the do-gooders will concentrate on the means; they will point out that these criminals are just misunderstood, have had too little guidance, suffer from coming from a poor background, a poor area, have single parents, little education. In other words, none of it is their fault, so nothing should be done about them. Except, of course, pour more money into leisure facilities, counsellors, corrective centres and so on.

"We must focus on the finished product, the end-game, the future state scenario, call it what you will. In other words, the *end* as opposed to the means. And it will be a painful process to get there, but well worth it. To do so we need to be prepared to put at risk part of a generation – those non-conforming to be banished for ever, irreversibly exiled. There would be mistakes, innocents swept up in the street-cleansing process. This would be unfortunate, but an acceptable risk for the overall benefit. I passionately believe that. We need to focus on that better world in the future – hopefully, the *near* future – where the good people can take charge of their simple needs and wants without fear and compromise. We need to insist that those who can achieve it for us do so, or move aside to make way for those who will. And in that better world, people like me will be justly castigated and repulsed for needlessly taking lives, instead of revered for doing somebody else's job."

The whole public gallery stood to applaud, in appreciation of the message.

"Thank you, Mr Lorimar," said Justice Templar as the ovation finally subsided, assuming that the prisoner had finished.

"If it pleases, m'lord," he said, and quickly continued, "I have one further piece of information to impart. And for withholding this until now I wish to apologise to you, to my Counsel and the Prosecution, and to the court in general. The story of the killing of the Bradys has been recounted accurately and objectively. But one detail of this case has yet to be revealed.

"My name is John Alexander Deverall. My death was reported three years ago. I am the son of Alma Deverall, the lady who took her own life three weeks prior to the death of her tormentors."

The courtroom was totally silent for what seemed a long time, and then erupted again, this time with incredulity. Dean Calvert and Penny Cartwright looked at each other wide-eyed before Dean looked down at the notes in front of him as if checking that he had not missed something obvious. Jo leant across to David and whispered in his ear, "Don't you dare look smug about this."

The prisoner waited until the room became silent again.

"I do not intend adding anything to my statement and I will not be pressed to do so. For the past three years I have been James Lorimar, but it does not matter what my name is. The only thing that is important is for the court to recognise the crime I committed and the reasons for doing it. I did it for my mother, Alma, and for the residents of Cullen Field Estate. *Please* do not lose sight of what is important here. We have all had a glimpse of what can be achieved by the removal of menace from the midst of decent people. I urge you to take up the cry as you already have done in this courtroom today. That is what is important. The future; a better future; a safer future."

It was a full minute before the judge tried to speak again above the sustained applause that followed. During that interlude he flashed several venomous glances at Charles Nicholson, sitting at the back of the courtroom, who returned them with a relaxed smile, which did nothing to lighten the blackness of his mood. However, when he finally did speak, after the room had become silent again, it was with calm authority.

"To say the least, Mr Lorimar, you are a man of surprises. I commend you for your heart-felt oratory. We also thank you, of course… " – this with kindly sarcasm – "… for your benevolent words relating to how we try to do our jobs. And I can assure you that, in spite of the revelation at the end of your speech, my mind is, as you requested, focused on the crime, including the whys and the hows. As far as this court is concerned you are James Lorimar, the man who has pleaded guilty to the violent, premeditated murder of Jimmy, Kevin and Karl Brady, and it is my duty to sentence you to a mandatory life sentence. This is the only sentence this court can impose. I recommend that you should serve a minimum of eight years after which time you should be considered for parole; the Home Secretary will then set the tariff.

"For what it's worth, Mr Lorimar, I empathise, if not totally agree, with much of what you said today. And I do hope some serious consideration will be extended to what I perceived to be an intelligent and well communicated argument."

The judge rose quickly, speaking as he stood up.

"Both counsels to my office immediately, please?"

The suddenness of his retreat took everyone by surprise. He was halfway out of the room before the rest of the gathering had responded to the Clerk's "All rise."

David and Jo watched as John Deverall was led away from the dock to the retaining cells, each acknowledging his smile with a nod of their head. He seemed relaxed and satisfied with the outcome, leaving behind a scene of high excitement, raised voices and animated gestures.

The press piled out of the court in one single mass as if the fire alarm had sounded, to collect their mobiles and such from the foyer and get to work on the new twist. Penny Cartwright immediately picked up her notes, anxious to follow the judge as quickly as possible, and was waiting impatiently as Dean Calvert exchanged angry words with Clive Granville, eventually joining her and strutting from the room. David and Jo made their way out of the building into bright sunshine. Neither had spoken since Jo's whispered comment earlier.

"Fancy a stroll along the embankment?" asked David.

"Yes, sure," said Jo. She peered intensely into David's face as if studying his expression carefully.

"This is satisfied," said David, "not smug."

"Mmmm, well it looks like smug to me."

They walked, in silence again, down to Ludgate Hill, turning right up to New Bridge Street then left towards Blackfriars and the river. They found a small bar near the Millennium Pier and abandoned the idea of the walk along the embankment, sitting outside and ordering beer and sandwiches.

"I think I'll ask Lorimar – Deverall – to put all that about tenacity and stuff in writing," said David. "I've got my annual appraisal with Allan next week. It might keep the subject away from my retirement, at least for a while."

"I have to say," said Jo, "he's a real collector's item. I think I might go and visit him in jail. Perhaps he'll take me out when they release him. I'll only be thirty-nine. I can't see him not fancying me, can you?"

"Not when he's been inside for eight years," said David. "He'll probably settle for anything."

"Well, thank you! You must admit though, he's a bit fit, isn't he? I guess it's okay to say that now that I've helped put him away."

"Not my type. But an exceptional guy all the same. That speech was something else, wasn't it? Even with six weeks to work on it. You know he spoke for over twenty minutes. I've never known the like before. Surprised old Templar didn't cut him short. Well, I'm not actually; I reckon he had been told to give him his head."

"That's just what I was thinking. Seemed to give up on the proceedings, didn't he? Like he just knew it was going to run and run, and nothing he could do about it. Tell you what though; he was certainly listening as closely as anyone."

"Perhaps it's his appraisal next week as well. His boss was there, you know. Charlie Nick was at the back of the court. Question is, now that it's over and the secret's out, is anyone going to work out how he managed to survive being blown up. Surely someone must be keen to know. I mean, he can't have faked his own death in those circumstances. Not in some canyon in Afghanistan. It must have been set up for some very good reason."

"Well if you're thinking of doing some more private detective work, I'll bet you won't get anywhere near anyone who can help you." She tapped the side of her nose with her forefinger. "Hush, hush; top secret; National Security."

"Even so, they can't stop us wondering, can they? He must have been reinvented for some very good reason."

"Perhaps to go around taking out people like the Bradys. Only we cocked it up by catching him."

"You don't really think that's possible, do you?" asked David, leaning forward with interest.

"Not a chance," said Jo, laughing. "I just figured you're up for believing anything right now."

"Right, that's it! Back to the station."

"Oh, come on, sir. Friday!" She checked her watch. "One-thirty. It'll be three before we get there."

"How come?" asked David. "We're only two minutes from the tube."

"Not at the pace I'm planning to walk."

David laughed.

"All right. But only if you get the next drink, and don't tell anyone I rolled over so easily."

"Sir!" said Jo, in a shocked voice, fluttering her eyelashes. "What *do* you mean?"

"Take it anyway you like, but don't forget it's *your* appraisal the week after next."

Jo waved to the waiter and pointed to the bottles in front of them, mouthing 'same again'. Half an hour later, they rose from the table, David picking up the whole tab for the refreshments, Jo wide-eyed with shock at his action, and her boss advising her not to expect it again. They started walking at a leisurely pace towards the tube station at Blackfriars.

"Actually, sir, I'm staying in London with a friend this weekend. Back on Monday morning; might be a bit late in – if that's okay, of course."

"No it bloody well isn't," said David. "So that's the reason for the delaying tactics. All this 'oo, sir, it's Friday, *please* can we have another drink?' It wasn't my company you were craving, just a way of saving a few quid on the tube. I'm deeply hurt, Jo, and I don't want to have your babies any more."

"That, sir, is a shattering blow, but what's done is done. I guess there's no going back for us."

"Definitely not! So come in whenever you like on Monday. I don't care any more. And in the meantime, have a great weekend; you deserve it."

He leant foreword and kissed her on the cheek.

"Thanks, sir," Jo smiled back. "You doing anything special?"

"No, nothing in particular – and that's by choice. Mainly chilling for two full days and three full nights, with a couple of sessions at the gym to keep the blood circulating. That's my idea of a great weekend."

"Actually, Detective Chief Inspector, that doesn't sound bad at all."

They went their separate ways.

★

Billy Wakeley opened the door and poked his head round. The office of the Recorder of London was large and high and impressive, with oak-panelling on the wall where the door was and floor-to-ceiling bookshelves lining the other three. Two crystal chandeliers hung from ornate ceiling roses. The large desk was covered in discarded wigs and robes, and the judge and two counsels, looking surprisingly ordinary now in just their normal clothes, were seated in three wing chairs around the table where Owen Templar and the LCJ had taken their earlier tea and biscuits.

"Lord Nicholson to see you, sir."

"Ask him to come in, Billy."

"Now, sir?"

"Now, Billy."

Charles Nicholson entered the room with what was obviously a pre-set beam on his face. This changed to a questioning look when he saw Owen Templar was not alone.

"Just need a few minutes with you, Owen," he said.

"You most certainly do, Charlie. Please, do sit down."

The Lord Chief Justice took the seat vacated by Dean's standing and politely waving him to it with an elaborate flourish. He waited a few moments, expecting his colleague to dismiss the barristers.

"Yes?" Owen prompted, inviting him to speak.

"Just a quick word."

"Oh, please feel free to speak openly in front of Mr Calvert and Ms Cartwright, Charles. They have been just as humiliated as I have." His manner was ultra polite and matter-of-fact, belying the bitterness in the actual words.

Lord Nicholson hesitated a moment and the muscles around his mouth tightened, as if he was going to take up the challenge, then he relaxed and sighed deeply. "Yes, you're right. You all deserve an explanation. I promise I'll tell you as much as I possibly can."

Dean and Penny, both feeling like innocent bystanders in this high-level crossfire, also sighed, audibly, with relief. Owen pressed a button on his desk and Billy appeared instantaneously, like a genie from a lamp, in the doorway.

"Could you get lunch for four please, Billy, and a chair for Mr Calvert."

"Yes, sir."

He disappeared for less than fifteen seconds before reappearing, effortlessly carrying another sizable wing-chair, which he placed next to where Penny was sitting.

"Lunch in ten minutes, sir?"

"That would be perfect. Thanks, Billy."

He turned to Lord Nicholson.

"Please enlighten us, Charlie."

"Okay," he said. "Everything I know, which, I will tell you now, is not everything there *is* to know. What I can tell you is that John Deverall – let's call him that now – is a very special person, one of only six in the world. Four of those six, including Deverall, are in the UK; one in the US and one in France. So everything I say is covered by the Official Secrets Act, and I will need each of you to sign a copy today. Okay?"

They nodded.

"Deverall was previously a top sniper attached to an organisation known as the Multinational Termination Unit. It's not an official group as such, more a virtual pool of expertise. Because of his outstanding ability he was recruited from the MTU by a clandestine section of G-Branch specialising in… well you can imagine, can't you, given his skill set. Before he could transfer to this section –

codename 'Pages', a derivative of Phoenix Agency – or 'Agents' – he had to adopt a new identity. This meant he needed to be killed off in Afghanistan."

"And then rose from the ashes as James Lorimar," said Owen. "How poetic."

"That's right."

"So, how did they do it?"

"I'm not party to what happened between the decision to transfer him and his arriving in London as Lorimar. But once here he was integrated into a normal civilian existence working at Germaine and Rolland. No-one officially knows – outside the Agency, of course – just how much this company knows and is involved. They are an investment company – that's a fact. But Lorimar is obviously not an investment expert – unless he's an exceptionally quick learner. He's required to be available as and when. However, it seems he chose to apply his skill for personal reasons, thus putting his whole operation at potential risk.

"And that's about it, then, as far as explaining the final revelation in court today. You know as much as I do now."

"That's fine, Charles, as far as it goes. We won't ask you anymore about his background and work. I think we all know enough about the importance of National Security to contain our natural curiosity. What I and, I'm sure, these good people are more interested in is why this had to be sprung on the court like that, instead of determining his identity before the trial and making it clear who he was then. Or, if this only came to light within the last couple of days, at least sharing it with us so we could manage the exposition more professionally? As it was, we looked like complete fools in there."

"Well, I didn't come up with the idea, Owen. Let me assure you of that. I sense that Deverall himself was pulling the strings. His real identity had to come out; there were bound to be people – possibly hundreds of people – who would recognise him. I mean, he's a pretty striking-looking bloke," Penny nodded, involuntarily, in agreement, "and there was no way they could keep him under wraps. So it was a case of when to pull the rabbit out. I understand it was he who decided to take it to the wire; wanted to delay this as long as possible while such a tide of emotion was surging along. He felt this would get his message across better than deflecting people with the sub-plot of who he really was. And I reckon he was right."

"I think he very nearly lost it at the end," said Owen. "I sensed a real confusion in the courtroom when he shared that bit of news. But I agree; I think he got away with it because of the momentum he'd already created. Good chap; shame he's not going to be around – within these four walls."

"Anyway, I was told only last night what I just passed on to you. In effect, 'the prisoner wants to address the court, and should be allowed as much time as he needs to do so'. End of directive. In fact, he wanted to speak *after* sentencing; I insisted it had to be before. Can you imagine the chaos if you'd passed sentence on Lorimar and were told afterwards he was Deverall? You see, Owen, it could have been worse. Oh, and just for the record, I was just as bloody livid as you were at being told what to do."

"I can understand that, but it still doesn't explain why you didn't tell us *beforehand*, when you and I met this morning, instead of just half of what you already knew."

"Couldn't trust you to go through with it, Owen," he answered with a sly grin. "You've got more integrity than I have. I couldn't imagine you sitting there pretending it was James Lorimar when you knew it wasn't. You'd have had to lie to the court, in effect. So I decided not to tell you. You're still squeaky clean; I'm the bare-faced liar. Or at least the bare-faced withholder of the whole truth."

The door quietly opened and Billy entered with the luncheon trolley. He pushed it up to the occasional table and began to hand out napkins.

"Thank you, Billy," said Owen. "We'll help ourselves. Time for your lunch anyway, isn't it?"

"Yes sir. Thank you, sir." He left, closing the door.

When they had helped themselves to Mr Wakeley's excellent fare, they sat back relaxed in their chairs, full plates on knees.

"Do you know why Deverall was allowed to call the shots, Charlie – no pun intended, by the way?"

"I assume because he knows some pretty important stuff. Certain people may have felt it was necessary to appease him, perhaps in exchange for his agreement to plead guilty. I mean, he's off limits now for people following up this identity thing. I suppose they probably wanted him put away. Though my guess is he won't be queuing for his gruel with the rest of the prisoners."

"That was my next question; they'll have to segregate him, won't they? They can't stick him in with a load of Bradys?"

"All I know is he's going to Pentonville. I don't know whether they have penthouses in Pentonville – it sounds like they should have – and if they do, I guess that's where he'll be staying."

They laughed at the play on words, all equals now.

"So basically," said Owen, "we just ignore the fact that this man is supposed to be dead, and just treat him as if the Lorimar story still applies?"

"Yes," said Lord Nicholson, with uncharacteristic brevity.

"One last question, Charlie," said Owen, smiling broadly now. "Who the hell managed to tell the Lord Chief Justice what he had to do in his showpiece courtroom?"

They all laughed as the person in question squirmed exaggeratedly in his chair.

"Oh, some big red-faced Brigadier chap in a loud checked suit. Looked like something out of a bloody Carry On film."

CHAPTER 12

At 10.00 am that same morning, Tom and Jackie met with Andrew in his office in the Norman Shaw Building. Their initial discussion centred on the first day of the Lorimar trial, but moved quickly on to George Holland's speech two days ago and the overwhelming media support it had received. Andrew was clearly desperate to add his Party's voice to the crescendo of demands for action. His 'significant hurdles' warning to Tom had long since been consigned to the waste bin and now his ascension to the bandwagon was absolute. Also, to Tom's surprise and contrary to his initial concerns at her involvement, Jackie seemed now to be supportive of his list of proposals, although this was mostly due to Andrew privately suggesting to her that she should put her own views aside 'for the good of the Party'.

The meeting ended at 1.30 pm, with Andrew charging his two colleagues to produce a joint message to share with the House and, as a consequence, the press, in two weeks' time, to coincide with the next debate on urban development just before the summer recess. Not a full-blown plan of attack, he said, but some preliminary details on intent, just to set the scene. As they were leaving the room, Andrew called Tom back. "Just a quick word, Tom." Jackie also turned, but Andrew gently dismissed her. "Have a good weekend, Jackie."

"You too, Andrew," she said, looking at Tom with suspicion. He returned her look with a shrug and closed the door after her.

"Not a happy bunny," said Tom. "I suppose she thinks I'm standing on her toes."

175

"Well so you are, and kicking her shins as well. But I've got a nice surprise for her. She's about to be unveiled, on Monday, as the architect of the New Justice Regime, which is what we are going to call your plan, Tom."

It took a few moments for Andrew's words to sink in, then Tom's own words came as a minor explosion.

"Yes, *my* plan, Andrew! You're damn' right it's *my* plan – mine and Grace's, anyway. I'm not sure where Hewlett comes in to it at all, never mind her being the fucking architect. She hasn't put forward one original idea."

Andrew leant back and smiled.

"Language, Tom, language. Do sit down and stop frothing at the mouth."

Tom returned to the seat he had only just vacated, prepared to be unimpressed by anything Andrew was about to say.

"The fact is, Tom – and this is between you and me and these four walls – we are not going to release a watered down, diplomatically diluted version of *your* plan the week after next. No, we are going to leak the whole fucking lot *next* week; Wednesday, to be precise."

Tom instinctively opened his mouth to respond before his mind had time to formulate any words.

"And with the name of Jackie Hewlett by then firmly stapled to it," Andrew went on. "Now, I am certain that the public's reaction will be a resounding 'yes' to the proposals, which will have the country counting down the days to the next General Election. In which case, the plan will pass seamlessly back into your capable hands, with full accountability to prepare for its implementation from the moment the last vote is counted. And from that point, this will be the fastest-tracked piece of legislation in this country's history.

"*But…* in the unlikely event that I am wrong – that we are *all* wrong – and the voters reel in revulsion from these barbaric measures, then I will reluctantly accept Hewlett's resignation, her position as the originator of such monstrous proposals having become untenable. I think this second scenario will prove to be a fairy tale. A bigger worry is that our proposals won't go far enough to satisfy the bloodlust out there. But, just in case, I am quite prepared to lose Jackie, but I'm *not* prepared to lose you. So your name can't go with it for that reason."

Tom continued to remain silent.

"Well?" said Andrew, getting a little agitated by the lack of response. "I take it you do agree with Jackie leading this now that I've explained the reason?"

Tom found his voice.

"Well, I think you've made up your mind, haven't you? Does Jackie know about this? Is she okay to go along with it?"

"Are you serious, Tom?" Andrew shouted this time, looking totally incredulous. "Are you completely fucking mad? Of course she doesn't know about it. Why do you think I let her go just now and called you back? She'd be an absolute fool to go along with something like this, wouldn't she? Except, of course, she's always whimpering about not getting enough recognition – 'it's always Tom Brown' and all that – so it would serve her right if the worst happened!"

"Bloody hell, Andrew," Tom said at last, "you are some ruthless bastard when you want to be. I hope I never become that dispensable or get on the wrong side of you."

"Well, at least you have the advantage of knowing what to expect if you do," said Andrew, with a friendly smile, but with no hint that he was joking. "Look Tom," he went on, "I need your commitment to this or at the very least your assurance that it will stay just between the two of us."

"Okay, I think I can live with that," he said, without any of the enthusiasm his leader was seeking. "After all, as we have said many times, it's the end that counts, less so the means."

"I think it was 'the end *not* the means' rather than 'less so the means' the last time you bored me with that quotation. I hope you're not softening your position, Tom. Anyway, I thought this would be right in line with your cavalier style – get it out there so people can embrace it, then we will *have* to deliver it, no matter what. Hewlett will have to support it and Greyburn will have to finance it."

Tom realised he was hearing more or less his own words repeated back to him.

"How did you… ?" he started to ask, and then thought better of it. "So what happens now? How are you going to leak it?"

"Well, to answer your first question, you go to work with Ms Hewlett, as we agreed, preparing the stuff for Thursday-week. As to your second question, you don't need to know that. Suffice to say, I shall spend an enjoyable weekend working on it – and the denial, of course. That needs to be ready at around the same time. I can't tell you how much I'm looking forward to this. Isn't it exciting, don't you think?"

Tom could see that he really thought it was. He felt a shiver of anxiety at the thought of the next few days, sitting across the table from Jackie, plotting her demise. Whichever way the public reaction went, she was to be sacrificed; either gently, moved to one side; or precipitously, with possible career-ending brutality. He rose to leave.

"Look at it this way, Tom," said Andrew, softening his manner, "unless we are completely out of touch with reality – in which case we *all* need sacking – the feedback we get will only confirm what we already know, and what the government already knows. You need to trust me on this; give me the benefit of the doubt that I'm acting for the best. After a few days we'll have a clear mandate, just as if we'd already been voted in. There's no *real* threat to Jackie, is there? The only thing that can go wrong is if Portman has secretly come up with something even more extreme. Community hit squads armed with Mini-Uzis racing through the streets machine-gunning any gathering of more then three people over the age of twelve. Let's hope, if he has, his plans are not as far developed as ours."

Tom gave a little laugh.

"Okay," he said, turning to leave and looking at his watch. It was just approaching 2.00 pm. "I'm going to get some lunch. A cheeseburger I think. I don't suppose you've ever had one, have you?"

"I must admit, I did *see* one once, but it didn't look like something I'd want anywhere near my mouth."

He stood up and reached across the desk to Tom, who shook his offered hand before turning to leave. As he opened the door, he nearly collided with a diminutive Chinese girl in a shiny gold mini-dress and impossibly high heels, who was about to knock and enter. The face turned up to his had a smiling mouth and large dark eyes, accentuated by a startled expression.

"Why, Mandy, we really must go on meeting like this," said Tom.

Mandy Lu, the Main Floor receptionist, gave a little laugh.

"That's fine with me, Mr Brown," she said. "You might like to hear this, actually."

She turned to Andrew.

"Just something in from the Lorimar trial, Mr Donald. Well, actually, it's not the Lorimar trial any more. Apparently the man isn't James Lorimar, he's," she consulted her notepad, "John Alexander Deverall. The son of the woman who… "

Tom gasped out loud and leant against the door jamb for support.

"Tom, Tom!"

He heard Andrew speaking a long way off.

"Mr Brown, are you alright?"

"Could you… errr… repeat that, Mandy, please," he said. "Are you absolutely sure you got the name right?"

Mandy looked again at her pad, screwing up her eyes as if this would give her answer more credibility. She said the name slowly.

"John… Alexander… Deverall."

"Christ!" said Tom.

"Is that significant?" asked Andrew, then, "Silly question; it obviously is."

"If it really is him, then he was my best friend and he was killed in action three years ago."

Mandy gave a little squeal, as if she'd just been told a particularly scary ghost story. Andrew offered an obvious explanation.

"Then he must be just *saying* he's this guy. That's more likely than someone coming back from the dead, after all."

Tom was staring into space.

"Alma Deverall," he said aloud to himself. "Of course. I just didn't make the connection!"

Andrew and Mandy said nothing, waiting for him to elaborate.

"No," he said. "It *is* him, definitely. There must have been some mistake over his death. Well, obviously… but why hasn't he been in touch?" He was talking to himself again.

"Best find out the details, Tom. There might be some really simple explanation. Memory loss or something. You know, the trauma of the trial bringing everything back. No point in guessing before you know a bit more."

"Christ," said Tom again. "I have to go."

"You were just leaving anyway – remember?" said Andrew, trying to make light of it.

Tom was pulling his mobile with clumsy haste from the pocket of his trousers. He switched it on as he walked from the room, totally swamped by what he had heard and what he was thinking, and not saying another word to the two people behind him. He had several messages, mostly from Grace. But it was one from Mags, received in the last few minutes, that he opened.

'Jad alive!' it said. 'Prob know already. Get in touch asap.'

He set off to walk the mile to his apartment to retrieve his car from the underground garage, responding to Mags as he went.

'On my way home. Can't believe it.'

He got as far as the corner of Abingdon and Great Peter Street, where, thinking better of it, he hailed a taxi and slumped into the back seat, eyes wide, mind reeling.

★

Brigadier Barry Henshaw carefully filled four cups from the large teapot shaped like an army tank, which had been presented to him when he had, officially anyway, retired from his last command for a quiet life in the garden. Never one for embracing deviations from tradition, his pouring was necessarily slow as the liquid passed through a small, delicate tea strainer, a utensil the like of which Vicky Barrowclough had never seen outside his office. She stood now and passed the filled cups to the other two people sitting around the Brigadier's desk – Peter Drake and Clive Granville. They all settled in their seats as the ceremony ended with the filling of the fourth cup.

"Well," said the Head of G2 Pages, "job done. Jolly good work, everyone. To bring you right up to date," he continued, "you need to know that Deverall will be isolated in Pentonville, ostensibly for his own protection, but also because during his period of remand prior to the trial, he was diagnosed with a rare wasting illness for which there is no known cure. He is, in effect, terminally ill and will die within the next two to three years."

The people in front of him nodded and sipped their tea.

"It's all been very unfortunate but, fingers crossed, no harm done."

He reached over the desk holding out a rectangular plate shaped like a landing craft – part of the same set – to offer a choice of Rich Tea or Custard Creams.

★

Tom picked up a newspaper from a vendor on Vauxhall Bridge Road after alighting from the taxi. It was an early edition and featured the arrival of the prisoner at the Old Bailey, with more pictures of the crowds lining the streets. He had the feeling he was looking back on history; that somehow the world had changed since this had been printed, and what he was holding were images of events that did not matter any more.

He was so overwhelmed and distracted by the news of his friend's reappearance that he initially doubted his ability to drive home. However, the prospect of the Friday afternoon scramble on the underground and then the train made him steel himself to try. He pulled out of the garage into Milton Street, then onto the main road which took him across the river, and past the Brit Oval to join the A3 for the long stretch home.

As he pulled into the drive at Etherington Place, he could remember nothing of the journey he had just made and was surprised to note that it had taken him less than fifty minutes. He came back to earth long enough to wonder how many times he had been caught on camera on the way. He knew it was impossible to achieve this time within the speed limits along the route. It also occurred to him that he had not thought to turn on the radio.

Mags came out to meet him, holding a small wad of printed sheets. They kissed briefly – on the lips – and Mags waved the papers.

"Just printed these off," she said. "E-mail from Tony Dobson; Lorimar's speech. Well, Jad's speech."

There were tears in her eyes.

"It's really true, then," said Tom, putting his arm around her, "he's alive?" His own voice broke a little as he asked the question.

"Yes. It had to be him, didn't it? We saw him yesterday."

"Why would he do it and not tell us?"

Mags said what they were both thinking as they sat together on the sofa in the front sitting room, each holding a glass of wine. "When I think of us at his funeral. He must have known how we'd feel, how upset – how *devastated* – we'd be."

"There must have been a really good reason," said Tom. "I mean, there had to be a lot of people involved, didn't there? You can't fake that sort of death on your own."

"But what about Alma? Unless she knew, of course. Perhaps we were the only ones there that didn't know. But she couldn't have done; remember how she was at the funeral. She must have thought he was dead, too. How could Jad do that to his own mother?" She was getting angry and upset.

"We'll have to wait and see, Mags. One thing I do know – Jad was – is – a kind and considerate person. Whatever the reason, it must have been a good one. Most likely out of his hands; a decision not of his taking."

They were silent for a while.

"You're right," said Mags, eventually. "Jad wouldn't have done anything to hurt us if he could have avoided it. What was I thinking?"

Her watery eyes eventually gave way to the tears behind them. They were neither tears of joy nor sorrow, just tears. An emotional jolt that had to be recognised somehow; crying seemed appropriate. Tom put down his drink and wrapped both his arms around her, holding her to him. They sat in silence like that for a few minutes.

"I'll say one thing for Jad," said Tom, at last. "He's lost none of his magic. He's only been alive again for a few hours and he's managed to get me the biggest cuddle I've had for ages."

Mags laughed through her tears.

"Aye to that," she said, leaning more closely against him.

They sat together like that for several more minutes, rocking gently back and forth, not wanting to move and lost in their separate memories.

The idyllic interlude was shattered by the crashing entry of their son. Jack Tomlinson-Brown, one month off his seventeenth birthday, was already as tall as Tom. Slim and athletic, with classical

182

good looks, he was a magnet for the attention of every girl in Bishop Adcock sixth form college, as well as those spread through all five years of the high school. He seemed to possess none of his parents' and sister's determination and intensity, and his enduring good humour was reflected in an ever-smiling face and an unswerving commitment to make a joke out of just about everything.

"Hey, did you see Uncle Jad has risen from the grave?"

He suddenly noticed their position together on the sofa.

"What's this, then? Mixed Sumo wrestling? My money's on the old man. You'll never get out of that one, Mum."

Neither of them made to move, but Tom could feel Mags shaking with silent laughter in his arms. He smiled across at Jack.

"Listen, if I give you some money, will you go to the movies?"

"Not when there's wrestling on the sofa. No way. Tell you what I will do, though, I'll top up your glasses while you work out how you're going to separate yourselves from each other."

"We're just fine," said Mags, still without moving, "but we'll have the top-up."

Jack went out to get the wine from the fridge, taking his time to return. Mags and Tom straightened up and looked into each others eyes.

"God, but you're beautiful," said Tom, his voice breaking slightly again. "Why can't we always be like this?"

"Don't know," Mags gulped out the words. "But I do know I'm only ever happy when we are."

They kissed gently but passionately, and when they stopped, Tom held her away from him as if to study her.

"God, but you're beautiful," he said.

"You just said that," she gave a happy, tearful laugh.

"I know, but it's the truest thing I can think of right now; apart from the fact that I do love you so much, Mags." He got suddenly serious. "You must know, when we argue, when I stomp off, or you stomp off – not that you ever do, of course –" he added hurriedly, making her laugh again "– I never stop loving you, not ever, not for a fraction of a second. You do know that, don't you?"

Mags smiled back at him.

"Of course I do, darling. It's you and me forever. That's what it is. That's what I want."

They were leaning together to kiss again when Jack, holding the wine bottle, spoke from the doorway.

"Would you mind pouring this yourself; I'm just going upstairs to puke."

"How long have you been standing there?" demanded Mags.

"Long enough," he said. "Oh, look," he added in mock surprise. "I've brought another glass in with the wine. Whatever was I thinking of."

"Let's all drink a toast," said Mags. "To a no-longer-absent friend."

Jack topped up their glasses and filled his own, raising it for the toast.

"A no-longer-absent friend," they said together.

Katey burst into the room.

"Hey, where's mine?"

★

"I think I only met him once or twice," said Katey, "just after you left the Forces. I don't have a clear picture of him at all."

What they called the 'family lounge' at the rear of the property was twelve metres square – the largest room in the house by a long way – and on two levels. In front of the floor-to-ceiling windows along the full length of the room, the lush carpet was just a few inches above the ground outside. On this lower level overlooking the large pond and wildlife area was a long coffee table with a four-seater sofa behind it and a huge armchair at either end. This was their favourite place to sit, and where the four of them had naturally gravitated after dinner – a rare event now for the widely diverse group they had become.

The remainder of the room was at two-steps-higher level, and was chaotic by comparison, with numerous sofas, armchairs, and tables seemingly spread at random around the floor area. Bookshelves covered the whole of the back wall opposite the windows.

"I only remember him from those couple of visits as well," said Jack. "Although he's my Godfather, isn't he? Presumably he was around when I was a baby. But I do know what he looks like – stubble, baseball cap, long leather jacket, carries a Glock 17 or similar… "

Mags gave him a withering look.

"John Deverall is a very special man," she said, "and it's one hundred percent down to him that you still have a father."

"Yes, tell us about that," said Katey. "I remember you saying when Uncle Jad was here that he was the man who saved your life. It didn't really register then, or since, I guess. But now he's back – and famous… "

"Yes, let's hear the story," said Jack.

"Are you two humouring me or something?" asked Tom, one eyebrow raised in suspicion. "This is serious stuff, you know."

"I'm sure they're not," said Mags, "and anyway, I'd like to hear it again."

"Yes, please, Dad," said Katey.

"Okay. Well… in March 2002 in Afghanistan, Jad and I were part of the UK contingent involved in something called Operation Anaconda along with US and Australian forces. The operation was an attempt to flush out Taliban and al-Qaeda rebels from caves at a place called Shah-e-Kot."

"Oh, I've heard of Shah-e-Kot," said Jack. "Really big battle, wasn't it?"

"How did you know that?" asked Katey, genuinely surprised. "I didn't think you knew *anything*."

"That's right, Jack," Tom continued. "It was actually the biggest land battle of the war up to that date. We were initially part of a group of sixty SBS and SAS personnel flown in to Bagram to pave the way for the Marines, and at first we stayed in Bagram to work with the medics."

"Better than being in the fight itself, I guess," said Katey.

"You'd think so, but that's not how it feels when you're there. There was just a stream of injured being flown in to the field hospital. They weren't people we actually knew; they were mainly US Navy SEALS, but they were our sister force and it was… well… harrowing to say the least – and frustrating.

"Anyway, eventually, an eight-man SBS team, including me and Jad… "

"*Commanded* by your father," put in Mags. Tom gave her a big smile.

"That's right. We were flown into the battle zone as part of the reinforcements, but as we landed the Chinook was virtually blown away from around us. God knows how we all survived that, but we did; only to find we were completely surrounded with absolutely no chance of doing anything useful. Some reinforcements, eh!"

"But that was hardly your fault," said Katey.

"Well, no. But it was bloody annoying after waiting that long to be involved."

"Annoying?" put in Jack. "God, that's not how I would have described it. Jean-shitting-scary, perhaps."

"Where do you get these expressions from?" asked Mags.

"Modern English course. Go on, Dad. What happened next? I can't wait to hear if you got out alive or not."

"For God's sake, Jack," said Katey. "Grow up!"

Tom shook his head and smiled.

"Well, we split up after a while and managed to get through the cordon one by one, arranging to regroup later on. And apparently, that's what everyone did – everyone except me, that is. I was last out and got separated from the others, then got pinned down by Taliban fire for nearly seven hours… "

"Seven hours! Christ!" Even Jack couldn't see anything amusing in that.

"… *And* got badly wounded. Two bullets in the chest. Sort of sideways on thankfully, so didn't go through the heart or any major organ, otherwise… "

"Stop!" said Mags. She was watching Katey go white. "Suffice to say, your father was near-fatally wounded."

"And it would have been fatally if it hadn't been for Jad," he continued. "Apparently, when they regrouped and realised I was missing, he went back to look for me." Tom's voice showed signs of breaking and he paused for a while. "It was a *crazy* thing to do, and God knows how he found me. But he did and he *carried* me – not helped me walk – I was all but unconscious by then – he *carried* me over a mile to safety across his shoulders. The Americans called it an escape from the jaws of hell. Not like the Yanks to make understatements, but really there was no way to describe… " his voice tailed off again.

Mags gave way to silent tears. "You see," she said. "We nearly lost him." She moved along the sofa to sit close to Tom and put both her arms round him. They were all silent for a long time.

"Nothing funny to say?" Katey snapped at her brother. Jack shook his head, tears in his eyes.

"Anyway," said Tom, regaining his composure and smiling at his audience. "Just for an encore, Jad went back a little way into the so-called jaws of hell to rescue a US soldier we'd passed on the way. And for that day's work, he received a Presidential Citation from a US General – he was the one, in fact, who used the term 'jaws of hell' – along with the Congressional Medal of Honour – which is the US equivalent of the Victoria Cross, no less. As your mum said, a very special man."

Katey got up and went to join Tom and Mags in the huddle. Jack walked over as well, standing behind the sofa and placing his hands on Tom's shoulders. "Thank you, God, for Uncle Jad," he said, half to himself.

"And you've got Uncle Jad to thank for *your* life as well," Mags said to Katey, when she and Jack had disengaged and returned to their chairs. "Your dad was airlifted to Bagram… "

"Back to the same place where I'd been helping the medics," said Tom.

"… then on to Kabul and home. He arrived back on the 22nd of April 2002." She looked sheepishly across at Tom who smiled broadly and nodded. "And nine months later, to the very day… "

Jack laughed as Katey blushed. "Well, thank you for telling me that, Mum," she said, smiling, "but any more details would be most unwelcome."

They all sat in contented silence for a while.

"It's always amazed me," said Mags eventually, "why he never had any sort of steady relationship in all the time we've known him. *Very* good-looking, charming, funny, seemingly empathetic with just about everyone. What a tremendous catch he would have been… "

"Yes, yes," said Tom. "Let's not get carried away. He's brave, I'll give you that, but in all other aspects I've always thought of him as being rather ordinary, to tell the truth."

Mags laughed.

"Well, of course, compared to you, I guess he is. But isn't everybody?"

"I suppose it is a little bit unfair to compare the rest of the human race with me," said Tom. "Everybody's going to come up short, aren't they? I mean, ask any of Katey's friends at school."

"Anyway," said Jack, "how come you haven't seen him in all this time? I would have thought an experience like that would have bonded you for ever."

"It's a good question. I was recovering at home for three months and Jad went to join Operation Ptarmigan, which was north of Kabul. Soon after I was back in circulation, he transferred to the SAS, and our paths just didn't cross, did they, Mags? He was on leave when I wasn't and vice versa. And then he joined this specialist group which kept him away pretty much all the time.

"When I left the Forces, I was around more when he was on leave and we met up a couple of times – that's when you remember seeing him. And then, of course… "

"You thought he'd been killed." Katey finished for him. "Have you any idea why that was?"

"None at all," he said.

"And it's not important," said Mags. "We thought we'd lost him. And I know it will be a long time before we get him back completely, but eight years is a lot shorter than forever."

★

The family home in the walled estate of Etherington Place, close to East Horsley, and a couple of miles outside the M25 ring road, had been vacated by Tom's parents when his father retired and moved with his mother to the Lake District. It was there where Tom and his three siblings had been born and where he had spent his first seventeen years before joining the army. Tom, Mags and Jack had taken over the place just two months before Katey was born.

The property was a grand Victorian mansion house which had originally stood in grounds of just over seven acres. Tom's parents had retained a plot of two acres for themselves and developed the rest of the land by building five new properties each with one manicured acre of its own.

Tom rose at 6.00 am and went out for his regular Saturday morning run. His route took him six miles, round the estate then the surrounding countryside, through a mature deciduous wood, past two ponds and across a rich meadow, before re-entering the estate, doing the same circuit of the five other houses in reverse, and home.

On the way, he thought about their love-making the previous night. It had been the first time for several weeks and had been affectionate rather than passionate; more satisfying than exciting. But it was pleasing and somehow appropriate for the circumstances, their minds still numbed by the revelations of the day.

It took him just under forty-five minutes to complete the run, a time he was reasonably pleased with, given the infrequency of his exercising these days. Back at the house, he poured himself fresh orange juice and went through to the living room where they had enjoyed the previous evening. Picking up the remote, he switched on the BBC News 24 channel. Just for a change, the story on the screen was as far removed from the Lorimar-Deverall saga as possible.

It was a piece about oil reserves in the Gulf of Mexico. What had been estimated as being the largest hydrocarbon discovery to date at the beginning of the century, with an anticipated extraction period of around twenty-five years, now looked like being exhausted six years sooner. The repercussions were staggering for Pet Euroleum, the main field operator, and its partner, Carbonium Oil. Tom watched in awe the pictures of a gargantuan platform, dwarfing the vessels anchored around it and reducing the personnel on its operations deck to virtual insignificance.

When the story moved onto the financial aspects of the case, Tom's interest gradually waned. Apparently, the implications for the partnership were huge, not least being the vast hardware commitment they had made for the full period, and the hit to pre-tax profits they would now take in depreciating the balance of its current value over a much shorter term. They would be seeking a buyer or buyers for the equipment, including the massive structure he had just seen, to reduce the overall costs of the operation down to manageable levels.

He changed channels and found he was even less interested in the latest unknown celebrity to be voted off a small cruise chip languishing in the Caribbean. He switched off without trying any other alternatives, and returned to the kitchen to replenish his drink.

It was just after seven o'clock, and Mags appeared in the doorway. In spite of her wearing no make-up, and her natural golden-blonde hair looking like she had been recently electrocuted, her overall appearance was stunningly beautiful, as always. She kissed him firmly on the mouth and helped herself to a bottle of water from the fridge.

"You lucky, lucky boy!" said Tom.

"What?" asked Mags.

"Just looking at you and talking to myself," said Tom. "Listen, that run has really wasted me. I'm thinking of going back to bed. What do you think?"

"I think it might be for the best; you can't be too careful at your age. I guess I should come with you to check that you're okay."

"Oh, would you, please?" said Tom, smiling broadly. "That would make such a difference to the next half hour."

They went back to bed together, but the sound of Katey already up and moving noisily around further down the corridor, caused them to revise their initial plans and just lie together contentedly in each other's arms.

"What time are you leaving for the office?" asked Mags, twisting to look at the clock on her bedside table.

"Taking a sicky today," he said. "Phoned Jenny yesterday on the way home. To be honest, I should probably have gone in, but I really couldn't face the thought of it yesterday afternoon."

"Good," said Mags. "Then when you've recovered from your exertions – and as it seems unlikely you'll be exerting yourself again in the next few minutes" – she added, as they heard Katey clumping about at the top of the stairs in her wooden-soled flip-flops – " I don't suppose you fancy a drive to the new nature reserve at Kings Leyburn? They've got over a hundred avocets that they think will be over-wintering there for the first time this year."

"Avocets?" said Tom, furrowing his brow. "That's a type of missile, isn't it? Very popular back in the Falklands War – or unpopular, depending which side… "

Mags pulled away and hit him with a pillow. Tom responded in kind and very quickly they had both rolled off the bed and were toe-to-toe swinging at each other, both with eyes closed and giggling like small children.

"What's going on in there?" shouted Katey, from behind the closed door.

"Your father's attacking me," Mags shouted back.

"Oh, right." They heard Katey going down the stairs, as if reassured by the statement.

They looked at each other and shrugged, then laughed.

"Look," said Mags, pretending to be serious again. "Surrender now or I'll start fighting my best."

Tom threw down his pillow and raised his hands.

"Okay. I give in on one condition. We have to consummate the cease-fire."

"Sounds fair," said Mags grabbing the front of his tee-shirt and pulling him on top of her as she fell back on the bed.

"What's going on in there?" It was Jack's voice outside the door. "Can I come in?"

"No!" they shouted in unison.

"Thought not," said Jack and clumped off down the stairs as well.

"This is hopeless," said Tom, shaking his head, and then kissing Mags long and tenderly. "Let's have breakfast and go and inspect these exocets. Just a minute, don't we have to go through Little Winton?"

"Well, I suppose we *could* go that way," said Mags, wide-eyed with innocence. "Or we could take a massive detour and go round by Dorking... "

"I love Dorking at this time of year... "

"... and the reserve closes at eleven," added Mags.

"Why?" said Tom, frowning hard. Mags thought for a moment.

"Missile practice," she said. Tom burst out laughing.

They both suddenly became serious, as if this last remark had reminded them of something.

"You know we haven't mentioned Jad yet?" said Tom.

"I guess we covered just about everything last night. What are you going to do about him?"

"Well, firstly, I'd like to understand what was behind his disappearance. I thought I'd make a few calls this weekend, you know, to try and find out what happened. Still got plenty of contacts in the SBS; that would be a good place to start. And if no joy there,

Dad might be able to pull a few strings with his old top brass buddies, at least get a few leads to follow up. Failing that, then… "

"There is another way," Mags interrupted.

Tom looked at her.

"You could ask Jad," she said.

Tom continued to look at his wife, shaking his head and with a smile spreading across his face.

"Who needs a brain when I've got you? Of course I could, and I will."

★

Jackie Hewlett phoned Tom at around midday, her name coming up on the display on the mobile which was sitting in the hands-free. He chose not to answer. He was currently showing off in his R8 with the top down weaving through the country lanes en route to Kings Leyburn via Little Winton. He looked in appreciation at the beautiful woman beside him. Mags was wearing the loose chiffon dress which Tom had always said was his favourite. Pulled in with a matching belt around her slim waist, it lifted the hemline to just above her knees. Right now, reclining in the passenger seat, she had pulled it up higher, revealing nearly all of her long slender legs. Tom reluctantly switched his attention back to the road.

"By the way," he said, as they squeezed through the narrow main street of the allegedly-threatened village past the Saturday market, "are you for or against a by-pass?"

"I haven't decided yet," said Mags.

Tom turned to look at her. She seemed deadly serious.

"You *are* joking?" he said.

She laughed.

"Yes, of course I'm joking. We're against it."

"Why? This is a gorgeous little village. Why wouldn't you want to divert the traffic round it?"

"Because just ahead is a notorious bottleneck at the junction with the A30, and it is absolutely certain that a by-pass will encourage far too much traffic for the junction to cope with and people will come through the village to avoid tail-backs on the new by-pass and try to join the A30 just north of… "

"Okay, okay, I give in!" said Tom. "That'll teach me to ask an open question. Anyway, good for you. It's obviously been argued through very thoroughly, and all I can say is, if it saves this village from the sort of stop-start we are experiencing at this precise bloody moment getting any worse, then I wish you every success." He leant over, gently patting her knee, and leaving his hand there. "I do actually mean that, you know."

"Well, thank you," she said. "Now will you please move your hand?"

He laughed and pulled his hand away. She grabbed it and placed it back on her knee.

"I didn't say *remove* it," she said, seductively. "I said *move* it. Perhaps a bit higher?"

He obliged, albeit quite a lot higher.

★

David returned from the gym at 4.30 pm and, with a bottle of Stella at his elbow, set out to read the *Guardian* cover to cover. His living room was not quite as spartan as his office, but still fairly minimal in its furnishings. A sofa and armchair were placed at ninety degrees to each other with a long low table in front and a matching side-table in the angle between them. The main feature of the room was a large multi-fuel burning stove at the side of which, in one alcove, was a drinks cabinet and in the other a forty-two-inch television. So far, his weekend had gone exactly to schedule – his *every*-weekend schedule. Saturday was the only day he bought a paper; never seeming to have time to do justice to one during the week. On Sunday he finished reading all the sections from the previous day.

He, like so many others that day, noted the similarity, now they were both set down in print, of Deverall's speech to the one delivered by George Holland just two days earlier. What made the likeness even more remarkable was the enormous difference in the two people themselves. They were as diametrically opposite as it was possible to imagine two human beings to be. One, an open, mild-mannered retired school teacher; the other a cool, calculating killer with a mysterious past.

His reflections were shattered by the arrival, unannounced, of

193

his daughter, Linny. Belinda Louise Gerrard was very tall and 'well-made' as she described herself. She had a plain but laughing, friendly face and exuded energy and joie-de-vie. She wore a loose dress over jeans, and her mass of hair was barely restrained in a make-shift ponytail. She was accompanied by her latest male exhibit, an even taller, good-looking young man whose natural expression appeared to be a wide beam. He was called Caz and seemed likeable enough, if not a little subservient, addressing David as 'Chief Inspector'.

After an hour of relaxed conversation, during which time his host on numerous occasions insisted Caz called him David, they rose to leave. Linny gave her father a big hug and an affectionate kiss on the cheek. Caz shook his hand warmly.

"Great to meet you, Chief Inspector."

"I give up," said David.

Linny laughed.

Caz beamed.

After they left, David microwaved and consumed a Cumberland Pie and settled himself in front of the television to watch *High Noon* on Sky Western Classics. To get himself suitably in character, he placed a newly-opened bottle of Bourbon and a shot glass on the side table next to him.

As he watched the approaching climax, with the Frank Miller gang walking line-abreast through the deserted streets of Hadleyville seeking their quarry, he imagined how similar the scene might have been in the minutes before the killing of the Bradys. The gang facing the cornered man in the cul-de-sac, believing there could be only one outcome to the encounter; the stranger's gun blazing, too quick for Jimmy to fire his own.

He checked his watch as the ex-Marshall and his new bride left town leaving his discarded badge in the dust. It was almost half past ten, and he was almost half-way down his bottle of whiskey. He decided to head for the bunkhouse.

As he switched off the set, his mobile rang.

CHAPTER 13

The Dog and Duck had been busy all day; there had hardly been a lull between the normally distinct lunchtime and evening sessions. A large number of the midday personnel, including all the Village Ramblers, returning from their regular Saturday walk, had stayed the course and, a little worse for wear but buoyant and happy all the same, had gathered themselves for the push to dinner and beyond. The atmosphere was one of celebration, with George still the centre of attention and enjoying his luminary status.

At just after 8.30 pm the pub phone rang in both bars and the dining room, like a warning bell in a fire station. One of the waitresses in the dining room picked up the receiver on the wall near the kitchen entrance. The diners listened to her half of the conversation with increasing interest and alarm.

"Hello, Dog and Duck… Sorry, could you speak up, please, it's really noisy here… Settlement Road?… What's happened?… Blocked off?… No, I don't know anything about that; it was open before. We've had a lot of people come… He's not here at the moment, just tell me again… Oh, right, blocked off by hay bales… Rolled across the road… You have?… Yes, okay, I'll find him and tell him… Yes, I'll do it right now… Yes, right away."

By now she had the attention of everyone in the room.

"What's happened, Lisa?" asked Alistair Neville, a local farmer, almost certainly knowing the answer.

"That was Redburn. He said someone has blocked off Settlement Road; rolled a load of those big round bales out of a field and – Redburn says – sealed off the village. He said tell Jed as quickly as possible, get everybody out... he said he's already phoned the police, but they won't be able to get through." She was starting to sound panicky herself, reflecting the looks of the people in the room listening to her. "What's it about?"

"Trouble, Lisa," said Alistair. "Find Jed, I'll warn them in the bar."

Most of the diners had risen from their seats. Alistair rushed out of the room, shouting as he went.

"They're back! They're coming! They've blocked off the road!"

As he was speaking, Fred Dawson came rushing in through the entrance from the car park at the back where he had been having a smoke.

"They're coming over the fields – hundreds of them!"

"Right!" Alistair Neville shouted above the increasing noise. "Everyone stay inside and lock and bolt the doors! Come on, Ben!" he turned to his brother who was leaning against the bar, a position he had occupied for several hours.

"What? Where're we going?" he slurred, eyes widening and struggling for balance and focus.

"Back to the house. Come on!" he repeated.

The two men left hastily through the front double-doors, Alistair half-supporting his brother. He turned back briefly.

"Don't forget, lock the doors. Do it *now*!"

They did as he said, then everyone crowded to the back room, looking through the rear windows at the gently rising field with the faint red-orange glow of the lights of the estate beyond and below it silhouetting the brow of the hill. The darkening skyline was broken by the bobbing shapes of figures descending towards the pub, getting shorter as they dropped below the brow, closing on their target. They re-appeared as the watchers' eyes adjusted and picked them out again, now against the backdrop of the slope.

Jed Smithers the landlord arrived, sweating, from the cellar. He pushed his way to the windows through the watching people. Talk amongst them was rising in volume with the increasing panic. Some seemed determined to make a run for it to the relative safety of their homes. Others were pointing out, rightly, that it was too late.

"Best get back from the windows," said Jed, but not loudly enough to be heard by everyone above their own frantic voices.

The crowd had now descended the field, dropping out of sight briefly behind the high fence at the rear of the pub car park before re-appearing again as they climbed over it. They were now only a few yards away, growing in numbers to around sixty or seventy, with more still waiting to climb the fence to join them. They ranged in age from pre to mid-teens, many tiny by comparison to others, sporting hooded tops, tee-shirts, designer jeans, leather jackets. They walked towards the pub through the cars parked along the fence, stopping to twist off a few door-mirrors. They spotted some crates of empty bottles which they lifted out, throwing them violently against the cars, cracking windscreens and smashing lights, then at the pub walls and windows. The people recoiled as several flew in to the room they were watching from. Three of them went down, blood streaming from cuts to their heads, necks and arms.

The crowd outside pressed up to the windows, leering in through the shredded panes and screeching threats and obscenities. Many of the women were now crying or screaming uncontrollably. Then one of the gang held up a hand to silence the mass behind him. He was a tall, well-built black youth, one of the oldest there and clearly the leader of the pack. He wore a leather jacket over a hooded top, the hood itself pulled well forward over his face. He shouted into the pub through one of the broken windows.

"We want one person, that's all! Otherwise we'll kill the fucking lot of you!"

The noise inside abated at the sound of his voice.

"George Holland, are you in there, you fucking little twat?"

Everyone turned instinctively to look at the person just named. George, who was at the back of the room and not visible to the youth, went deathly white; Irene clung to him and starting sobbing, her whole body shaking with fear.

Jed was the first to react.

"He's not here! Go home; the police will be here any minute!"

"Not unless they come in fucking helicopters."

There was a sinister chorus of jeers and laughter.

"Get into the front," said Jed, "as many behind the bar as we can squeeze in. The rest can stand on the stairs. At least they won't be able to hit us with anything."

They all did as they were bid; two of the people who had been injured were helped through the small hallway, away from the crowd gathered at the back, and made as comfortable as possible seated on the stairs. The third they laid gently on the floor. She was bleeding profusely, with a jagged piece of glass protruding from her throat and had all but passed out. Jed phoned the police from his mobile, asking for ambulances as well, and tended her the best he could using the first aid kit from behind the bar. The wound was such that there was little he could do to stem the flow without restricting her breathing.

"I really hope Ben and Alistair got home safely," someone muttered, bitterly.

As they entered the main bar area, they could see that many of the gang had already gone round to the front of the pub; the place was completely surrounded. The wail of police sirens could be heard – from a large number of vehicles – but it was obvious that they must be stationary – the sound was constant, not getting any louder. Missiles now rained in through the front windows, this time including bricks and lumps of concrete. One youth had picked up a garden spade from the pub yard and was crashing it against the double front doors like a sledge hammer, shattering glass and splintering wood.

Suddenly, above the deafening noise of this and the gang's shouting and whooping, came the even louder sound of an explosion. It was obvious from the sudden end to the hostilities that this was not of their doing. Everyone outside stopped and looked down the road towards the centre of the village. The booming voice of Alistair Neville filled the temporary calm.

"Next one takes someone's fucking head off!"

The gang fell back from the front of the pub and spread out across the road facing the sound of Alistair's approach. The gang leader shouted back.

"You George Holland?"

"What if I am?" Alistair's voice again.

"Then you're fucking dead! Anyway, you're not him. And this has fuck-all to do with you."

Inside the pub, people realised what was the source of the explosion.

"Oh bloody hell," said Jed, peering cautiously out, "it's Al and

Ben with a couple twelves. What the hell do they think they're doing?"

"Jesus!" said someone else. "Ben's as pissed as a newt."

"I've got to go out there," said George. "Somebody's going to get killed."

They all shouted down the idea, and Irene clung more tightly to him, but he made a move towards the door.

"I'll come with you," said Fred. "Look, no-one should say which one is George. But he's right, it's not the Nevilles' fight and they're out there and we're in here."

"We'll all go," said Clive Taylor. "All together. Come on. Now!"

They pulled open the damaged doors and almost everyone spilled into the road, including many of the non-residents of the village. The scene before them was reminiscent of another time, another place. The Cullen Field mob, probably a hundred strong was fanned out across the road, several deep, to their left. To their right, the two brothers were walking steadily towards them, Ben holding a twelve-bore to his shoulder, pointed straight at them, Alistair reloading his own.

George stepped out into the road, facing the Nevilles, arms raised.

"Hold it, boys," he said.

The two farmers towered over George. They were both huge men with barrel chests and broad shoulders, each with a mass of wild hair. Alistair had a red bushy beard streaked with grey; Ben was sporting about three days' stubble.

"Stand aside, George!" boomed Alistair.

"Oh, so this is George!" shouted the tall black youth. "Well, nice of you to come out to see us."

The rest of the people from the pub had followed George to stand with him in front of the two brothers. They all turned to face the gang. 'The Thin Grey Line', as one paper would later describe them.

"Jokey!" shouted the youth at the front. A small boy pushed his way through the front line to stand beside him. His black angelic little face was wide-eyed and shining with excitement. He wore a small backpack.

"Okay, Denny!"

The gang's leader and a smaller white youth in a black military-style jacket and white jeans and with a scarf tied behind and pulled up to cover the lower half of his face, reached into the bag and each pulled out a handgun. Without hesitation the black youth raised his arm, aiming directly at George, no more than ten yards away. But as this was happening, the Nevilles burst through the rank of villagers, with Ben firing as he moved quickly forward.

His shot took away half the leader's face, splattering those behind him with pellets, blood and human tissue. Amazingly, he did not go down immediately. The villagers screamed and gasped in horror as the youth seemed to look at them in surprise with his remaining eye as it glazed over in death and he slumped, almost in slow motion, onto the road.

His gun had flown from his hand with the impact of the shot, and even before he hit the ground, it had been grabbed by another of the gang. The white youth with the other gun looked across in disbelief at his dead companion. He turned back towards George, eyes flashing in raw, uncontrolled anger. Holding the gun with two hands, arms stretched out on front of him, he aimed at George again and took a few steps towards him, ignoring the threat from the shotguns.

Alistair was shouting as loudly as he could above the mayhem. "Stop this! Stop! No more! Go!"

The villagers broke ranks and started running; only a few stood their ground to try to stop the incident escalating further. George was frozen with fear, looking directly into the barrel of the handgun, now just a few yards away.

The youth squeezed on the trigger.

Someone screamed, "No!" and threw themselves at George to push him aside.

He fired, from no more than three yards.

A body hit the ground.

Ben loosed off his second shot, and the youth with the gun went down, badly wounded but holding on to his weapon.

He raised it and fired at Ben this time. The bullet hit him in the throat, bringing a fountain of blood.

Ben dropped the shotgun, slumping to his knees, coughing and grasping the wound with both hands.

Alistair stepped forward and swung the butt of the shotgun in a wide arc, clubbing the youth hard on the top of his head with a sickening thud.

He looked across anxiously at Ben, and then shouted again.

"Let's stop this now!"

Salvoes of missiles were being thrown from the back of the crowd when at last the sound of the sirens increased in volume as the police cars breeched the barricades.

In the no-man's-land between the two groups all eyes were now on Jokey. He had been the one who picked up the gun which the leader had released in his death throes. He now stood motionless, his face still with the same look of exhilaration, but with his beautiful big eyes now leaking tears. He was holding the gun with both hands and pointing it straight at Alistair. The farmer smiled, speaking gently to him, "Now then, Jokey. That is your name, isn't it? Please give me that. You don't want to hurt anyone, do you?"

"Give the man the gun, Jokey," someone else said. "It's okay; you won't get in to trouble."

Alistair walked slowly up to him with deliberate steps, and reached out his arm.

"Jokey... "

The boy closed his eyes and pulled the trigger.

Alistair was dead before he hit the ground, shot between the eyes. Ben cried out in grief and anguish, almost choking on his own blood and dragging himself across the ground to his brother. Jokey placed the gun carefully on the ground, turned and ran towards the rest of the gang, who were rapidly dispersing as the first police vehicle came into sight, followed by three anti-riot vans and an ambulance. Someone grabbed him by the hand and ran after the rest, round to the back of the pub, to climb back over the fence and return across the field.

Ben was howling loudly, his voice distorted into an unearthly, high-pitched rattle. A few yards way, George Holland, with less sound and more dignity, cradled his wife's head in his arms as her precious life slipped away.

★

David Gerrard wasn't sure whether he said "Shit" just before or just after he pressed the 'answer' key on his mobile, so his opening words were extra polite just in case.

"Hello, David Gerrard here. Who is it, please?"

"Detective Chief Inspector, it's John Lawrence," said a familiar voice, a uniformed inspector from Parkside. "Sorry to bother you at this time, but thought you'd want to know. We've had a multiple killing in Meadow Village. A bloody gunfight, it seems, like the OK Corral. Four dead, five more injured, three of them seriously."

"Meadow Village! Bloody hell," said David. "What happened?"

"Big gang from Cullen Field, witnesses say probably over a hundred, two shooters carried by a young kid. Couple of farmers from the village with twelve-bores... Happened outside the Dog and Duck."

"So who are the dead?" asked David.

"Two of the Cullen Field gang, one of the farmers and – here's the real sickener, sir – Irene Holland, George Holland's wife. Hit by accident. It seems the gang had gone there to get George – called him out from the pub."

"Are you in charge there, John."

"Yes, sir."

"I'll come right down."

"Okay. I thought you should know first. This must be linked to the other killings. Shall I send a car for you?"

"Thanks, John, but I'll make my own way down. What's happening there now?"

"Ambulances have taken all injured away, and Mrs Holland; just three of the four dead remaining. SOCOs looking for bits and pieces, but we've around forty witnesses and no mystery. Only issue is who fired the first shot, seems like it could have been one of the villagers, but I guess that's academic anyway. The kids came armed and intent on killing – so no question who started it. We're still taking statements."

"Okay, be right with you; you can fill in the details when I get there. By the way," – David couldn't help himself – "isn't it always the baddies that shoot first?"

"Not necessarily, sir. They always *draw* first, but the good guys are usually quicker and beat them to it."

In spite of the sick feeling in his stomach, David managed a brief chuckle at the spontaneous reply. Inspector Lawrence probably watched the same films he did.

"See you soon, John. Anything else I should be getting my head round while I'm on my way?"

John thought for a few moments.

"Well, I'm not sure if this is something that *anyone* can get their head round, but the kid who fired the last fatal shot was, we think, about eight-years-old."

"Jesus!"

Having turned down the offer of a lift, David had to decide how to get there. Omar Shakhir was his best bet, he thought, the only one of the group he knew for certain would not have been drinking that evening. Omar was both the joker and the genius of David's team. In addition, he was tall and very handsome, further enhancing his popularity with the girls in the team and with the wider female population at Parkside. He was also happily married and teetotal which somewhat hampered their opportunities for developing his social life.

He scrolled through the 'contacts' on his mobile, found Omar and pressed 'call'.

The Detective Constable answered quickly.

"Sir?" he said, seeing David's name on his display.

"Sorry to phone at this time, Omar. Do you fancy a spot of overtime? And before you answer that, I mean right now. If you can't make it, that's okay."

"Hold on, please, sir."

He was obviously checking with his wife. David sensed the discussion was relaxed, even though that did not stop him feeling guilty.

"That would be fine, sir. Where do you want to meet? At the station?"

"No, we're back at the Killing Fields, I'm afraid, or close by anyway. Could you pick me up? You know where I live, don't you?" A rhetorical question.

"Of course, sir. About fifteen minutes."

"Fine. Thanks, Omar. Please give my apologies to your wife."

★

Katey and Jack were both out when Tom and Mags arrived back at the house just before 6.00 pm. Jack phoned at around half-past.

"Hi, Mum. Just to let you know, I'm eating round at Gilly's and staying over. Is that okay?"

"Yes, that's fine, just as long as I know where you are."

"Oh, come on, Mum," he said, teasing her, "I'm letting you know out of courtesy and consideration, not because I *have* to, you know."

"So why did you ask if it was okay?" said Mags.

"Just part of the aforementioned courtesy and consideration," replied Jack.

"And it's very much appreciated, my love," said Mags. "Have a nice time."

"You, too, Mum. More Sumo wrestling planned for this evening?"

"Mmmm, you never know."

Jack laughed.

"See you tomorrow."

A little later, Katey returned with two of her friends for an evening in and a sleep-over. They would make themselves a meal, Katey said, leading the raiding party into the kitchen. As usual, her friends seemed more interested in spending the evening with Tom than with Katey. It took a gargantuan effort to extract them from her father's personal space and into her personal lounge, which adjoined her bedroom. This was in spite of the room being fitted out like a film-cum-recording studio with a massive wall-mounted television screen and a wireless sound system featuring eight speakers invisibly set into the walls.

After the girls had finally left them alone, Mags reclaimed the kitchen to prepare a stir-fry for the two of them. Tom remembered Jackie's call and listened to her message.

"Tom, sorry to call you at home. Just checked your website and noticed you've no surgery today. Wondered if you could phone me when you get the chance. Andrew's been in touch this morning, told me I'm fronting this New Regime thing, and said he's already told you. Look, I know I've been going on a bit lately about who's responsible for what. Put it down to insecurity, if you like. You've not been on the wrong side of Andrew yet; you don't know what it's like. But this just doesn't seem fair; these are your ideas, your proposals. I'd like to talk to you about it, if you've time, before Monday. Even get together and make a bit of a start, if possible. Anyway, sorry about the long and rambling message. Speak later. Bye."

Tom was thankful he had not picked the message up earlier during their day out. It would certainly have put a damper on the enjoyment, because his immediate reaction was an overwhelming feeling of guilt about his and Andrew's plan to deceive her. He knew how much it would mean to her to be trusted with the Party's proposals. It would be a massive personal sacrifice if she were to decline the opportunity on the basis of wanting to see fair play.

He opened his laptop and logged on to Corporate Time to check their schedules for the coming week. Then he phoned her back, relieved that the call went straight through to voicemail.

"Hi, Jackie. Thank you for the call and my apologies for the delay in replying. Just to reassure you, I am perfectly okay with you leading this thing. It should be you, and I'm looking forward to working with you on it. Unfortunately I can't make a start this weekend, but we both seem to have some time available Monday and Tuesday mornings, and Wednesday afternoon. I've booked that on CT. Hope that's okay. Enjoy the rest of the weekend. Bye, Jackie."

After their meal, Mags and Tom settled together on the sofa in the small front sitting room where Jack had burst in on them the previous afternoon. It was their favourite room in the house, because it had no TV, no hi-fi, no PC. Just a sofa and two armchairs round an occasional table, a couple of wing chairs in the bay window looking out onto the front drive and garden and, very importantly, a drinks cabinet. A room designed just for each other's company, as Tom described it.

They were on the point of turning in, and had just popped their heads round Katey's door to say goodnight, with much giggling and eyelash fluttering from her friends, when Tom's mobile rang. He saw that the call was from Jenny Britani and checked the time – 11.10 pm. It had to be something important or urgent or both. He sat down on the bed and pressed 'answer'.

"Yes, Jenny?"

"Oh, Mr Brown, I'm so sorry to call you at this time, but I've just made the last check of your voicemails at the office and there's one from Chief Constable Rayburn, phoned a minute or two before eleven. No message, but she left a number for you to call." She read it out and he wrote it down on a notepad on his bedside table. "I thought I'd better pass it on."

"That's fine, Jenny. You did the right thing, thank you. I'm sorry that you had to interrupt your Saturday evening."

"I don't mind. Hope it's nothing bad. Night, Mr Brown."

"God, what's this about?" he muttered, going downstairs to make the call. Afterwards he went back upstairs to Mags.

"What's the matter?" she asked, as he appeared, white-faced, at the bedroom door. "Not Jack?"

"No, no," Tom re-assured her quickly. "Nothing like that."

"What then?"

"It's Irene – Irene Holland. She's been… murdered, shot down outside the pub in Meadow Village. God, poor George – well, poor Irene, of course, but… God… I should go and see… " although he was not sure what or who.

"How?" asked Mags. "When?

"Tonight, not long ago. A big gang from the estate attacked the village. They were after George; apparently Irene just got in the way. Oh, God, I can't begin to think what George must be feeling. She is – was – a really wonderful lady. Look, I must go to the village tomorrow – can't do anything tonight. Will you come with me? Please."

Mags hesitated, just for a moment.

"Of course," she said. "Come to bed. As you say, there's nothing you can do tonight."

"Yes, yes, you're right."

★

David and Omar arrived at 11.15 pm. The pub was illuminated by the flashing blue lights of a dozen police vehicles and several portable search-lights trained on the area where the action had taken place. As he approached, David's first impression was that it looked like an out-door disco experiencing a problem with the sound system. In the centre of the scene were three small tents each surrounded by movable posts on circular bases with crime-scene tape stretched between them. SOCOs in white hooded all-in-ones were searching the perimeter whilst others were crawling around close to the tents. Camera flashes added to the light display.

Omar's vehicle was stopped 100 yards or so short of the pub then waved through as the police constable recognised the DCI before he had chance to show him his ID. John Lawrence walked over to the car as Omar pulled up alongside one of the police vehicles. The inspector was tallish, well built, and with a friendly face dominated by a large moustache.

The front of the Dog and Duck was totally wrecked. All the downstairs windows were smashed and several in the living accommodation upstairs. One of the double-doors was lying inside the entrance; it had fallen away when the customers had come out to face the gang.

"Thanks for coming, sir," he said as David got out.

"No, thank you for the early heads-up. You know DC Shakhir?"

"Yes." The two men nodded to each other.

"So take me through the carnage, please, John."

The inspector told the story from when the waitress had taken the call right up to the delayed arrival of the emergency forces.

"What were those things they'd used to block the road?" asked David.

"They'd rolled about ten big hay bales onto the road from a field and dumped them on their sides. Impossible to get them upright again by hand. Another farmer from the village, Redburn Price – the one who made the call to the pub and the initial one to the police – he ran to his place and got his tractor and shoved them off the road. It's a good job he did; not sure what would have happened otherwise."

"And Mrs Holland? Did you say she died instantly?"

"No not instantly, but in the ambulance at the scene. They took her away. The other three bodies are still here."

"And the injured? How are they doing?"

"One woman got a shard of glass almost through her throat. She's lost a lot of blood – touch and go apparently with her. The guy Ben, Alistair Neville's brother – Alistair's the one the young kid shot – got hit in the throat. He should be okay, looked a lot worse than it is – bad enough, mind. And two more with minor cuts on face and arms. Seems likely that there could be quite a number of the gang with minor injuries as well – sprayed by the shot that killed the first one. One's been taken to hospital with eye injuries. We found him afterwards in the car park, staggering around, blinded and screaming. Paramedics couldn't say whether it would be permanent; they won't know for a while."

"And the young kid who fired the last shot?"

"Yes, we haven't got a full name yet. They called him 'Jokey' – presumably a nick-name. We think he's the brother of the one doing all the talking – the first one who was killed. If that's true then, obviously, once we ID one of them, we'll know the other. We're all over the place down there right now." He pointed in the direction of the estate, where on the skyline the usual orange glow was supplemented by blue flashes.

"Quite a few seem to know who they are but won't give us a name. But they reckon the young lad is eight years old."

David shook his head sadly.

"What sort of reaction are we getting on the estate?" he asked.

"Too early to tell, really. Shock and disappointment, so far, but not sure how they'll react when it comes out that one of the villagers has killed two kids."

"Well, they were ecstatic enough when Deverall killed three of them. Why would this be different?"

"It might not be; just waiting to see. It would be a shame if the good feeling between the village and the estate was to end. One thing for certain, there seems to be a massive amount of sympathy for Irene and for George. He's a real popular figure there; he's said a lot of good things about Cullen Field since the Brady thing."

"Let's hope it'll be enough to get the honeymooners through it with their marriage intact," said David.

He looked around at the scene.

"Can we move the bodies now, sir?" asked the Inspector. "Do you want to see them first?"

"No, I don't want to see them, but I guess I should."

He looked briefly into the three tents. It was something he had never got used to.

"They can go now," he said. "We'll just have a mosey round."

The ground was marked out to reflect the last act with its shattering climax. David recognised one of the SOCOs.

"Hi, Karen," he said.

"Oh, evening, sir," said Karen Eccleston, standing up and pushing back her hood to reveal a mass of blonde hair tucked down the back of her suit. She was small and sturdy, with a round, pretty face. "Bad job."

"You said it. Where does everything fit?" he asked looking round.

"Well, that's where Ben Neville was shot, and he crawled over to his brother there," she pointed as she spoke to a pool of blood spread over a large area, where Ben had initially gone down, and a trail leading to one of the tents.

"That's where Mrs Holland died," Karen went on, indicating another pool of blood. Then she pointed to the tent covering the first youth who had been hit. "That guy lost half his head," she said, "It's all around here." She swept her arm round the gory mess close to the tent where tissue from the scalp and head cavity mingled with the splashes of blood.

"And that's where the second kid was clubbed," she explained, indicating the third tent. David gave a shudder.

"If you think this is bad," said Karen, "I suggest you give the pub a miss. A poor woman in there nearly had her head taken off by flying glass. Blood's about a foot deep."

"Thanks, Karen; we'll take your advice. Thanks for the sightsee."

"You're welcome, sir."

They walked round to the back of the pub, crunching over broken glass. A crate had been placed on its side against the fence to provide a step for the police and SOCOs to climb over it. He eased himself over, followed by Omar, and they walked up the field to the brow and looked down onto the estate below. The scene was similar there, with police vehicles in many of the streets nearest to them, blue lights strobing everywhere. He turned and looked back down to Meadow Village along the route the attackers had taken, visualising the tranquil country scene in the gently fading light, suddenly transformed into a battlefield running with rivers of crimson.

David looked at his watch.

"Midnight," he said aloud. It triggered a thought. "At the lost and found," he added.

Omar looked at him questioningly.

"Meatloaf," said David.

"Oh, right," said Omar, nodding his head vigorously, as if that explained everything.

★

The oldest fifty or so cottages of Meadow Village dated back about 250 years. Between then and the present day, more than three times that number of houses had been added to the early settlement, but they had, in effect, just filled in the spaces between the original buildings. So the village had not grown in area, just in density, and the houses themselves had been tastefully integrated into the surroundings. In addition to the Dog and Duck public house, the village also boasted a church, community hall, shop-cum-post office, and a few small working farms. All these were clustered together in a tight residential area and surrounded by fields, which were used mostly for grazing sheep, cattle and horses.

Tom and Mags's visit to the stricken village on the Sunday morning was intended to be brief, personal and unreported; a plan which seemed naïve in retrospect for two people with such a high profile in the public eye. They drove there immediately after an early breakfast, leaving a note for Katey who, along with her friends, were still asleep upstairs.

They arrived just before 10.00 am. The police, recognising Tom, waved them through the barrier at the top of Settlement Lane, and they pulled up outside the pub in almost exactly the same spot where the taxi had dropped him off when he met George just before the 3AF debate. The memory brought a sick feeling to his stomach and standing tears to his eyes. Mags reached across to him and squeezed his hand as they opened the doors to get out.

The village was overrun by people. There were still four police vehicles there and a team of SOCOs had returned to view the scene in the daylight. In addition, there was now the expected media circus, this being an extension to the headline chronicles of the past couple of months and an incident which brought together the two previously parallel-running stories in a dramatic collision. Several huge vans representing all the major TV news channels were parked at the side and back of the Dog and Duck. Many reporters and technicians were standing around chatting and drinking coffee – supplied by the pub – whilst even more were setting up equipment. Newspaper journalists were out in force, along the full length of Main Street, the village end of Settlement Lane, and were hurrying around intercepting residents for interviews.

Mercifully, the area outside the Dog and Duck had been hosed down and there was none of the graphic evidence of the slaughter from the previous evening. The shattered windows were boarded up except for one where the pane was already being replaced. Jed Smithers was directing operations and did a classic double-take when he looked across at the new arrivals.

"Tom – Mr Brown," he said, recognising him, "I'm Jed Smithers, landlord."

Tom smiled and shook the man's extended hand.

"Yes, I remember, Jed. This is my wife, Maggie."

Jed had not taken his eyes off Mags since his double-take.

"Pleased to meet you, Mrs Brown," he said.

Mags smiled back at him.

"Terrible business, Jed," said Tom, drawing the landlord's gaze away from his wife. "Have you seen any of the villagers this morning?"

"Just those passing to go for the papers. People can hardly speak, they're so upset. It'll never be the same again, I don't reckon. Unless you can build a wall round that bloody place."

He pointed in the direction of the estate.

"Has anyone seen George? I can't begin to imagine how he must be feeling."

"I saw Fred Dawson earlier. He'd called in to see him. Said he looked just about dead himself. Poor Irene; she was a lovely… " His voice broke and he turned away.

"Yes, she was," said Tom. "A lovely lady. We're just going to have a walk round. Which is George's house – just in case we decide to call in to pay our respects?"

"The white cottage with the arch over the gate."

Tom followed the direction of the landlord's pointing finger.

"Okay, thanks, Jed."

They walked further into the village, initially escaping the attention of the press. A local radio crew, a girl reporter and male technician, were doing a piece live outside George's house.

"I wonder how long all these have been camped in the village?" said Mags.

"Most of the night, probably," said Tom, as they came up to George's cottage. "The story's twelve hours old now. We'll call in on the way back," he added, wanting to avoid the radio crew. Then he seemed uncertain. "Do you think I should? It won't look like a publicity thing, will it?"

"Not if we try to call when there's no-one around, only I think that might be difficult." She nodded towards the pub where Jed was talking to a few of the television people and directing their attention towards George's house. "He's probably telling them right now that you're here," she added. "Anyway, if they do ask you for comments, you can say this is a private visit to a personal friend and you have nothing further to say today. I think most people would respect that."

"Most people," Tom repeated. "This is the press, not 'most people'. But that's a good idea, Mags. Let's go."

He turned back suddenly, putting an arm round Mags's waist and steering her behind the reporter through George's gate. He heard her say, "A couple, as I speak, are going up the path presumably to pay their respects to the bereaved campaigner. Just a minute, I do believe… "

Tom turned to her as she spoke and put his right forefinger to his lips in a request for secrecy. The reporter seemed taken by surprise and stopped in mid-sentence.

"I'll just check that out," she said, recovering quickly but not giving away the visitor's identity.

Tom mouthed 'thank you' and turned to the door, pressing the bell.

Fred had not exaggerated when he described George's appearance to Jed. His face was ashen and his eyes were red. He really did look more dead than alive. He seemed not to recognise Tom at first, not expecting to see him on his doorstep like this, but when he did, he managed a weak smile and stepped back with a whispered, "Come in."

Their visit was brief and personal, as intended. Tom introduced Mags, wondering, albeit too late, whether her presence would accentuate George's loss. However, he seemed comforted that she had taken the time to visit. They did not speak of the incident; George seemed incapable or unwilling to refer to it. They sat mainly in silence with their own thoughts. After several minutes he offered, half-heartedly, to make them tea or coffee and seemed relieved when they both declined. They left after about ten minutes, which seemed a lot longer. Tom and George shook hands and then embraced, a little self-consciously, and Mags kissed him gently on the cheek. Tom said the only thing he could think of.

"If you need anything, George, please get in touch."

As they parted at the door, George spoke hoarsely, fighting back his tears, "They won't get away with it, you know. I'll do it for Irene. I'll make sure they get what they deserve."

Neither had time to respond as he closed the door quietly behind them. As they walked through the gate, the radio reporter stepped up to them. She was in her late twenties, tall and slim and casually dressed in a brown fleece jacket and faded jeans. She had a pleasant rather than pretty face and her dark hair was tucked into a fleece hat which matched her jacket. She wore no make-up, unlike her counter-parts interviewing for television.

"Excuse me, Mr Brown. I haven't reported that you're here and the mike is turned off at the moment. I don't want to intrude, but would you mind very much if I asked you just a few questions on air? I'll tell you what they are beforehand, of course. I promise there is nothing political about them. They're just about this dreadful incident."

"Yes, very well," said Tom, sighing but feeling the girl deserved some response just for sensitively respecting his position. She must be new to the job, he thought cynically. "Go ahead and ask; I'll trust you to be gentle with me."

His winning smile, even diluted by adversity, was enough to make her blush a little.

"Thank you," she gave him her widest smile back. She checked a large watch hanging like a pendant round her neck. "Back live in… six seconds. Jez, count down for transmission, please."

"Three, two, one… go."

"This is Clarisse McCarthy, reporting for Thames Plus Radio one-nine-two. I'm in Meadow Village outside the cottage of Mr George Holland, the campaigner for community reform, whose wife was so tragically shot dead last night. It seems Mr Holland himself had been the intended victim, and his wife was hit by accident as she stepped forward to protect him.

"With me now is the Member of Parliament for Princes and Marlburgh, Mr Tom Brown, whose constituency includes Meadow Village, and his wife, Mrs Maggie Tomlinson-Brown.

"Mr Brown, what is your reaction to the terrible events of last night?"

"Well, I think, Clarisse, that our reaction," he put his arm again around Mags's waist, this time to very clearly include her in the response, "is the same as any civilised human being, that it is frightening that a pleasant evening among those closest to you could end in such an appalling loss of life."

"And you are, I think I'm right in saying, a personal friend of Mr Holland?"

"That's correct. I have a great personal liking and respect for the man, and his wife was a very lovely lady."

"You have just been to see Mr Holland. How is he coping with his tragic loss?"

"Very much as you'd expect, I think. He seems stunned and confused. But I believe he will come through this with an even stronger determination to combat these forces of evil which he has clearly set himself bravely against."

"And do you support his stance in this campaign, Mr Brown? The permanent removal of these forces of evil, I mean?"

"This is a private visit to a personal friend, Clarisse. I have nothing further to say today," Tom replied, repeating Mags's exact words.

Clarisse silently mouthed the word 'sorry'; Tom nodded that it was okay. The reporter then held out the microphone tentatively towards Mags, raising her eyebrows, questioningly, about a possible response. Mags nodded and leant forward.

"Have you anything you would like to add, Mrs Tomlinson-Brown?" said Clarisse, picking up the cue.

"Only to endorse what my husband said. We are shocked and

dismayed at what has happened. Mr Holland is a brave and good man, and it must seem to him right now that there is little justice in this world."

Mags leant away to indicate she had finished.

"Thank you both for taking the time to talk to us. This is Clarisse McCarthy for Thames Plus Radio in Meadow Village."

She indicated three-two-one silently to her technician with a diminishing display of fingers on her left hand. He cut the sound on cue.

"Thank you, Mr Brown, Mrs Tomlinson-Brown. Sorry if I stepped outside our contract. Must be an occupational disease."

"An occupational requirement, not disease," said Tom. "Now you can do us a favour, if you don't mind. You see that silver Audi parked outside the pub?" Clarisse nodded. "Could you go and get it for us, please, and drive it over here so we can make our escape? That way we won't have to talk to any other reporters and you get an exclusive; and I get to tell everyone that Clarisse McCarthy drove my car. What do you think?"

Clarisse's fragile show of cool professionalism evaporated in a little-girly squeal.

"Really?" she said. "Yes, of course."

She took the keys from Tom and went to retrieve the car. Tom chatted casually with Jez whilst the technician kept his eyes riveted on Mags. Clarisse returned with the car, driving a little more quickly than the 150 yard journey merited.

Tom and Mags shook hands with them both, Clarisse leaning forward inviting a kiss on the cheek – an invitation Tom declined. They drove slowly and quietly past the media crowd at the pub, looking pointedly away to reduce the chance of recognition. They were just past when Jed caught sight of them and Tom put his foot down and gunned the car out of the village. Behind them, Jed ran into the road, followed by a few others, pointing after the car as if he had just seen Tom steal it. They were soon well on their way home. Tom slowed down and they drifted gently along the quiet roads.

"Feel okay, darling?" asked Mags after a while.

"Yes, I do, actually," said Tom. "Better than I thought I would." He paused a few moments.

"Thanks for coming, Mags. I really appreciate it. You're the reason I'm feeling okay. I couldn't have done that on my own."

Mags smiled at him, and then added, mischievously.

"It doesn't do anything for my peace of mind, you know, seeing that young hussy with the microphone squirming and melting under your gaze. Are you like that all the time? I think I'd better insist you come home every night."

"Just part of the job," said Tom. "Actually, it's the part I hate most, but it's got to be done."

"Oh, yes, I could see it was agonising for you."

"And anyway," said Tom, "what about the landlord – and the technician – I could actually *hear* them dribbling. Just try to make yourself a bit less sexy next time we go out, would you?"

"Hey, you've no idea how hard I had to work to look as bad as this," she said. "Anyway, that landlord got my name wrong. Who the hell's Mrs Brown? Even so, perhaps I shouldn't have fluttered my eyelashes and pouted at him. He was rather good-looking though, don't you think."

"Absolutely not, and whatever you did, just don't do it again – except for me, of course."

They both laughed.

"Just one more thing, Mags," said Tom, becoming serious again. "You know when you spoke to that journalist?"

"Yes," she said, a little anxiously.

"Thanks for not mentioning the Little Winton by-pass."

She gave him a very severe frown.

"It's a good job you're driving," she said.

"I wouldn't have dared say it if I wasn't."

★

Jack and Katey retired early that evening, tactfully leaving their parents to themselves. Before going to bed, however, their daughter gave Tom some 'feedback', as she called it, from one of her friends.

"Joss would like you to sign a pledge saying that if you ever divorce Mum you'll wait until she's old enough and then marry her. What shall I tell her?"

"Tell her fine, but let's try and keep it out of the school newsletter for the time being."

"Okay. Goodnight."

"She'll do it, you know," said Mags, after their daughter had left. "She'll tell her tomorrow."

"Well that'll teach you not to do all that fluttering and pouting and flirting again."

They smiled at each other affectionately in silence for a while.

"I hope they both go to sleep before we do tonight, don't you?" said Mags.

"Me too," said Tom. "Then Sumo to a finish this time."

CHAPTER 14

At 9.30 on Monday morning, Jo Cottrell watched as DC Murray Davenport passed the two computer-generated images across the desk. The face of the tall black youth who had led the attack had been gruesomely constructed from a photograph of the surviving half of his face. The other, of Jokey, was the product of an abundance of information from eyewitnesses.

Stephen Davies, headmaster of Princes High School, leant forward in his chair and looked at the two pictures. Then he shook his head and turned away.

"Dillon Enderby," he said. "Fifteen years old. Hasn't been in school for a long time. Eight weeks or so, I believe."

"Thank you, Mr Davies. Do you recognise the other boy?"

"Not for certain," he replied, "but I think you'll find that it's his brother, Joaquin." He pronounced it 'Wa-keen'. "He attends Gosforth Road Primary School, which shares the same site as us – across the playing field. The head teacher is Mrs Julia Braden. This is all so terrible."

"Do you know why Dillon hadn't been attending school?"

"No, we've been round to the address in Dewsbury Close a number of times; members of staff – including myself – and community police officers. There appears to be no-one living there at present." He shook his head again.

Mr Davies was in his mid-fifties, medium height and thin. His face was drawn and pale. What remained of his hair was long and grey and combed straight back, hanging wispily and curling up over the collar of his jacket at the back. He wore a grey suit and white open-necked shirt. The overall impression was of a man who was monochrome and battle-weary.

"What about the other boy who was killed? Do you know who he is yet?" he asked.

"Yes, his parents identified him this morning. I'm afraid he was a pupil here as well – Denzel Jones."

"Oh, God. Actually he hasn't been in school either."

"Did you know they were friends, Denzel and Dillon?"

"Yes, I'm afraid they were both part of a particularly violent and disruptive group."

"And could you provide us with the names of other members of this group, Mr Davies?"

"Yes, I suppose I could."

"Good, I'll send an officer to see you as soon as possible. You see when we went round to Denzel's house and searched his room, we found a rather disturbing collection of weapons hidden under the base of his wardrobe." She checked her notebook. "Three different types of handgun, a quantity of long-bladed knives, and a Mac-10 machine pistol. That last item is capable of delivering over a thousand rounds per minute. You can't even begin to imagine what damage that could do. So it's important we track down these kids, in case they're all keeping a stash like that somewhere."

"Yes, I'll do what I can, obviously."

"Thank you, Mr Davies. I'm sorry it's such bad news. Do you have a photograph of Dillon we could have? It might be useful in finding his brother."

"Yes, of course. It might take me a while to get one."

"That's okay. I think we're ready to see Mrs Braden now, anyway. If we call back in, say, twenty minutes?"

Jo and Murray walked the short distance across the playing field to the primary school.

"Where do you think the nickname Jokey come from?" asked Murray.

"From the spelling I suppose," said Jo. "J-o-a-q-u-i-n."

Murray screwed up his face in thought. "Of course, as in Joaquin Phoenix. Except up to this moment I've always called him Jo-kin Phoenix."

Mrs Braden could not have been more different from Mr Davies. In her early thirties, vivacious and smiling, she had long blonde hair, streaked with pink highlights, and an eyebrow stud. She wore a short flared black dress with white spots over black leggings. Jo wondered whether she represented the 'before' and Mr Davies the 'after' of a career teaching in Cullen Field. She was, however, clearly affected by the events of two days ago, especially when they produced the image of Jokey.

"Oh dear," she said, with a catch in her voice. "Yes, it's Jokey all right. He is the most lovable kid – when he's here, that is. His big eyes, his smile. He's cheeky, I know, but he's not bad. Very popular with the other children and the staff. But it's always the same with younger siblings; they invariably want to be like their big brothers. And I'm afraid Dillon is a very bad lot… "

"*Was* a very bad lot," said Murray. "I'm afraid we've just identified him as one of those killed on Saturday."

Julia said nothing for a long time as if she was choosing her words carefully. "I guess I should be shocked and saddened," she said, "but it just might be the only way Jokey will have a chance. Does that sound really bad?"

"We can't help what we feel, Mrs Braden," said Jo. "Only what we do. And I don't necessarily disagree with you. You just said 'when he's here'. Has he been absent recently?"

"Yes, for a long time, I'm afraid. Probably a couple of months. People have been round to the house, but no-one seems to be living there."

"And how old is he?"

"Just eight. We all sang 'Happy Birthday' to him in assembly just a day or so before he stopped coming in."

"Thank you, Mrs Braden. Do you think we could have a photograph of Jokey, please?"

"Yes, of course." She turned to her PC and with a few touches of the keyboard a sheet was emerging from the printer next to it. Another contrast with Mr Davies, Jo thought. She took the A4-size image from the headteacher.

Walking back to the high school gym where the Parkside MIT incident room had been established, Jo's phone sounded.

"DC Cottrell speaking… I see… When?… Thank you." She

ended the call. "Emily Burton just died," she said. "The lady who got the glass through her throat. Five dead now."

★

DC Drury knocked on the door of 16 Dewsbury Close, clutching the photographs of the Enderby brothers. The large man who opened the door was unshaven, unkempt and, seemingly, unwashed. But not unfriendly.

"Detective Constable Drury," said Geoff, "and this is DC Wheeler." They held up their badges. "Mr Grainger, isn't it?"

"That's right. Jerry Grainger. Come in."

The detectives glanced at each other in surprise. They had been preparing for having to talk their way into the house. The man gave the impression he was used to visits from the police. He turned and led the way into a living room which met all the standards of cleanliness and order that Mr Grainger set for himself. "It's about next door, I suppose?" He waved to a couple of chairs at the dining table and sat down opposite them.

"Why do you say that, Mr Grainger?" asked Siobhan

"Jerry, please. Well, when I saw it on the tele yesterday about the village and about the two black kids involved, I started to wonder, like."

"Are these the two you mean?" Geoff put the photographs on the table.

"That's them. Although we haven't seen them for ages. Probably a couple of months."

"The whole family or just the boys?"

"The lot of them. The kids weren't always at home anyway, stayed out nights on end. And when they did come back it was sometimes midnight or after. Not right for a seven or eight year-old, is it? Always in trouble as well. Dillon used to have real big fights with his dad – you could hear them through the walls, crashing about, screaming and shouting. Dad was always pissed, mind. Although, the few times I saw him when he wasn't, he seemed like a decent bloke, really. Your lot always round here; sometimes had to nearly break the door down before they'd open up. Made our lives a misery – well, everybody's in the close. Wife's

221

been really bad with the worry and all. We were glad when they left – I can't tell you how much."

"Have you any idea where they might have gone – the parents, I mean?" said Siobhan.

"None at all, and I doubt if anyone else could help you either. People tended to stay out of their way. Obviously the kids were still around somewhere though." He shrugged his shoulders and gave a mirthless little laugh. "It's coming to something, isn't it, when the parents run away from home."

★

Over breakfast, Tom watched the outrage unfold on the morning television news programmes. He left early for Westminster, his first meeting with Jackie timed for 8.30 am. He wondered just how productive it would be given the inevitable discussion on what was being described as the 'Meadow Village Massacre'.

As he opened the front door to leave, his personal paper-boy arrived at the gates with the morning delivery. Tom left a couple of the dailies for Mags, and piled the rest on the passenger seat of the R8. As he pulled away, he noted the imposing headline on the top paper, the *Daily Mail*:

'BROTHERS IN ARMS!'

That's pretty good, he thought, in spite of the seriousness of the event. It captures the essence perfectly; like the Earps and the Clantons in probably the most famous gunfight of all.

Parking under New Palace Yard, he went along the walkway to Portcullis House and to Jackie's office where they had arranged to meet. She was already there.

"Andrew wants to see us in his office," she said. "I think it might be about Meadow Village."

"Everything will be about Meadow Village today, I guess," said Tom. "I went there with Mags yesterday; private visit to see George Holland."

"Really? I'm surprised it wasn't picked up by the media," she said. "I didn't see or read any mention of it."

"A Thames Plus Radio exclusive," said Tom, smiling, "in exchange for their helping us to escape the rest of the media. I'll tell you about it later. Better go and see the boss."

They left Portcullis House and walked to the Norman Shaw Building next door.

"Do sit down," said Andrew, bounding to his feet and waving to the two chairs in front of his desk. "Coffee? Yes?" He poured two cups from the coffee pot on the table next to the door and carried them across on a tray, with milk and sugar, setting it down on his desk between Tom and Jackie. Then he sat back down in his chair facing them.

"Well, what a weekend," he said, beaming. "Talk about playing right into our hands."

"Oh, you mean the brutal slaying of Irene Holland?" said Tom. "Yes, what a stroke of luck that was!"

Andrew seemed to suddenly remember himself, and held up his hands in apology.

"Yes, I'm really sorry, Tom. I know she was close to being a personal friend – through George. That must have seemed very callous; I didn't mean it to sound like that. I guess I'd moved on past the actual incident to look at the ramifications; the fall-out. And, without apology this time, I have to say it will ultimately work in our favour, and… " – he held up his hand to stop Tom interrupting – "… for the benefit of all those people, at the scene and subsequently hearing about it, who will have been traumatised by this event."

Andrew looked across at Tom, raising his eyebrows, inviting him to speak. Tom remained silent; not appeased, but unwilling to pursue it.

"All the more reason to get on rapidly with this proposal," Andrew continued. "Did you two have a chance to meet yet?"

"No, but… " started Jackie.

"Jackie wanted to get started, but I couldn't make it this weekend," said Tom.

"We've put time aside over the next three days," said Jackie.

"Oh, well," said Andrew. "Shame, but no matter. Possibly my fault for not making it absolutely clear how urgent it is." He smiled humourlessly across at them. "Well, I won't delay you; you've got some catching up to do."

Tom stood quickly and walked to the door, holding it open for Jackie, and closing it behind them without another word.

"God, I wish we had a Party boxing competition," said Tom. "I know who I'd love to get in the first round."

They walked back to Jackie's office.

Portcullis House was a relatively new addition to the accommodation at Westminster, providing more spacious offices than the limited space in the Palace allowed. The Shadow Home Secretary's office was large and well appointed with matching desk, filing cabinets and bookcases. There was also room for a separate sitting area with a couple of armchairs facing each other over a low table.

"We didn't drink his coffee," said Tom. "Shall I go back and get it?"

They both laughed.

"I think the stuff out of the machine will taste better," said Jackie. "The enjoyment depends as much on the company you keep as the quality of the bean."

"Why, Jackie," he said, giving her his best smile, "what a lovely thing to say."

They laughed again and walked down towards the vending machine.

Their meeting went well and they produced the full skeleton of the presentation. With that complete, they set about applying the flesh, and were ahead on their tight schedule by lunchtime. At 1.00 pm they left the building and went in search of food. They strolled along the Embankment, enjoying the warm midsummer sunshine. Tom took off his jacket and carried it over his shoulder.

"By the way, Jackie," said Tom, after a while, "what exactly did you mean about getting on the wrong side of Andrew?"

"I wish I hadn't said that, actually. It seemed pretty disloyal afterwards. After all, he made me what I am – even if it is only a yes-woman. At least it's a fairly senior yes-woman."

"You didn't answer the question," said Tom.

"It's nothing really specific. It's just that he scares me at times. I'm not sure how far he would be prepared to go to get his own way. I think he's dangerous – and I can't believe I'm sharing all this with you. Why do you think that is, Mr Brown?"

"Perhaps we've both found a new friend," said Tom, seriously.

"I hope so," said Jackie. They walked on for a while without speaking, checking out the eating places.

"What about here?" said Jackie, indicating a mobile kiosk with a few chairs and tables spread across the wide pavement. "Hot dog?"

"Excellent idea," said Tom.

"You sit down over there and I'll get them," said Jackie, pointing to one of the two empty tables. "What do you want?"

Tom looked at the limited menu which comprised hot dogs of various sizes, with or without chips.

"I'll have a Monster-Dog with chips," said Tom.

Jackie gave a little laugh and walked over to the kiosk, which sported the sign 'Top Dog' over the serving hatch. Tom watched her go, appreciating what a good-looking woman she was; trim figure, shapely legs, nice swing of the hips, and a pleasant face. As always, she was immaculately and fashionably dressed; today in a dark suit with a short straight skirt and double breasted jacket. The same age as himself or thereabouts, he guessed; she was someone you would like to be seen with, be proud of, but without pub landlords and sound technicians drooling and fantasising over her.

She headed back towards their table balancing three items, a Midi-Dog, a Monster-Dog and a very large polystyrene tray full of chips.

"If we eat all this," she said, "we won't have room for any pudding and we can convince ourselves we declined through self-control."

Tom laughed.

"Good spin, Jackie. You should be in politics."

They spoke very little for a while, mainly due to incapacity born of the eating challenge in front of them. When they had done the most damage they could to the dogs and chips, Tom got them two coffees from the same kiosk and they sat relaxed and comfortable with each other's company.

"What's your afternoon looking like?" asked Tom.

"Cross-party group meeting with His Highness the Mayor on City of London congestion charges; a review there-of," she answered. "Thinking of reducing them, believe it or not. Traffic wardens up in arms about potential job losses if we don't do something to entice motorists back onto the double yellow lines."

Tom threw his head back and laughed.

"What about you?" she asked.

"I'm going over to the constituency office," he said. "As you know, I cancelled Saturday's surgery and I might just pick up a few people this afternoon. They know my car; I'll stick it outside and they'll see it and some will no doubt pop in. Actually, the reason for the cancellation was the Lorimar-Deverall thing. I assume you got the whole story – of course you did. I actually know John Deverall really well… we served together, he was a very close friend. My kids call him 'uncle' for Christ's sake."

"Wow, what a shock that must have been." She thought for a moment, and then went on. "Listen, Tom, I don't know whether you intend telling Andrew this, but if you do, I can only imagine he's going to want to exploit it somehow. Try to display you as carrying on your friend's work or something. I know how his mind works. It could get a bit tacky for you. Just a thought; I'm not trying to interfere."

"No, it's a good point. I never thought of it, but the job's done anyway, I'm afraid. He was there when I found out and I just blurted it out. I mean I was really shocked, like you say. Interesting that Andrew never mentioned anything about it this morning. Or saw it as a reason I might not be working over the weekend."

"Interesting, but not surprising. I'm not sure in which part of the brain the facility for empathising is located, but I'd bet my life Andrew has that part missing."

Tom laughed. "Anyway, it might be exactly what Jad – John Deverall – would want. Someone acting as his representative on the right side of the law. I guess it will all come out about our friendship anyway whether Andrew takes a hand or not."

"Yes, I guess it will," she said. "Anyway, I'd best get going. I've enjoyed today, Tom. I didn't think I would but I really have. Until tomorrow then."

They stood up. Jackie hesitated before leaving. Tom leant across and kissed her gently on the cheek.

"I've enjoyed it, too, Jackie."

★

John Alexander Deverall sifted through the selection of Monday's dailies on the small dining table in front of him, checking that he had read them all. He had followed the Meadow Village story as it was breaking on the local radio the previous day with an increasing sense of shock and remorse. It was an absolute fact, he told himself, that Irene Holland had died as a direct result of his killing the Bradys. The links in the chain connecting the two events might be numerous, but they were laid out in a straight line from one to the other.

He got up from the table and checked his watch – 11.15 am. His visitor was late, but he guessed that punctuality wasn't a problem for them any more. He looked round his new home. He had to admit, it was a lot closer to an upmarket studio apartment than a prison cell. Although it comprised just one room, which included living, sleeping and dining accommodation, the room itself was a reasonable size and in the shape of a long rectangle, so the three areas were naturally separated. The bathroom off the bedroom was large and more than adequate.

The feeling of incarceration was real enough, however. The three windows were not much more than horizontal slits well above head height designed to let light in, not to let him look out. This was because most of the room was below ground level, and the windows were only just above the height of the ground outside.

He moved across to where a three-seater sofa faced a large wall-mounted TV screen and clicked the remote. The channel was Thames Plus Radio 192. What had shaken him just as much as Irene's death was hearing yesterday the voices of Tom and Mags being interviewed as they left the Hollands' house. More guilt consumed him; just as intense. He remembered how he'd discretely watched them both at his funeral service, beside themselves with grief, and how he'd cried himself at their pain. Now his secret was out, he craved the opportunity to see them again; to grovel for forgiveness.

At 11.25, the door opened and his personal warden stepped inside. "Mr Granville," he said, then immediately withdrew.

"John," said the solicitor extending his hand limply.

Jad shook his hand, or rather his fingers, and they sat down at the table.

Clive opened a document case and removed some papers. "Some stuff here for you to sign; and some information about what happens next. I have to tell you, the Brigadier is not well pleased."

"Really," said Jad. "I thought he'd be delighted."

The solicitor looked at him over the top of his glasses and raised his eyebrows.

"It was a joke, Clive. You know – sarcasm. I do realise I'm in disgrace; I don't need you or anybody else to tell me."

"It's not killing the Bradys, John. It's getting caught that's the issue. I'm not saying that it was okay to do it, of course. It was wrong. An abuse of trust… "

"If you're here just to tell me stuff I already know, Clive, than perhaps I can be signing whatever you've got there while you're doing it; seeing as it won't be necessary for me to listen."

Clive looked at him and shook his head.

"We're still on the same side, John – and that's the same side as Henshaw as well. Don't lose sight of who your friends are."

Jad didn't answer; just looked away.

"Okay, let's get it over with," said Clive, pushing the documents across the table and placing a pen in front of Jad.

After he'd signed them, Jad stood up and stretched. "Is that it?"

"Yes, that's it. Except to say it's been decided that we won't release details of your illness yet. We think it's best to wait until your profile has diminished somewhat. At the moment it's even bigger than your ego. Thank God we don't have to wait for *that* to reduce in size."

He put the papers back into the case and rose to leave. There was no proffered hand this time, limp or otherwise. He pressed a button at the side of the door, the warden opened it and he left with deliberate haste.

★

Jo was already waiting at her desk when David arrived at Parkside. She followed him into his office, checking her watch – 8.15 pm.

"Christ, Jo. We might as well move in here permanently. What have we got?"

"A Mrs Gayle Lucas got in touch with Romford police this

afternoon; this was even before we'd put out the kids' names. Said she was worried that the boys might be her nephews. Apparently, eight weeks ago her sister and brother-in-law – Mary and Winston Enderby – had asked for the use of their caravan at Long Beach Caravan Site near Southend and had turned up at her house without the children to pick up the key. She asked where the boys were and was told they were staying with friends. It seems her sister was very vague about it, but Mrs Lucas knew about the problems they'd had with the children and thought perhaps they'd been taken into care or custody or something and that her sister just didn't want to tell her. Then with the news over the weekend about the two brothers, along with their descriptions, she put two and two together."

"And we've picked them up?"

"Yes, they're already here, waiting in Room Four. I spoke to Sergeant Clark Morden, the detaining officer at Romford. They picked them up at the caravan at… " she checked her notes "… 7:10 this evening. They hadn't heard of the Meadow Village thing, and Morden said that when he explained the circumstances, they seemed more upset at being found than being bereaved."

David shook his head. "Okay, we'd best get down there to talk to them. Have they had coffee and such?"

"Yes, they've been made as comfortable as possible."

They joined the couple in the same room where they had interviewed John Deverall, and made the appropriate introductions. The Enderbys were both small and slim, and dressed casually in lightweight outdoor clothes, as if they had been planning an evening stroll when the police had picked them up. They looked a picture of total despair, each with a frightened, apprehensive look in their eyes; nothing like the troublesome neighbours that Jerry Grainger had described.

"Would you mind if we recorded this?" asked Jo. "It saves us a lot of writing and you a lot of reading later." The couple nodded.

David and Jo didn't need to ask many questions; the words came pouring out of Mary Enderby.

"We knew something like this was going to happen. It was the only way it was going to end."

"What was… ?"

"Dillon. The way he was. Completely out of control. We tried

229

everything, didn't we, Winston? He was really bright at school. At first he used to read, do his homework, everything. We did our best to encourage him and get him interested in hobbies and the like – sport mainly. Winston took him fishing, to football matches; even got him interested in climbing – he was a good climber, wasn't he Winston? And he got really in to fishing when he was Joaquin's age – entered a couple of competitions – for juniors, like.

"But as he got older, he got ridiculed and bullied for doing that sort of thing. Winston kept trying to encourage him, didn't you Winston?"

"Like pissing in the wind." Her husband so far had been sitting with his head bowed in a posture of abject misery, and didn't move to answer his wife.

"But Dillon just turned on him. Actually pushed him away and punched him when he was trying to talk to him." She reached across and took her husband's hand. He gripped it tightly. "Anyway, he joined the gang about a year or so ago, for his own protection as much as anything, at the time. But soon we were hearing all the bad things he was doing… "

She broke down and the tears came. Winston sat up and put his arm around her. "What can you do," he said, "when trying to get them doing something useful actually puts them in danger? Parents are supposed to make sure their children are safe."

David shook his head. "I don't know, Mr Enderby. I don't know what you can do. I'm so sorry." After a pause he went on. "And Joaquin. What about him?"

Mary composed herself. "He just idolised Dillon. Wanted to be like him. You know, all the kids on the estate looking up to you and that. He'd do exactly what Dillon told him, even though sometimes you could tell, he'd just want to stay home and play." She began to cry again.

"What did you do about the children?" asked Jo. "Did you try and get some help with them? Report what was happening to anybody?"

"We didn't have to," said Winston, bitterly. "We had half the neighbourhood reporting them."

"Well, it must have been bad for them all," said Mary. "All the noise; you and Dillon fighting. The police always round… "

"Aye, and me pissed all the time," said Winston, quietly, fighting back his own tears.

No-one spoke for a while, then Jo asked, "I understand the boys were away from home quite a lot?"

"All but left home," said Winston. "No idea where they were most of the time. We went to the police ourselves, you know. They said they couldn't do anything unless we could show that they'd done something wrong. I mean – Joaquin was seven yours old, for fuck's sake! Oh yes, and they told us they just needed a firm hand. What a joke!"

"As if it was all our fault," said Mary. "Anyway, we'd just about given up, couldn't face it any longer. So we asked Gayle – my sister – if we could borrow her caravan. We tried to find the boys – we planned to take Joaquin with us – but they were nowhere… "

"We thought if we got Joaquin away from the estate, there might still be a chance for him," said Winston. "You, know, while there was still time. But we couldn't find them, and, well, we went anyway. We just meant to be away for a few days, but… Everyone is going to think we're really bad parents aren't they?" His voice broke. "I just don't know what else we could have done."

"For what it's worth, Mr Enderby," said David, "I for one don't think you are bad parents. And, like you, I don't know what else you could have done." He only just managed to stop himself from adding, 'but there was a bloody lot more that we could have done.'

"As Winston said, we only intended to go there for perhaps a week at the most," said Mary. "But it was so peaceful. We managed to get passes so we could go walking on the island, Winston did some fishing – even got a little job down by the jetty at Shoeton Point helping with the boats – repairs and such. And another thing," she went on, "he hasn't touched a drop since we've been there, right love?"

Winston nodded. "That's right."

They were all silent again for some moments.

"Would you be able to provide us with names and addresses of Dillon's and Joaquin's friends?" asked Jo. "We've probably seen them already in the door-to-door enquiries we've been making, but it would be useful to know anyway."

Mary and Winston looked at each other. There was no hiding

the anxiety in their eyes. "No, I'm afraid we don't know their names," said Winston. "They never mentioned any one in particular, and anyway, they all seemed to live out on the streets."

David and Jo said nothing, hoping the silence would encourage a different response. "Okay," David said at last. "If you do think of anything or anyone, please call me or Detective Sergeant Cottrell." They each handed over a card with their contact details. "In the meantime, we'll take you home and request that you stay there until we find Joaquin. It could be that without Dillon, he may try to return home. And speaking of Dillon, I'm afraid I'm going to require you to identify your other son at the morgue. Either one or both of you will be fine. I'm very sorry to have to ask."

"No, we understand," said Winston. "I'll do it right away, if someone could stay with Mary until I get back."

"I'll do that, Mr Enderby," said Jo. "We'll take Mrs Enderby home and drive you there afterwards."

★

It was after 10.00 pm when David and Jo finally left the station. To end the day, they each drove the couple of miles to Meadow Village and parked round the back of the pub.

The Dog and Duck had been externally resurrected with new window panes and replacement double doors at the front. Inside it felt like the morgue David had just visited. Not that it was deserted – there were quite a number of people in the main bar – but no-one was talking. People were sitting around, with glazed expressions directed at full pints most of which, given the lack of anything that looked like a decent head, must have been standing there untouched for some considerable time.

Jed Smithers nodded his recognition when David approached the bar. Jed was an impressive-looking character; mid-thirties, tall and well-built, with a shaved head and stubble beard. He had broad shoulders, a flat stomach and looked like he worked out quite a lot.

"What can I get you, Chief Inspector?" He inclined his head at Jo with an appreciative smile. "Your assistant scrubs up well," he added, oblivious to the mild racist inference in the remark.

Jo smiled back politely, not understanding the joke but enjoying the attention.

"This is Detective Sergeant Cottrell," said David. "DC Shakhir's got time off for good behaviour."

He ordered a pint of bitter and a half of cider and looked around the bar as Jed pulled them.

"You've done well to open up again in less than two days, Jed," he said, "and it was important you did. The village needed this, needed to see they can survive. How've people been?"

"A lot better today than yesterday. Sunday was worse than a wake, as if people just had to come to check that it was all true but didn't really want to be here. I wasn't actually open, but nobody wanted a drink, anyway. I've not opened the back room again yet. Not sure what to do; that's where Emily got hit in the throat." He shook his head sadly, then walked off along the bar to serve someone else.

David and Jo took their drinks and went through into the snug next to the main bar. It was empty. They sat in silence for a few minutes.

"What did you make of Mr and Mrs Enderby?" asked David.

"I liked them, a lot," she replied. "And I feel so sorry for them, as well. I really believe they did their best; that it wasn't their fault. What do you do when you know that if your kids look anything like being half-decent, they'll get beaten to a pulp every time they go out? How can you deal with that?"

"I agree," said David. "It's too bloody easy to say 'they just need a firm hand.' Can you imagine how they must have felt going to the police for help and being told that – after they'd tried absolutely bloody everything? First Alma Deverall – daren't come to us because she knew we'd let her down and then, as if to prove she was bloody right, these people *do* come to us and – guess what – we bloody well let them down! What the bloody hell do we get paid for, for Christ's sake?

"You're getting on your 'bloody' roll again, sir," said Jo. "Have another pint and relax; I'll drive you home and get a taxi back here to pick my car up… "

"Thanks, Jo… "

"… on expenses!" she added.

"But of course," he said, smiling now and relaxing already. "Tell you what; get me a large Macallan instead."

Jo raised her eyebrows.

"I'll pay," said David, pulling a ten pound note from his wallet and tossing it on the table.

"Great," said Jo, picking up the note. "I'll just go and find Jed. I may be gone for some time."

★

'SECRET PAPERS REVEAL RADICAL PROPOSALS FOR NEW JUSTICE REGIME'

A secret document leaked from the Shadow Home Secretary's Office, reveals details of the extreme measures the Opposition Party will introduce if they achieve power at the next General Election in fifteen months' time. It is believed these have been discussed as a matter of urgency over the past several weeks, primarily in response to the growing public demand for new initiatives to curb what Jackie Hewlett, Shadow Home Secretary, has referred to as 'Domestic Terrorism'. These measures will include:

- *'Absolute Zero Tolerance' relating to the behaviour of street gangs*
- *Police powers to arrest and hold yobs causing a disturbance for up to three days without charge*
- *Powers for the courts to give custodial sentences to trouble-makers without the current need to prove guilt of a specific crime; cumulative evidence of nuisance value will suffice*

And the measures, to be component parts of what Ms Hewlett terms the 'New Justice Regime' – the NJR – will go much, much further for extreme cases of wrong-doing

- *New sentencing which will lead to the permanent separation of those failing to respond to more conventional measures of control.*
- *The creation of a 'Life Exile' (LE) status whereby such people will be permanently relocated off-shore in custom-built detention facilities, with no opportunity for return*
- *The creation of an intermediate 'Deferred Life Exile' (DLE) status for individuals under the age of sixteen (and over the age*

of twelve) who will be monitored for three years or up to the age of sixteen, whichever period is the longer, at which point a decision will be taken on whether they will be confirmed as 'Life Exiles'. During this deferred period they will also be completely isolated. This designation – DLE – would also be available as an alternative to immediate LE status in certain mitigating circumstances.

'Whereas these measures will be designed specifically for those individuals rejecting their communities by their behaviour and attitude, a number of specific crimes could receive DLE or LE designation. Such crimes have not been clearly identified as yet but may include:
- *Drug dealing*
- *Aggravated burglary*
- *Using a weapon whilst under the influence of drugs or alcohol (DLE only)*
- *Rape*
- *'Active' paedophilia*

'New facilities for the monitoring of offenders will also be part of the NJR. These are particularly extreme and include:
- *The indefinite electronic tagging of all DLEs should they be released after their deferment period.*
- *Such tags will be surgically inserted close to the heart of the offender, rather then attached to them mechanically*
- *Tags will be used not only for locating offenders but could also impart an electric charge which would have the effect of immobilising them and aiding recapture if necessary*

'The document includes many more details on a new structure for the judiciary, which would incorporate, as a key component, fully trained jurors selected from a pool who will serve a period of three years and who will receive payment for their role. It also provides for a significant increase in the number of police officers, a reduction in administrative pressures, and more flexibility for the deployment of resources across traditional inter-force boundaries.

'Although these changes are extreme and go much further than

any previous proposals for tackling these serious national issues, the Opposition are confident that, with an early indication of election success next year, they can be preparing for government with a view to introducing these measures within six months of taking office.'

★

Jackie and Tom were summoned to Andrew's office at just after 4.00 pm. Without preamble, he read from the paper he was holding.

"'The leak came via an email with the document attached. It seems the source of the communication was a privately-owned PC whose email address was terminated immediately after transmission. The message, however, is clear regarding its origin, stating 'from the office of the Shadow Home Secretary; at last, someone with the bottle to stop the persecution of the innocent!' Interesting, don't you think?"

He refolded the copy of the *London Evening News* 'Special Edition' to show the front page, and tossed it across the desk towards them as they stood awaiting an invitation to sit down. Jackie gasped as she read the headline.

"Please feel free to read it all," Andrew went on, "but I can save you the trouble by telling you it's word perfect," he said, "However, so we don't all fall out of friends, let's not worry right now about how this happened. I trust you guys have worked discreetly and carefully; I can't believe it was down to anything you've done in the last couple of days. So this isn't a witch-hunt."

As he spoke, he waved them to be seated. At the same time he got to his feet and began pacing round the room

"What we need to decide, however, is what we say, if anything, at this stage. The press are going to ask us if all this is true – obviously. Well, we can't exactly say it isn't, can we? Because, as I said, it's virtually word-perfect. We'd have to back-track on everything we've done to date on this if we denied it. So that's not an option. What I believe we need to say is that we have, of course, with the greatest urgency, started to conduct an internal investigation as to the source of this information. And put up the shutters with 'at this stage we have no further comment to make.'

"Because," he went on, "this could work big-time in our favour.

236

If we *can* stone-wall it for a couple of days – perhaps even just twenty-four hours – we'll get a really good feel for the reaction out there.

"Worst case scenario, in the face of outrage and anger, we have ready a suitably indignant denial. 'How could the public seriously believe we would suggest such extreme... etcetera'. Best – and expected – outcome, they all shout 'bring it on!' and we prepare for government."

Jackie was white-faced and appeared not to be taking in much of what Andrew was saying.

"And how do we address the issue of the leak itself?" she asked.

Andrew stopped pacing and sat down again.

"Well, we may not have to. If the reaction is positive then... "

"Then let me be more specific," interrupted Jackie. "How do we address the issue of the leak if the reaction is *not* positive?"

"Well, as I say, Jackie, I'm not ready to address that yet. I think I said just a few moments ago, if you were listening, this is not a witch-hunt... "

"No, but it will be, just as soon as the first bit of negative feedback reaches you. Would you like me to resign now, or would you prefer to sack me?"

Andrew seemed temporarily unsettled by the confrontation, but he quickly recovered his poise and responded with his customary cool menace.

"You must do what you think is appropriate. But let me make it clear that it will be *your* doing. I have been deliberately conciliatory in this meeting when, I believe, I could have been forgiven for blowing my top. I have no idea where you get the idea from that I'd sack you, Jackie," he went on, just a little more warmly, "I have only days ago made it clear that I want you to lead on this new strategy. Why on earth would I do that if I saw your position as that tenuous?"

"Very well," she said, "let's leave it for now, as you say, and concentrate on the holding statement. Might I suggest that we make this an official press release read to camera by Press Liaison? That way we don't get drawn into a wider debate and we can limit what we say. Jim McIntyre's a good stone-waller; he should do it."

"Good idea, Jackie," said Andrew. "Let's agree the wording between us."

They sat for a further twenty minutes, Tom and Jackie first reading through the newspaper article and then the three of them drafting the message. Jackie read out the final release.

"'A statement from the office of Mr Andrew Donald, Leader of Her Majesty's Opposition. Mr Donald will be conducting a full enquiry into the recent communication, allegedly from the office of a Shadow Cabinet Minister, to the *London Evening News* on Wednesday 14th July. He hopes to conclude this investigation within the next few days, at which time he will decide what action to take. In the meantime, there will be no further statement on the matter from this office.'" Jackie looked up. "I think that is okay as far as it goes, but to state the blinding obvious, the overwhelming interest will be the content of the leak not where it came from. This won't go anywhere close to satisfying the press even for a day or two. And what about the House… ?"

"Well, Stone-Wall McIntyre might have to work overtime for a start, and as far as the House is concerned, then we'll hide for a couple of days. There'll be no-one on the Front Benches who can answer the questions. It's just a day or two until we get the feedback, and in the meantime I'll put together a denial statement – which I am certain we won't need. Okay?"

"Can I see the denial statement when it's ready?" asked Jackie, more as a demand than a request.

"Well, as I say, I don't believe we'll need to issue one," said Andrew. "But, if you'd like… "

"I would," she snapped back. "Is that everything for now?" She made to stand up.

"Yes, I guess."

"Then if you'll excuse me." She turned without speaking again to either man and walked quickly from the room.

Tom had risen from his chair, his instinctive old-world reaction to a woman rising from hers. He watched her leave not knowing what to do.

"I'd better catch up with her," he said, turning to Andrew. "Still got to finish the proposal. We'll need to have the official version even sooner now, I guess."

Andrew was relaxed and smiling again, back in total control.

"Sit down for a minute. Let her get her knickers untwisted first," he said. "What was all that about? Stupid bitch! She can't see further than the end of her big nose!"

Tom did sit down, but leant across the desk towards Andrew, springing instinctively to his colleague's defence.

"Bloody hell, Andrew. I thought she took it pretty well. Can you imagine what she must be thinking right now? You could show a bit more sympathy for your victims!"

"God almighty!" said Andrew, throwing up his arms in exasperation. "I don't know what the matter is with everyone today. I've done nothing that you and I didn't agree on Friday. I've even given Ms Jackie a bloody vote of confidence, for God's sake. How the hell is that screwing up her life?"

"Your problem, Andrew, is that you can't see past your own priorities. You can't accept that anyone who doesn't see things *exactly* how you do has any value whatsoever. Let me tell you a secret. Jackie Hewlett is a very nice human being. Not only that, but she's bloody good at her job. Oh, and another thing," he added, "if you bother to look at her closely, you'll see she does *not* have a big nose."

Andrew's mood lightened at the final remark.

"Well, well," he said, with a sneer. "You and Jackie Hewlett. Who would have thought it? And here's me just assuming that you'd be banging Grace." He raised his hands in appeasement before Tom could respond. "Just joking."

He smiled broadly, mainly at Tom's discomfort.

"You'd better *not* be giving Grace one, by the way," he added, as if to make it clear that he really had been joking.

Both men were silent for a while, but with the tense atmosphere persisting. Tom eventually got to his feet.

"Best get going," he said, and left the room with neither man bothering to say goodbye.

He walked back to Jackie's office in Portcullis House. She was sitting with her back to the door swinging back and forth through a semicircle on her tilt-and-swivel, obviously deep in thought.

"Jackie, are you alright?"

She swung fully round to face him.

"Oh, hi, Tom," she said, "Sorry to rush out like that, but that smug bastard was really getting to me."

"You caught him off guard today, though, Jackie," said Tom,

smiling. "I think for a moment he considered tending his own resignation."

Jackie laughed.

"No, not even for a split second. But I admit to having enjoyed not simpering along and slinking out backwards, curtsying all the way. And do you know something – I don't give a shit what he does; I don't trust him one iota any more. Because I'm certain I know where the leak came from. I mean, this works perfectly doesn't it – and it wouldn't be the first – or last – time it's been done. Leak something controversial and wait, with a prepared denial, for a reaction. Then tear it up if everyone likes what they hear.

"It has to be him, doesn't it?" Jackie went on. "He actually said in there, didn't he – 'I don't believe it's either of you' – or something like that. He wouldn't say that if he didn't know who *has* leaked it. I mean, who knows about this stuff – in that sort of detail? You, me and Andrew – oh, and Grace Goody. No-one else. And what you also need, for the plan to work, is a scapegoat if it goes wrong – a fall guy. Or a fall girl in this case. He's not going to sacrifice you, is he? And Grace just isn't a big enough meal to feed to the vultures… "

"Well," said Tom, astonished at her perceptiveness and firming up his loyalties, "we're a team, Jackie, and in team sports, all the members get relegated together. So he can have a fall-couple this time."

Jackie beamed a smile at him.

"Why, Tom," she said, mimicking his recent words to her, "what a lovely thing to say."

CHAPTER 15

Joaquin Enderby turned up at his house at 6.00 pm that evening as if he had never been away. He knocked on the front door, which was opened by Winston. The boy walked into the living room, seating himself on the sofa and picking up the remote from the floor in front of where his father had been sitting. His parents stood together in the doorway watching him for several minutes in silence as he flipped through the channels without saying another word.

Mary phoned the police before sitting next to her son on the sofa.

"Are you hungry, love?" she said.

"Starving," said the boy.

"What would you like?"

"Fish fingers and chips," he said.

"Fish fingers and chips – *what*?" asked his father.

"Fish fingers and chips, please," said Joaquin.

"Good boy," said Winston. He looked across at Mary with a wide smile.

Jo arrived fifteen minutes later with Geoff Drury and Judy Standitch, a Care Liaison Officer. Joaquin was seated on the sofa with Winston's arm around him. They were watching some sort of game show, just as if it was what they did every evening at this time.

Twenty minutes later, the three officers left, deciding to postpone questioning the boy until the following day. Joaquin had already fallen asleep in his father's arms.

"We'll be here at nine o'clock in the morning," said Jo. "But I think it's only fair to tell you this, Mary, Joaquin will have to be taken from you for a while, to undergo psychiatric assessment; to see what can be done to help him. I hope it won't be for long."

Tearfully, Mary saw them out.

As they drove away, Jo sighed and shook her head. "That's just about the cutest cold-blooded killer I've ever seen," she said.

★

Stopping in a lay-by ten minutes from home, Tom sent Mags a text to let her know of his imminent arrival. For a full five days now, in the wake of the revelation about Jad, the subject of their discord had not been mentioned. Perhaps, he thought, they had put that behind them. Perhaps Mags was prepared to moderate her opposition to his work for the benefit of their personal relationship; and the leak to the press would have no effect one way or the other.

The previous two evenings that same text message had prompted her appearance on the steps in front of the house as he pulled in through the gates. Today she was conspicuously absent. He put his car away in the garage – something he rarely did these days – to give her a bit more time to emerge, just in case she had simply mistimed her coming out of the house. He went in, making more than sufficient noise to announce his arrival.

"Mags!" he shouted. "Daddy's home! Mags are you okay; where are you?"

"In here." The flat statement came from just a few yards away in the front room – *their* front room. Tom went in. Mags was sitting at one of the chairs in the window with her back to him; she didn't turn round.

Tom kept trying.

"Hide and seek, eh? How exciting."

"Have you read this?" Mags said, without changing her position, but raising the folded paper above her head for him to see.

"Well, no… "

"But of course, you don't need to, do you, because you wrote it."

"No I didn't actually; Harriet Bradley wrote it," said Tom, referring to the name of the reporter.

"But it's yours, isn't it?"

"It's a rather tabloid-ish attempt to trivialise a great deal of very serious work with which I have been involved, if that's what you mean," he replied.

"Did you leak it?" asked Mags

"Of course I didn't," he said, but with no indignation, which Mags was quick to pick up on.

"But you knew it was going to be leaked." Mags's voice was quiet, almost a whisper, and all the more threatening for it, like a stealth attack which carries insufficient impetus to meet it decisively head-on. He sat down in the chair next to hers and tried to look into her face. She turned away, avoiding any chance of eye contact.

"Mags... darling," he said. "You knew I was working on this. You've known for weeks, months. I thought we'd reached a sort of truce; accepting our differences. Don't tell me you haven't enjoyed the past few days as much as I have. Why has that got to change?"

She sprang to her feet, taking a few steps away from him and then spinning round to face him from the centre of the room.

"Because this is obscene!" she said, hurling the paper at him. "I can't believe you're planning to put kids away for ever, when they haven't even committed a crime. Or perhaps I've read that wrong – five or six times! You want to turn this country into a police state, for God's sake! Well, I'm not voting for you and I'll never vote for you again. And I'll make sure that everyone *knows* your wife is not voting for you! I can't believe it! Inserting bombs into people that you can activate by remote control – that's right isn't it?"

Mags was going red with rage, shouting almost hysterically at him.

"That's absolutely *wrong,* in fact!" he yelled back. "And I'd really like to know where you got that from. You've had access to all this stuff all the time I've been working on it. It wouldn't surprise me if it was *you* who leaked this!"

Mags was shocked at the accusation; it seemed to stabilise her for a moment.

"Oh don't be ridiculous! Why would I do that?"

"I don't know," said Tom. "Maybe because you think everyone out there thinks like you do. To try and disgrace me, or something."

"Thanks very much," sneered Mags. "That's what you think of me, is it?"

"Jesus Christ! You just said you're going to tell everyone on the fucking planet that you're never going to vote for me again. Is that supposed to be a public demonstration of marital solidarity?"

Mags didn't speak. Tom went on.

"You didn't say what a bastard Jad was when he said all this stuff. He's a bloody hero; George is a bloody hero; I'm a bloody barbarian! How does that work? Andrew thinks… "

"Oh, let's not talk about Andrew! If it was eighty years ago in another country, he'd be dressed from head to foot in black leather and goose-stepping to work in jackboots! I thought you were a notch or two better than that! I just can't see what you can possibly achieve with these… well, you said it – barbaric tactics; other than alienating a whole generation of innocents!"

"*Innocents!* There's that fucking word again! Bloody hell, Mags, you only ever read or hear the bits that add to your case, don't you? We're talking about the really, *really*, bad few that contaminate the vast, *vast,* good majority who are, at the moment, too scared not to follow them. We're trying to *save* a generation, if you'd only open your eyes and ears. And seeing as you've asked the question, what we – and I mean me, John Alexander Deverall, the recently widowed George Holland – whose wife was brutally murdered by a group of your *innocents* – and similar heathens – what *we* want to achieve is a world where the bad guys are scared of the police and not the other way round. And if that's a police state, then bring it on!"

Mags turned away from him, making to leave the room.

"Listen, Mags," said Tom his voice softer now, "if the reaction to this is adverse, then I'll drop it. If the public throw their arms up in horror, like you, then I'll resign – do something else, help you with the business, whatever. I only want to do this because I honestly believe it's what people want. If I'm wrong then that's an end to it. That's a promise. You and I are more important than anything."

Mags had stopped. She turned back to face him.

"And what if the reaction *isn't* adverse, as you put it? What if everyone – or the vast majority – go for it? What then?"

Tom hesitated.

"Then I'd have to go ahead with it," he said.

"I see," said Mags, quietly again. "So just let me get this right. We – you and I – are more important than *anything*. But that's only if people don't support your proposals. If they do, then you'll put the feelings of the electorate before those of your wife, and, presumably, in such a case, you and I are *not* more important than anything."

Tom sighed; that was exactly the message he had just delivered.

"So basically," she went on, "whether or not our relationship survives will be decided by the voting public. I suppose I should feel privileged that our future is important enough to be the subject of a national referendum. But, for some reason, I don't feel that way at all."

He watched her leave the room, not knowing what to say.

★

David Gerrard was raging around his office at Parkside like a wild bull. It was 9.05 am and he had just taken a call from Jo, who had informed him that the Enderbys were not at home, and their car, a blue Renault Clio, was missing from the close outside.

"Bloody brilliant!" he had yelled down the phone. "We told them they were about to lose their little boy, and then buggered off home and went to bed! Why in Christ's name didn't we leave someone watching the bloody house?"

Jo pulled the car into Long Beach, with Geoff calling out directions from the map of the site to get them to Mary's sister's caravan. Judy Standitch was in the back. There was no sign of the blue Clio outside and no-one was inside the caravan itself. The people next door said they'd arrived very late last night but had left again by the time they had got up.

Jo phoned David.

"Suggest you check Shoeton Point," he said. He was calmer now. "Mary said Winston had a job there and did some fishing. Get out there."

Five minutes later, they were speaking again.

"They're not at the Point," said Jo, "and no-one's seen them here this morning. Where was that place she said they went walking?"

There was a pause while David checked the transcript of the interview on his screen.

"She said 'the island'. Does that help?" he said.

"There are a few islands here – some are sort of pseudo-islands, but they still call them islands. Didn't she say something about managing to get passes?"

There was a few moments' silence, as David checked again.

"Yes, that's it, must be Skoalness! The island's owned by QuanTechnick, government research agency. They'd have to have passes to get on there. Listen, I'll get the chopper boys out to search the area for their car. I suggest you head out there anyway. I've got a feeling that's where they'll be."

Jo set off again, finding the single lane onto Skoalness Island. They showed their IDs at the visitors' lodge where the attendant confirmed the blue Clio had been through the check point, and set off along the six mile track towards its furthest-most point. The island was predominantly farmland and mostly below the level of the highest tides. As a consequence it was protected by a sea wall, and was a popular area for birdwatchers who mainly strayed beyond the wall onto the sandbanks and mudflats which built up against it.

They had only been going about five minutes when a helicopter raced past them towards Skoal Head, the north-east tip of the island.

"Christ that was quick," said Jo. "Very impressive."

Geoff and Judy craned their necks to watch it go by.

"That's S-and-R," he said, "not one of ours."

"Oh, please God, no," said Jo, speaking for all three of them.

By the time they got there, all three bodies had been set down just inside the wall. Shocked birdwatchers and walkers, observing the scene from a distance, were speaking in hushed, distressed tones as the plastic body bags were unrolled ready to receive their tragic cargo.

An elderly couple were talking to the coxswain of the inshore lifeboat. Jo slumped forward in the driver's seat, hands on wheel, head on hands, and sobbed uncontrollably. Geoff got out from the car and went across to the couple and the lifeboat man. Judy leant over from the back seat and placed a comforting arm around Jo's convulsing shoulders.

Geoff showed his ID.

"I think I know who these people are," he said. "We came here looking for them. Can you tell me what happened?"

The coxswain turned to the couple who were clearly very shaken and distressed.

"Would you like to tell the detective what you just told me?"

The man nodded.

"And you are?" asked Geoff.

"Peter Grantham and this is my wife, Elizabeth. We're birdwatchers. We were just panning round over there, watching some Whimbrel flying across that spit of sand" – he pointed – "and we noticed these three people. They were up to their waists already – the child nearly to his shoulders. It's a lovely spot but really dangerous if you don't know it. The tide pours in behind it making it into an island, then… "

He choked momentarily at the recent memory.

"That's what we thought must have happened today at first," he went on. "We shouted to them but they just didn't respond. Just stood there with their arms around each other." His wife had started to cry quietly. "We called 999 and within a few minutes the lifeboat and the helicopter arrived. But too late. They'd disappeared into the water by then. They did a fantastic job – the helicopter winch-man got all three out in no time, but… "

"The really strange thing," said Elizabeth Grantham, "was that it looked like they wanted it to happen; like they wanted to drown."

★

Tom was in Jackie's office, just after midday, when Jenny phoned him on his mobile.

"Mr Brown, I have Detective Superintendent Allan Pickford from Parkside on the office line. Would it be convenient to speak to him right now?"

"Do you know what it's about, Jenny?"

"Yes, it's to do with the missing child who was involved in the Meadow Village shootings."

Tom looked across at Jackie, pointing to his phone. Jackie nodded.

"Yes, Jenny. Ask him to phone my mobile, please."

In less than a minute his phone sounded again.

"Mr Brown?"

"Speaking, Allan – and I think it was 'Tom' last time we met."

"You're right, Tom, it was. I'm afraid we've had a rather tragic development in the search for Joaquin Enderby. You know we found the parents… "

"Yes, Monday, wasn't it?"

"That's right, in a caravan at Southend. Well Joaquin turned up last night. Just walked into the house, apparently, as if he'd never been away. Anyway, it was a bit late to speak to him then – he was just about asleep by the time we got a couple of officers round there. Cut a long story short, by the time we got round this morning, they'd gone – back to the caravan, it turned out. And this morning – well, all three drowned off Skoal Head; apparently cut off by the tide."

"Christ, that's awful… "

"But that's not even the worst of it, Tom. It seems it was deliberate. Eyewitnesses said they just stood there together and let the sea take them."

"God, those poor people. What could have been going through their minds?"

"I thought you should know because of… well they're your constituents, of course, and it's part of this whole sickening Meadow Village thing. Right now the official line is 'tragic accident', but I don't know how long we can keep it to that. It seems the people who saw it happen don't really believe that and we can't stop them talking to the press. They'll almost certainly be asked about it."

"Okay, thanks, Allan. Appreciate the call."

Jackie had been listening wide-eyed to Tom's half of the conversation.

"And then there were eight," he said, half to himself, as he ended the call.

"They're sure it's directly related?" asked Jackie, when he explained what had happened.

"I don't know what the psychologists will make of it, but I do know for certain in my own mind that if the incident hadn't happened last Saturday, eight more people would be alive today."

"Should we tell Andrew?" Jackie asked.

"No, let him find out from someone else. I can't face the prospect of his spinning this off the cuff into something positive.

I'm afraid I might hit him."

"Oh, come on, then," said Jackie. "Let's go tell him!"

Tom allowed himself a brief smile. Then he checked his watch.

"I'm heading over there for the surgery in a few minutes. Do you think I should go to the estate again?"

Jackie shook her head.

"To see who? There are no Enderbys there to sympathise with."

★

Just after 1.00 pm, in Parkside MIT operations room, Geoff Drury brought the team up to date with the events of the morning. Missing from the meeting was DS Jo Cottrell. She had been inconsolable since their sighting of the bodies and David had sent her home accompanied by DC Baxter, who had since returned. Also present was Judy Standitch, whom Geoff had invited along with the DCI's permission.

David listened to the account of the events from their visit to the Enderbys the previous evening up to Geoff's conversation with the couple who had reported the tragedy. His expression left no-one in doubt about his displeasure, but he was on his best behaviour in front of Judy.

"I believe it was the right decision not to interview the child last night," she said. "He was almost asleep when… "

"I'm not claiming to be a professor of hindsight, Judy," interrupted David. "God knows there are enough of those around. But that's not the point at all."

"I just think it was important not to appear to harass the family when they had just been reunited," she went on. "In my opinion, Detective Sergeant Cottrell… "

"And we *are* interested in your opinion, believe me. But putting a police car at the end of Dewsbury Close, out of sight of the house even, does not constitute harassment, but it would have been a good example of common sense. That was not your responsibility, Judy; that was most definitely ours. You have nothing to reproach yourself about.

"But what we had was an eight-year-old kid who was potentially very unstable – or whatever the PC term is for a child who's been homeless for two months and who has just shot someone dead. His parents, who were so far past the end of their tether that *they* actually ran away, had just been joyfully re-united with him. They were then told they'd better expect to lose him again. Now if that's not a recipe for a fucking calamity, then I don't know what is!"

Judy's face reddened.

"What will happen now, sir?" asked Omar.

"We get back to rounding up as many gang members as possible," David replied. "What Detective Superintendent Pickford has decided to do, if anything, I am not party to as yet. I assume you did mean what happens next about the cock-up, Omar?"

"About anything, sir," said Omar. "I was just worried about the sarge, that's all."

"Well, you'd hardly expect me to discuss DS Cottrell with you, Omar, or with anyone else for that matter."

He looked round the room, feeling the team's collective anxiety like a material presence.

"Look, hands up anyone here who, at some time or other, has made an error of judgement," he said, raising his hand.

Everyone in the room followed David's example.

"There you are then," said David. "That's what it was, Omar – an error of judgement. So don't worry about Jo, but I appreciate your concern. Thanks for the briefing, Geoff and Judy. And now," he added, "let's get back to the mean streets."

The team left the room and he went into his office. Before he had time to sit down behind his desk, Allan Pickford appeared in the doorway.

"Just caught the back end of the meeting, David," he said. "What are you going to do about Jo?"

"Well, I'd be grateful for any thoughts you have, sir, of course, but if it was just down to me, then probably nothing."

"I think something has to be said to her, I mean… "

"What exactly, sir?" David interrupted. "There is nothing that we can say to her that she doesn't already know. The girl is devastated. I don't believe there was any indication whatsoever that something like this could happen. If there had been, Jo was more likely to pick up on it than anyone else in my team, including me – and, with respect, you as well, sir."

"I don't doubt it, David, but it was pretty clumsy to say the least to leave with a parting shot that they were about to lose their child again. I'm sorry, but if you won't say something to her, then I feel I must. She's a good cop, David, and whatever else is said, then that fact should be clearly communicated. But I actually believe she'll get over this more quickly if she has that conversation with someone – and it would be much better for *her* if that someone was you."

Allan turned to leave.

"Think about it," he said.

"Okay," said David, with a deep sigh. "I'll do it. But I'm not sure this is the right time, sir."

"Do it now, David," said Allan. "Straight away. I don't think there is a right time for this, so better to just get it over with. No need for paperwork; nothing to go on her file."

He left the office, closing the door behind him.

David picked up his notepad and quickly wrote down a few words on it before placing it in his jacket pocket. He looked at the photographs standing on the desk in front of him – six in all. Five of these were facing him and were of his family; two each of his son and daughter – as babies and teenagers – and one of himself with his wife and both children before their divorce ten years ago. The sixth one faced outwards so it could be seen by anyone entering the office. He picked this one up and studied it, smiling at the memory. It had appeared on his desk a few days after an outdoor team-building day and showed him standing next to Jo and towering over her, both of them liberally spattered with mud after a mountain-biking session. The caption at the bottom read:

'Hobbit meets Cave Troll'

(A scene from 'The Fellowship of the Ring')

After looking at it for a long time he replaced it, then scooped up his keys from the desk and left the office, passing through the empty MIT room and out of the building.

★

Jo was reluctant to let him in at first. It took a lot of persuasive words into the speaker at the front door before she gave in.

"Wait a minute, then," she said.

It was well over the minute before David heard the buzz of the lock being activated. He pushed open the door into the foyer. He could see a door being opened and left ajar at the top of the curved staircase. He climbed the stairs and went in. The neat apartment in the small complex of Brantingham Villas had a long passageway through to the open plan living room-cum-kitchen, with doors off to two bedrooms, a utility room, and a bathroom. He went straight through to where Jo was half-standing, half-leaning against the back of an easy chair facing the door. Her eyes were red and her face looked sore from wiping her tears, but she had done a good job in composing herself and returned his smile.

"Hi," she said, in the softest of whispers. "Thanks for coming."

She turned and sat down on the chair, David taking a seat at the end of the sofa nearest to her.

"Would you like a drink – tea, coffee?"

"On expenses, of course," said David, extracting a brief laugh. "Yes, I will, but let's have a chat first. I'm here because the whole team's worried about how you are, but also officially as well."

"Oh dear," she said, quietly, looking down at her clasped hands.

David reached across and put his own hand over them.

"You are the best cop on my team, Jo. Possibly the best I've ever worked with" – she looked up at him and smiled – "so let's get the official shit out of the way quickly. Okay?"

"Okay," said Jo, tears welling again, knowing the gist, if not the detail, of what was coming.

"Don't read anything into the fact that I'm going to stop holding hands with you for the time being," he said, leaning back and withdrawing his hand. Jo sobbed out a laugh this time, tears flowing again.

"Just so long as you'll hold them again afterwards," she said.

"I promise. Firstly," he said, "nothing about what we say will go on your file. It's just between us – the Boss-man has been absolutely clear on that."

Jo looked at him, horrified.

"God, the Super's been involved? Oh, no! What did he say?" She slumped forward into a near-foetal position.

"He said it was important that I spoke to you about the incident, which I am doing; that it was unwise for you to leave the family at

252

a time when they would be confused, if not very distressed, without watching out for them. And I agree with him. That was a mistake, Jo, not putting a watch on the house overnight, especially knowing that they had somewhere else to go."

Jo had not changed her position, but her shoulders were shaking.

"Having said that, no-one in the world could have anticipated that something like that would have happened. And the Super agrees with me, that if anyone on the team was likely to see the signs, it would have been you. *And* he also said" – he reached into his pocket and took out the notepad, reading from it – "'she's a good cop, David, and whatever else is said, then that fact should be clearly communicated.'" He replaced the pad, pausing to let Allan's words register with her. "We need you, Jo – this is me again, by the way, but I'm speaking for everybody; you are the beating heart of this team; we can't function properly without you."

Jo had stopped crying but did not move. They remained in silence for a long time before David continued.

"And another thing, Jo – and this is an honest observation and not just for your benefit – if they hadn't been able to leave, if someone had been there to prevent them, they could easily have done something in their own home. Tablets, gas fire, something. There are easier ways than standing waiting to be drowned."

Jo looked up as if to say something, but David went on.

"*Also* – hear me out. Are we absolutely sure they committed suicide? Perhaps they genuinely got cut off and simply saw no way out. So they stood together like that and waited for the good Lord to take them. We don't know otherwise for certain."

"Oh yes we do, David," said Jo, more composed. "They did it deliberately. I'm never going to believe anything other than that and if I'm going to get over this, then that is what I have to come to terms with; not hide away behind something I know isn't true. But thank you for all that; I can't tell you how much it means to me."

"I do really mean it, Jo."

"I know you do."

They sat for a while in silence. Jo looked across at him, eyes red but now dry.

"I'm not sure I can come back, sir. People will say it was, quote, 'just an error of judgement' unquote. Some will say it to be kind – some will really mean it. But it's as you've said a number of times recently, they come to us for help and we let them down. Those poor people, feeling so bad they… What if they thought I meant we were going to take Jokey away for ever? What if they linked what I said to what they'd been reading in the papers; seeing on TV? They probably felt… "

"I don't believe that for a nanosecond," said David, with real conviction, reaching forward to take her hands again. "I'd bet my life that they knew nothing of the leak; they didn't have time. It was less than twenty-four hours since it hit the press – a lot less. They wouldn't have known. Please, please, don't be a victim of this thing, Jo. We've got loads of victims; we don't need another one. What we do need are people who can prevent more victims."

"Could I have time off to think, sir? I don't think I'd be much use right now anyway."

David did not answer immediately.

"Okay," he said. "Compassionate leave – not holiday. You'll be wanting all your holidays when you come back. Right?"

Jo looked sadly at him, shaking her head.

"Right," she said. There was a further silence, both wrapped in their own thoughts.

"Now," said Jo, suddenly, "tea, coffee? Please stay a little longer."

"On one condition," said David.

She raised her eyebrows with the unspoken question.

"Biscuits, as well."

"You drive a hard bargain."

★

"Hi, it's me," Tom said into the phone.

"I know," said Mags.

"Just to let you know I'm coming back tonight. Surgery finished early."

There was no answer.

"Have you seen the news? That poor kid, drowned with his parents."

254

"It seems your New Justice Regime has got off to a flying start."

"Mags, that's a *terrible* thing to say. That little guy was eight-years-old. How the hell can this have anything to do with the NJR?"

"The NJR!" she scoffed. "So it's a coincidence, is it? The new measures for taking children permanently away from their parents are announced, and less than twenty-four hours later one of the prime candidates for separation ends up dead – deliberately drowned along with the parents. Now that's what I call real impact!"

"I can't believe what I'm hearing!" he said. "There is no way that the two things are connected at all and I don't believe you think there is either! He was eight, for Christ's sake – way too young to be affected. And anyway, where do you get the idea from that it was a suicide? The police haven't said that it was."

"No, but just about every reporter has on all the news channels. It seems they just stood there and let the sea come in around them…" Her voice had changed, was breaking a little.

"I'm really sorry," he said, meaning he was sorry she was upset.

"A bit late for that!" she snapped again. The phone slammed down. He called back immediately.

"What!" she snapped, but with a tell-tale hoarseness to her voice.

"Please, Mags," he said. "I am sorry you are so upset – I hate that, you know it – but please don't accuse me of being accountable in any way for that young boy's death. That is so cruel; I am truly devastated, believe me. I'm not trying to duck responsibility for the New Justice Regime; if that's what you are pissed off with me for, then guilty as charged. But not Joaquin Enderby. It's the ones we want to put away for good who decided his fate before he was even born… "

There was a click as the phone went dead again at Mags's end.

★

Tom and Mags had dinner in almost total silence; just the two of them. Mags went upstairs immediately afterwards, taking her nearly empty wine glass, and settling into her study-cum-studio. She used this as an office for managing the business and her local campaigning work, and also for her hobby of landscape water colours; there were always two or three easels with partly finished pictures spaced around the room. This evening, she closed the door and sat with a book in the wing chair by the window, facing out over the front drive.

Tom followed her a few minutes later, and knocked gently on the door. There was no response; he opened it quietly and leant into the room.

"Top-up?" he said, waving the wine bottle like a white flag.

Mags turned to him and then immediately away, but held up her glass. Tom walked over, gently holding her raised hand as if to steady it as he replenished the glass.

"I won't interrupt you if you'd rather be alone," he said, "but can I just ask you a couple of things."

She half-turned towards him with an exaggerated sigh.

"Will you come with me to Irene's funeral tomorrow, please? It's at eleven; I won't be going on afterwards to the buffet, or anything; we should be back here for one at the latest."

Mags did not answer at first.

"Yes, okay," she said, eventually.

"Good. Thanks, Mags," said Tom.

"You said a couple of things."

"Yes, I'm going to arrange to see Jad. I assume you'd like to come with me."

"No thank you," said Mags. She turned back to the window and raised her book to indicate that the conversation was over.

"But why not?" asked Tom, his brow furrowed in surprise. "I thought you'd want to see… "

"I do, but not this time," she said, her voice hardening.

"Yes, but why? That's the question. Why? Not when?" He was now getting frustrated himself.

"I just don't want to get in the way," said Mags, turning to him again with the now-familiar blaze in her eyes. "You'll find it much easier to work out how the two of you can carve up the world without me sitting there, quite possibly – heaven forbid – not agreeing with every syllable you say! Now please, can I get on with this book? You said you wouldn't interrupt me if I wanted to be alone, and I *do*!"

"Right! Fine!" said Tom. "Can I suggest we go separately to

the funeral tomorrow? I couldn't stand two hours of silent righteous indignation while I'm trying to concentrate on driving. I'll leave you the postcode for the satnav and see you there. Okay?"

Tom closed the door, not waiting for an answer.

CHAPTER 16

The funeral of Irene Holland attracted over 800 mourners, almost half of whom were from the estate. In addition, around fifty or sixty members of the press were present, all respectfully inconspicuous. The Meadow Village church, St Mary's, could accommodate around 150 at a squeeze. The remainder stood reverently outside listening to the service over the loudspeakers organised by Tony Dobson at Fred's request.

Tony himself, like Tom, was there as a friend and not in his work capacity. In the end, Mags had travelled to the village with Tom, via Westbourne Avenue, where she had spent an hour at the apartment whilst Tom attended an early meeting with his local constituency team. They spent the day under a veneer of shared politeness, an unspoken cease-fire, in deference to the business of the day rather than any mutual empathy. Anyway, they both decided – privately – it was better than the exertions of continuous battle.

They chatted with many of the people – almost all of whom were Tom's constituents – after the funeral. There was only a brief opportunity to speak to George himself, and they politely declined his invitation to attend the wake at the Church Hall.

The journey back to Etherington Place passed in silence, but this time out of respect for two very nice people – one deceased, one bereaved. Other people's anguish often serves to put one's own problems into perspective, and so it seemed that afternoon. As Tom and Mags parted, they exchanged a brief kiss – hesitant, but tender and gentle all the same.

The funerals, four in all, of the rest of the direct and indirect victims of that fateful Saturday took place during the first half of the week following Irene's. Those for Alistair Neville and Emily Burton at St Mary's were relatively modest affairs, attended by their families and other villagers. In Alistair's case, the mourners included his brother Ben, in a hi-tech hospital chair, accompanied by two nurses and a complex collection of tubes and wires to assist with his breathing and feeding, and for monitoring his vital indicators. Denzel Jones's funeral was also essentially a private event.

The Enderbys' was very different.

Hundreds of people lined the streets of Cullen Field as the cavalcade of three hearses – the brothers' coffins lying heart-wrenchingly side by side in the third vehicle – took the family from their home in Dewsbury Close to All Saints Church near the centre of the estate. Jo Cottrell was present, accompanied by David Gerrard, Geoff Drury and Judy Standitch. George Holland was among the mourners as was Tom Brown, who had attended all three previous funerals, subsequent to Irene's, in a semi-official capacity. His was a feeling of relief that this depressing sequence was over, as he left the still thronging crowd at around noon for Westminster to be present for Prime Minister's Questions. The morning had been unseasonably cold, dark and wet; a suitable backdrop for the final act of such a dreadful series of tragedies.

Except, it was not quite the final act.

★

After the public's overwhelming endorsement of their leaked plans, Andrew had ceremoniously torn up his prepared denial. It was a hollow and over-dramatic gesture, Tom and Jackie agreed afterwards, given that the document was set in e-concrete on his hard-drive. Eight days after the leak, Jackie gave an exceptional performance in the House, presenting the main points of the official version of the Opposition's proposals at the scheduled debate on urban development.

The following day, Friday 23rd July, the House started its summer recess. Before they went their separate ways, Andrew, Tom and Jackie, along with Grace, met in the Shadow Cabinet room in the Palace of Westminster.

"Well, with apologies to Richard the Third," said Andrew, "I think that 'now is the summer of our content.' All the more satisfying, I would suggest, because Gormley and Co will be agonising over this oil supply crisis. Almost makes you believe in God, doesn't it? Only worry is we get recalled to help them out."

"And what will you be doing?" asked Tom. "Where has Isobel decided you'll be taking her on holiday?"

Andrew smiled benignly at Tom, not allowing anything to spoil his mood. "Probably a private beach somewhere, at a very expensive hotel. As long as I can relax and read, I don't really care. I think I'll take Jackie's speech from yesterday with me. It doesn't get much better than that."

He smiled across at the Shadow Home Secretary. Grace cleared her throat expressively, and the two women exchanged frosty glances. Andrew seemed to be enjoying himself,

"Anyway," he said, "I think we can all be pleased with our efforts over the past few months. I won't delay you."

He rose to his feet, prompting the others to do likewise.

"Could I just borrow you for a minute, Grace?" he said.

Tom and Jackie left together.

★

On the Monday of the first week of the summer recess, both George Holland and Tom Brown separately requested a meeting with John Deverall. The meetings were scheduled for two days later, on the Wednesday, with one immediately following the other. Jad was dressed formally in shirt and jacket, and was wearing a tie, normally not allowed in such circumstances. He was taken from his quarters to a small, windowless meeting room with bare white-washed walls and ceiling, and a metal floor. It contained only a table and two chairs facing each other across it, all three items secured to the floor with steel brackets. He noted when he was left to await his first visitor that the room door was locked but no-one remained outside. He had an eerie feeling of being totally abandoned, as he listened to the receding metallic footsteps.

The man who stood before him when the door opened again was much smaller than he expected. He had only seen pictures of George's face and the occasional head-and-shoulders, and his assumption regarding the man's stature, he realised, had been moulded by his massive impact on the national stage.

Jad stood and stretched out his hand as the visitor entered and walked over to the chair opposite him. He looked pale, thin and drawn compared to his pictures in the press taken during his tour. They held the handshake for several moments, neither man speaking as if each was in awe of the other. The silence was broken by the voice of the guard.

"Thirty minutes."

He closed the door, leaving it unlocked.

Jad waved his free hand to the chair, inviting George to be seated, and breaking the silence as he did so.

"Thank you so much for coming, George," he said. "It means a lot, you thinking of me at this awful time. I am so sorry about your wife. I can't… " His voice tailed off as the words failed him, choked by sympathy and the memory of his own bereavement just a few months earlier.

"Thank you, John. I know you lost your mother recently. You must still be hurting from that."

Jad nodded, and they sat in silence for a half a minute or so, each absorbed with his own grief.

"I just felt I had to meet you," said George, at last. "I guess I should be thanking you for seeing me."

"Well, you were very lucky," Jad replied. "When you asked, I'd just got a slot in my appointments calendar – a late cancellation – that allowed me to squeeze you in… "

Both men laughed and the atmosphere changed instantly.

"I promised myself," said George, smiling, "that I would not ask you anything to do with how you came to be two people. But, seeing as how I'm here and consumed with curiosity, I might just give it a go… "

"Don't even think about it," said Jad, smiling back. "Just one person now – John Deverall."

There were a few more moments of silence, relaxed this time.

"I guess my main reason for coming was to ask a favour," said

George, becoming more serious. "You spoke so passionately in court on the subject that I guess you know I desperately believe in; the same topic that I've been talking about myself for the past couple of months. It just seemed right that you and I should get to know each other. I believe – I *know* – there is a massive will for change across the country – for looking after the good guy, for protecting the little people. You're the one who kick-started that, John, and I have to make sure that it happens – I have to – I promised Irene that I would. I mean, I promised myself *for* her after she… " He hesitated, losing his thread briefly with the emotion. "So I guess we're a sort of team, and if what has happened – these terrible events – ultimately leads to something better, then there's some consolation in that, isn't there?" The inflection on the last two words made it into a genuine question, as if he were searching for assurance.

Jad nodded, but George continued before he could speak.

"What I want to do is get as many people as I can, committed to the cause – to voting in this New Justice Regime. Because that's what the vote is – what's coming up next year is a referendum, not an election. It's the people voting for a revolution – for kicking out the bad guys – not for a new government. Right now, just that one thing is enough.

"I might have the chance – probably *will* have the chance now, after the leak and then the official confirmation of the proposals a week ago – to reach around forty percent of voters through this retirement web-com system. If I can get them aligned, into like a block vote, then we can virtually carry this election ourselves. Any day now I think I'll get confirmation to go ahead, and then… well, who knows?"

"Wow," said Jad. "You said something about a favour, but I'm not sure why you need me, or anyone for that matter. You seem to have everything sorted out. That's a point, actually. Isn't it in the bag already? From what I read and hear in the press, there doesn't seem to be anyone actually against this NJR. Nobody who's speaking out, anyway."

"Not at the moment, but right now we're fifteen months off voting for it. That period might be reduced, but there'll still be plenty of time for things to change. For a start, there are a lot of human rights issues for the campaigners to get their teeth in to. I reckon they're just riding out this initial wave of euphoria, and waiting for their moment. I'm not even sure how it will sit with European Law. It seems to fall outside the provisions of at least Articles 3 and 6 of the Human Rights Convention, maybe others as well. This could be just bravado by Donald and Hewlett; they might not be sure they can deliver; might be just jumping on the bandwagon. But if nearly half the electorate are rock solid behind the proposals, they'll have to implement them – they'll have to keep their promise.

"But... there's an oil crisis just round the corner. People's priorities will shift very quickly if we get into power cuts and rationing. This government could still save themselves if they deal with that really well – to everyone's satisfaction. I just want belt and braces... "

"... and string and elastic," put in Jad.

"... and staples and super-glue," said George, smiling and relaxing again, drawing breath at last.

"I'm right there in your corner, George, but I can't see for the life of me how I can help."

"I want to put your name to this campaign," George replied. "I'd like to call it 'The Deverall Plan' or something like that. You're the one who's grabbed the public's imagination. I'd like to be the one to – sort of – carry on your good work. Excuse the cliché, but... "

"Hold on, George." Jad raised his hands in a 'slow-down' gesture. "I'm really flattered that you want me to help, but don't even think of using the name of a convicted murderer as your standard – standard as in flag, I mean. It deserves better than that. And anyway, the Opposition have taken up the cry; I'm not sure you need to call it anything. I'll do whatever I can to support you, and I really am genuinely touched that you want to include me. So please, let's think of what I can usefully do – accepting that I'm not likely to be given time off to wander round Piccadilly wearing a sandwich board or carrying a placard."

His visitor produced a weak smile.

"What about this?" said Jad, trying to keep the momentum going. "Why not write a book? You just need to put down on paper and expand on what you said during your lectures and you have a readership-in-waiting of millions – probably tens of millions – out there. If you got your skates on it could be ready for the Christmas rush! Seriously, George, that is something I could help with – proof-reading, research – demographic data, for example – just feedback on the text. I think I really could make a contribution with something like that.

"And if not a book, then perhaps a series of articles – or both. You'd get into any major newspaper, the letters section at least, but I reckon they'd give you editorial space. What about tapping up this guy Tony Dobson? He seems to have become a sort of groupie of yours, from the accounts of his that I've read. Please don't take this the wrong way, George, but now has got to be the optimum time for reaching out to people; whilst the whole nation is still weeping with you over Irene."

George remained silent for a long time, a little uncomfortable at the suggestion that he should exploit Irene's death. However, he knew it made sense. After all, he had asked for this man's help; he was only responding with ideas for achieving what they both so passionately wanted.

"I always fancied writing a book," said George, rather absently, as if this was suddenly the most important thing he could do.

"There you go then," said Jad. "I was joking about the Christmas rush, by the way," he added. "That's strictly for celebrities cashing in on their fame. Anything real and meaningful wouldn't stand a chance batting against those."

They both smiled.

The door opened.

"Two minutes!"

Both men got to their feet together and exchanged the same warm handshake and smiles as when they had first met. George stepped outside the room, waiting whilst the guard closed the door, and listening to the footsteps of two people approaching from the world outside.

★

David Gerrard was seated in a comfortably upholstered wing chair across the desk from Allan Pickford in the latter's large, carpeted office on the SLT corridor above the MIT room. The office was in stark contrast to David's own, with a number of tasteful pieces of free-standing furniture in natural oak and one wall given over completely to shelves in the same wood, filled to capacity with important-looking books no-one ever touched.

"I know how you feel about these annual meetings, David, but I thought we could use this one – if you agree, of course – to cover off a few issues that I think are perhaps more pressing at the moment. Okay?"

David did not answer, his silence inviting clarification.

"Three things, actually," Allan went on. "Firstly, the situation regarding Deverall; I just want to make it absolutely clear that the case is over. Okay?"

"Yes. Unless my memory's playing tricks on me, I seem to remember we won, didn't we? We caught him and put him away. Case over, as you say. That's how it usually works, isn't it? Sir?"

"Thank you for clarifying the rules of engagement, David, but I think you know what I mean. Deverall's identity is *not* our concern. It might be fascinating – tempting even, as a mystery to solve – but we leave it alone. Are we clear about that?"

"What's all this about, Allan? You told me this when I got back from 'oop' north; after I'd been to see the kid who knew Deverall. Are you implying that I've been sneaking around trying to find out more? Because if you are, then you're totally wrong. Or very badly informed," he added, thinking the unthinkable, that Jo may have shared his ongoing interest with his boss. He dismissed the thought almost before the words were out of his mouth.

"No, I'm not saying that," said Allan. "I'm just passing this on, because it's been re-affirmed to me only yesterday."

"I'll tell you what, though. I'm not happy about it. I think we've been made to look bloody foolish as a result of this. And I would very much like to find out more. I won't, of course, if you tell me not to. But can I be so bold as to ask why? I mean, if I'm being warned off, can't someone at least have the courtesy to tell me the reason. I think I'm owed that much."

"I can only tell you what Heat-Ray told me," he said, referring to their Chief Constable, Heather Rayburn. "Her message was very clear. In the interest of national security, we must let alone the reasons for the deception. If, apparently, anyone were to uncover the background to his change of identity, it puts an extremely delicate operation at risk. As far as *I'm* concerned, David, that's good enough for me. And it has to be good enough for you."

"Well, at least you've given me a bit more information than you did the first time – the 'national security' bit. That was Jo's take on it; I guess I knew as well. But it's nice to be told," he added, smiling in mock gratitude.

"DC Cottrell," said Allan, "that's the next point. Where are we with her coming back to work?"

"Well," said David, trying and failing to fit this into the context of his own performance review, "she's been off for two weeks, that's all. She was shattered by what happened; blames herself, like you'd expect her to do. Always prepared to take the blame, uncomfortable with the accolades. You know what she's like?"

"I do," said Allan. "She's bloody good; in fact she's more than that. I'm not sure what you said to her but it certainly had an impact. The wrong impact. I never thought I'd see her run away from something like this… "

"Now just a minute!" David leant a long way across the desk. "I said to you, very distinctly, that I believed it was *not* the right time to give her a disciplinary. You as good as ordered me to go against my own judgement, with my own sergeant, and now I'm getting blamed for the outcome? That's not like you, Allan. What's going on?"

The Superintendent raised his hands to calm his colleague.

"Sorry, David, that's not how it was meant to sound. I'm not blaming you – if there's any blame, you're right, it's down to me. It's just that the timing of this couldn't have been worse. You know – we've discussed it – the Chief Super has been monitoring Jo over the past eighteen months or so; taking a close interest. Well, he's just on the point of promoting her to Inspector, when this happens. Credit to him, he's more concerned about getting Jo back and promoted than he is about the Enderby thing. Feels it's just one of those things; error of judgement. And the reason for the urgency?" Allan went on. "Point three on the agenda. Your retirement."

"What retirement?" asked David. "When have I ever said I wanted to retire?"

"What age are you, David – as if I didn't know?"

"Well you tell me, then."

"You're fifty-three in two months' time. You started with the force when you were nineteen. You've done nearly thirty-four years; you've earned a full pension already. There are lots of other things you can do out there; another life. I just think you should give it some thought, that's all."

"But it isn't all, is it? If that was all, then it wouldn't be linked with Jo's promotion."

"Big G Hookway feels that we can't justify simply adding another Inspector-level position to the MI team at Parkside once Claire comes back off maternity leave," said Allan. "We'd need to reduce numbers above DS. One way of doing that would be to lose the DCI level position and go with two DI's."

Allan looked agonisingly at David for a response.

"Understood," he said, simply. "Not sure why I had to bloody drag it out of you, Allan. I'm not an unreasonable person, am I?"

"No," Allan smiled, relaxing. "Not in the least. But it's not something I really want – you retiring. But I do want to keep Jo. So you see the dilemma? Jo gets promoted to DI and she has to move somewhere else."

David looked thoughtful for a few moments before he spoke.

"Can I just add one small item to the agenda, please," he asked.

"Of course."

"My performance in the job. Forgive me for being naïve enough to think it, but I had just the vaguest suspicion that this was what the meeting was going to be about. Don't ask me why – it must have been something to do with it being called 'David Gerrard's Annual Appraisal' that triggered the thought… "

"David, I… "

David held up his hand with a smile.

"Sorry, Allan, just a release for my sarcasm. The stuff we've talked about is really important. You know I want the very best for Jo – because she deserves it – pure and simple. But are you in any way dissatisfied with my work? I mean, is that a factor in trying to accelerate my leaving?"

The answer was instantaneous, and reinforced by the shocked look on Allan's face.

"Absolutely not!" he almost shouted. "Christ, David, how could you even *think* that? I can't think of one single thing I could pick you up on in pretty much all the time I've known you. Surely you didn't really believe that?"

"I guess not – hoped not. Thanks, Allan, I really appreciate your saying that. Although I could probably help you to identify some things to pick me up on if you thought that might lead to a more balanced view."

Allan laughed.

"So basically," David went on, "I would need to retire before Jo got promoted – or soon afterwards, or Big G would move her out. Straight away?"

"Well, I'm not sure about immediately. There might be some flexibility in the timeframe."

Both men sat in silence for a while. Allan spoke first.

"I've just thought, you know. I'm coming at this totally from a selfish point of view. Just think about it; Jo will get her promotion whether you retire or not. She might even *prefer* to move somewhere else, especially after this lot. It might even be the best for her, might get her back to work sooner. So it's just me, isn't it? I don't want to lose her so I'm making the link. Right?"

"Well, I think you're wrong about Jo wanting to go somewhere else, because you were *right* about her not being the type to run away. I believe she'll want to come back here, or" – he paused, fixing his eyes on Allan's – "she won't come back at all. That's a possibility."

"I hope she does," said Allan, shaking his head sadly, "for her sake more than anything else. How long before we'll know, do you think?"

"I don't know. But let's look at agenda items two and three together. What about this? I'll agree, right now, to retire when I'm fifty-five – exactly two years from this coming 14th of September. You have to fix it with our Gavin that you'll carry an extra DI for that period, a sort of hand-over, with me coaching Jo as her mentor – I mean, she'll be working on different cases to me, won't she, so she'll be doing the job? So there'll be no increase in head-count at Parkside, just a different ranking profile for a relatively short time. You can fix that, can't you?"

"I guess I probably could", said Allan. "Only probably, mind," he added.

"Fine. I'm sure you can," David continued. "And I can handle that – a set date when I'll be going, with time to get used to the idea, and no more talk about it in the meantime. That's okay. Now, what I can tell Jo is that her future is part of a bigger picture. I can only retire if she comes back. Of course, I won't put it to her quite like that – that would be a bit like blackmail. But it might be the sort of thing that could get her to think more objectively – more constructively – about her future."

He leant back, looking pleased with himself.

"Do we have a plan?" he said.

"You never cease to amaze me, David."

"Well, make the most of it. You've only got two more years of ceaseless amazement left."

Allan laughed again,

"There's just one thing, though," he said, with a sly smirk.

"What's that?"

"You really will have to move out of your office this time or Jo won't have anywhere to work. I knew I'd get my own way in the end."

★

Tom and George exchanged silent nodded greetings through the bars of the iron door. The sombre surroundings seemed to actively discourage the use of words. The bars slid noiselessly open and they crossed with a snatched handshake before going their separate ways.

The guard opened the door of the small cell.

"Thirty minutes," he said, nodding towards the interior of the room, like a pimp ushering a client into a boudoir.

As Tom entered, Jad was already off his chair walking the two or three steps towards him. They didn't speak at first, as if they were each coming to terms with the other's presence, then they shook hands, briefly, and embraced tightly.

"You look great," said Jad, at last, hoarse with emotion.

"So do you, all things considered".

They seated themselves, neither taking his eyes off the other.

"Almost unbelievable, isn't it," said Jad, "how paths that run together for so long can end up so far apart."

Tom didn't speak for a while, the words refusing to come out, trapped inside by sadness. Then he smiled.

"I guess so; though I'm not sure which one of us is calling the shots right now. I do know it *should* be me, but… "

They laughed.

"You really do look great," said Jad, again.

"And, as I said, so do you. I hope I look as good as you when I've been dead for three years."

Jad did not laugh or even smile at this.

"I guess you could say I owe you an explanation," he said, quietly.

"An explanation and an enormous apology," said Tom, just as softly.

"I can't tell you everything, Tom. Not even you. You'll find out a lot more when you become PM or whatever next year." He gave a brief laugh, then hesitated, not knowing where to start.

"I cried at my funeral, you know," he said. "I cried for you and Maggie… Oh God, I haven't asked yet, how is Maggie?"

"Fine; sends her love, of course. Please, carry on."

"I was supposed to be miles away, in a 'safe' house. But I couldn't stay there. I had this stupid idea that if I could get you – both of you – on your own, I could explain, then just sneak away. How mad is that? Well, I got as far as the gates of the churchyard and I saw you two standing together – well, more leaning on each other than standing, crying your eyes out… "

He stopped speaking, his own tears falling onto his shaking hands. Tom reached across, grabbing them, his hands soon moist with his friend's tears.

"It's okay, Jad, really. Just go on, please."

He looked up and smiled through his reddened eyes.

"That's the first time for five years I've heard the name 'Jad'. It sounds good."

He reached for his handkerchief and wiped his eyes; putting it away he smiled again, embarrassed but composed.

"That's when I cried," he said, "seeing how much you were hurting. It affected me more than seeing Mum upset, somehow. It was her disowning me that made me do it; so she shouldered part of the blame. I don't mean I thought 'serves her right' or anything like that. At least I don't think I did… "

"Made you do what, exactly?" asked Tom, trying to get him back on track.

Jad paused. "As you know, up to the time of my... death, I was sniping for the MTU. Alma couldn't live with it; she gave me an ultimatum – give it up or she'd disown me – denounce me as her son – cut off my inheritance, sort of thing. Well, I couldn't give it up, not just for an elderly lady, even if it was my own mother, who didn't – and wouldn't even *try* to – understand why I was doing these so-called terrible things or who I was doing them to. So she told me she had no son and I was never to return. I tell you, Tom, I've been shot on four separate occasions, but what she said hurt more than anything I've ever experienced." His voice again broke a little, but he went on.

"Then I was assigned to a different role, one which required a new identity. And so I was killed off in Afghanistan. I became James Lorimar. So there you are."

"And that's it; that's all you can say?"

Jad thought for a moment.

"Look, why don't you ask me questions, and I'll answer as much as I can."

"That's fine with me; I've got about a hundred. For a start, why couldn't you let us know?"

"Because John Deverall was dead. It had to be like that. I couldn't write to you and say, 'by the way, Tom and Maggie, I won't ever see you again because I'll be pretending to be someone else'. It had to be absolute – that was the deal. I guess I could have said no to the whole thing, but I needed it, in a way, after the thing with Mum and – well, other reasons. I really am sorry, Tom. Remember you lost me, but I lost you as well. I couldn't get in touch, and if you think about it, it was actually harder for me. I knew where you were, what you were doing. My Godson growing up, and his little sister. I could have been part of all that... "

"And what you're doing now, was it worth it?"

"What, languishing in prison – no definitely not," he said with a weak attempt at levity. "But what I did before – yes, certainly. I believe I've made a difference and that's very important – to me. But it came, like most important things, at a price. A new life without friends, in this case."

"Christ, Jad. It must have been *really* important for it to be worth that."

"Yes, that's right," Jad said it quietly, almost to himself.

"So what's this about you being an investment strategist? It seems you have hidden depths, Mr Deverall."

Jad laughed. "Nothing like that. I have a work double; someone who does everything I'm supposed to be doing, so all the stuff is there to prove I'm what I say I am. I think of him as a sort of inverted stuntman; I do the dangerous bits and he takes over when I have to sit behind a desk."

Tom laughed at the imagery. "And 'the dangerous bits'?"

"That's what I can't tell you, but you know what I did before, so I'm sure you get the general idea."

Tom nodded. "So what made you... come back? Was it just the Bradys?"

"I guess so. After a couple of years, living and working – for most of the time – only twenty or so miles away from Mum, I just had to see her again; check she was alright. I wasn't supposed to, and I didn't actually intend meeting up with her. But... well... she wasn't alright; she was anything but alright. She was being terrorised. So I took her away – well, you know the story, don't you?

"And we had a great time, some of the best days of my life. Her apartment was just a short distance away from mine and I saw lots of her. She never mentioned my work again; didn't even press me too much about how come I was still alive but somebody else. She was just glad to have me back, and I was glad to be back. I think she really enjoyed the subterfuge of my having a different name. She kind of joined in the adventure. We actually created a new name for me just as a secret between the two of us. Alex Anderson. Get it? *'Alexander'*, her *'son'*. She said if she could call me that, it would be like having me back completely. What I can't believe is that I gave the police that name – when I told them I was a carer. How stupid was that? As if they wouldn't have checked it out...

"Anyway, when the six months was nearly up on the lease she got a bit down, but then she said she was ready to go back. God," his composure slipped again, "I should have pressed her more as to whether she was sure..."

He was silent for a full minute. Tom waited, moved by his own thoughts on the tragedy that followed.

"Two days before she was due to go back to St George's Close, I found her... "

Tom still made no comment, but his own guilt swamped his feelings for a while. Thinking how he passed by so close to where she lived at least twice a week on his way to the office, and didn't realise what was happening to her just down the road on his own patch.

Jad's voice cut into his thoughts.

"I didn't decide straight away. I'm not sure when I made up my mind. But the Bradys had to pay. I watched them over a period of a week or so after she died. Saw what they did, how they treated the kids – how they used them, where they drank, who they dealt drugs with; built up a picture. They were unbelievably evil, Tom. I've never known the like. In the end, it was the easiest decision I ever made to take them out."

"Why do it so publicly though, Jad? You could have done it anywhere, without being seen at all, most probably. Why take that sort of risk?"

"Because, as I said in court, I wanted it to be as dramatic and high-profile as possible. For people to know what was happening – or what *had* happened. I seriously thought about taking them out in the pub, you know. But I wanted to be sure I got away, and that no-one else got hurt. And three bad guys just found in an alley wouldn't have had anything like the impact without the build-up beforehand. You have to say, it worked! I certainly didn't expect all this."

"And you really believed you'd get away with it?"

"Absolutely. Why not? I wasn't even a real person. I just planned to fade back into the black hole."

"So how did it go wrong?"

"Accident of timing. I can't take anything away from Gerrard and Cottrell – they did their job better than I did mine. I just figured they'd be through with scouring the estate by the time the house went up for sale. But the council were real quick with the sign. From what I understand – and I'm not supposed to know this – Gerrard and Co went back to my mother's house the day after the council put it up. If they'd gone two days earlier – or the council had done it two days later – they would never have seen it and quite possibly they'd never have gone down that route. Unlucky, eh?

"But then, to their credit, they put the story together really fast. They picked me up at the grave. I'd been twice every week since her funeral. And I'd planned that to be the last visit for a while, just in case they were getting close. Again, unlucky, but careless all the same. Even more ironic, the undertaker had assumed she would be cremated, but it was always Mum's wish that she should be buried. Without a grave there'd have been no obvious place to visit and for the police to stake out."

Tom smiled in spite of the seriousness of the topic.

"Christ, Jad, you know a bit about generating excitement, don't you? And why the drama in court if you intended to reveal who you were anyway? I can understand why you had to admit your real identity – somebody, like me, was going to recognise you anyway. But why take it to the wire like that?"

"I'd got up such a head of steam as Lorimar; I just didn't want anything to get in the way of the message. Actually, I thought I'd blown it for a moment. When I told them who I really was, they looked at me like I'd sort of betrayed them. As if what I'd said didn't mean anything because suddenly it wasn't the right guy saying it. Difficult to explain – but it was okay, I think."

"You *think*! I should say it was. You really can't begin to imagine the mood out there, Jad. And the press can't truly reflect it either, not for all the superlatives. Everyone was talking about what you said – and what George said, as well, of course. It was just about the only topic of conversation up to the leaked document – which only mirrored what you'd both been saying anyway. What do you think of our little revolutionary, by the way?"

"I like him a lot," said Jad. "I mean, what is there not to like? He's an amazing guy. When you think of what he's just been through, and how he stays focused on his goals. The guilt alone of what happened would stop most people. How do you live with the fact that somebody died saving you?"

"I guess we had to, didn't we, all the time."

"But that was totally different. The ones who died in that situation signed up for danger, knew what they were getting in to. This was just a nice lady… " The sentiment briefly robbed him of words again.

274

"I'm still not sure why all this is happening," said Tom. "What is so different about the Bradys, about the way they were killed, about Cullen Field? We have this problem country-wide. I mean, it's not on every street, or every estate; it's not even in every town. But where it does exist, it affects hundreds of people. And that means – cumulatively – thousands – in fact, tens, most likely hundreds, of thousands; perhaps even millions. Does this mean that all we've ever needed were a few vigilantes to take matters into their own hands and we'd get a government elected with a mandate to take over from them? Has it always been that simple?"

"I know what you mean," said Jad, "but I don't believe it's like that. I think the factors were stacked up to work in our favour." He began to count on his fingers. "Cullen Field is packed with decent people; there was a very strong gang leadership, and, within the estate, it seems just the one gang; the killing hit the press at a time when people were gagging for a solution, and the news was slow elsewhere; our esteemed Opposition party" – he nodded towards Tom – "were quick enough and ready to exploit it; Meadow Village – one of the affected areas – had an exceptional man in a position to develop and spread the message.

"There's probably other stuff as well, but I believe all those things being lined up in place contributed to this – well – phenomenon wouldn't be too strong a word, would it? Like you just push one domino over and end up with a spectacular display. So I reckon it was just lucky – right thing, right place, right time. If it had happened on another estate, in another area, half a dozen others could have been ready to step up to the plate, or another gang taken over. Remember the summer riots back in 2011. The police took out the ringleaders then, and there were scores of young pretenders stepping into their places. Inexperienced, wild, out of control. Made the situation even worse. Here there was just a vacuum, and the good folk on the estate seemed to fill it, took over their own streets. For a time, anyway."

"Well, whatever," said Tom, with a sigh. "You've quite probably got us elected, and… "

"Hey, not me," said Jad. "The wee guy who you probably passed in the corridor. He's the man. He's actually *planning* the election right now, wielding a block vote of forty percent of the electorate.

Easy, peasy for you. You won't need to bother with a manifesto or campaigning or any of that time-consuming stuff. Saint George will get you there by himself. I hope you're going to give him a job in government when you take over."

Tom smiled. They were silent again for a while.

"Come to think of it, Jad, you've always been a mystery." Tom mimicked Jad's finger-counting. "Good-looking, articulate, sensitive, empathetic, charm by the ton-load. Mags and I were talking about this the other week; it's amazing you've never had a meaningful, lasting relationship. God knows you've had plenty of opportunities and potential takers. Or have we missed something? I suppose that might just have been John Deverall; perhaps James Lorimar's been putting himself about big-time."

Jad laughed.

"No, he hasn't. Not allowed. The fact is, Tom," he said, frowning pensively at the ceiling, "I guess I've just never found anyone good enough. I set astronomical standards, you know."

"That's not an answer," said Tom, still smiling, but sadly now, "but I guess it's none of our business. Although I think it's a shame – almost a tragedy as far as Mags and I are concerned – that the person we love the most outside the family – the person we owe more to than any other human being – should prefer a life of isolation to one of close friendship. And I mean close in the geographical sense, Jad; I know we couldn't have been closer spiritually. You said it's been five years since you heard someone call you 'Jad' – I guess that must have been me or Mags. Well, you've only been dead for three years – that's a full two years you just didn't get in touch. Why was that?"

"Yes, I could have handled that better, I suppose," said Jad, considering his answer carefully before replying. "The fact was that I'd become a target myself. On a couple of occasions, while I was on leave, I got the distinct impression that I was being watched. Turned out I was right – watched by MI5 who'd had a tip-off there was some sort of contract out on me. Apparently, they – the bad guys – figured I would be easier to isolate and eliminate away from the front line than on it. And our guys had intelligence that I was going to be hit back in the UK. I just couldn't put anyone else at risk – especially your family – who were virtually *my* family in all but name."

"But why didn't you say?"

"Because you'd have tried to persuade me just to carry on as normal. And I wouldn't have taken much persuading. But I knew it was too big a risk. Easier just to stay away and say nothing."

The door opened and the prison officer leant into the room.

"Two minutes," he said, stepping back and this time leaving the door open. Tom called after him.

"Could you make that ten – or twenty?"

There was a brief pause.

"Fifteen minutes; no more." The reply came and the door was closed again.

"Good, because I have to ask you this," said Tom. "You were always real cagey about that incident in the Hindu Kush. Did you really have Abu el Taqha lined up for oblivion and the Yanks stopped you firing? The story gets bigger and better and less plausible the more it's told. Last time I heard it, the US guy threw himself in front of el Taq to take the bullet."

Jad laughed.

"The Shadow," said Jad. "It wasn't quite like that."

"Why the Shadow, anyway?" asked Tom.

"The Turks called him 'Golgesi' after the bombings in Istanbul in 2003, which means 'the Shadow'. There's an ancient Turkish belief that if a man is evil enough, his shadow alone can bring death and disaster. It doesn't stand up to close examination as a piece of folklore, because for the shadow to be there the guy casting it has got to be as well. But anyway, as you know, for quite a while el Taqha was Bin Laden's right hand; 'the hand that rocks the world'; reputed to be the one co-ordinating their world-wide terror campaign and also the main conduit to the affiliated al Qaeda-inspired attacks. And as such, he was almost certainly linked – directly or indirectly – to the carnage in New York, Bali, Madrid and London. Quote – the man who turns al Qaeda dreams into global nightmares – unquote."

"Actually, I didn't know all that," said Tom. "So what happened?"

"It was later in the same year as Shah-e-Kot; I was with Ptarmigan trying to flush out the Taliban. To be honest there wasn't much action at all. They were spread too thin; small groups difficult to track. Then one day we were out on patrol with a US group; overall commander was a Major Marty Kade. Good guy; newly promoted. We decided to split up into two groups – SBS and SEALS – to cover more ground more quickly, not expecting to see anything. We went east; they continued north."

"You were still SBS then?"

"Yes, last mission before transferring across. Anyway, after about thirty minutes we got intelligence that Abu el Taqha was close by, less than a mile from our current position, but quite a bit further away for the Yanks. So we headed straight there and got there well ahead of Kade. El Taqha was down in this basin with around fifty guys; we got to this ridge above him less than five hundred yards away." Jad was becoming agitated with the recollection. "He was standing on the back seat of this jeep, the others in a semicircle in front of him. I had a clear shot; he wasn't moving; easy peasy!"

He paused. Tom waited.

"And… " he said eventually. "What happened?"

"VTI, that's what fucking happened."

"VTI?"

"Our patrol leader contacted Kade and told him the situation. Asked him for permission to take him out. I could hear his side of the conversation. Anyway, long story short, Kade said to wait for them to arrive – *only* twenty fucking minutes away, they said. Our guy asked why; Kade said VTI – verification of target identity! For Christ's sake! Too late by the time they arrived. He'd moved; no target. I nearly shot Kade instead!"

"I thought you said this Kade was a good guy… "

"Not his fault. Never stopped apologising; he was just as pissed off as we were – and we were *really* pissed off. Just following orders, he said."

"And the reason for the orders? As if I didn't know – or couldn't guess. Same as Tora-Bora."

"Something similar. At Tora Bora it was – allegedly – insufficient air cover. This time, if you want my opinion, it was because they wanted one of the Yanks to get him. Show the folks back home that *they* were getting their own back for 9/11. Not leaving it to the Brits or the Aussies.

"In both cases, though," Jad went on, "it was somebody behind a desk in Washington who took the decision – a political rather than military one. And who knows how many lives could have been saved in Bali and Madrid and London. Possibly none at all, but maybe also hundreds. Whatever the truth, I can't tell you how much I regret not disobeying orders and taking him out."

His recounting of the story had taken its toll on Jad and his mood had dipped dramatically.

"I think that's why I didn't hesitate to get the Bradys," he went on. "Different scale, same principle. Remove the few and save the many."

The door opened. "Two minutes."

"You'll come again?" asked Jad, anxiously, as Tom started getting to his feet.

"Of course. I'm going to keep a close watch on you from now on. Probably bring Mags next time."

Jad shook his head.

"I'm not sure I really want her to see me in here, Tom. But I'll leave it to you – and Maggie – to decide. Give her my love, won't you? What is she doing with herself these days? I see her picture all over the place. Business journals, conservation stuff, human rights... She must be one of the most photographed women in the country. I could never understand why she didn't become a model."

"Well, she had her chance," said Tom. "In her late teens she was offered the opportunity; really big bucks, as well. Anyway, she was in her 'down with the sexual exploitation of women' phase at the time and turned it down. She wasn't always the shy, reticent weakling she is today, you know."

Jad laughed. "I can't imagine she's very supportive of your new justice plans – I am right in saying they're yours, aren't I? Not really Jackie Hewlett's."

"Right on both counts," said Tom. "They *are* my plans and Mags is *not* very supportive. In fact, that is the biggest understatement I've heard this century."

Both men laughed.

"Well, perhaps the second biggest," he added, becoming serious and showing the emotion in his eyes. "Number one has got to be what Mags said the night we found you again. She said 'John Deverall is a very special man.'"

The guard stepped in again and then back, not speaking or looking at them but leaving open the door as a clear signal for Tom to leave. Both men stood up, Jad swallowing hard to control his tears.

"Look," said Tom, "if there's anything you want me to do – apart from springing you, of course – then just ask. I owe you more than I could ever repay."

They did not shake hands this time; just repeated the long embrace. There were tears in both men's eyes as they parted.

CHAPTER 17

Twenty-five days after his near-death experience outside the Dog and Duck, Ben Neville was taken by ambulance from the hospital back to his farm. The damage to his neck and throat had healed, but the experience had left him frail and weak. Although there were no medically assignable causes, he was now unsteady and slow compared to his previous robust self.

With him in the ambulance were one of the nurses who had attended him during the previous ten days in the recovery ward, and an occupational therapist who would be carrying out a survey of his property to assess to what extent he would need ongoing assistance, and whether any modifications to kitchen, bathroom, stairs or bedroom would be required.

Following the ambulance was a police car with two uniformed officers, which parked in front of the house, its occupants still inside, as the survey was carried out. Some time afterwards, a pink Toyota Yaris pulled up and disgorged a very large dark-haired woman in a navy-blue pin-striped trouser suit carrying a calf-skin brief case. She walked over to the police car and identified herself.

"Shaney Levenbrooke," she said. "Mr Neville's lawyer. I assume he's home." She nodded at the ambulance.

"Hospital staff are just checking out the place," said the driver. "Shouldn't be long now. They've been in there for nearly an hour."

"And what exactly are you here for?" asked the lawyer. It was more of a challenge than a question. "Are we to expect a twenty-four hour watch on him from now on?"

"We're not sure, ma'am," said the other officer. "We'll do as we're told, as always. We sort of assumed it was for your client's protection."

He looked away with obvious distaste. Ms Levenbrooke bristled, and then turned back to her car.

"I guess I'll wait until they've finished," she said, half to herself, and squeezed back into the driver's seat.

When the medical staff had departed, the lawyer spent a couple of hours with Ben, leaving around 3.30 pm. She told him she would return at 10.00 am the next morning to accompany him to Marlburgh Central Magistrates Court, where he would be formally charged. As she walked from the house to her car she looked across at the police vehicle and nodded goodbye. The driver waved a friendly hand while his passenger looked pointedly the other way.

At 4.30 pm Ben's GP arrived, leaving at 5.15, just as his afternoon carer pulled in through the gate to make his evening meal. The police watched the comings and goings with cynical amusement.

"Christ, you're never alone with a murder charge, are you?" said the driver.

"Too right! If you want to be waited on hand and foot, seems you've got to either win the lottery or blow somebody's head off."

★

The following morning, Shaney arrived promptly at 10.00 am and knocked on the door of the farmhouse. She noticed a different police vehicle, this time occupied by two women officers, both of whom gave her a rather over-enthusiastic wave of welcome.

The door was opened by Ben's morning carer, who had found him in low spirits but at least up and dressed and ready for his breakfast. Twenty minutes later all parties left the house, Ben finding his lawyer's mode of transport even more cramped for his bulky and less flexible frame than she did. The short convoy of vehicles – the carer's small 4x4, the Yaris and, lastly, the police car – bumped through the farmyard gate and up the rutted track to Settlement Lane, turning right and leaving the village.

Ben pleaded guilty to the charge of murder and was remanded on bail pending an appearance at Stansbury Crown Court in six months' time. By 11.30 am he was back at the farm; Shaney left at 11.50, ignoring the occupants of the police car.

★

Jo Cottrell walked unannounced and unexpected into the Parkside MIT room exactly three weeks to the day from when DC Catherine Baxter had taken her home. She was greeted with three seconds of absolute silence followed by half-a-minute of sustained applause. All the composure she had carefully constructed before entering was washed away on the wave of sound and she slumped onto a chair, tears flowing above the widest of smiles.

David sprang from behind his desk and raced out of the office to embrace her, finding himself about seventh in line in an enthusiastic queue for the same privilege. It was worth the wait; she clung to him as his turn came and gradually retrieved her poise and dignity. There were friendly cries of "Speech! Speech!" followed by laughter as Jo waved her arms in a gesture declining the invitation.

"Well, *I'll* make a speech," shouted Omar above the rabble, climbing onto a chair. "Jo – ahem, I mean, Detective Sergeant, ma'am," – more laughter – "we are *so* pleased to see you back, and if I may be so bold, you look absolutely *gorgeous!*"

There were cheers and whooping all round. Jo pointed to her wet face, striped by lines of still-running mascara.

"I always suspected as much, DC Shakhir, but now I know for certain. You're a bloody liar!"

They suddenly noticed Detective Superintendent Pickford in the doorway and the noise abated. Omar dropped down off the chair; Jo turned away briefly and wiped her face with a tissue hastily taken from her shoulder bag. Allan stepped forward as she turned back to him and shook her hand, holding on to it as he spoke.

"Great to see you again, Jo. Welcome home. And just for the record" – he addressed the whole gathering – "suspending protocol for a moment, I totally agree with DC Shakhir."

He reached forward and kissed her lightly on the cheek. There were more cheers and whoops, suggestive ones this time. Allan stepped back and raised his hands.

"Right, that's enough!" he growled. "Protocol back on again."

The mood was perfect. Her appearance had lifted the whole group; top to bottom.

★

The round-the-clock watch on the farm continued for a week, after which it was reviewed in the light of there being no interest shown by anyone near the property, except for a stream of well-wishing visitors, all of whom were required to identify themselves until they became familiar to the police. A decision was taken to stop the continuous surveillance and replace it with regular drive-bys every four or five hours. This was just about sustainable up to Ben's court appearance; 24/7 was definitely not.

Ben had not yet been told of this change as the last of the two-person shifts parked up just inside the farm gate to relieve the overnight pair at a few minutes before 8.00 am on the final morning of the watch. So – it was later concluded – what followed was simply a coincidence with respect to timing.

The officers – one male, one female – got out of the car to conduct their inspection of the grounds around the property – a task which each team was required to do a couple of times during their shift. As they set off across the yard they heard a shot from inside the house. They raced to the front door. It was locked.

"Mr Neville!" Police Constable Lisa Milner shouted as she pushed hard against the door. She was a tall, powerfully-built woman, but could make no impression on it. Her companion, PC Aidan Connor, peered in through the window next to the door, hands held above his eyes to reduce the reflection from outside. He could not see anybody in the kitchen and ran to the next window – the main living room. There was no-one there either. Lisa was still throwing her shoulder against the big oak door and shouting frantically. "Ben! Ben, open up!"

Aidan raced round the back. The rear door to the house was also locked but presented no problem. An elbow through a pain of glass and a turn of the key – still in the lock – gained him access. He checked the two rooms at the rear of the ground floor – dining room and large utility room – no-one there either – and then went to the front door to let Lisa in. The morning carer was just pulling into the yard.

They both shouted from the hallway.

"Ben! Ben! Where are you?"

"Are you okay?"

After checking out the two front rooms again, and, satisfying themselves they were empty, they ran upstairs, Aidan leading, his long legs taking the stairs three at a time. The smell from the gunshot took them straight into the largest bedroom at the rear of the house. They both reeled back and spun out through the door onto the landing, hands covering their mouths. There was not much left of Ben above his chest. He was lying on his back on the bed with his legs over the edge just reaching the floor. The shotgun lay at his feet. The force of the blast had thrown him backwards from his sitting position on the side of the bed.

Aidan slumped to the floor on the landing, his back against the wall. Lisa unhitched the radio from her belt and called in, her free hand clutching the banister at the top of the stairs for support. The carer appeared white-faced at the bedroom door and then fell forward in a dead faint without uttering a word. One of the oak panels on the bedroom wall had been pulled away, revealing an empty cavity behind it.

★

The following morning, David Gerrard was sitting with his head in his hands when Allan walked into his office.

"You alright, David?" he asked.

"No," said his Detective Chief Inspector, looking up. "Most definitely not."

"Look, it's not anybody's fault," said Allan. "We couldn't have expected the search team to start taking the walls apart. Remember, they'd found and removed two shotguns and two rifles; that's six guns altogether counting the two that were used on the night. There was absolutely no reason to suspect he would have another stuck behind a wall. So don't start beating yourself up – or beating anyone else up, either."

David sighed. "You're right, sir, but so soon after the Enderbys… "

"Don't even think of making that link, David. Not now we've

got Jo fully back on board. Don't let's risk her slipping back. This is completely different anyway. It wasn't up to us to decide whether he was fit to be on his own. I'm not throwing bricks at anyone else, by the way, but it's most definitely not *our* fault. So let's not try to takest away the sins of the world. That's someone else's job."

David managed a smile at the irreverent quote as Allan left the room. Jo slipped in after he had gone and sat on one of the chairs in front of the DCI's desk.

"You alright, sir?" she asked.

"Everyone's very concerned about my well-being," he replied. "I think I'll have to issue a bulletin or something."

"Well, speaking for myself, what with all that's gone on, I've still not had my appraisal; so my asking is just plain creeping."

David gave a little laugh.

"Well, to be honest," he said, "I wasn't feeling all that great until a few minutes ago. But my two closest colleagues have just made me feel a whole lot better."

"It wasn't anybody's fault, you know," said Jo. "You could hardly expect the search team to start ripping down walls and... "

"Hey, just a minute!" put in David. "Those are the exact words I've just heard from the Super. Have you two been rehearsing this?"

"Discussing, not rehearsing," said Jo, sheepishly. "We were just concerned you might react like I did with the Enderbys. You know, 'God, it's all my fault', when – like you told me – if it hadn't been the gun it would likely have been something else. Please, don't be a victim, sir. We don't need any more victims... " She paused, staring into space as if deep in thought and tapping her chin with her forefinger. "Now where have I heard that before?"

"Might I just remind you, young lady, that even when you get your promotion – *if* you get your promotion – I'll still outrank you. So let's have a bit more respect, if you don't mind."

"Sorry, sir, but I've been working hard on my sarcasm lately. I wouldn't want the lack of such a basic requirement blocking my career path."

"Okay, we'll cover that in your appraisal, but if you want a sneak preview, I can tell you you're doing just fine."

They laughed again, before David became serious.

"I hope this is the last bloody chapter though, Jo. That village has taken a pasting, hasn't it? I was talking to Jed Smithers yesterday. He was telling me that five years ago, both Ben and Alistair were doing really well; farms flourishing and getting involved in a bit of land development – you know, selling a few acres for more houses. And since then, both spouses have died, and now both brothers. God knows what will happen to the farms now. I guess that's nobody's problem any more."

"I can't see that there are any more likely victims," said Jo, "so let's hope this is an end to it. Nine in all now, from that one attack a month ago."

"I don't want to tempt providence," said David, "but I'm still worried about George Holland. They tried to get him once; why not again? He's not exactly backed off, has he? In fact he seems to have taken over from Deverall. He'll be wearing a black baseball cap next and packing a Glock."

He was interrupted in mid-sigh by the appearance of an excited Allan Pickford in the doorway.

"I've just got in some great news for both of you, and I'd like to share it while you're together." He closed the door. "I'll do this formally afterwards, but very briefly – David, I can confirm you're application for retirement at age fifty-five has been accepted." He gave David a wide smile and then swung it round on to the Detective Sergeant, like the beam of a torch. "And, Jo, I am delighted to be the one to tell *you* that, effective from the 1st of September – that's two weeks on Tuesday – you will be promoted to the rank of Detective Inspector. And you will be transferred with immediate effect... " he paused dramatically "... to right here." He pointed to David's desk.

★

Jad's symptoms had been initially discussed during his time in custody prior to the trial, but there had been no official diagnosis. His first full assessment took place the week after Tom's visit. However, extensive analysis of the test results failed to throw any light on the situation. There appeared to be no carcinogenic evidence, no cardiac issues or any sign of respiratory problems. The only indication of any illness at all was a slow reduction in weight and fleeting periods of short-term memory loss. Best guesses put it down to a form of accelerated aging with no known precedent; in the absence of which there was no immediate prospect of a cure or any treatment at all.

Jad himself appeared unconcerned, focused as he was on his important work with George, who had been making good progress with his book, sharing many of the passages with Jad and taking his feedback. He had decided, with Jad's agreement, to use his speech from the dock, verbatim, as the prologue to his text. Furthermore, the survey was now taking shape.

In addition to the meetings with Tom and his regular dialogue with George, another frequent visitor was Vicky Barrowclough. Given that she – like Clive Granville – was a member of the G2 team, he was able to entertain her in what he referred to as his 'apartment'. She informed him of the company's intention to keep open his position at Germaine and Rolland for a while before deciding on whether to recruit a replacement. Really good investment managers, with such specialist skills, were difficult to find these days, she told him with a straight face.

★

Andrew called Tom to a pre-meeting in his office in the Norman Shaw Building the day before he was due to announce the structure of his 'task force', as he called it, the extended team which would work on the plans for the NJR's implementation. As Tom entered his office, Andrew was reading from one of the morning papers.

"Hey, Tom, we're still in the news and, according to the *Guardian*, unstoppable. Listen to this. 'The events of these past few months' – they mean the Bradys, Meadow Village and all that – 'can be likened to the destabilising of a mountain top, creating a political and social avalanche of awesome, overwhelming power. As it cascades, unstoppable, in its devastating surge, it now seems certain that everything in its path will be either swept along with it or buried irretrievably beneath.' Now, how about that?"

He put the paper down and waved him to a chair.

"Listen, Tom," he said with an apparent warmth that had been missing from their recent encounters. "I've been thinking a lot about the leak and, more particularly, the fact that absolutely nothing was done about it."

"But, surely… "

Andrew continued as if Tom had not spoken.

"When we get close to the election I don't want anybody throwing in our faces the accusation that we will not be tough enough to carry these changes through, and not taking action on the leak is just the sort of thing that they will latch on to as evidence. It was something that could have destroyed the Party with the wrong public reaction. It could have been that serious. I don't feel I can just sit back and pretend it didn't happen because the public's response was positive."

Tom was astonished to hear Andrew referring to his own actions in such a way, as if he had actually started to believe someone other than himself was responsible for them.

"So what… ?" he said.

"I'm going to take Hewlett off the team and take away her Shadow Ministerial role."

"What the hell for?" said Tom, angrily. "It's over, for God's sake; we got through it; nobody cared – or cares! I can't see… "

"No, you can't!" Andrew yelled. "No further than your fucking charismatic nose-end!" He almost leaped out of his chair and began pacing furiously back and forth behind his desk. "Why don't you grow up, for Christ's sake? This isn't the fucking Boy Scouts, and you'd do well to remember that! And just listen – I mean really *listen* to what I'm saying – like you're actually *interested*. It's not *now* that I'm concerned about. It's when we get to the in-fighting at the election, when the barbed arrows start flying around. *That's* when it will matter!"

"Okay," said Tom, speaking calmly as Andrew stormed about the room. "I understand what you're saying and I must bow to your experience. But let me make my position clear. I will need to consider my options very carefully – based on my own conscience – if you do this to Jackie Hewlett. Because we three know, don't we, that she didn't leak the document? And at least two of us know who did."

He stood up and turned to leave the room. Andrew called after him.

"Tom, get back here and let's have this out. I can't afford – in fact, I won't allow – a split right now. Not when we've already won, for God's sake."

Tom turned to face him.

"Yes, *we*," he said. "You and Jackie and I – and Grace. If you are planning to subject Jackie to that sort of indignity after the massive contribution she's made, then I don't think I want to be part of this new team. On the other hand, if you want me to continue to work *with* her, then I'll give it absolutely everything to ensure we deliver." He paused. "Your decision."

Andrew had stopped pacing. He glared at Tom through half-closed eyes, breathing heavily as he fought to control his anger. He took a long time to respond.

"I don't like being blackmailed, Tom," he hissed.

"Blackmailed?" said Tom, eyes wide with genuine surprise. "How does that constitute blackmail? I merely want to keep the team together that has got us this far."

"Or you'll reveal who leaked the document… "

"Where the hell did that come from?" asked Tom, his voice rising again.

"You just said – your exact words – 'I have a conscience… I must consider my options… because we both know who leaked the document… ' If that isn't blackmail, then I've spent a lifetime not knowing the meaning of the word!"

"Well, firstly, those were *not* my exact words, and what I meant by my options, as I went on to explain – very clearly, I think – is whether I would be prepared to continue without Jackie on the team. That's all. Look, Andrew, isn't it in the Party's interest to have the strongest team in place? Isn't it more important to show solidarity *now* than to worry about what someone *might* say in the future?"

Andrew did not reply for a full minute. Tom became increasingly uncomfortable, but waited out the silence.

"I'll think about what you said and get back to you," said Andrew, flatly, without expression. "And in the meantime just remember who else was party to leaking the document."

He sat down again at his desk. Tom stepped forward and leant a long way across it, clenching his hands and supporting himself on his knuckles. His voice was barely above a whisper, "I don't like being blackmailed either, Andrew. Just you remember that."

There was another long, strained silence as the two men glared into each other's eyes, before Andrew looked away.

"That's all for now," he said, picking up his desk phone. The meeting was over.

★

George Holland had received the official approval for access to the REP database in July, just over two weeks after Irene's funeral, and five days after his first visit to Pentonville to see John Deverall. Henry Moorhouse's contact at the DWP had been wrong in believing the request would be turned down, but that had been before the wave of sympathy following George's tragic loss. After all he had been through, it was almost unthinkable that he should be denied anything.

He and Jad, mainly via email, worked together on the proposed mail-out with the considerable help of Pro-Poll, the UK's leading market research agency, who assisted them with the design of the communication, reducing it to a small number of tick-box questions with a single 'Comments' box, and a high clarity index for the text. Pro-Poll's costs, thanks to Tony Dobson's influence, were met by a national tabloid newspaper in exchange for the opportunity to be the first to publish the results of the survey – or 'referendum', as George continued to call it.

On 1ˢᵗ October, the questionnaire was emailed to just under sixteen million people on the Register between the ages of fifty-five and eighty; a total of around nine million residential addresses, including care and nursing homes where communal PC facilities were available. It was sent, at Pro-Poll's suggestion, as a simple email, not an attachment, as George and Jad had originally planned. They were asked to respond by 18ᵗʰ October. Two weeks after that date, the full report had been compiled.

As agreed with their sponsor, copies were sent with a letter from George simultaneously to Ellen Gormley and Andrew Donald and – allowing one day for them to receive and absorb the findings – the report was published by the tabloid the day after that.

★

Andrew, Tom and Jackie met on the morning of Friday, 5th November to discuss the results. The two men sat in silence in the Leader's office as they waited for Jackie. There had been no further reference to the blackmail issue, but the aftermath of the conflict was evident in the colder climate of their subsequent meetings. Her arrival eased the tension in the room.

Andrew had George's letter in front of him.

"I won't read it in full," he told his colleagues, "but just listen to these numbers and rejoice.

"Target population: just under sixteen million.

"Number of respondents: fourteen million – that's eighty-eight percent, and Pro-poll predicted one-third. Make a note never to use them for anything we do.

"Of the fourteen million, over ten-and-a-half – three-quarters – agreed with *all points* for change – remember these are *our* points for change.

"Out of the remaining three-and-a-half million or so, two-and-a-half agreed in *principle,* although most of this group voiced concern over one or more of the extreme measures… " He looked up, frowning. "Extreme measures? I must have missed that bit of the proposal.

"Fewer than one million – around seven percent – of respondents opposed the changes."

He looked across at them, smiling broadly. "And here's the big finish. *Ninety-one percent* of the respondents, which, George informs us, is exactly eighty percent of the *whole* target population, answered 'yes' to the final question, which was, 'Will you hereby commit to casting your vote in favour of the Party at the next election who will themselves commit to these measures?'

"This is just too easy; and to think I entered politics for a meaningful challenge. By my calculation, this means that just over one third of the electorate has just voted Gormley and Co out of office." He beamed across the desk at them. "Who needs fireworks? Well, team, what do you think of *that?*"

"Well, obviously, it looks very promising," said Jackie, "but let's remember, no-one has voted for *this Party*. They have shown their

292

support for an ideal, which, admittedly, aligns closely with our own objectives. But when push comes to shove, entrenched party loyalties will override this hysteria for millions of people. I'm not even sure if this survey will prove more beneficial to the government than to us. What it has done is clearly define – and quantify – what they have to do to stay in power; the extent to which they need to move in either challenging or adopting our proposals. I'm sure Ellen Gormley will be concerned about the results, but she'll also be extremely grateful for the information."

There were a few moments of silence before Andrew responded.

"You're absolutely right, Jackie," he said, taking both her and Tom by surprise. "Complacency is the one thing that we cannot afford. We have the high ground – I'm sure Tom will like the analogy – and we must diligently and, if necessary, ruthlessly defend it."

He put the letter down on the desk and continued.

"Another piece of news. I have it on good authority that the government will be calling a General Election next June. Could be better, of course; we were hoping for the spring. But, never mind, at least they've shifted it by four months. Poor old Ellen must be really teed off right now. All this brilliant work to resolve the oil crisis and she can't claim a single brownie point because she's been publicly insisting all along there wasn't really a problem. You really have to feel sorry for her, don't you?"

★

The Queen's speech on 16th November passed with the traditional surfeit of ceremony and lack of passion. The annual commitment was made to improving community life...

"My government will introduce legislation to protect communities from antisocial and threatening behaviour by street gangs and organised crime, which will include significantly greater penalties for repeat offenders and for those who carry weapons and deal in illegal drugs... ."

Andrew pointed out afterwards that the statement should have started with the words "My *next* government will... "

★

A week after the Queen's Speech, the Leader of Her Majesty's Opposition held a small 'reception', as he chose to call it, as both a thank you for the work carried out by the task force, and a celebration of the results of the REP survey. Tom, Jackie, Grace and Reggie, along with a couple of dozen people who had provided them with legal advice, administrative support, data-gathering and number-crunching, were invited to join him in one of the committee rooms at Portcullis House for champagne and canapés.

It was a measure of their Leader's inability to display the common touch that the room was devoid of beer, lager, wine or any suggestion of real food. Nevertheless, the gesture was well received and the group was clearly appreciative of the recognition. It was also Friday afternoon, and a good way to end the week. Mobile phones had been duly switched off to comply with Andrew's socialising protocol.

Three-quarters-of-an-hour into the party, Andrew's PA entered the room. Shirley Topliss was in her late twenties, a small, slim girl with tightly-curled ginger hair and freckles. Her natural expression was famously one of pending doom, but right now she was looking noticeably more agitated than usual and beckoned Jackie over to her.

"Mrs Hewlett," she said in a low voice, "I've just had a call from a Mrs Manners. She'd like you to phone her back as soon as possible."

Jackie's face drained of colour.

"Did she say what it was about?"

In spite of the hushed delivery of the message, everyone in the room had stopped speaking and was listening to the exchange, alerted by Shirley's anxious expression.

"Something about Lucy. You need to call her right away."

"Oh, God!"

"Jackie," said Andrew, walking over. "Are you alright?"

"My child-minder," said Jackie, retrieving her mobile from her shoulder bag and switching it on.

She slumped onto a chair as she keyed the number. Then stood up again and almost ran from the room as the phone connected. Outside she leant against the wall of the corridor.

"Danni," she said, "what's wrong?"

"I'm not sure, Jackie, I went to pick up Lucy and when I got there, her teacher said she had left with somebody about twenty minutes before the end of classes. They said that you'd phoned at lunchtime to say that she would be picked up early, and that you had described the person – a young man. Apparently he had ID and everything and a note from you on your official letterhead. They showed it to me. They all seemed perfectly relaxed about it, so I came home. It wasn't until afterwards I thought… well… you would be bound to let me know if you'd made other arrangements. Oh, please tell me it's alright… "

Jackie was unable to say anything for a few moments. Tom had followed her as far as the door and watched her face contort in an agony of fear. He stepped forward as she slumped to a sitting position, back to the wall.

"Jackie, Jackie, what is it?"

She turned to him, seeming to take a few moments to recognise him.

"Tom. It's Lucy." She dropped the phone onto the floor. Tom picked it up and, crouching beside her, spoke into it.

"Hello. It's Tom Brown here. What's happened? Is Lucy hurt?"

"No. Well I don't know. Someone picked her up from school and… well… "

Jackie took the phone back from Tom, recovering a little. Andrew and Shirley had joined them and were standing behind him. Jackie checked her watch; it was 3.55 pm.

"Listen, Danni, I didn't phone and that note wasn't from me. I'm going to call the police. Can you go back to the school; I'll send the police there. I'm on my way."

Tom helped her to her feet. She leant unsteadily against the wall and her hands were shaking as she keyed the emergency number.

"I need to go," she said to the group, her voice trembling. "I need to get… "

"I'll drive you," said Tom.

Grace had joined the group.

"No need," she said, "we'll get her there with a police escort… "

"I'll come with you anyway," Tom said. He looked across at Grace and wasn't sure whether or not he detected a brief scowl. He gave her the benefit of the doubt.

Jackie was speaking to the police. Andrew himself hurried down the stairs to the ground floor reception and told them to get a car round as soon as possible, giving the destination as Jackie's home – she could redirect it to the school as they got closer. He also asked for the police escort. "A serious emergency," he said, without elaborating.

Jackie and Tom joined him almost before he had finished delivering his message. The car pulled up outside within two minutes, a police motorcycle half a minute later. They set off at 4.03 pm. It was already getting dark, making the situation seem even more desperate.

On the way, Jackie called her husband, telling him what had happened and to go home in case Lucy turned up; then Lucy's father – her first husband. He could do nothing – he lived in Ayrshire – but just in case Lucy called him. She contacted the school, explaining the situation, and telling them that her child-minder and the police were on their way. They assured her that the police were already there and had started asking questions, and Danni arrived as she was speaking. Jackie phoned her PA, Cindy Pearce, at her constituency office to check whether anyone had asked for some of her letterhead notepaper. Not as far as Cindy knew, but she would ask around.

Then, biting her lip as she asked, "I don't suppose Lucy's there, is she?"

"No, I expect she's with Danni," said Cindy. "Why, what's wrong, Jackie?"

Jackie told her, the effort destroying her composure. Her voice broke and Tom took the phone from her.

"Hi, it's Tom Brown. We're on our way to Lucy's school, Cindy, we'll keep you posted. Let Jackie know if anything happens at your end."

"Of course. Oh, God!"

Jackie took the phone back from him and made calls to the homes of three of Lucy's friends, more to fill the time than with any real expectation or hope of a positive outcome. No-one had seen her.

They were just ahead of the rush hour and with the police out-rider they made it to the school in thirty-seven minutes, not much more than half the time it usually took, arriving at 4.40 pm.

Jackie ran inside, past the two police cars parked in the playground. Tom followed, asking their driver and the out-rider to wait. The staff had provided a good description of the man – tall, late twenties to mid-thirties, close-cropped hair, black-rimmed glasses, well-dressed in a lounge suit and tie, pleasant, well-spoken. There had been nothing about him to arouse suspicion, except in retrospect – he was wearing gloves; they noticed when he handed them the letter. Even though it was nearing the end of November, it was still very mild. The police had acquired a digital photo of Lucy from the school's computer records, and Jackie okay-ed their circulating this to patrol cars in the area.

Most of the staff were in tears and Lucy's own teacher was inconsolable. The Security Supervisor was being questioned by DI Keith Warnock, the investigating officer, and looked completely shattered by the event. He had actually spoken to the man, exchanging friendly greetings, as he entered the premises alone and when he left shortly afterwards with Lucy.

They asked Jackie about a possible misunderstanding – a mix-up on dates, for example – just for the purpose of eliminating the obvious. However, nothing as straightforward as that would explain the phone call and a forged letter. Jackie was unable to identify anyone from the description, at least no-one specific.

Inspector Warnock took Tom to one side. The questioning of Jackie and the staff was taking place in the school hall; the policeman led him through to the foyer. In the year-six classroom off it, helped by a teaching assistant, police were carefully checking Lucy's desk and the PC she shared with three other pupils. The inspector was a tall, well-built man with strong features, and an air of authority and reliability. But in spite of the feeling of confidence he inspired, he was clearly very concerned.

"This doesn't look good, sir," he said. "Whoever did this took an enormous risk. He must have known there was a good chance the school would phone Mrs Hewlett back to confirm the arrangements after receiving the call. That's what they should have done, in which case we'd have been here waiting for him when he arrived. He must have been very confident of the plan and very convincing in the role. We've checked the call; from a mobile reported stolen earlier today. The school record all incoming calls and keep them for a week, just in case – standard practice now. This one had loud traffic noise virtually drowning out the caller. Obviously to mask their voice."

"What would he – they – want her for?" asked Tom. "It doesn't bear thinking about."

"I don't think it's anything to do with sex if that's what you mean," the policeman replied, "because it's been so well set up and carried out with a lot of bottle. She's obviously been targeted and it's most likely something to do with the mum."

At 5.50 pm, Jackie's mobile phone rang; it was Cindy and she sounded very excited.

"Jackie, I've got someone here who would like to speak to you… "

"Hi, Mum! Cindy said I had to phone you… "

"Lucy!" shouted Jackie. "Oh, darling, where have you been? Are you alright? What happened? How many times… ?" she broke down crying and Danni took the phone from her.

"Hi, Lucy, it's me… "

"Is Mum okay? What's wrong?"

"Yes, she's okay, it's just that… well, she'll tell you… just a minute… "

Jackie recovered and took the phone again.

"I'll tell you later, darling," she said. "Could you put Cindy back on for now?"

"Okay, see you soon."

"Hi," said Cindy. "She just walked in a couple of minutes ago. She's got a letter for you that this guy gave her. I've not opened it, obviously, and I haven't asked her anything about where she's been. What do you want me to do?"

Jackie looked at Inspector Warnock.

"Can we all go home?" she asked.

"Yes, of course," he said, "but we'd like to come round right away. It's important we talk to Lucy as soon as possible, while everything is fresh in her mind."

Jackie nodded, and spoke into the phone again.

"Cindy, can you take Lucy home? Eddie's already there and I'll set off right away."

"Okay. Thank God!"

"I'll get going back, then," said Tom.

"No, please come to the house," said Jackie.

"It would be useful just to have a few words," the Inspector put in.

"Okay," said Tom. "The car's waiting outside."

"That's alright, sir, Mrs Hewlett can travel with me. Perhaps you could follow on behind."

Tom thanked and dismissed the motor cycle escort, and the small convoy of two police cars and Tom's car headed off for the joyous reunion.

An hour later, as he was being driven back, Tom phoned Grace to tell her what had happened. She answered the call straight away.

"Hi, Grace."

"Hi. What's happened?" her voice seemed flat and indifferent.

"Well, no panic," said Tom. "Lucy's back with Jackie. No harm done. This guy who picked her up at school just took her round a few places – the zoo at Benton Woods, exhibition of Russian children's paintings, McDonald's. She seems to have had a really good time, in fact. Then he dropped her off at Jackie's office. Didn't touch her at all, but left a letter for Jackie."

"Really."

"Sorry, Grace, is this a bad time to talk? You seem a bit distracted."

"No, go on. What did it say?"

"I've got a copy here – the nice policeman let me have one. I'll read it to you. 'Your child has been taken away for just over two hours. I trust, and hope, that this short experience has been agonising for you. By now you have been reunited and she is with you again to love and cherish. Before returning to your heinous work, stop a moment to consider the feelings of those parents whose children you will remove for ever. I sincerely hope it will not be necessary to reinforce this message.' What do you think of that?"

For the first time, Grace showed some active interest. "So what is she planning to do?" she asked.

"I'm not sure I know what you mean," said Tom. "I guess she'll talk to the school again to make sure they are more diligent and the police will probably… "

"It doesn't matter," said Grace. "I guess it must be quite a shock. She'll have to think carefully about it."

"Right," said Tom. "Oh, and could you let Andrew know? I guess he'll be anxious to hear the news."

"Okay," she said.

"Doing anything exciting this weekend?" he asked.

Grace brightened up.

"Nothing at all, exciting or otherwise. I don't suppose you can suggest anything, can you?" He seemed to be listening to a different person.

"Nothing that I can specifically help you with, well not this weekend, anyway. But if I think of something, I'll get in touch."

"That's very selfless of you. I'll never let the phone away from my side. Actually, I was planning to go into the office tomorrow; will you be there for your surgery?"

"Yes."

"Good. I'll see you there, then."

"I'll look forward to it. Good night."

"Night."

He sat back in his seat, slipping the copy of the letter into his pocket. Then he thought about something Inspector Warnock had said. He phoned Mags.

"Hi," she said.

"Hi. Is Katey with you?"

"Yes, she's right here. We were just talking… "

"Good."

"Do you want to speak to her?"

"No, it's alright."

There was a pause. He could imagine Mags trying to work out what was going on.

"Are you okay? Are you on your way back?"

"I'm fine. See you soon."

He ended the call, wondering how he was going to explain it later.

★

Andrew phoned Jackie on her mobile on Saturday morning. She noted his name on the display and waited for a long time before answering.

"Yes, Andrew."

"Jackie, are you okay? I heard from Grace last night that Lucy was returned unharmed. God, what a shock it must have been."

"Yes, but everything's alright now. Thanks for phoning… "

"Listen, Jackie. If you need to take a few days next week, that's fine. I don't suppose you want to let her out of your sight right now."

"Well, thanks. I might just… "

"And what was this about a letter Lucy had been given?"

"Just someone trying to scare me, that's all. I'm not going public with this, Andrew. I've told the police to keep it out of the press."

"What did they say to that? It's sort of tying their hands a bit, isn't it?"

"That's exactly what they did say, but I don't want to start attracting every crank with a point of view about the NJR."

"The NJR? What's that got to do with Lucy's abduction?"

"Can I talk to you next week, Andrew? She's right next to me at the moment. Okay?"

"Of course. Keep her right there, Jackie. Just come back when you're ready."

"Okay, thanks."

★

On Thursday morning, Jackie handed a letter to Shirley Topliss requesting that she pass it to Andrew as soon as possible. She talked briefly with Shirley about the events of the previous Friday and thanked her for her concern and good wishes. At around midday, Andrew walked into Jackie's office with the letter in his hand.

"Jackie, are you absolutely sure about this?"

"Absolutely." Her eyes searched his face for a reaction.

"Well, I completely understand, of course. Tom told me what the letter said, and I half expected it. And, naturally, under the circumstances, I accept your resignation from the Shadow Ministerial role and the task force. But I would like you to continue as Member of Parliament. I know Tom would like that as well. I hope you don't mind, but we discussed it at some length."

She shook her head. "I don't know, Andrew, I think perhaps… "

"Just look at it this way, Jackie. You seem to want to keep the whole issue with Lucy low profile. I can understand that. But it will beg a whole lot of questions if you suddenly give up everything. If you just relinquish the senior role and the working group, we can say that you feel you have taken the proposals for reform as far as you need to be involved, and are concerned that you have neglected your local commitments in recent months. So you have decided to concentrate on your responsibilities towards your constituents – or something like that. That should satisfy the press and it also sends a clear message to the person who wrote that letter. In effect, he's succeeded in warning you off."

Jackie sighed. "I'll think about it, okay?"

"But that does make sense, doesn't it?"

"Yes, I suppose it does." She looked at her watch and stood up. "Now if you'll excuse me, I have a meeting in five minutes' time."

★

When Tom arrived in Marlburgh for his afternoon surgery an hour later, Grace was buzzing around the place in a rare state of animation.

"What have I missed?" he asked, as she followed him into his office.

"Nothing, why?"

"Well you just look rather too happy for there not to be something going on."

"Not at all," she said, smiling widely at him. "But every so often I stop to think how lucky I am to have such a meaningful job and such a wonderful boss."

"Well, I can't argue with that," he said, smiling back. "Oh, by the way, Jackie has handed in her resignation and Andrew has accepted it."

"Oh, well," said Grace, with no pretence at surprise. "You and I managed perfectly well without her before. I'm sure we'll be able to struggle along."

She turned and almost danced out of the room.

CHAPTER 18

The snow was still falling gently onto the gleaming white blanket that already covered the churchyard and the surrounding streets. The lights in the church illuminated the dancing flakes passing close to its windows, producing a wonderfully seasonal picture. In contrast, the single bell tolled mournfully in recognition of the solemnity of the occasion.

The streets around All Saints were heaving with people and the church itself was filled to well beyond its intended capacity. Jad had been smuggled there early in the day – well before the service was due to start at 11.00 am – to avoid his having to be driven through the crowds.

Inside, the church was bedecked with Christmas decorations including a huge tree covered in twinkling lights to the left of the front pew. On each side of the packed congregation, three plain-clothed prison officers stood line-abreast throughout the proceedings, their backs to the wall, never once taking their eyes off their charge who was seated between Tom and Mags in the front row.

The latter held his hand throughout the whole of the service. Also on the front row, in seats reserved for them, were Jack and Katey, George Holland, and Lucille and Barney Ambrose. At the back of the church, David Gerrard and Jo Cottrell were squashed in with the rest of the general public. Whether the massed crowds had turned out to 'celebrate the life of Alma Deverall', as the presiding vicar put it, or just to catch a glimpse of her son, was irrelevant. Either way, Alma finally received the send-off Jad felt she deserved.

As the service neared its end, the vicar nodded towards Jad, who rose and stepped forward past the Christmas tree and climbed the short curving staircase to the elevated pulpit. He opened the Bible on the book-stand in front of him and addressed the congregation.

"A reading from the book of Psalms, Chapter 37." He lowered his eyes and read from the text.

"Do not fret because of the wicked:
do not be envious of wrongdoers,
for they will soon fade like the grass,
and whither like the green herb

"Yet a little while, and the wicked will be no more:
though you look diligently for their place, they will not be there.
But the meek shall inherit the land,
And delight in abundant prosperity.

"The wicked plot against the righteous,
and gnash their teeth at them:
but the Lord laughs at the wicked,
for he sees that their day is coming.

"The wicked draw their sword and bend their bows
to bring down the poor and needy,
to kill those who walk uprightly;
their sword shall enter their own heart,
and their bows shall be broken.

"The righteous shall be kept safe forever,
but the children of the wicked shall be cut off.
The righteous shall inherit the land,
and live in it forever."

He raised his head and looked again at the sea of faces in front of him. The lights on the tree were reflected in the tears standing in his eyes. His voice was hoarse but carried easily to the farthest corners of the church.

"Let this be Alma's legacy. Amen."

After a moment's silence, the whole congregation responded.

"Amen."

Afterwards, Jad was taken out through the vestry entrance, but with people a dozen or so deep surrounding the church, it was impossible to keep him from the public's attention. Extra police were speedily drafted to the scene, abandoning the plan for low-profile control of the event, and three motor-cycle out-riders – in an arrow-head formation – were needed to part the crowds ahead of the security vehicle returning him to Pentonville.

★

The Multinational's Global Headquarters resided in Chicago, Illinois, in spite of its name suggesting it should be somewhere else. The Hilton Düsseldorf, then, would not seem the most obvious venue for a high-level meeting involving key members of the Company's Board. The Senior Vice Presidents for Finance, Operations and Logistics had flown in to Schipol Airport early the previous day for a pre-meeting at the company's European Head Office in Amsterdam, and then travelled the 140 miles across the border to the hotel in a chauffer-driven car during the evening. The effects of jet-lag had been completely off-set by the prospect of the meeting – unprecedented in the experience of any of the participants and with potentially huge significance for both parties.

The meeting the following morning began at 10.00 am, after a late breakfast, and business was concluded by 1.30 pm. The deal was struck, smiling handshakes were exchanged and papers signed. The two groups went their separate ways. The US contingent adjourned to the hotel's luxurious Axis bar for a celebratory drink and light lunch. Theirs would be an early night at the hotel; the following morning they would catch the Lufthansa flight from Nordrhein-Westfalen Airport direct to Chicago. The previous two days' exertions and excitement began to catch up with them, and two of the three were asleep in their designer chairs by the time the rolls and salads arrived.

The three-strong UK delegation stepped out into the freezing cold and walked along Georg-glock-strasse, towards the Rhine. They crossed the Kaiserwerther Strasse and weaved their way through the streets to the embankment, heading south along Robert-lehr-ufer flanked by the river on their right and Rheinpark to the left. The temperature was around thirty degrees Celsius lower than in the Board Room on the mezzanine floor of the hotel and it took the whole of the mile-and-a-half walk to the Canoo Restaurant for their lungs to get accustomed to the change. They had just about stopped hurting when they took their seats at a table overlooking the delicate structure of the Oberkasseler Bridge, crossing the river just a little further upstream.

They ordered drinks – a Becks each – and chose starters and mains from the extensive lunchtime menu. One of the two men excused himself – 'a comfort break', he said – and left the room. The other two members of the party looked smilingly into each others eyes, their expressions reflecting both the success of the meeting and their delight in each other's company.

★

The convoy of four unmarked vehicles made its way northwards as inconspicuously as possible along the M6, stopping briefly at the same motorway services where Detective Chief Inspector David Gerrard had purchased his sandwiches six months previously. The vehicles were directed to a secure area, cordoned off by high boards. In addition to the armed guards in the escort, a dozen local police officers from the Special Firearms Unit awaited their arrival in the screened-off zone. Half-an-hour later they resumed their journey, soon leaving the motorway and heading north-east into the dramatic winter landscape of the West Pennine Moors.

Two of the vehicles parked up on the outskirts of the small town, the others picking their way through the narrow streets before crawling silently and carefully up the short ice-covered lane to the terraced house which was their destination. The door of the house was already open; a young man wearing a heavy military overcoat sat just inside the doorway in a wheel-chair, nervously wringing his hands and occasionally wiping tears from his anxious face. John Deverall looked across at him from the rear seat of the leading car as it stopped at the curb, and his own tears ran freely. The young woman sitting by his side reached over and held his hand, her own eyes fixed on the figure in the doorway.

EPILOGUE

On the morning following the broken mug incident in the kitchen at Etherington Place, bleary-eyed through lack of sleep, but with a renewed sense of purpose, Tom Brown slipped into the chauffer-driven 700 series BMW which had crawled silently up the drive to his house at 6.30 am.

His errant children had informed Mags by text at around 3.00 am that they were staying over with friends and going directly to college the next day. He had finally slipped into bed in his room – he was now separated from Mags by half the house – at around 4.00 am, placing the half-dozen pieces of the mug on his dressing table and setting his alarm to wake him at 6.00. It was cutting it a bit fine, perhaps, to make the 6.30 pick-up, and so it proved; it was a few minutes before 7.00 am when he descended the three steps to the driveway.

"Morning, Paul," he said. "Sorry to keep you waiting."

"Morning, Home Secretary," his driver replied, opening the rear door with a brief salute. "And don't worry, sir. I'll get you there in time."

Paul Webster closed the door as Tom settled into the leather sofa which served as a rear seat. He had not had time for any breakfast, but he had shaved and showered, and coffee and croissants would await him at the meeting. As they pulled out of the drive, a second vehicle, with two Special Branch officers inside, slipped in behind them to escort them to Westminster.

Within a couple of minutes he found himself slipping into a shallow sleep. As he drifted off, his last conscious thought – of a group of young men heading fearfully into the unknown – faded then re-formed into a vivid memory from his own past.

★

Sierra Leone, September 2000. He was with the SBS involved in a coordinated rescue operation – official codename 'Barras', but dubbed 'Operation Certain Death' by the Special Forces involved. Their objective was to free soldiers of the Royal Irish Regiment, who, whilst on a UN peacekeeping mission, had been captured by units of the rebel militia, known as the 'West Side Boys'. Eleven hostages had been taken, of which five were subsequently released. The remaining six had been tortured and held to ransom, the rebels making various demands of the British authorities for money, arms and concessions in return for their release.

They were being held in Geri Bana, one of three villages fifty miles east of Freetown on the Rokel Creek River, where the rebels were encamped. Tom was in command of one of two integrated SBS-SAS observation teams who, using inflatable raiding craft and under cover of darkness, penetrated the jungle upriver of the camp. They successfully delivered intelligence on rebel numbers and positions and, vitally, information that ruled out either a land or river operation. As a result of this, it was decided that a direct aerial assault, although very dangerous, was the only option. The main attack would be carried out using Lynx helicopter gunships to fire on rebel positions and Chinooks to land Paras close to where the hostages were imprisoned.

As the observation teams set off, Tom, seated at the front of the leading Raider, looked over his shoulder at John Deverall just a few feet away. As with all the high-risk operations they had shared, the anxiety showed on his face. He returned Tom's look with wide eyes but without the hint of a smile.

★

The vivid recollection of that fearful look on the face of his best friend briefly dominated his consciousness as he awoke suddenly from his disturbed sleep. In his mind's eye, he saw that expression,

308

intensified a thousand times, transposed onto each of the faces of a group of young men – a group with a similar age profile to the one he had commanded on that day.

They too would be heading across the water into the unknown; but theirs would be a feeling of utter hopelessness rather than anxiety; a feeling fully warranted by their circumstances. They would not be clinging to the hand ropes around the edge of a Rigid Raider, but to a hope that they would soon awake from their nightmare. They would not be bouncing precariously against the surge of a rushing river, looking forward to the completion of their mission, but gliding smoothly towards a living oblivion from which there was no possible return.

"... the children of the wicked shall be cut off... "

Jad's words from the pulpit came back to him. He checked his watch. In less than two hours' time, at 9.00 am, the irreversible step would be taken, and the start of the process would mark the end of everything for the occupants of the vessel. He had been to the place himself. He remembered it well, how he had stepped forward and been greeted with 'Look out, lads, here comes the Hotel Inspector.' There had been a touch of genuine humour at the time; not today.

He was momentarily shaken; a rare and unnerving experience for a man whose entire life had been driven by absolute certainty in the justification of his actions.

He reached for his phone.

"Hello, Grace Goody."

"Hi, Grace. It's so good to hear your voice. I'm really sorry to call you this early but... "

"That's okay. I told you – any time – day or night. What's wrong?"

"I'm not sure, to tell you the truth," he replied. "I just don't know where to start. I have to talk to you." His voice was almost a whisper, aware of Paul's presence a few feet away, even though the front and rear seats were separated by a sliding glass window, which was currently closed.

"Do you want to meet?" she said. "I thought you were with the PM this morning."

"I'm on my way – seeing him at eight at the House. No, it will have to be on the phone. Are you okay to talk right now?"

"Yes, of course. Please tell me what it is. You're really worrying me." Her voice was almost pleading. She had never heard him talk like this before.

"It's just that I can't get the thought of those guys out of my mind."

"Which guys?"

"The ones we're shipping out today. They'll be loading them right now."

There were a few moments of silence as Grace tried to absorb what he was saying; too many moments for Tom.

"Grace, are you still there?"

"Yes," she answered, "but I don't understand what you mean."

"I keep seeing their faces, what they'll be thinking, how frightened they'll be, not knowing what... "

She interrupted, her voice strict and business-like.

"I see, so when you say 'those guys', you mean 'those guys' who have taken it upon themselves to dedicate their lives to heaping misery on everybody else; 'those guys' who have been given every opportunity to change their ways; 'those guys' to whom it has been made absolutely clear what would happen to them if they didn't take those opportunities. You haven't forgotten, have you, Tom, in all this soul-searching, *why* we are doing this to... *'those guys'*?"

Now there was silence at Tom's end.

"Look, you're probably imagining your own kids in that situation. But these are not your kids – nothing like your kids. And you want yours to grow up in a better – safer – world, don't you? Do you know what my least favourite cliché is, Tom? Yes, of course you do, don't you? 'No pain, no gain', but it's often right, isn't it? If – and I do mean *if* – we have to grieve a little for a few lost souls, then it's a price we must be prepared to pay for the much wider benefit. For God's sake, listen to me! It's a bit early in the morning for me to repeat *all* your speeches back to you, but I'm happy to do it if it helps."

There was still no reply.

"Tom! Are *you* still there?"

"Yes, I'm here."

His voice was much calmer now.

"I knew it was a good idea to phone you, Grace. It's always a good idea, come to think of it – day or night."

"Now you're just guessing," she said, teasingly. "You've never phoned me at night."

"No, but I've thought about doing it quite a lot."

"Doing what exactly? Phoning, you mean?"

"No, not just phoning."

Neither spoke for a while.

"Listen, Grace," he said, "you know I'd like to carry on talking to you, but… "

"It's okay," she interrupted again. "Are you alright now?"

"Yes, thanks to you. You've made the nasty bogey man go away. I really don't know how to thank you." It was a deliberate feed and it was not wasted.

"Oh, *I* do," she said, in a sensuous whisper; then, "Good luck with his Highness. See you later."

The BMW turned off Kensington Road into Westminster Bridge Road, and the familiar sight of his place of work just a few minutes away brought him back to timely reality. As he switched his attention to the meeting with the Prime Minister, his mind let in the noise of the bustling streets with the suddenness of an explosion. He checked his watch; Paul had made it with over five minutes to spare.

They crossed Westminster Bridge before the car turned into St Margaret's Street and slowed almost to a stop in front of the gates of New Palace Yard. Their progress was all but halted by a swaying corridor of photographers and reporters waving microphones, shouting out a hundred questions which blended together to make each individual one unintelligible.

He smiled and waved but on this occasion made no verbal response. The police cleared a route through the crowd and the car entered the Yard, turning left then right past the line of trees with their buds barely open, showing just a hint of their early spring green. They swung right again at the end of the Yard, and pulled up at the Members' entrance. Tom stepped out of the car and stood for a full minute taking in his surroundings as if he was seeing them for the first time.

HOTEL ST KILDA

The story continues in

HEAVEN'S DOOR

Read the first chapter now...

CHAPTER ONE

Week 1; Monday, 23 March…

The detective inspector replaced the desk phone on its cradle and looked across at his sergeant.

"Come in, number three."

"Sir?"

"That's the third one …" he checked his watch "… in twenty-two hours who's agreed to come and talk to us. Almost as if they were conferring, don't you think, given their intransigence over the last five weeks?"

"Do we pick him up or is he going to claim fifty quid for a taxi?"

The DI snorted a laugh. "I think we play it softly-softly for the moment. I offered to bring him in – he said he'd make his own way later today."

"And the other two?"

"Should be here late morning unless they change their mind again. They told me they were coming yesterday afternoon."

"Should we chase them up, do you think?"

"Not sure. We don't want to seem to be pushing too hard, but the worry is they could easily choose to disappear again. I mean, there's nothing in it for them really, is there?"

"Revenge, I suppose?" offered the sergeant.

"That's true, but revenge usually takes a different form in these cases, doesn't it? I still don't understand why three unconnected people – well, seven, I suppose you'd have to say – would chose to do it this way. Anyway, let's just leave them for now and see what happens over the next couple of days."

The two men were sitting across the desk from each other in the

315

DI's office, which was small and modern. The beech-finish desk was L-shaped, incorporating a PC work station on the short leg of the 'L'. Down one side of the room was a line of matching cabinets and on the wall on the opposite side was a large screen with a back-projection facility for the computer and which doubled as a dry-wipe board.

The senior man clicked a few keys on his keyboard and the screen came to life. He got up from his tilt-and-swivel and stretched, then stepped over to the collage of images and words on the screen. He was of average height and build, and untidily dressed in a grey suit which had seen better days. His thinning grey hair made him look older than his forty-two years.

"So, what have we got so far?"

★

Two days later
Week 1; Wednesday, 25 March…

"Welcome aboard, as they say."

The large man in the dark blue uniform smiled and extended his hand to each of the two visitors as they walked up the ramp at the rear of the vessel.

"Thank you, Captain …"

"Oh, I'm not the captain. Calum Nicholson at your service, Chief Prison Officer at Lochshore. Captain McLeod is on the bridge doing his final checks. I'll take you to see him later."

The man who had spoken to Calum was tall, in his mid-forties and distinguished-looking, with a mane of steel grey hair. He was well-dressed in a short reefer coat worn over an expensive lounge suit, shirt and tie, and shining black brogues. The other man was much smaller, around average height and in his mid sixties. He wore a thick waterproof coat over a round-necked fisherman's jumper and, with his grey beard and woolly hat, looked much less out of place preparing to enter the bowels of a ship than his companion.

"Lawrence Harding," the tall man introduced himself, "Parliamentary Under-Secretary of State for Prisons, and this is Mike Needham, chief designer of Alpha. We are here *only* to observe and absorb – nothing else. And we're very grateful to you for finding time to show us round."

Calum checked his watch. "You're very welcome, but I'm afraid we don't have long. We start embarking at seven, so that gives us just thirty-five minutes. Please ask any questions as we go round."

He turned and they followed him onto the vessel, stopping just inside.

"The ship is a specially-modified passenger ferry," said Calum, "previously used to take people to some of the most beautiful places imaginable. Back then it was called *Spirit of St Columba* and where we're standing now was the vehicle deck. Now it's known as PTV1 – short for prisoner transfer vessel one."

In front of them were two walkways. Calum took them along the one on the port side.

"What we have are one hundred and fifty separate, two-metre-square cabins, each with three solid metal walls and one outward-facing wall with steel bars and a sliding door. The cabins are linked together in four lines – two lines of forty back-to-back down the centre of the ship and a line of thirty-five on both this and starboard sides. As you can see, each line sits separately on rail tracks so they can be moved on and off the vessel like a giant flexible cage on a fairground ride. This and the other gangway run the length of the deck between the outer and central line of cabins on either side."

"Amazing," said Mike Needham, looking round like a little boy in a toy shop. "I can't wait to see the link-up to the lifting platform, especially how it's done in heavy seas or high winds."

"Well, speaking personally," said Calum, smiling, "I hope you *don't* get to see that on this trip – the heavy seas and high winds, I mean."

Lawrence Harding was peering into one of the cabins. Calum continued.

"Each cabin has a bench along one side, a small swing-out table, like those on passenger airlines, and a TV monitor." Calum was pointing out the furnishings. "And behind the plastic curtain across the corner there's a chemical toilet and small wash-hand basin. A bit basic and spartan, but it's just for a single one-way trip of twenty or so hours."

"And the television," said Lawrence. "What's that for?"

"Not for Sky Movies, I'm afraid. We'll be showing them a training film during the second half of the trip. A thirty-minute programme on a continuous loop, covering aspects of life on Alpha. Not sure myself whether it's a good idea. More likely to scare them than educate them, I reckon."

"But they've had their training already, haven't they?"

"That's right, but the thinking is that it's all a bit unreal at that stage."

"A *bit* unreal." Lawrence raised his eyebrows.

"Well, whatever. At least it's something for them to look at if they want to."

"And meals?"

"Once we've got them installed they'll get trays with coffee, a cereal bar and sandwiches. We slide them under the doors of the cabins."

"But they'll get other meals?"

"Three today and breakfast tomorrow morning. Although I can't imagine many of them having much of an appetite, can you? Let's go up here."

He led them up some metal stairs and along to the monitoring centre on the deck above, where they would be able to observe proceedings on the array of CCTV screens. Calum took them over to a map on the wall.

"Here's where we are now." He pointed to the map. "After we leave Loch Fendort we go round Kerrera into the Firth of Lorne and head north-west through the Sound of Mull. From there we'll cross the Hebridean Sea and skirt the southern tip of the Bishop's Isles, before heading north-west again into the open Atlantic for a further sixty miles. That will take us twenty miles south-west of here." He pointed to the island group which represented the farthest outpost of the British Isles. "The entire trip is planned to take around twenty-two hours, so we should be there around seven tomorrow morning."

"Will I need any seasick pills?" asked Mike.

"You'll have to ask the captain," Calum smiled. "I've been too scared to ask him myself."

★

The first fifty yards of the walk passed calmly enough. After all, the young man was in a familiar building where he'd been moved around frequently during the past three weeks. He knew this was different, of course, but it was only when they reached the outer double doors that this awareness surfaced in the form of violent panic.

The doors were open and fastened back. The metal walkway stretched ahead in a straight line. Along and round the quayside the lights shone brightly in the early morning gloom and were reflected in the still waters of the harbour. The ferry, two hundred yards away and looking huge against the flotilla of smaller boats, was facing directly away from them with its rear ramp lowered. The walkway split into two just before it mounted the ramp and disappeared into the stern of the vessel.

He was no more than average height, slim and wiry with long fair hair, wearing a baggy grey jogging suit over a black tee shirt. The two security officers he was handcuffed to were huge men in dark blue uniforms, with hard faces and short cropped hair. As the prisoner stepped through the doorway, the sight of the vessel and the cold morning air hit him at the same moment. He lunged at the man on his right causing him to crash heavily against the rail of the walkway and slump to the floor. He kicked wildly at him, karate-style, with the heel of his foot, the steel bracelets tearing at the skin around his wrists as he tried to pull himself free. The second officer gripped him round his chest from behind, squeezing hard as his colleague scrambled up and grabbed his flailing legs.

"Needle – now!" he yelled as they held him still.

The prisoner screamed at the sudden stab of pain in his thigh as a third man stepped forward and jabbed the syringe hard into the muscle. The guard holding the prisoner's legs turned to the medic.

"Tell Gally to show them all that thing – or the biggest one you've got – and make sure they know you're going to stick it in them if they don't behave themselves and walk nicely for us. How long will this take to kick in?"

"About four or five minutes; should last for up to six hours. I'll tell Gally, but it's supposed to be a fall-back measure, that's all."

"Just tell him!"

He turned back to the writhing young man.

"Settle down, son," his colleague was saying. "Don't make it even rougher on yourself."

"You're breaking my fucking arms, you fucking bastards!" he spat the words out at them.

"I'll break your fucking neck if you try anything like that again," the other guard shouted.

They eased him onto the walkway, laying him face down and moving his arms so they could rest naturally at his sides. His rapid breathing slowed as the relaxant did its work. After a few more minutes they helped him to his feet and guided him along the walkway and into the vessel, locking him into his cabin.

★

It was 7.55 am. The man got out of his chauffer-driven BMW at the Members' Entrance in New Palace Yard and breathed in the fresh March morning air as he gazed up at the ancient walls of Westminster Hall, which still retained some of the original building dating back a thousand years. He waited until the first of the sixteen strokes which counted down the hour sounded in Elizabeth Tower close behind him before pushing his way through to the entrance foyer.

The man was tall and slim, with broad shoulders and an upright military bearing. He was impeccably dressed in an expensive light grey suit, a shirt which matched the colour of his twinkling pale-blue eyes and a navy and yellow striped tie.

"Good morning, sir."

He beamed down at the prime minister's diminutive, freckled PA.

"Morning, Shirley, you look lovely today, as always."

"You're in Committee Room 14."

She escorted him in silence to the meeting room on the first floor. It was exactly eight o'clock.

Committee Room 14 was set out with a table on a dais at one end and three rows of facing benches down each side. Along the outside wall, were a number of leaded windows reaching almost to the ceiling. The room was also known as the Gladstone Room and around the other walls, above the wood panelling, was a series of paintings showing parliamentarians who served during his terms as prime minister.

"Ah, the Home Secretary; at *last*."

Andrew Donald was seated on his own at the table on the dais, with the thirty members who represented the top level of his government occupying the seats closest to him. With the exception of the man who had just spoken they all rose to their feet as Tom Brown entered the room.

"And good morning to *you*, Prime Minister."

He took his seat on the dais next to Andrew – the signal for the others to sit down – and opened his briefcase to remove a red leather-bound folder, which exactly matched those in front of each person in the room. The thirty-two attendees opened the folders in perfect synchronisation.

"As you know," said Tom, "we've made remarkable progress against the NJR targets. In fact, we've met them all."

★

Andrew brought the meeting to a close one hour later and the members began to close their folders and open their briefcases. Tom rose to his feet to stem the exodus.

"If I may, Prime Minister, whilst we're all together, could I just share a thought as to how we might move on from here?"

★

The prison doctor stood behind the consultant, looking over the woman's shoulder at the pale, thin figure she was examining. The room had bare white walls and contained four beds lined abreast with a small cabinet at the side of each. Just one of the beds was occupied. After a few minutes they both walked away to the corner of the room. The consultant spoke in a low voice, almost a whisper.

"Very slight deterioration over the last couple of days but significant all the same, I'm afraid. We need to get him weighed again. Not a lot else we can do except make him comfortable. And they can take his name off the door in there – he won't be going back."

"We'll need to move him from here if that's the case," said the doctor. "He can't stay indefinitely in the hospital."

"I'll arrange that," said the consultant, looking at her watch. "Ten-fifteen. Might even get him in somewhere today if I can catch someone right away."

"Thank you, but I don't think we can move that quickly at this end. I'll start the ball rolling right away but we'll need approval from on high, given who he is – well, *what* he is. Although he doesn't look much of a danger to anyone now, does he?"

"Shame. This is one of the good guys, whatever the official record will say about him."

They left and the duty nurse pulled the curtain around the bed.

★

"I wish you wouldn't spring things on me like that, Tom. I don't like being backed into a corner."

Committee Room 14 was empty except for the two men. The prime minister was an inch or so taller than Tom, with a bulky frame, and a round face under dark brown hair which was combed to the side with a ruler-straight parting. As always, he was fashionably dressed in an Italian suit and silk shirt and tie, and carried his surplus weight well.

"I just felt with all the positive feedback we are about to give," Tom replied, "this would pre-empt anyone saying, 'Okay, so far so good, but what next?' We don't want to look like we think the job's done …"

"The job *is* done, Tom. The job being the successful implementation of the New Justice Regime. What happens next *within* that regime is part of the new process of law."

"I can't see how this can possibly hurt us, though. It was in our manifesto, so no-one can say …"

"Actually, it wasn't *part* of the manifesto, if you remember. It was *mentioned* in the manifesto as a future possibility – no more than that."

"So you're saying … well, what exactly? The Cabinet agreed to go with it. They're expecting it now. Are you going to reconvene?"

"No, we're going with it and if the whips do their job in the intervening four hours or so, we won't get the wrong reaction from at least *our* side of the House this afternoon. But you've got Latiffe to thank for that – *he* swung the meeting, not you. And if the initial reaction of our own cabinet members is anything to go by, this could knock the shine off the massive positivity of the NJR feedback."

"Then why did you …"

"Agree to it? Because in principle it's the right thing to do. It's just the timing I'm not entirely comfortable with. And the spontaneity, if I'm honest. No testing of the water."

"And how did you propose to do that, Andrew? The usual way? Leak it through the press and prepare a disclaimer just in case? And this time it would have to be me that resigned, I suppose?"

Andrew glared at him. "Don't get carried away with your own importance, Home Secretary. That was *not* what I meant, and you know it!"

"Yes, my apologies," said Tom. "I guess I've never lost the cavalier instincts which brought us to power. We seemed to be another Party then."

"We *were* another Party," said Andrew. "We were the fucking *Opposition* Party trying to become the government! Can't you understand the difference?" He rose from his seat to signal they had finished. "Look," he added, "*I'll* raise this in the House at the end of your report. You just finish as planned after the feedback. That way I can cut off any discussion today and leave it for debate next Monday. Any more surprises?"

"None, Prime Minister. Oh, except that I was going to call for special prayers tomorrow for the Exiles. That's if …"

"As you please," said Andrew. "But let's not forget that those bastards are getting exactly what they deserve and exactly what we promised them."

★

Calum checked the time on the large wall clock in the monitoring area. It was 12.55 pm and they were exactly three hours into their journey.

"Well, gentlemen," he said, turning to his two guests, "time to call on the captain, I think. You can ask him about the weather," he nodded at Mike Needham.

They climbed the stairs to the deck and Calum noted that the wind had increased and the waves were slightly higher than before. Captain Douglas McLeod waved for them to join him on the bridge. Calum and Douglas were very much alike in appearance. Both large men in their early fifties, with broad muscular shoulders and arms, and barely any surplus weight in the places it normally starts to accumulate at that age. Even their uniforms were similar – both dark blue, although Douglas's sported white flashes on the cuffs and shoulders. He also had the captain's compulsory full grey beard.

Calum introduced Lawrence and Mike.

"So you're the guy who designed Alpha," Douglas said, smiling at the smaller man. "Have you seen it in situ at all?"

"I've spent most of the last two years of my life on it but I haven't seen the finished article fully functional yet."

"Well, you're in for a treat," said Douglas. "And talking about a treat…"

He pointed across to the island on their left no more than a mile away. Two rows of brightly coloured houses were reflected in the calmer water of the bay. A dozen or so small boats languished in the harbour along with a large ferry taking on vehicles and early season tourists. Above and behind the houses stood a sandstone hotel, which looked like an old castle, and beyond that some low tree-covered hills.

"Tobermory. Beautiful, isn't it?" he said. "And that," he pointed ahead, "is Ardmore Point, northernmost tip of Mull. After that, well, it's more or less the Atlantic Ocean. We'll be slowing down when we get into open sea, but we're right on schedule."

"Mike wants to know if it's likely to be rough," Calum said, with a faint smile.

"No, smooth as a mirror," said Douglas, smiling back in a way that left the three men wondering whether he meant the exact opposite.

★

"Afternoon, Tom."

Tom looked round with a start. He was sitting out on the Terrace, having just finished a cold lunch of smoked salmon and salad, and was staring absently out across the river. The generously proportioned figure of Gerald Portman, ex Home Secretary, now Shadow Chancellor, beamed down at him and gestured towards one of the empty chairs next to his table. "Do you mind?"

"Not at all," said Tom.

"Le jour de gloire est arrivé, n'est-ce pas?" Gerald was of medium height, but everything else about him was larger than life. He carried most of his weight in front of him, stretching the material of his pinstripe suit and white shirt. His tie and his general manner were as flamboyant and pleasing as ever.

"Not sure how glorious it is," replied Tom, who had been picturing in his mind the scene on the transfer vessel and coming up with some uncomfortable images.

"I thought this was your dream, Tom. Not having second thoughts, I hope. I mean, it's a bit late …"

Tom laughed.

"Not a chance, Gerald. After you completed the easy bit, I have nothing but smug satisfaction for the way we finished the more demanding part of the job. But it would be churlish not to acknowledge your contribution. So if *you* want to call it glorious, I've no objection."

Gerald chuckled.

"That's more like it, I thought you'd gone all melancholy for a moment." He stood up. "Well, I guess you weren't sitting here all alone on the off-chance you'd get picked up by a Shadow Cabinet Minister. You must have a few things still to think about. And anyway, it's bloody cold. So I'll leave you in peace and go and finish rehearsing my spontaneous one-liners."

Tom laughed.

"Go, by all means, but please not on my account. I can't do any more now in the next half-an-hour. If you like, I'll send for a hot water bottle and a blanket, and we can go in together in a few minutes."

"Okay, I'll be brave," he said, sitting down again.

ACKNOWLEDGEMENTS

Thanks are due to the many people who contributed in different ways to the production of this book.

To those who provided me with factual information on aspects of the story: David Burrow, David Gibbons, Andrew Garner, David Monks, Ben Shatliff and, in particular, Alan Isherwood, who gave up his time on several occasions to help me.

To all my friends who showed such an enthusiastic interest in the book and whose encouragement made it unthinkable that I should not complete it, even when the stream of ideas had reduced to barely a trickle. And especially to Marian Sample, who gave me essential feedback on the manuscript at the beginning which set me on the right course.

To Gary Smailes of Bubblecow for his detailed editorial critique and invaluable advice following on from this.

To my family who never doubted the outcome even when I did myself – son Daniel, daughter Hannah, daughter-in-law Annette and brother Geoff. Also, grandchildren Thomas and Ellen who both contributed with ideas for the cover design.

Lastly, and mostly, to my wife, Carol, for her unstinting support and for putting up with years of my feeling sorry for myself when things were not going as planned.

MICHAEL KNAGGS was born in Hull in 1944. He moved to Thurso, Caithness, in 1966 to work as an Experimental Officer at Dounreay Atomic Power Station, and relocated to Salford in 1968 to complete a degree in Chemistry. From 1970 up to his retirement in 2005, Michael worked for Kellogg Company – the global breakfast cereal manufacturer – latterly as Human Resources Director with responsibility for pay and benefit policy across the company's European organisation.

He lives in Prestwich, Manchester, with his wife, Carol. Their passion is hill-walking and they undertake at least one long distance walk each year. They have two children and two grand-children.